Goodnight, God Bless

(DI Alex Peachey 2)

Ann Bloxwich.

Red Dragon Publishing LTD

ISBN: 978-1-7394066-2-2

This book is a work of fiction. Any resemblance between these fictional characters and actual persons, living or dead, is purely coincidental.

RED DRAGON BOOKS

THIS BOOK IS DEDICATED to everyone who has ever been abused in any way, whether it be as a child or as an adult. It is never your fault, despite what you may believe or have been told. You are not a victim; you are a survivor, and you are not alone.

Chapter 1.

Then.

    The little girl tucked the bottom of her blankets in and carefully lined her toys up along the edge of the bed, with the biggest bear she could find nearest the door. She hoped that Edward Bear would prove to be a better protector than Sally Doll had been. The green monkey with the long arms had been stuffed at the back of her wardrobe, and she planned to get rid of it as soon as possible.

Satisfied that all the sides of the bed were protected, she climbed in and scooted down as far as possible without covering her head. She drew her feet up inside her nightdress, pulling the fabric over her feet to enclose them completely.

She hummed a song that had been playing on the radio earlier but tried not to be too loud. She knew the best way to keep the monster out was to pretend to be asleep.

A creak on the landing outside startled her, and she ducked under the covers, eyes tightly shut.

She lay as still as she could, praying under her breath but it was no good.

The door handle began to turn...

Chapter 2.

Now.
Alison Munroe breathed a sigh of relief as she pulled up outside the house. The upstairs window was closed, so it looked as if Mark had gone out. She was glad of the chance to have the place to herself. Mark hadn't left the house since he came out of hospital, but the doctor had said to give him some space and he would go out when he was ready. It was easy for him to say, but it was really beginning to get on her nerves.

The doctors had diagnosed Mark with severe depression, but Alison had soon realised that Mark was only ill when it suited him. The minute he got his hands on his benefit cheque, he was suddenly well enough to go out and blow the lot on computer games and junk food. A teacher's wage wasn't huge, and Alison was sick of supporting him. Mark always looked at her like a lost puppy when she asked him for money to cover his half of the bills, saying he'd got carried away and forgotten to save any. At first Alison had let it slide, but soon realised she was being taken for a fool. She had confronted him about it one evening before she went out. Seeing his meal ticket sliding out of his grasp, Mark had done what he always did when backed into a corner; he'd taken an overdose. He always made sure to ring someone, so he was discovered before it was too late, and the last time it had been his sister, Molly, who had been on the receiving end of the call. She'd rushed over and found him unconscious on the floor, with an empty pill bottle in his hand. An ambulance was swiftly sent for, and Mark was whisked off to hospital, with Molly by his side. Alison had been spending the night at a friend's house, and only

4

found out about it when Molly sent her a text afterwards, telling her Mark would be home the next day.

Mark's mother had been furious and had blamed Alison. She frequently left nasty messages on the answerphone, threatening all kinds of things if Alison dared to send Mark back to her.

'He was fine when he lived here with me,' she shouted one evening, when Alison had foolishly answered the phone. 'You just don't know how to treat him right. He should never have moved in with you!'

A loud sniffling noise had ensued, then Mark's mum had changed tactics, going for sympathy instead.

'Fine, have him back then.'

'I don't want him moving back here, I'm too old to deal with his problems! You're a cruel, heartless wench, inflicting all this grief on a defenceless old woman!'

Alison had laughed out loud when she heard that. Mark's mother was the proverbial battle-axe, and nothing scared her at all. It was plain to see where Mark had got his acting skills from.

Alison had held the phone at arm's length, letting the old bag rant until she ran out of steam, then calmly replaced the handset and told Mark he had a week to get out.

A month had passed since then, and Mark was still here.

Alison climbed out of the car and opened the boot. The shopping bags had spilled some of their contents, so she repacked the loose items and heaved the bags out. It took two trips to get the boot unloaded, but Alison was pleased with the amount of stuff she'd got for her money. Alison had also treated herself to a new hairstyle, the short blonde bob suiting her far more than the old brunette shoulder-length style she'd had for years. The soft honey-coloured highlights complemented her dark blue eyes, making her look younger. She'd put a little weight on recently, but decided it suited her better, despite Mark's comments to the contrary.

Alison put the shopping away then made herself a well-deserved cuppa. She stood looking out of the kitchen window and sipped her tea, thinking what a mammoth task tackling the overgrown garden was going to be; something else Mark had promised to do. The sun was shining, so Alison carried her drink outside and perched on the low wall. She spotted what looked like the dying embers of a bonfire at the far end of the garden and wandered over to see what Mark had been burning whilst she was at the shops. She picked up a stick and poked at the remains, turning over old bits of paper, most of which looked to be unpaid bills. Alarmed at seeing her name on some of them, Alison dragged the unburnt pieces of paper out of the embers and waited for a few seconds for them to cool down before picking them up. The name of a credit card company could still be seen on the corner of one, and her heart sank.

Alison went back into the house, put her half-full mug on the counter and rushed upstairs. Mark had fitted a large padlock to the outside of the spare room door, something else Alison hadn't given him permission to do. Alison looked at the hasp. It wasn't screwed down properly, so Alison popped back to her own room to retrieve the screwdriver from her bedside drawer. She kept it there to threaten Mark with if he ever got any ideas about trying to climb into bed with her, which was a shame because their sex life had been amazing.

She had the hasp unscrewed in a few seconds and carefully opened the door, smiling to herself when a piece of paper fell out from between the door and the frame. Mark had clearly been watching spy films again. She tucked it into her pocket and went inside.

Alison wrinkled her nose in disgust at the state of the room. Piles of dirty clothes were scattered all over the place, some on the floor, some hanging off the back of the chair and some on the unmade bed. The sheets looked as though they hadn't been washed in a month and she really didn't want to know what that foul smell was. There was a stack of empty cardboard boxes leaning against one wall. Mark clearly hadn't made a start on packing up his stuff. Alison picked her way across the room to the small desk under the window, being careful not to disturb anything. She booted up the computer, which Mark had decided was going into the spare room with him. Alison had been too tired to argue at the time.

The computer wasn't password protected; Mark probably didn't think he needed one. 'Silly boy,' Alison mused. She glanced through some of the things on the desk while the screen loaded. Mark had certainly been busy she thought; there were loads of email addresses and phone numbers scribbled onto scraps of card, and Alison took out her phone and photographed them. If he was doing anything illegal she wanted to be sure she had proof before she acted. She carefully put everything back where it had been.

When the computer was finally ready, Alison quickly scrolled through the browser history. She couldn't believe how much crap Mark looked at; events pages for trucks, motorbikes and classic car shows, fan pages for several Z-list movie and TV stars, and a few social networking sites. She checked his email next, which wasn't difficult as he used the same password for everything. Mark had loads of emails from people asking him to share photographs, and some pointing him to websites he might like. He hadn't deleted anything in the past few months and Alison knew it was risky to try and read them all now. She selected all of them and forwarded them to herself, including the deleted ones, then copied and forwarded all the contacts and saved files until she had everything he'd ever sent and received. Just as she was about to log off, a new email came in.

Alison couldn't resist opening it, knowing she would have to delete it afterwards so he wouldn't know she'd been there. It was from someone called Glam53, asking if he was still wanting to meet up that evening. There were contact details attached so Alison forwarded this also, then deleted it and logged off. A quick look around the room assured her that Mark wouldn't know she had been in, so she closed the door and reattached the hasp, remembering to put the piece of paper back. She went into the bathroom, stripped off and took a hot shower, scrubbing herself as if she were contaminated.

Alison changed into a pair of faded blue jeans and a pink sweat-shirt. She picked up her old brown leather boots and was heading downstairs as Mark came in. He was carrying bags from the local computer game shop and music shop in one hand, and a large paper bag from a fast-food outlet in the other. He spotted her and had the cheek to look guilty. As he tried to sidle past her on the stairs, Alison stood firmly in the way, and he was forced to stop.

'Looks like you've had fun. I don't suppose you have any money for me, do you?' Alison folded her arms and watched him squirm.

'I needed to get some stuff. I'll give you some next time,' Mark said, trying to sound like it wasn't a big deal. He made to squeeze past her, but she blocked his way and shook her head.

'Not good enough, that's the same thing you said last time, and the time before that,' Alison stated. 'There is food in the house, and I doubt very much those computer games are a necessity either. I want some money, Mark, and I want it now.'

Mark's face darkened. 'For fuck's sake, that's all you want me for! It's not my fault I'm depressed, just fuck off and leave me alone!' He tried to push past her, but Alison stood firm, and he stumbled back down two or three stairs, dropping his food, which spilled out all over the hall carpet.

'Now look what you've done, you stupid bitch!' Mark picked up the scattered fries and chicken nuggets, throwing them back into the bag. Alison came slowly down the stairs towards him, her eyes never leaving him. Mark started to look worried. He shouted and swore a lot but was a complete coward when someone faced up to him. He stayed kneeling on the ground and Alison stood over him with a scathing look on her face. A long minute passed, then she stepped past him and went into the kitchen, trying not to let him see how much she was shaking. She heard him go upstairs and let out the breath she'd been holding in.

'I bet you still eat that food despite it being on the floor, you dirty bastard,' she muttered to herself. Mark had some vile habits, none of which had been present when they first moved in together. She shuddered when she recalled some of them. Picking his nose and wiping it off in his pocket or the arm of the sofa – and a few times eating it – picking up cigarette butts and scraping the leftover tobacco out to make roll-ups, going through public bins and taking things out.

The final straw had been when she'd come home one day and caught him urinating in the kitchen sink. 'It's not my fault, I was desperate,' he'd said when she asked him what the hell he was doing. He seemed to think it was highly amusing. Alison had been disgusted and had bleached the sink twice afterwards.

Loud music started blaring out from upstairs, and Alison closed her eyes in despair. Still, no time to worry about him now, she had a meeting to get to. She slipped on her boots, grabbed her jacket and bag, and left the house.

Chapter 3.

My latest subject lies strapped firmly to the old wooden bench, unable to speak thanks to the superglue I applied to its lips. I want it to know how it feels to be paralysed by fear, unable to speak or move. Its eyes search my face, silently pleading for me to show mercy. Did it show mercy at the time? No of course not. So why should I?

Now, how to proceed? I decide to begin with the fingers. I pick up the nutcrackers and apply them, closing my eyes and sighing with satisfaction as I feel the knuckles collapse under the pressure. It tries to pull away, but the heavy-duty strapping holds it firmly in place and discourages movement. Its face is bright red, eyes rolling back and sweat coating its brow. Strange noises are forced down its nose due to the mouth being sealed. I do hope it doesn't choke to death. That would be unfortunate when I haven't even begun yet.

Chapter 4.

D etective Inspector Alex Peachey stood in the shower and groaned as the scalding water hit his skin. He ached all over from where he'd slept on the sofa, but he really couldn't get used to not having his wife beside him in their bed.

He rolled his shoulders under the stream, trying to ease out the knots that seemed to have become a permanent fixture. He knew he had some important decisions to make but really didn't know where to start, so was going to pop into work on his way to the hospital and have a chat with his boss.

Alex switched the shower off, dried himself and got dressed, choosing a dark grey suit and white shirt. He selected the blue tie that Jayne had given him for Christmas and put it on. He wandered through the bungalow that only a few weeks ago had felt new and exciting but was now an empty shell. Alex put the kettle on and stroked Jack, who rubbed around his ankles in false affection as he waited for Alex to give him his breakfast.

'Here you go mate,' Alex murmured as he placed a bowl of food on the floor. 'I hope it tastes better than it smells.' The big black and white cat sniffed it suspiciously and looked at Alex with an accusing stare.

'Take it or leave it pal, there's nothing else.'

Realising that no alternative was forthcoming, Jack crouched down and took a mouthful before strutting away with his nose in the air.

'Everyone's a critic,' Alex remarked. He made himself a mug of tea and leaned against the low worktop to drink it. Sunlight streamed through the oversized windows, lighting up the spacious kitchen. Looking around, Alex could see why his son loved the place so much.

Designed and built by Alex's brother, the bungalow was a few hundred yards from Dave's own house. Everywhere was wheelchair accessible so Joel could live independently if he chose to do so, but a separate, self-contained annexe had been included in case live-in carers were ever needed.

Joel's cerebral palsy had been caused by birth negligence, and the family had successfully sued the hospital, winning Joel substantial compensation. The money had been used for various things over the years, such as specialist equipment, private physios etc., and more recently the new bungalow. Asperger's syndrome had been diagnosed when Joel's behaviour started to become a problem in his teens, and his mother often bore the brunt of his violent outbursts. When Joel had headbutted her and broken her nose, Alex had insisted they involve social services, but Jayne argued she didn't need their help. Things had come to a head a couple of weeks ago when Alex arrived home after work to find Jayne unconscious on the floor and Joel sitting nearby, covered in blood, and crying, insisting he was sorry.

Jayne had been rushed to hospital, where she was found to have a broken elbow, a dislocated shoulder, a shattered cheekbone, and a fractured skull. She also had a blood clot close to her optic nerve, so doctors had placed her in an induced coma to allow the swelling on her brain to go down before they could operate. Despite the assurances from the medical staff that this course of action was safe, Alex was terrified that Jayne wouldn't wake up again. Alex's brother, Dave, had driven him home and stayed with him until he had fallen into an exhausted sleep on the sofa.

The drive to work was uneventful, the roads quiet now rush hour was over. Alex parked in his usual spot in the car park of Wolverhampton police station and sat with his eyes closed for a few moments while he gathered his thoughts. A sharp tap on the window startled him, and he opened his eyes to see DS Craig Muir grinning at him, looking like a model in a black designer suit and cream shirt, his dark hair expertly gelled into place. Today's silk tie and matching handkerchief were in a rich shade of amethyst. He looked like he'd just stepped out of a James Bond film.

'Morning, boss. What are you doing here?'

'Hello Craig,' Alex said, getting out of the car and shaking his friend's hand. 'I'm going to speak to the DCI about coming back to work. I can't do anything at the hospital, and I can't sit at home twiddling my thumbs, so I thought I may as well come and see what you lot are up to.'

'Well, it's good to have you back. How's Jayne?'

'Whether I'm back or not depends on how this meeting with the DCI goes. Jayne's still the same. The breaks are all healing well, and they are doing another scan today to see if the swelling on her brain has gone down. Once it has, they can decide what to do about the blood clot.' Alex's voice cracked, and Craig put a hand on his shoulder to comfort him.

'I was going to ask how you're doing, but I know it's a stupid question,' Craig said. He waited as Alex locked his car and they walked into the station together, only parting company at the top of the stairs outside the room which housed the Major Crimes Unit.

'Craig, let the team know that I'm popping in, but fill them in so I don't have to answer loads of questions,' Alex said as he set off along the corridor towards the DCI's office. 'And tell Les to get the kettle on.'

Craig grinned at him. 'Righto, boss.'

By the time he knocked on DCI Andrew Oliver's office door, Alex's face ached from smiling at people he'd encountered on the way.

'Alex, come in,' Andy said as he got up from behind his desk and shook Alex's hand. 'Would you like a coffee?' He was a tall slim man, with a halo of prematurely white hair and a ready smile. Alex shook the proffered hand but declined the drink and took a seat in front of the desk. Andy poured a coffee from the heated jug on the sideboard before sitting back down in his chair. Alex filled him in on his wife's condition.

'Well, she's getting plenty of rest while she's sedated, which also means she's not under any stress. Have you seen Joel since he's been with your brother?'

'No, I haven't,' Alex admitted. 'To be honest, I can't bring myself to. He will tell me he's sorry to my face, then scream abuse at me like he always does. I'm not in the right frame of mind to deal with that just yet.'

'Have you decided whether or not to press charges?'

'I want to, but Dave and Carol are right when they say it's Jayne's decision to make, not mine. Joel is highly intelligent, and I know he's aware of what he's done. The question is, was it an accident as he claims, or was it intentional?'

'That's the kicker, right there. Jayne's been on the receiving end of Joel's temper many times, but until she can tell you, then you will just have to go with the flow.' Andy looked at his watch. 'Sorry to rush you, but I've got to go and speak to the Chief Constable. If you need more time off, or if it gets a bit much, then please come and see me.' He stood up and walked Alex to the door. 'There is no point whatsoever in pushing yourself too hard, but if you feel ready, then I'm sure acting DI Redwood will be glad that you're back. They've got a particularly strange case, a mutilated body found up at the old aircraft hangars.'

'What's strange about it? That's the norm for us.'

'I'll leave your team to bring you up to speed. It's an unusual one, that's for sure.'

'I'd best get on then. Dawn left me a voicemail the other day, telling me to stop skiving or she'd send Barney round to chew my arse off.'

'She wouldn't do that, she loves that dog too much to expose him to old meat,' Andy replied with a wink.

'Hey, speak for yourself, you're no spring chicken,' Alex laughed.

'Tell me about it, I received my bowel testing kit through the post the other day. Just the kind of thing to make you feel your age.' Andy shook Alex's hand again. 'Go and see your team and tell them the good news.'

'I'll just stay for an hour or so today, so they can bring me up to speed. I've got an appointment with Jayne's consultant this afternoon, but I'll be back in properly from tomorrow.'

'Just do half days for the time being, that way you can spend some quality time with Jayne without spreading yourself too thinly. DS Redwood is more than capable of leading the team in your absence, and if there are any problems, she can always come to me.'

'Thanks, sir, I appreciate that.'

Chapter 5.

Wolverhampton City Council were working hard to clean up the city, but it was no easy task due to many of the dilapidated buildings being listed or of historical importance, so they had to be preserved or restored. They had cleared vast amounts of wasteland where they could, obliterating the abandoned scrapyards and factories so the land could be sold on to developers. The old jam factory in Wednesfield had been renovated and was now the Kingswood Community Centre. The centre had three function rooms of various sizes for hire, a kitchen, toilets, and private offices, and was used by a wide variety of people for things like clinics, parties, wakes, slimming clubs and occasionally as a temporary blood transfusion centre.

Twice a week, the smallest room belonged to Alison's group, and she strived to make it as comfortable as she could. Alison busied herself rearranging the chairs into an inwardly facing circle, then straightened the cushions. She dimmed the lights a fraction and made sure the curtains were firmly closed. The women who came to the group were extremely vulnerable and needed to feel completely safe away from the outside world. This was where they talked about their deepest secrets, opening their hearts, and hoping to find some form of peace.

Tracy Downey breezed into the room, huge smile on her face and a bag of goodies in her hand. She had been in the last group and had got so much out of helping others as well as herself that she had been the perfect choice to run the group with Alison when Sonia Jameson had retired. Alison had welcomed her with open arms, and they had become firm friends.

'Oh wow, what's in that bag? It smells divine,' Alison asked, her mouth watering.

'I stopped off at that little bakery near the fire station; it was about to close so I got a load of Danish pastries for half price, and I snagged the last couple of sausage rolls for Brian's lunch tomorrow. I picked up some milk and biscuits from the corner shop, too. What time did you tell everyone to be here?' Tracy headed into the small kitchen, put the milk in the fridge and arranged the snacks ready for break time, then came back in to see if Alison needed any help.

Alison looked at her watch. 'They should be here in about half an hour. We've got seven women this time; one dropped out at the last minute.' She glanced through her notes. 'They're a nice range of ages, too; the youngest is in her twenties and eldest is almost sixty.'

Tracy nodded her approval. 'That's a really good mix. Hopefully, the younger ones will make the older ones feel more comfortable. They always seem embarrassed to talk about anything sexual.'

'I think it's a generation thing, so many subjects were taboo back then,' Alison said as she placed a pile of paper and some coloured pencils on the table. 'Jean was a bit like that last time, do you remember? She was slow to join in but once she got over her shyness, she made amazing progress. Did you know she went for that promotion? Jean would never have pushed herself like that before; she used to let them walk all over her. Rumour has it that she's gone from a mouse to a lion, and boy can she roar.'

Tracy laughed out loud. 'That's fantastic, good for Jean! I knew she would go far.' They heard the doorbell ring and Tracy looked at the wall clock. 'Blimey, there's fifteen minutes to go yet. Someone's keen.' She went towards the kitchen to put the kettle on, leaving Alison to open the door.

At first, the new group were hesitant, but the kind nature of the two leaders soon helped them to settle.

'Hello and welcome to our survivors' group. My name is Alison, and this is Tracy. We started out just like you, so we know how you must all be feeling. We hope to help you come to terms with what you've been through, and to show you that is not normal, not acceptable, and never, ever your fault. The person or people who hurt you are the ones to blame, despite what they may have told you at the time. No one on this earth has the right to take your dignity and self-worth the way they did. We are here to help you get that back.'

Alison glanced at Tracy and saw her nod her appreciation. The first meeting was always a tough one; you never knew what kind of people you would be seeing and how they would react to a group session. This was Alison's fifth group, and all the women who had attended had been able to face their demons and come out as winners.

Angie Mathieson had been the one exception.

Even after seven years, Alison still blamed herself for Angie's death. They had met when they had both attended the group and had become firm friends. If Alison hadn't suggested going out that day, Angie would never have spotted the man in the shopping centre. Time had appeared to slow down as Angie walked calmly up to him and stabbed him in the neck with a pen in front of his family. He had bled to death on the way to hospital while the police had searched for Angie, who had run off after the attack. Alison had been taken to the police station, but after what seemed like endless questioning the police had let her go. She had returned to her car on the rooftop car park to find Angie standing on the ledge. As Alison ran towards her, Angie smiled then stepped off. The only good thing that came out of Angie's suicide was the knowledge that she was finally at peace.

'We'll start by introducing ourselves. As I said just now, I'm Alison, and I was abused by my dad's friend, who we called Uncle Geoff. He used to babysit for me and my little brother when we were young. We'd go into the bathroom, and he would get me to touch him. He used to say it was a puppet and if I was good, it would dance for me.

I had no idea that it was wrong, I just thought it was a fun game. It went on for months until my brother asked my dad why he never got to play with Uncle Geoff's puppet in the bathroom. My dad confronted him, but he denied it and said he'd done nothing wrong. We never saw him again after that, my parents just said he'd moved away. Back then, sexual abuse wasn't really talked about like it is nowadays, so it was all swept under the carpet. I pretty much blanked it out until I was older and began to realise what he had done. I lived with the guilt until I was around fifteen, when I started drinking and fell in with a bad crowd. My parents didn't know how to deal with me, and I ended up in care for a while. When I first heard about this group years later, I didn't want to know, the thought of talking about it was painful, but I eventually came to realise that what happened to me was never going to go away, so decided to give it a go. I did the ten-week course twice before my group leader, Sonia Jameson, asked me to help run it. We worked together ever since, until she took early retirement. This is Tracy's first time as my co-worker and right-hand woman. I'll hand you over to her now, and she can tell you her story.'

By the time the interval came, everyone looked more relaxed than they had when they first arrived. Tracy made tea and coffee, and Alison handed round the snacks whilst the women chatted amongst themselves. When the session ended, Alison handed out cards with her mobile phone number on, in case anyone wanted to talk more privately. It didn't take long to tidy up afterwards, and soon they were heading out the door themselves.

By the time Alison got home she was shattered, but in a good way. She opened the front door and was met with silence. Mark must have gone out again. Resisting the temptation to double lock the door, she headed upstairs for a soak in the bath and an early night.

Chapter 6.

Alex stood outside his wife's hospital room, trying not to listen to the nurses as they dealt with Jayne's various drips and tubes, but getting more and more agitated by their loud conversation.

'I don't know what I'd do if it were me. I mean, how do you choose between your partner and your child?' the first one said.

'I know, it must be awful. I mean, to be saddled with a kid like that to start with, then for them to grow up and try to kill you. It doesn't bear thinking about,' the other replied.

A blur flew past Alex and threw the door open, startling both nurses. 'You two might want to think about winding your necks in before I report the pair of you! Half the bloody ward can hear you, not to mention Mrs Peachey's husband, who is standing right outside the door, listening to you two picking his family to pieces. Now, get out!'

'But we need to finish...' was as far as one got before seeing the fury on Carol Peachey's face. The nurses left hurriedly, heads bowed so they wouldn't have to look Alex in the eye as they passed him. His sister-in-law stood with her hands on her hips, her face like thunder.

'Thanks Carol, I appreciate that,' Alex said, planting a kiss on her cheek. He offered her the comfy chair on one side of Jayne's bed, taking the plastic one on the other side for himself.

'You're very welcome. Those two will have a rocket up their arses once I've finished with them,' Carol replied, taking her coat off. She kissed her sister-in-law on the forehead before sitting down.

'Leave it Carol, while they're talking about us they're leaving everyone else alone,' Alex said, stroking Jayne's dark hair. The bruising was almost gone now, but Jayne's face still looked misshapen. Alex hoped it was just the tape holding the breathing tube in place. He placed his forehead gently against hers and prayed she could feel his thoughts.

'You look posh, have you been into work?' Carol asked. She looked tiny in the big hospital chair. She wore faded blue jeans, a yellow zip-up hooded sweatshirt, and a pair of black trainers. She rummaged in her pockets and pulled out a couple of boiled sweets. She offered one to Alex and took the remaining one herself.

'Yes, I thought I should probably go in and show my face. To be honest, I was going spare at home,' Alex said, opening the sweet and popping it into his mouth. 'If it weren't for the cat, I'd just stay here all the time.'

'It does you good to step away, Alex. You'll be no use to Jayne when she wakes up if you're knackered.' She looked at him and waited a moment before she spoke again. 'Joel said to ask you if he could come home.'

'I don't bloody think so, do you?' Alex snapped.

The machines attached to Jayne started to beep, making them both jump. A nurse came in and pressed some buttons on one of the various pieces of equipment that Jayne was hooked up to.

'I think she heard us.' Carol leaned over the bed and spoke into Jayne's ear. 'Joel's fine darlin', don't you worry. Me and Dave are looking after him.' The beeping stopped, and the nurse smiled at Carol before leaving again.

'Sorry, Carol. I didn't mean to bite your head off.'

'Hey, no need for apologies. I think we've all heard enough of those recently.'

'How is he otherwise?' Alex asked. 'Apart from wanting to come home.'

'He's okay,' Carol said. 'He's quiet most of the time. He's working his way through Wayne's jigsaw puzzle collection.'

'I don't want to see him just yet.'

'That's understandable. Dave and I can manage in the meantime. Speak of the devil,' she smiled as Dave walked in, bringing the smell of winter with him. His breath came out in little clouds and his cheeks glowed red from the cold.

'Bugger me, it's nippy out there,' he said, plonking himself on the end of Jayne's bed. He ruffled Alex's hair. 'How's it going, little bro?' he grinned.

Alex smoothed his hair down again in mock annoyance. 'Fine until you got here, knobhead.'

'Ah, you love me really,' Dave laughed. He was a taller, stockier version of Alex, and older by a couple of years. His ruddy complexion came from being outside most of the day, overseeing his team of builders, but he still had the ramrod-straight posture he'd had since his army days.

He studied Jayne for a moment, then poked her gently in the leg. 'Oi, lazybones, move over and let me lie down, I'm knackered after a hard day's graft. It's alright for some, lying around all day while the rest of us are outside in all weather.' He winked at Alex, his booming laugh echoing around the room.

'Shut up you twat,' Carol said. 'You'll have the sister in here if you're not careful.'

Dave rubbed his hands together with glee. 'Now you're talking, a nice sexy nurse to look at my throbbing joints.'

Alex stifled a laugh as Carol aimed a slap at Dave's head. 'You'll have a throbbing earhole if you don't behave yourself.'

'Steady on, I was only joking,' Dave said. He pulled a sulky face and looked at Alex. 'Can I have her done for spousal abuse?'

Alex laughed. 'You could, but Carol would beat us both to a pulp.'

'That's true,' Dave agreed, throwing a cheesy grin at his wife before turning back to look at Jayne. There was no sound for a moment, except for the rhythmic beeping of the machines.

'The bruising's faded a lot,' Dave remarked. 'Have they said when they are going to wake her up?'

'I was meant to see the consultant, but they've had to rush off to an emergency that came in just now.' Alex picked up the clipboard hanging at the bottom of Jayne's bed and flipped through it before putting it back. 'I'm not even going to attempt to read that, it's all gobbledygook to me.'

A nurse came into the room, holding a notebook. 'Hello folks, I'm Lisa, I'll be looking after Jayne this week,' she said, her Irish lilt both melodic and soothing. 'I was just about to come in and do Jayne's observations and heard what you said, so I thought I'd bring you this.' She handed the notebook to Alex. 'We keep a diary in layman's terms of what treatment our patients are receiving; we encourage families to write things about their loved one too, such as what their favourite food or drink is. If you like, we can have a radio brought in and tuned to her favourite station, and you can bring a soft toy or item of clothing sprayed with her favourite perfume and we'll place it close by so she can smell it. When we wake her up, she may feel quite disorientated, so something familiar will help to keep her calm.'

'That's a lovely idea, I'll bring something in for her tomorrow,' Alex said. 'She likes sixties music, especially The Beatles, so if you can find a station that plays that sort of thing, she will be happy.' He gave a nervous cough. 'Do you know when you'll be waking her up?'

The nurse looked at the chart. 'According to this, she had a scan earlier. The results aren't on here, so I'll go and see if I can track them down.' She bustled out of the room again.

'I'd forgotten she'd had that done today. Now I feel like a complete shit for not asking when I arrived,' Alex said, rubbing his face.

'Come on bro, you've got loads on your plate, no doubt I would have forgotten too if I were in your shoes,' Dave said, slapping Alex's shoulder. 'Once the nurse has been back with the scan results you should go home and get some sleep. If Jayne wakes up and sees you looking like that, you'll scare her back into a coma. Your eyes are like piss-holes in the snow.'

Alex laughed. 'Okay, I'll go and get my head down as soon as I know what's going on. Will I see you tomorrow?'

'No, Joel's got double clubs tomorrow, then I've got to drop Wayne off in town before I go and do the shopping, but if we can pop round the day after, that would be great.'

'Sounds good,' Alex replied. He noticed Dave and Carol exchanging glances. 'Is everything okay?'

'Everything is fine, we just wanted to have a chat with you about something. It's nothing to worry about, it can wait.'

'Sounds ominous,' Alex commented, looking around as the door opened and the nurse came back in.

'Sorry about that, I was waylaid by an anxious relative,' she said, 'But I have the results of Jayne's scan now, so if you'll bear with me, I'll tell you what it says.' She read through the paperwork in her hand before addressing them.

'The blood clot is stable; it hasn't changed shape at all. The swelling on her brain has reduced slightly, a little slower than we would have liked, but at least it's going down. Once it's reduced enough the surgeon will operate to remove the clot.'

'What if they can't remove it? Will Jayne go blind?' Alex asked, fear creeping into his voice.

'Let's cross that bridge when we come to it,' the nurse said. 'No point worrying at this stage, let's just get her through this part first.' She smiled at them all and left the room.

'Well, I don't feel as if I'm any the wiser than before,' Alex complained.

'I know darlin', but there's nothing to be done about it just yet,' Carol said. She stood up and hugged him before picking up her bag and signalled for Dave to open the door. 'Let's all go home and get some rest while we can, because she's going to need all of us when she wakes up.'

Chapter 7.

When Alison got up the next morning, Mark was either already out or hadn't come back the night before. Alison suspected the latter, seeing the door chain still off. She went into the kitchen and put the kettle on. The doorbell rang and Alison hurried to answer it, wondering who it could be at such an early hour.

Jean Harrison stood on the doorstep, nervously looking around. She was smartly dressed in a blue two-piece trouser suit, white blouse, and black court shoes. Her mid-length grey hair had been blow-dried straight and fastened back with a silver clip.

'Hello Jean, what a lovely surprise! Come in, you're just in time for a cuppa.' Alison hugged her. 'Congratulations on the promotion, you deserve it.'

Jean said nothing but walked through to the kitchen. She sat on one of the stools at the breakfast bar and watched as Alison sorted drinks out for them both.

'I'm afraid I can't chat for long; I've got to get to work,' Alison said as she handed Jean a mug of coffee.

'It's okay, I won't keep you. I'm so sorry, but I need to ask you something personal.' Jean seemed anxious and the mug trembled in her hands.

'Sure, what do you need to know?'

'You know the work we did when I came to the group – the charts, drawings, and worksheets? What happens to it all afterwards, once the course is over?'

Alison looked surprised. 'I transfer all my notes onto my computer and keep the handwritten ones in my filing cabinet. Everything else is destroyed.'

'You don't share them with anyone else, do you, like on the internet?'

'No, of course not. Only the person who is running the group with me gets to see it. We usually arrange a meeting, where we can go through everything in private. That way, if someone is struggling with a particular issue, such as your phobia with snakes, we can work out how best to help them.' Alison looked concerned. 'What's wrong Jean? Please tell me.'

'This arrived in the post today.' Jean opened her bag and took out an envelope, containing a piece of card. There was a picture of a dead snake on the front. On the back were the words 'Goodnight, God Bless' and a row of numbers. Jean began to cry, big loud sobs that made her entire body shake.

Alison grabbed the kitchen roll, tore off a few sheets and handed them to Jean. 'What a horrible thing to do! I'm so sorry, Jean; I don't know what to say.'

'I'd barely got over the shock of opening that, when the police called. They want me to go in for an interview this morning to answer some questions about a body they've found. I was hoping that you'd come with me. I don't think I can face it alone,' Jean said, wiping her eyes. Her words were punctuated with hiccups from crying so hard.

'Of course I'll come with you, I'll just ring the school and arrange to have the morning off,' Alison said, giving her friend a hug. 'What about your mum? Will she be okay?'

'The carers are there now, and Mary next door has said she will take over from them until I get back.' Jean smiled. 'Thank you for this, you're a good friend.'

'You're welcome,' Alison said. She called work and explained she had a personal issue to deal with, then picked up her bag and followed Jean outside. They climbed into Alison's car and set off, leaving Jean's car on the driveway.

'Have you any idea who the dead person could be?' Alison asked as she turned out of the lane onto the main road.

'Not a clue,' Jean sniffed. 'Apart from those of you I met at the group and a couple of work colleagues, it's just me and Mum.'

Alison looked puzzled. 'But if you don't know who it is, why would the police want to interview you?'

'I guess we'll find that out when we get there.'

Chapter 8.

When Alex walked into the office of the Major Crimes Unit, the whole team gave him a round of applause. Tears pricked at his eyes, and he coughed to clear the lump that had formed in his throat as he looked around the room. There were two teams in the Major Crime Unit, and when the police had acquired the newly converted flour mill, Alex had been in the right place at the right time and had snagged the top floor office, with Charlie Baldwin's team taking the one on the floor below. The room consisted of a large open-plan space, with desks at one end and a small kitchen and rest area at the other. In the centre of the room was a large table, used for briefings, etc. Along one wall was all the technical stuff – photocopiers, printers and so on, with Alex's office tucked away in one corner. The huge windows were the original ones from a more industrial age, and despite being set very high up the walls, they allowed plenty of natural light to flood in.

'Thanks everyone, it's nice to know you've missed me, but I'm back now so there'll be no more slacking,' he said, causing a ripple of laughter. 'We'll have a proper catch-up in a bit, but for now I'm going to reclaim my chair and let DS Redwood bring me up to speed, while Les makes me a brew.'

DC Les Morris sighed theatrically. 'Why is it always my turn, why can't Gary do it?'

'Because you're older than me,' DC Gary Temple replied with a grin.

'No, it's because he is going to fetch the doughnuts,' Alex said to everyone's amusement except Gary's.

'Ah, boss, that's not fair!'

'If you weren't so lippy maybe you wouldn't have to. Anyway, the exercise will do you good, you've got a wedding coming up.'

Gary's face lit up as he slipped his jacket on. 'Aye, you've got me there. Come on, get your money out, guys.'

'I'll get these,' Alex said, handing him a twenty-pound note. 'Get a box of twelve assorted, and make sure there's a lemon meringue one in there for me. I could do with a sugar hit.'

'Righto boss, I shan't be long,' Gary said as he disappeared through the doorway.

Before Dawn could speak, the phone on her desk rang, and she went to answer it. 'Mo, can you bring the boss up to speed while I get this?'

'It will be a pleasure.' DC Maureen 'Mo' Ross walked over to the incident board. 'We got a call yesterday to say that a body had been found in one of the old aircraft hangars at the back of RAF Cosford.'

'Who found it?' Alex got his notebook out ready to jot down anything useful. 'Surely not a dog walker? That's a restricted area.'

'No, it was a construction crew. The hangars are being demolished to make way for a new airman's accommodation block. One of the guys thought it was a present for him at first, because of the wrapping.'

'Wrapping?'

'The body was inside a box that had been gift-wrapped. It looked like a huge birthday present, and one of the guys had just turned forty. He got the shock of his life when he opened it.'

'Bloody hell, I bet he did! I hope they didn't throw the wrapping paper away.'

'No, as soon as they realised what it was they backed off and called us. They even set up cones to keep people away from the area.'

'Maybe all these police dramas are starting to teach people some common sense at last.' Alex scratched his head. 'Do we know who it is? The body, I mean?'

'Not yet, but we do have a lead of sorts. There was a gift tag on the parcel with a name and address on.'

'You're kidding!'

'Nope, and the woman it was addressed to is coming in this morning to talk to us.'

'Excellent.' Alex looked at Mo, noting the walking stick. 'How are you?'

Mo shrugged. 'I'm getting there, some days are better than others. I'm having physio, but it's going to be a long road.'

'Car chases are all very well if you're auditioning for a Hollywood blockbuster, but in real life they are highly dangerous. Dare I ask about your car?'

Mo winced as she thought about her precious Ford Capri, which had been badly damaged when Mo had chased a suspect along the M54 motorway. The suspect had rolled the car she was driving and had ended up in Mo's path, leaving her nowhere to go but straight into her. Mo had walked away with whiplash, cracked ribs and a sprained ankle. The suspect hadn't been so lucky and was pronounced dead at the scene. Mo still felt guilty, even after she'd discovered that Michelle Simmons had died from a broken neck when the car rolled, so was already gone before Mo had collided with her.

'It's a sorry mess, I can tell you. My brother was furious at first, but he was glad I wasn't hurt too badly. I'm so grateful he fitted those extra safety features when he restored the car. I'd be a goner if he hadn't.'

'Can he rebuild it or is it too far gone?'

'He's confident he can fix it as it's mainly bodywork, but it's getting hold of parts, that's the problem. Not many places carry stock for a 1979 Capri.'

Alex gave her a gentle hug. 'I'm sure he'll work his magic and you'll soon be reunited with your baby. Do you have a car you can use in the meantime?'

'No, my ankle isn't strong enough yet, but the rest of the team are taking turns giving me lifts to work and back. Isobel doesn't have a car, so I'll have to look at getting something reasonably priced to keep me going until the Capri is back on the road.'

'I'll keep my ears open and let you know if I hear of one going cheap,' Alex said.

'Cars don't go cheap, budgies do,' Craig piped up from behind his desk.

'Ha ha, very funny – not,' Mo said, throwing a pen at him.

'Hey, that's police brutality! Boss, do something!' Craig protested.

Alex winked at Mo. 'I didn't see a thing.'

'Oh, I see how it is,' Craig retorted. 'Just you wait until you're
better, I'll have you doing my paperwork for a month – or not,' he
added, seeing Alex's face. 'Only joking, boss.'

'You'd better be,' Alex warned, trying not to smile.

Dawn put the phone down. 'That was Faz, he has a preliminary
report for us so I'm going to pick it up before my interviewee gets
here. Do you fancy coming with me?'

'Sure,' Alex said. 'Les, forget that tea for now, I'll have a fresh one
when I get back.' Alex followed Dawn out of the door as Les came
out of the kitchen area with Alex's drink. Craig nearly fell off his
chair laughing at the expression on his face.

'Every bloody time,' Les muttered. 'Ah well, waste not want not,'
he said, taking a slurp.

The city mortuary was on the other side of the large green area
next to the police station, alongside the magistrate's court. It made
life much easier to have all three important buildings close together,
the old mortuary having been part of New Cross Hospital in
Wednesfield, and it saved time not having to travel back and forth all
the time when there was a case to solve. The fourth side of the quadrangle was home to trendy cafes and restaurants, all vying for trade
from one of the busiest areas of the city.

Alex and Dawn walked across the green, chatting idly about anything and everything.

'How's Barney?' Alex enquired.

Dawn's face lit up at the mention of her precious German Shep-
herd. 'He's great, he enjoyed his holiday in the countryside. Loads of
places for him to run around and explore.' She laughed. 'You should
have seen him when he came across a rabbit though, he hid behind
my legs like a frightened puppy.'

Alex laughed at the thought of the huge dog fearing something so small. 'He's a special egg, that one.'

'He is, but he's my special egg, and I love him. Pets are wonderful, they never judge you, they're great listeners, and they always know when you need hugs.'

'They do, we wouldn't be without Jack. He's like a little old man; so grumpy but so lovable at the same time.'

It's a shame you can't take him to see Jayne, it might help her recovery.'

'If it would I'd do it in a heartbeat.' Alex tried to smile. 'But she'll soon be fighting fit again.'

'She will, so you'd better be keeping on top of the housework or you'll be for the high jump.'

'There's only myself and Jack to look after at the moment. Joel is still at Dave and Carol's.'

'Have you seen him since it happened?'

'No, and I'm not sure I want to.' Alex gave a mirthless laugh. 'I've heard he's insisting it wasn't him, but let's face it, Jayne didn't beat herself up.'

'It must be really tough. If you need to talk to anyone...'

'Thanks, Dawn. I really appreciate that.'

'I was going to say talk to someone else,' Dawn laughed.

'Thanks, pal,' Alex grinned back, grateful for the humour.

They reached the mortuary building and Dawn opened the door for Alex. 'Age before beauty.'

'You cheeky bugger!'

'You love me really.' Dawn spotted a familiar figure coming towards them. 'Look who it is.'

'Alex!' Dr Matthew 'Faz' Farrow called out when he saw his old friend walking along the corridor towards him. 'About time you came back, the place hasn't been the same without you!'

'Faz, good to see you too.' Alex was enveloped in a bear hug so tight it threatened to cut off his air supply. He extricated himself, eyes glistening as he grinned at the coroner.

'Don't mind me,' Dawn added drily. 'I'll just stand here and look pretty.'

'Detective Sergeant Redwood, you always look pretty, you don't need me to tell you that. I choose not to say it though as you'll arrest me for sexual misconduct.'

'Fine, you're forgiven,' Dawn smiled. 'But I wouldn't arrest you, I'd just beat you up.'

'And I'd pretend not to enjoy every minute,' Faz winked. He held out a slim file. 'It's not much, I'm afraid. I'm still waiting on some stuff, tox screen, hair analysis, etc., but the basics are in there.'

Dawn flicked through the contents then passed it to Alex. 'It makes for grim reading,' she said.

'It certainly is. Someone took their time with this chap; in the end it was exsanguination that killed him.'

'These injuries are brutal.' Alex handed the file back to Dawn. 'They must have kept him for hours in order to cause so much damage.'

'Agreed. Anyway, I can't stop because I've got a family coming in to sort out paperwork for the release of their loved one. Text me when you're free Alex, and we'll go for a curry and a catch up.' Faz patted Alex's shoulder, smiled at Dawn and strode off towards his office.

Dawn's phone pinged with a text from Craig to tell her that her interviewee had arrived, so they headed back towards the station.

'Do you mind taking the lead while I take notes?' Dawn asked as they walked along.

'Sure,' Alex said. 'Your shorthand is much better than mine. I'm going to head off after lunch if that's okay. I want to go to the hospital and see how Jayne is, then I've got some stuff to sort out at home be-fore Gary and Craig come round later.'

'Is it roleplaying night?' Dawn asked.

'Yes, Jayne bought me the new Deathwatch RPG for Christmas and tonight's as good a time as any to start, seeing as we finished our last game when you lot were out with Jo on her hen night.'

'RPG? Is that where you dress up and run around in the woods?'

'No, that's LARP, it stands for Live Action Role Play. RPG means Role Playing Game. We play with multi-faceted dice – some with as many as twenty sides – and score sheets.'

'Ooh, very retro,' Dawn smirked.

'Sometimes the old ways are the best. Now, let's go and do this interview.'

Chapter 9.

Alison took Jean's hand in hers as they waited for Alex and Dawn in one of the interview suites. These rooms were usually reserved for interviewing children, vulnerable people, or victims of sexual or domestic abuse. It was a large, airy room, painted in a sunny shade of yellow, with a feature wall decorated with floral wallpaper. Cream-coloured blinds hung at each of the two wide rectangular windows, and the floor was covered with dark-grey carpet. A huge yellow circular rug was at the far end of the room, on which stood a child-size plastic table and chairs. Boxes of children's books and toys lined the wall under the windows. The day was cold but bright, and sunlight poured in, making the room feel welcoming. Alison put her arm around Jean and could feel her trembling with fear.

Jean jumped violently when the door opened and the two officers walked in, but their warm smiles and easy manner as they made their introductions helped to calm her nerves. She squeezed Alison's hand to let her know she was okay.

Once everyone was introduced and refreshments sorted out, Dawn opened her notepad and glanced at Alex, waiting for him to begin.

'Mrs Harrison, thank you for coming in,' Alex said, smiling at them both. 'We've just a few questions to ask you if that's okay.'

Jean nodded and swallowed hard. She closed her eyes and took a few calming breaths to steady herself, an exercise she had learned in Alison's group sessions. 'I'm ready,' she said.

Alex opened a slim file on the coffee table in front of him. It contained a few pages and some photographs, but Alex was careful to keep these covered up for the time being.

'I'm not sure how much you've been told, so I'll start from the beginning,' Alex said. 'The body of a man was discovered yesterday afternoon, in a disused hangar near the private airfield near RAF Cosford. His remains had been placed in a large wooden crate which was gift-wrapped, with a tag bearing your name and address attached to the outside. Do you have any idea why someone would do this, or do you know who the victim could be?'

Jean reached into her handbag, pulled out the envelope she had shown to Alison and handed it to Alex.

'I don't know, but I received this in the post this morning,' she said.

Alex opened the envelope and took out the card. He looked at both sides carefully before passing it to Dawn.

'Do you know what it means?' Alex asked.

Jean started shaking. She looked at Alison with pleading eyes. 'You tell them, I'm going to be sick,' she said as she leapt up and ran for the door. Dawn dropped her notebook and hurried after Jean, leaving Alison and Alex alone.

'It's not my story to tell, but I'll give you the abridged version if you'd like to take notes,' Alison said. She waited for Alex to pick up the notebook and to retrieve the pen which had rolled under the table.

'I run a group for survivors of childhood abuse. It's a ten-week course, all designed to help the attendees work through their abuse and learn how to deal with issues that are a direct result of the trauma they experienced,' Alison explained. 'Everything we talk about in that group is strictly confidential, nothing leaves that room. Jean came to the last group, which finished several weeks ago. She was abused by her uncle when she was five years old, he had a shop and he used to molest her in the storeroom. He had a tattoo of a snake on his arm, and he used to tell her that it would bite her if she told anyone. She's had a phobia of snakes ever since.'

'I see,' Alex said, looking at the card again. 'Do you think that this picture was sent by him?'

Alison shook her head. 'I don't think so, it looks a lot like the one Jean drew a picture of as part of her therapy. Whoever sent the card knew about her phobia, which means that they either wanted to frighten Jean, or...'

'Or what?'

'Or they wanted to let her know that he can't hurt her anymore. That's why the snake is dead.'

'What about the numbers?'

'Those I have no idea about. Maybe Jean knows.' Alison looked towards the door as Jean and Dawn came back in. Jean looked like she'd been crying again.

'Sorry about that,' Jean said. She sat down and picked up the glass of water on the table, hands shaking as she took a sip.

'No problem,' Alex assured her. 'Are you okay to continue?'

'Yes, please carry on.' Jean nodded and took another drink of water.

'Alison has explained to me what the picture represents, so we don't need to discuss that just now. Can you shed any light on the other details?'

Jean looked at Alison before answering. 'The numbers don't mean anything to me, but the message does. One of the things we discussed in our group were memories that made us happy. I used to spend a lot of time with my grandparents during my childhood, and when my grandma tucked me into bed at night, she used to kiss me and say 'Goodnight, God bless'. I always slept like a log when I stayed there because I knew I was safe.'

Dawn looked up from her notepad. 'So, the phrase could mean that you can sleep safely now,' she said.

'That's what I'm thinking too,' Alex added.

'The only time I've told anyone about that was in the group, and when we did the drawing therapy, I wrote those words on my work because they represented happier times,' Jean said.

'Are you able to give me the name of the person who abused you?' Alex asked gently.

Jean's face paled. 'I can't,' she said. 'What if he finds out?'

'He won't find out, because the police are not allowed to tell him, are you?' Alison said, looking at Alex and Dawn, daring them to disagree with her.

'No, we're not.' Dawn leaned forward and took Jean's hand in hers. 'I know you're frightened, but if you can't tell us his name, could you possibly give us a description of him instead?'

Jean wiped her mouth with a tissue. 'I suppose I could do that. I don't know how tall he was, but he was bigger than my dad. He had greasy blond hair and horrible blue eyes.' Jean shuddered. 'I remember those eyes boring into mine, they were so cold and cruel.'

'That's great, Jean,' Dawn prompted. 'Anything else? Does he have any distinguishing marks?'

'Yes, he had a big mole on the right side of his neck, about here.' Jean pointed to her own neck and Dawn wrote it down. 'He also had a tattoo on his left bicep, it used to terrify me.'

'Why's that?' Alex asked.

'It was of a cobra, reared up like it would strike. You have to realise that I was quite young, so I believed him when he said it would bite me if I didn't do as I was told.'

Dawn and Alex exchanged glances. The body in the morgue was a match to the man Jean had described.

'Thank you, you've been a huge help,' Alex said. He decided to take a risk.

'Jean, if I tell you that you will never have to worry about him ever again, would you reconsider giving us his name?'

'I don't know, I'm scared he will find out.'

'I don't think you need to worry about him anymore. We can't say for certain until there's been a formal identification so this is off the record, but the description you've given us matches the body recovered from the hangars. I think someone's left you his corpse as a gift.'

Chapter 10.

Then.

Tracy groaned and bit down on the hand towel as the pain ripped through her body. The tiny foetus finally gave up its fight for life and was expelled into the watery grave below. Tracy flushed the loo quickly, before she was tempted to look.

The bathroom door rattled, and a whiny voice called out. 'Mum, make her hurry up, I'm going to wet myself!'

'Tracy, are you still in that bathroom?" Her mother's words cut into her thoughts like a razor blade. "Hurry up, you're going to be late for school again! Gemma's been waiting ages; you'll make her late too if you don't get a move on!'

'Give me a minute will you?' Tracy roared back. 'I'm nearly done!' She cleaned herself up as best she could, sluiced her face with cold water and wiped it dry. She looked in the mirror at her pale reflection, her dark brown hair plastered to her face. Opening the door, she stuck her tongue out at her little brother as he shoved past in his rush to get to the toilet.

'About bloody time! You'll never make it before the bell at this rate.' Tracy's mum looked at her suspiciously. 'What's wrong with you now? Always something these days, I dread to think what your exam results will be like.'

Tracy shrugged, ran her fingers through her damp hair and grabbed her school bag. 'If you must know, I've got my period, and it's a messy one. What do you care about my exams anyway? As long as I get a job and bring money in you couldn't give a flying fuck!' The slap was expected but still stung her cheek.

'Watch your mouth or I'll really give you something to complain about.' Tracy's mum turned to Gemma and smiled. 'Sorry about that, chick,' she said, 'But she drives me round the bend some days. I bet you don't give your mum any trouble do you?'

Gemma shook her head with an embarrassed smile and headed for the door. Tracy followed, throwing her mother a dirty look before slamming the door behind her. Both girls breathed a sigh of relief as they walked quickly away from the house.

'Jeez Tracy, how do you put up with it?' Gemma asked, puffing to keep up with her friend. 'It would do my head in.'

Tracy laughed despite the thudding ache in her stomach and hooked her arm through Gemma's. 'Fuck her, she's a stupid cow. Come on, let's move it or we'll have that dickhead Docherty moaning at us as well.' They picked up speed until they were almost running. Tracy kept her eyes forward but knew from the burning sensation on the back of her head that she was being watched from the upstairs window of her house.

BOBBIE DUCKED AS THE shoe flew over her head. She ran for the stairs, but the coarse, grating voice of her mother drifted after her.

'You little whore, you wait till I catch a hold of you!'

Bobbie pulled a bag out from under her bed. She'd been secreting food and money in it for a while, waiting for the right opportunity to leave, and from the fury in her mother's voice, she knew that the time had finally come. She would have preferred to hang on for a few more weeks to scrape a bit more money together, scavenged from her mother's and sister's purses, small amounts that wouldn't be missed, but her time had run out when she'd been caught washing her sheets, stained with the evidence of her shame.

'You can't stay up there all night,' the voice taunted. 'You have to come down sometime, and when you do, you'll get what's coming to you, you filthy little slut!' The front door slammed and a welcome silence fell.

Bobbie was so engrossed in her packing that she jumped when her sister came into the small bedroom they shared. She took one look at the bag and grabbed Bobbie by the shoulders, shaking her.

'How long has it been going on?' she demanded. 'Tell me!'

Bobbie refused to look at her, her cheeks red with embarrassment. After a few minutes, Angie let go and Bobbie sank down onto the bed. 'A few weeks.'

'I don't fucking believe it!'

'It's not your fault, Angie.'

'No, it's not, and it's not yours either.' Angie picked up a pillow and threw it against the wall, her eyes blazing with anger. 'I'll kill her!'

'Please, don't do that! You'll get into trouble and they will take you away. You can't protect me if you're in jail.' A single tear rolled down Bobbie's cheek.

Angie's face softened and she hugged her sister tightly. 'Fair enough, but it stops tonight. Don't worry about her,' she added, seeing Bobbie's scared glance towards the door. 'Trust me, by the time I'm finished, she'll be the scared one.'

THE STUDENTS RUSHED from the room, oblivious to the teacher's shouts to slow down. As Julie went to leave, Mrs Birch called her back.

'Are you okay, love? You look a bit peaky. Should I phone your mum and get her to come and pick you up early?' The teacher brushed Julie's hair back off her face and felt her forehead. 'You're a bit warm, why don't you take that cardigan off?'

'No, it's okay. Thanks, Miss.' Julie pulled her cardigan around her, her voice so low that the teacher had to lean in close to hear. 'It's just a headache.'

'Maybe you're dehydrated. Why don't you go and get a drink of water from the fountain, then go and sit in the medical room for a bit?' Mrs Birch studied the young girl intently but Julie continued to stare at the desk in silence. Sighing, she let her go, noticing the way Julie held her ribs as she walked.

Julie grabbed her bag and hurried out of the room before the teacher could ask any more awkward questions and headed towards the water fountain outside the gym. She rubbed her arm where the bruises were starting to turn yellow. She should have known better than to struggle, it just made things worse. Leaning over the fountain made her catch her breath in pain, so Julie cupped one hand to catch the water that shot out of the spout, whilst holding down the button with the other.

'Hey, skiver!' a voice called along the corridor, making Julie jump and spill water down her front. Julie's heart sank when she spotted Lydia Duggins walking towards her. Her skirt was rolled up to show her pudgy thighs, and her dark-blonde hair was pulled up in a rough ponytail.

Lydia laughed when she saw the girl's wet skirt. 'Ha, you've pissed yourself! Shall I fetch your mummy to change your nappy for you, you little baby?' Her irritating laugh was like nails down a black-board, and it echoed down the hallway.

Julie tried to walk away, but the bully stepped in front of her and refused to let her pass. 'Have you got any money?'

'No,' Julie muttered in a soft voice.

'What did you say to me, you little bitch?' Lydia grabbed Julie by the shirt front and pulled her close, her green eyes full of cruelty. Julie recoiled at the smell of stale cigarettes on the girl's breath. She noticed a blackhead on Lydia's oversized nose but didn't mention it in case the girl punched her.

'I said no, I haven't got any money.' Julie winced as Lydia pushed her away again, causing Julie to bang her sore arm on the water fountain.

'We'll soon see if you're lying,' Lydia sneered. She grabbed Julie's bag and upended it, laughing as the contents spilled out all over the floor. She pulled a face when she didn't see any money.

'Fucking useless, that's what you are!' She threw the bag on the ground and stalked off, leaving Julie to pick everything up.

'What's going on?' A stern voice asked as the door to the gym was flung open. The PE teacher stood, hands on hips, glaring down at Julie as she picked up her things.

'Nothing Miss, just dropped my bag. I'm sorry.'

'Well, hurry up and get to class before I give you a detention.' The door was slammed closed again.

Julie felt tears pricking at the back of her eyes but blinked them angrily away. She crammed the last of her belongings into her bag, heaved it onto her shoulder and headed for her next lesson, the pain in her ribs burning like fire.

Chapter 11.

Now.
Alex sat at his desk and mulled things over in his head.
Jean Harrison had eventually given up the name of her abuser, and
Mo was currently seeing what she could dig up about him. Jean had
been unclear about his age, but if there was anything to be found
about Alan Stanley, Alex knew that Mo would find it.

He picked up the card again and studied it. The sequence of
numbers seemed familiar, but Alex couldn't remember where he'd
seen it before. He stood up and went to the door of his office.

'Les, have you got a minute?'

Les looked up from his computer screen. 'One sec, boss.'

Alex had just sat down again when Les came in. 'Sorry about
that, I was just putting in a request for Alan Stanley's phone and financial records. I'm also running him through HOLMES.'

'Anything interesting?'

'Not so far, but I've only looked in our area. Do you want me to
widen the net?'

Alex shook his head. 'Not yet, I'll speak to Andy Oliver first and
see what he says. It will no doubt come down to budget, so let's just
concentrate on our own area for now.' He passed the card to Les.
'What do you make of those numbers?'

Les looked at them for a minute. 'I'm sure I've seen something
similar before, but I can't think where it was.'

'That's exactly how I feel.' Alex looked at the clock. 'Blimey, is
it that time already? Right, gather the troops and we'll have a quick
briefing before I start on Gary's transfer paperwork.'

'Righto.' Les opened the door and almost walked into Craig. The two men did an awkward dance as they tried to get past each other. In the end, Craig stepped back and allowed Les to leave before he entered.

'Are we still on for tonight?' Craig asked, plonking himself into a chair.

'Yes, we are. I'm going to brief everyone, then I need to see Gary before I go. It'll be a flying visit to the hospital today, I've got stuff to do before you two arrive later.'

'Anything we can help with?' Craig asked.

'No, I just want to pop over to the old house and check everything is okay, and to pick up any mail that might have slipped through the redirection.'

'Have you decided whether to sell it or are you still considering renting it out?'

Alex thought for a moment. 'I'm still not sure, but there's no mortgage so I'm not losing any money by keeping it on. The utilities bills won't be much either as it's empty. I'd planned to talk it over with Jayne once we were settled in the new bungalow.'

'If it's not costing you anything then I'd wait and see if the market picks up,' Craig said. He stood up to leave but Alex stopped him.

'Has Gary heard back from the promotions board yet about whether or not he passed his sergeant's exam?'

'No, not as far as I know. Do you want me to ask him?'

'No, I was just curious. I would've liked him to find out before he transfers, so if it's bad news he has us around to console him.'

'He'll be on honeymoon for two weeks after the wedding, that should take his mind off everything else.' Craig stood up and opened the door, waiting for Alex to go first. They walked across to the big board, where all the details of the case were displayed. Alex called everyone together.

'What have we got so far?' Alex asked as he leaned against the edge of an empty desk.

Dawn cleared her throat. 'Identification has been confirmed as Alan Stanley, a 63-year-old retired shopkeeper from Oldbury. He was married with two grown-up sons.'

'I see,' Alex said. 'Craig, what did you and Gary find out?'

'We spoke to the construction company as well as the company that are responsible for removing the rubbish from the hangars, but no one saw anything suspicious. Now he's been formally identified, I was thinking we'd go and talk to the neighbours and find out what he was like, whether he's had any visitors and so on.'

'Take Les with you, I need Gary to go through his transfer paper-work with me. Mo, find out if Alan Stanley has an online presence, especially look for links to anything dodgy,' Alex said. 'Meanwhile, Dawn can have a chat with the vice squad and see if they've had any reports of anyone threatening sex offenders.' Alex looked at the clock on the far wall. 'I don't know if any of you remember, but we've got a new colleague joining us tomorrow. I think you'll all get on like a house on fire – once you've got used to her,' Alex said, with a twinkle in his eye.

'I'm not sure I like the way you said that,' Craig said, a hint of sus-picion in his voice. 'What's wrong with her?'

Alex laughed. 'Nothing's wrong with her. She's just a bit...enthu-siastic.'

'Oh Christ, now I am seriously worried,' Craig muttered as he stood up and put his jacket on.

'Relax, you'll soon get used to each other,' Alex grinned. He stretched, his back and knees popping in harmony with each other. 'Gary – let's get this paperwork done so I can go and see my wife.'

Chapter 12.

Mark Rodgers sat in the swivel chair in his room, feet on the desk and head tilted back. He stared idly at the peeling paint on the bedroom ceiling as he tried to think of ways to get Alison to let him stay. Sex had worked for a while; he was an adventurous lover and drove her wild in bed, but she didn't seem interested now. He frowned, wondering whether she had found someone else. The idea made him angry, and he felt the familiar rage start to bubble up inside. He stood up quickly, grabbing the large knife that was impaled in the desktop, and stabbed hard at the surface in temper. He picked up his leather jacket and put it on, patting the inside pocket with satisfaction as he felt the bulge of the notebook and photographs that were hidden there. He grinned to himself. If she didn't want him, there were plenty who did.

He went downstairs and into the kitchen. He grinned as he unzipped his jeans and relieved himself in the kitchen sink. Once he was finished, he did his jeans up, then lifted down the old biscuit tin that sat on the top shelf of the dresser. He took the lid off and stared at the piece of paper inside.

'If you're looking for money, you're out of luck. Try getting a job and earning your own.'

Mark roared and threw the tin across the kitchen, knocking over a plant pot. It fell off the counter and smashed, scattering soil and broken pottery all over the floor. He strode through the mess and out of the front door, slamming it hard behind him. 'Fucking bitch,' he thought to himself as he kicked the garage door repeatedly. The rage in his chest swelled and he knew he needed to get it under control fast. He climbed on his pushbike and pedalled away, leaving the next-door neighbour peering nervously at him from behind her net curtains.

When Alison arrived home a couple of hours later, she listened intently as she pushed the front door open. All was quiet, much to her relief. She hung up her coat and bag and walked along the hallway, stopping dead when she saw the mess in the kitchen. The pale blue hallway carpet was ingrained with soil and tiny shards of pottery from where Mark had stomped through it. Her face fell when she spotted her precious violet, lying on the floor next to the biscuit tin.

Alison gently picked up the little plant and checked it to see if it could be saved. Apart from a few bruised leaves it seemed unharmed, so she set it on the draining board and went out to the shed in the back garden to see if she could find a new home for it. Rummaging through the various assortment of pots, Alison found one that looked about right, and filled it with compost. She took it back indoors and replanted the violet, all the time trying to keep her temper under control. When she had finished, Alison put the kettle on while she attended to the rest of the mess.

The front door opened with a bang as Mark came in, a fast-food bag in his hand. Alison glared at him, but he avoided all eye contact and started to go upstairs.

'Hold it right there,' Alison snapped. 'Would you care to explain this lot?' She pointed to the dirty floor.

'It wasn't my fault,' Mark began. 'It was an accident. I knocked the pot over as I was going out.'

'And you didn't think to clean it up at the time, you just decided to walk the dirt through the house instead?'

'I was in a hurry; I was going to clean it up when I got back.'

Alison shook her head at him. 'No, you weren't, and this was no accident, unless the biscuit tin has learned to fly off the top shelf. You were planning to steal from me again, weren't you?' She looked at him as if he were a bad smell. 'Well, you've pushed me too far now. If you're not out by the end of today, I'll have you removed.'

Mark dropped the food bag and rushed towards her. He grabbed her by the shoulders and slammed her against the wall, knocking the wind out of her. He tried to kiss her, but Alison brought her knee up sharply between his legs and he sank to the floor, clutching his testicles.

'You bitch,' he hissed. 'You'll pay for that.'

'No, you will,' she said, brushing her hair out of her face. 'I'm calling the police.'

PC Penny Marshall pulled up outside Alison Munroe's house and got out of the car. She had bumped into Mo as she left the station, and when she heard where Penny was going, Mo had insisted on coming along in case the incident had anything to do with their case.

'Are you okay?' Penny asked as Mo struggled to get out of the car.

'Yes, I'm fine, it's just aching a bit, the damp weather makes it worse.' She smiled at Penny's concerned expression. 'Really, I'm okay.'

Penny smiled back as she rang the bell. 'As long as you're sure.'

Alison flung the door open. She looked flushed but otherwise uninjured.

'Thank you for coming so quickly. He's still upstairs, but I think he's packing his bags. There's a lot of noise coming from his room.'

'No problem. I'll go and speak to him while DC Ross takes a statement from you,' Penny said.

Mo followed Alison through to the kitchen whilst Penny made her way upstairs, following the sound of loud music. She knocked on the door.

'Mr Rodgers, this is PC Penny Marshall. Do you mind if I come in?'

The music cut off swiftly, leaving an almost equally deafening silence. Penny knocked again and repeated her request.

The door inched open, and Mark peered out. Penny stood patiently, saying nothing but letting him know that she wasn't going away. Eventually, he opened the door wider, and she stepped into the room. She tried hard not to gag at the smell of sweat and mouldy food.

'Miss Munroe called us to report an assault. Would you care to tell me your version of events please?'

Mark's clothes were damp with sweat, and his hair was sticking up. 'I told her it wasn't my fault. I didn't mean to break her stupid pot. She kicked me in the balls, I should be reporting her.' He sat down on the swivel chair and rested his head in his hands.

'Miss Munroe has also stated that she has asked you to vacate the premises on several occasions. Is that true?'

'Yes, but she's always saying that. She doesn't mean it.' Mark looked at Penny from under his fringe, a shifty look on his face.

'Well, this time she does, and she's fairly insistent that you leave today. Have you somewhere else to stay?'

'No, and she knows it, the stupid bitch. Sorry,' Mark added, seeing Penny's stern look.

'What about your mother? Miss Munroe mentioned that she lives in Bilston.' Penny was beginning to tire of the man's attempts to look hard done by and struggled to keep her voice level.

'Well, yeah, but I don't want to go there.'

'Regardless of what you want, Mr Rodgers, Miss Munroe says that you leave today; or she will press charges of assault.' Penny glanced around the room. 'So, I suggest you start packing.'

When Penny went downstairs she was grateful to see a pot of coffee on the kitchen counter. Alison poured her a cup and Penny held it close to her face so she could inhale the delicious aroma. She still had the stench of Mark's room in her nostrils and had to take several deep breaths to get rid of it.

'It's vile, isn't it, the smell up there?' Alison said, screwing her nose up. 'God knows how long it will take to clear.'

'It's pungent, that's for sure. He's packing now and should be out by the end of the day.' Penny sipped her coffee. 'Wow, that's really good.'

'Thank you, a friend of mine went to see her family in Yorkshire over Christmas, and she bought me a hamper of goodies back from Betty's tea rooms. Try the shortbread, it's heavenly.'

Penny did and had to agree with her. 'Crikey, I'd be the size of a house in no time if I lived near them.'

'They have an online shop, so maybe you should treat yourself.'

'I might do just that. Now, what's the situation with Mr Rodgers?'

Alison told them about the stealing, and the damage to the plant pot. 'It was one of my late grandmother's plants. He knows how much it means to me. I've had a lot of things disappear recently; I think he's responsible.'

'What sort of things?' Penny asked.

'Jewellery, money, and I think he's taking my mail, too. I've been waiting on some important papers from my grandfather's estate that I need to sign, and they haven't arrived.'

'Could they have got lost in the post?' Mo asked.

'That was my first thought, but the solicitor says he sent them recorded delivery, and the post office say they were signed for. He has nothing to gain by stealing them, I just think he did it to spite me. I've asked the solicitor to draw up a duplicate set, but I'll have to take a day off work so I can go to his offices in Oxford to sign them, as I don't trust them not to disappear again. Like I said, Mark loves to cause me grief.'

'I can ask him to turn them over if you like,' Penny said, standing up again. 'But you'd better pour another coffee for me to sniff.'

Penny went upstairs, listening intently. Mark was talking to someone on the phone, and it didn't sound good.

'I know she's a bitch, but she'd better be careful because I will get my own back, don't you worry. I know exactly how to frighten her.'

Penny stepped on a creaky stair and the conversation stopped. 'Hang on, I think the nosy cow is listening. I'll call you later, babe. Yeah, me too.'

The door flew open, but Mark stopped dead when he saw Penny standing at the top of the stairs.

'Oh, it's you.'

'Sorry if I interrupted your call,' Penny said, 'But Miss Munroe says you have some important paperwork that belongs to her.'

'No, I don't. She's lying if she says I've taken it.' Mark took a step closer to Penny, his stare so intense that it felt like it was penetrating her soul. She took a step back, aware that she was close to the edge of the top step.

'No one is accusing you of taking it. Maybe you just forgot to give it to her, which would be easy to do, especially if you've not been getting on.' Penny turned and started to go downstairs again, wary of turning her back but hoping her instinct was right. 'It could be that one of the neighbours had signed for it, not you as Alison thought. I'll speak to the sorting office tomorrow and they can check to see who signed for it.' She went downstairs, aware he was watching her.

When Penny got back to the kitchen, Alison looked at her hopefully.

'I have a feeling that your paperwork will turn up very soon,' Penny smiled. 'Now, where's my coffee?'

Chapter 13.

I watch the flames lick the sides of the incinerator; mesmerised by the hypnotic dance they perform. This one had been easier to subdue, more willing to drink the coffee so it could get down to business. I'm always fascinated by the look of confusion on their faces when they start to lose control of their bodies, particularly when they see the way I'm looking at them like the vile scum they are.

I just need to deposit the carcass, but I can't recall where it used to take its prey. I'll need to spend a quiet evening re-reading the notes I copied. I'm sure the police will have made the connection by now, but I hope they won't work out who I am before I finish my list. I can never repay the debt I owe, but I hope this goes some way towards reducing the balance.

A piece of material floats up out of the fire and I poke it back down again, where it sticks to something greasy and catches alight. I stir the fire idly and watch the body parts turn black and sizzle as their juices are released. They will soon be nothing more than ash, and I will begin the next project.

Chapter 14.

Alex had just finished a load of laundry when his brother knocked the door. He set the basket of wet clothes on the floor and went to let Dave and Carol in.

'Hey, knobhead,' Dave said, slapping Alex on the back of the head. 'Get the kettle on.'

'You put it on, I need to get the washing in the dryer before I go to work,' Alex said, shoving past Dave. He went into the utility room and loaded the tumble dryer then went back into the kitchen. Carol was making coffee and Dave sat at the breakfast bar, reading something on his phone.

'I thought I told you to do that,' Alex said, punching Dave's arm and smiling at Carol.

'It's fine Alex, you know what a lazy git your brother is,' Carol said. 'If we wait for him, we'll die of thirst. He makes terrible coffee anyway.'

'Oi, I'll have you know my coffee is great,' Dave replied, with mock indignance.

'I wouldn't know, it's been years since you made one,' Carol said, winking at Alex.

'That's because it's so good, you'd start bowing down to me,' Dave grinned. 'I'm saving you from the wear and tear on your back.'

'Twat,' Carol replied, laughing at his logic. She sat down next to Dave and turned to Alex. 'Any updates on Jayne's condition?'

'Not since yesterday, but I've rescheduled my appointment with Jayne's consultant for today. I know they plan to operate as soon as they can.'

'That's great news isn't it Dave?' Carol said. Dave grunted his agreement, his mouth full of the biscuit he'd helped himself to from the tin on the counter.

'You said last night that you wanted to talk to me about something,' Alex said.

'Yes, that's right,' Carol nudged Dave, who swallowed hard then drained his mug to clear his throat.

'Okay, I'm just going to come right out and say this, so don't interrupt me until I've finished,' Dave said. Alex nodded and stood with his back against the worktop, arms folded and a neutral expression on his face. It was a pose he used at work to make criminals feel more at ease.

Dave took a deep breath and held it for a second before exhaling again. 'It's Joel. He's lonely and confused, and he wants to come home. He knows his mum is in hospital, and that you're angry with him. He's incredibly stressed, and I think – we think – that he should be allowed to move back into the bungalow.'

Alex opened his mouth to speak, but Dave held his hand up. 'Let me finish,' he said. 'If Joel was allowed to come home, Carol and I would move in here and become his carers until professional ones could be found. This place is plenty big enough for all of us, and it would mean that when Jayne comes home, she would never have to be alone with Joel again.'

Alex stood in silence as he absorbed what his brother had said. He was still angry with his son and knew he would have to deal with it sooner or later.

Eventually he spoke. 'To be honest, I haven't given any thought to what happens next, I've been so worried about Jayne. I'm not sure that having the two of them living in the same house is good for either of them, even if other people are there. I want to know for certain what happened before I let Joel anywhere near her again.'

'Understood,' Dave said. 'We just want you to know that, as much as we love you, Joel is still our nephew, and we refuse to abandon him.'

Alex could feel his anger start to bubble over. 'I've not abandoned him, but I can't face him either. I need to understand why my son would choose to assault the one person who refused to give up on him when things got tough. She wouldn't even accept help from you two and look where it's got her – lying in intensive care with a fucking great blood clot on her brain! I know he's sorry, but all the apologies in the world won't undo what he's done. I don't believe for a minute that it wasn't him as he claims, so maybe if he could admit that it would be a start.' He scratched at a patch of stubble on his chin that he'd missed that morning.

'Look, the last thing we want to do is put you under more pressure,' Carol said. 'So, for the time being we'll leave everything as it is. Hopefully, Jayne will be awake soon, then we can decide what to do from there. In the meantime, you concentrate on work and leave Joel to us. I should mention that I'm getting in touch with social services though. I know Jayne didn't want them involved, but I do, and whilst I'm looking after him I'm going to get as much help as I can.' She stood up and put her coat on, hugged Alex and headed outside, but not before Alex noticed the tears in her eyes.

'If you need to talk, ring me,' Dave said, pulling Alex close and putting his arm around his shoulders. He rubbed his knuckles against Alex's head, making him yelp. 'Doughnut!' he shouted, laughing as he dodged Alex's punch.

Once they had gone, Alex rinsed the mugs and put them in the sink, ready to be washed up later. His head was all over the place as he tried to keep track of it all. He glanced around the spacious kitchen. Only a few weeks ago they had been looking forward to living here, now it was the last place he wanted to be. He picked up his jacket, grabbed his keys and walked out, slamming the door hard behind him.

Chapter 15.

Craig parked in the station car park, being careful to avoid any overhanging trees. He was as meticulous about his car as he was about his wardrobe, and heaven forbid a bird should leave him a little present. Craig went around to the passenger side to let Mo out.

'You don't have to wait on me, you know. I'm quite capable of getting out by myself.' Mo stifled a groan as she turned her upper body.

'It looks like it,' Craig said. 'Come on, old girl, let me give you a hand.'

Mo glared at him but took the proffered hand. 'You wait until I'm back on my feet again, I'll kick your backside for you.'

Craig grinned. 'You'll have to catch me first.' They started to cross the car park towards the door, just as a huge black motorbike roared through the gates and bore down on them. Craig grabbed Mo and dived across the bonnet of Gary's car with her as the bike swerved to avoid him. He stood up, a look of fury on his face when he saw the dirty marks on his clothes. He brushed himself down and marched across to where the biker was climbing off the powerful-looking machine.

'You bloody idiot, you could have killed us!' he roared. 'Look at the state of my clothes – they're completely ruined! Who do you think you are – Eddie Kidd?'

The biker removed their helmet, unleashing a cascade of long, frizzy light-brown hair and turned to face Craig.

'Sorry about that, I didn't expect anyone to walk out in front of me,' the woman said in a broad Yorkshire accent as she stuck her hand out. 'No hard feelings I hope.'

Craig still looked angry but shook hands. 'It's a car park, not a racetrack, so bear that in mind. You're lucky I was here to save my colleague. She's recovering from a car accident and can't move as fast as I can.'

The woman looked contrite. 'I'm really sorry, it was rare to see anyone in the yard at my old place. I guess I'll have to be more careful here.'

'Yes, you will,' Craig scolded. He looked at her more closely. 'Are you transferring in?'

She gave them both a huge grin. 'That's right. I'm Lizzie Brewster, the new DC.' She looked Craig up and down with a twinkle in her eye. 'I reckon I'm going to like working here if they all look like you,' she said, punching him playfully on the arm and almost knocking him over.

Mo wrapped her arms around her ribs and bent forward. Craig put a hand on her shoulder in concern, but when she stood upright again, she had tears of laughter rolling down her cheeks.

'Stop it, it hurts like hell,' she spluttered. She held her hand out to Lizzie and introduced herself. 'I love the wheels. 2010 Triumph Bonneville if I'm not mistaken?'

'That's right,' Lizzie beamed. 'You know your bikes. I'll have to take you for a spin sometime.'

'I'll definitely be taking you up on that, but you'll have to wait until I'm fully fit again,' Mo said.

'No rush, just let me know when you're ready and we'll do it. I hear there are some great places to see nearby.'

'There are, once you get out of the city,' Mo said. 'We've just picked up a new case, so your timing is perfect. Come and meet the rest of the team.'

They walked into the office to find Dawn and Les huddled together at his computer, concentrating on something on the screen.

'Is the boss around?' Craig asked, making them both look up.
Dawn burst out laughing when she saw Craig's filthy suit.

'Quick, someone call the nearest tailor! DS Muir needs an emergency appointment!'

'Ha ha, very funny! You can blame Evel Knievel here,' he said,
pointing at Lizzie.

'I have no idea who that is, must be before my time,' Lizzie admitted. Craig's mouth fell open in shock.

'World-famous motorcycle stuntman, he once leapt over the
Grand Canyon,' Les told her.

'Is he anything to do with that other bloke, Eddie something or
other?'

'Eddie Kidd?' Les asked. 'He was also a stunt rider. Tragically, he
sustained a brain injury when one of his stunts went wrong.'

'Cool, I'll have to look them up. Nice to meet you both,' Lizzie
said, once introductions were done. She looked around the room and
nodded in appreciation. 'I've heard good things about this place, all
of them true by the look of it. Your team's reputation is brilliant.'

Dawn laughed. 'Really? That's good to hear. The city is in a bit
of a state, but improvements are slowly being made. The new bus station went up a few years ago and the train station is ongoing. Hopefully soon they will get rid of all the derelict buildings and drag us
into the twenty-first century.'

'Sounds good. What's the case?' Lizzie asked, gesturing to the incident board.

'Murder of an alleged paedophile, possibly by a vigilante,' Les
said.

'You don't waste words, do you?' Lizzie said with a smile. 'I like
that in a man.'

Les looked flustered. 'I'll make a brew. Who wants one?'

Craig laughed. 'Les, are you offering to make the tea without being asked? That's a first.'

Les stuck his tongue out at him. 'Bugger off and change your clothes, you're making the place look untidy.'

'It's a good job I keep a spare change of clothes here. I can drop these off at the dry cleaners on the way home.' Craig glanced at Lizzie. 'I should make you pay the bill, seeing as it was your fault.'

Lizzie pulled a bulging wallet out of the pocket of her leather jacket. 'You're right, I should. Here you go,' she said, 'Let me know if it's any more than that.' She winked as she handed him a bundle of five-pound notes.

'Ta very much,' Craig smiled. 'I'm going to get changed, I'll be back in a bit.'

'Are you feeling flush?' Mo asked. 'Or do they pay more up north?'

Lizzie put her wallet away again. 'I doubt it. It's my prize money from the weekend,' she said. 'I haven't had a chance to go to the bank yet.'

'Prize money? What was it, horses, dogs or online poker?' Dawn asked.

'I'm a wrestler,' Lizzie said, making them all laugh. 'It's true,' she insisted.

The conversation was interrupted by Gary coming in, a bulging carrier bag from the local bakery in his hand. 'What's so funny?' he asked, putting the bag on the table.

'DC Gary Temple, meet DC Lizzie Brewster – your replacement,' Dawn said.

The two shook hands. 'Blimey, you've got quite a grip there,' he said, flexing his fingers.

'Lizzie was just telling us that she's a wrestler,' Mo said.

'Really?' Gary said, not sure if he was being wound up. 'Show us a couple of moves then.'

Lizzie shook her head. 'I don't think that's a good idea, I might hurt you.'

'Don't be daft, you're only a girl...' was as far as Gary got before finding himself face down on the floor in a half-nelson, with Lizzie kneeling on him.

The rest of the team applauded loudly. 'Wow, that was superb,' shouted Mo.

'For you maybe, but it wasn't for me,' Gary grunted, trying to throw Lizzie off his back.

Lizzie got up and offered Gary her hand, pulling him up with a jolt. 'I did warn you,' she said. 'Just be glad I went easy on you.'

Gary rubbed his neck. 'It didn't feel like you did. I hope you haven't bruised me, or my fiancée will be wondering what I've been doing.'

Lizzie laughed. 'You'll be fine, nothing a bit of muscle rub won't cure. When's the wedding?'

'It was supposed to be in March, but we've had to bring it forward because we're moving to Norfolk,' Gary said, a grin spreading across his face. 'Jo's landed a great job, teaching psychology at the University of Anglia, and they need her to start at the beginning of spring term.'

'That's terrific, congratulations to you both. Right, I'll pop and get changed out of these leathers if someone will tell me where the lockers are,' Lizzie said.

Dawn stood up. 'I'll show you; I need to pee anyway. Gary, can you dish out the bacon rolls?'

By the time the two of them returned, Dawn knew that Lizzie was the perfect replacement for Gary. She had a wicked sense of humour, which certainly helped in a job like theirs.

Les was just putting the phone down as they walked back in. 'That was uniform. They've got another body.'

Chapter 16.

'Poor Jean, she must have been terrified!' Tracy said as she
helped herself to a slice of Victoria sponge cake. She knew she
shouldn't, she was hoping to lose her post-Christmas weight before
their holiday in April, but the invitation to afternoon tea in Gee-
Gees Café had been too tempting. She took a huge bite, licked jam
off her fingers and turned her attention back to Alison.

'She was, but I was so proud of her,' Alison said. 'She did rush
off to the loo to be sick, but afterwards it was though someone else
had taken over. She answered all their questions in a calm manner,
and they seemed to believe that she was innocent of any wrongdoing.
The only time she wavered was when they asked her for her abuser's
name.'

'Did she have to formally identify the body?'

'No, which I'm pleased about because she shouldn't have to look
at that monster ever again.' Alison lifted the teapot and refilled both
of their cups before choosing a fondant fancy from the remaining
goodies left.

'I'm going to have to stop coming here, everything is too good.'
Tracy sighed happily as she swallowed the last of her cake. 'So, what's
the big news you said you had?'

'Mark's gone,' Alison said, smiling over the rim of her cup. 'Or at
least as good as. I called the police yesterday after he attacked me.'

'Wow, wait a minute, what do you mean he attacked you? Are
you okay?' Tracy sat forward and scanned Alison's face for bruises.

'Calm down, he didn't hit me. He pushed me against the wall
and tried to kiss me, so I kicked him in the balls.' Alison smirked

at the memory of Mark's face as he'd sunk to the floor. 'He'd been mooching around the kitchen whilst I was out, looking for money. The tin where I used to stash it was empty, so he threw it across the kitchen and knocked my violet plant off the counter. Luckily, it's okay but I would have killed him if he'd damaged it. It's the one my gran gave me. When he came back, I had a go at him and told him to get out. He thought he could get around me by trying to kiss me, but that didn't end well for him.'

'What did the police do?' Tracy asked.

'A couple of police officers came out and told him he had to leave, as per my request. They told me to let them know if he didn't comply, and they made sure he knew it too.'

Tracy drained her cup. 'Did he leave?'

'I told him he had to move out by the end of the day, but that I'll give him a week to organise collecting his stuff. He hasn't got a lot to pack to be honest, but it gives me a chance to snoop through what he does have and make sure he's not taking anything of mine.' Alison waved at the waiter for the bill. 'I've a feeling I'll need to redecorate that room and replace the carpet. It absolutely stinks in there.'

As they left the café and walked out into the crisp winter air, Alison spotted a woman and a young girl aged around ten years old, watching her from across the road. Alison waved but the woman pulled her coat collar up around her face and hurried away, forcing the young girl to run after her.

'Who was that?' Tracy asked as she pulled her gloves on.

'I thought it was one of the women from the new group,' Alison said. 'In fact, I'm sure it was, but I didn't know she had any children.'

Tracy shrugged. 'I wouldn't know, I haven't learned enough about the new lot yet. I'll try to read their notes properly before the next meeting.' She gave Alison a hug. 'Let me know if you need a hand cleaning Mark's room once he's gone.'

'Will do. It feels good to know that he will soon be a distant memory.'

Alison strolled back to the car park, feeling positive for the first time in months. Her smile slipped when she spotted an envelope tucked under her windscreen wiper and her heart sank. The last thing she needed was a parking ticket. She opened the envelope, took one look at the card inside and threw up.

Chapter 17.

Alex pulled into the station car park just as Dawn came outside, followed by a woman he'd not seen before. He wound his window down as Dawn approached.

'What are you doing here?' she asked.

'There's no change, so I thought I'd be of more use here.' He looked past Dawn at the other woman, who had hung back to allow them to speak privately. Dawn followed his gaze and beckoned Lizzie forward.

'This is Detective Constable Lizzie Brewster. She arrived this morning and has already made quite an impression on the rest of the team,' Dawn said with a smirk.

'Really? I look forward to hearing about that at some point,' Alex smiled back. He stuck his hand out through the window and Lizzie shook it, making him wince.

'Sorry, boss, I forget my own strength sometimes.'

'No problem. Where are we going, Dawn?'

'We've got another body, this one's down by the canal near the canoe club,' she said. 'I thought I'd take Lizzie along.'

'That's a good idea, throw her in at the deep end, so to speak – the job, not the canal. Trust me, you really wouldn't want to swim in that.' Alex shuddered at the thought. He gestured for them to get in. 'We may as well all go.' He pulled out of the car park and negotiated the busy ring road with ease, heading north towards Oxley. Dawn filled Alex in on Lizzie's interactions with the rest of the team, which had him roaring with laughter.

'Poor Craig,' he said. 'I bet he was traumatised.'

Lizzie grinned back at him. 'He wasn't happy, that's for sure. He had to rush off and get changed. Can you believe he keeps a complete set of spare clothes in his locker? I bet he even has extra pants!' This made Alex laugh even harder, so by the time they arrived at the Canoe Club in Oxley Moor Road, Alex had almost forgotten the earlier stresses of the day.

He parked up and they all got out. Forensics had beaten them to it and were already unloading boxes of equipment in preparation for whatever awaited them. Alex, Dawn, and Lizzie each took a paper suit and put them on, then walked down the towpath towards the body, being careful to use the footplates that had been placed to protect any evidence that may have been left behind.

Faz had been crouching over the body, but stood up on hearing their approach, a beaming smile splitting his face almost in two as he walked towards them.

'Alex, impeccable timing as always!' Faz said, his green eyes twinkling as he pushed the hood of his suit down. His dark ginger hair had gone curly with damp and Lizzie blushed as they were introduced. Faz was keen to hear all about her other profession, but Alex indicated that they should concentrate on the job in hand.

'Quite right Alex. Now, let me tell you what I've found so far,' Faz said. 'I should warn you, he's a bit of a mess.'

They walked over to the body and stood for a minute or two, surveying what used to be a human being lying on the ground in front of them, partially wrapped in a body bag. The man's limbs had been twisted so badly that he now resembled a pretzel.

Faz pointed out some of the injuries sustained. 'This poor soul was tortured quite extensively before he died,' he said. 'I can't specify what with as there seem to have been several different implements used. I can't even tell you which injury caused his death because there are so many of them.'

'That body the other day, that was tortured too, wasn't it?' Lizzie asked.

Faz grinned at her. 'Brains as well as brawn – my kind of woman,' he said. 'The hands, tongue and eyeballs are missing, so I think it's safe to say that the same person killed this chap.'

'How can you be so sure?' Alex asked.

Faz crouched down next to the body again and shone his torch inside the body bag so Alex could see. 'It's unlikely there are two killers who like to remove their victim's genitals while they are still alive.'

Alex inhaled sharply and crossed his legs. 'Yikes, that's a bit extreme.'

'It depends on how you look at it,' Faz replied as he zipped up the body bag and signalled for his colleagues to take it away. 'As a doctor I'd say it seems brutal, but as a father I'd say he got what he deserved.'

'I know what you mean,' Alex said, 'but we can't let our personal feelings get in the way. It's our job to stop criminals, not encourage them.'

Dawn called out to Alex, and he walked over, leaving Lizzie talking to Faz, whose delighted chuckles told Alex that Lizzie must have been telling him about the antics in the office earlier. He smiled to himself, glad that she seemed so eager to fit in.

'What have you got?' Alex asked Dawn when he reached her.

'They think this was pinned to the box that the body was in as it was found close by. The heavy rain must have dislodged it.' She handed him an envelope; the writing on the front was smudged but some parts were still legible.

'Okay, let's go back to the office and add this to what we've already got. Can you ring the woman who runs that group and ask her if she knows who the recipient is?'

'Sure. Do you want me to tell her why?'

'You may as well mention it's to do with another victim, she'll find out soon enough anyway now the vultures are circling.' He pointed to the news crew standing on the bridge, desperately trying to get a peep at what was inside the white tent via their long-range cameras. They made his stomach turn the way they descended, eager to be the first to break the news and not caring who they hurt in their bid for glory. He resisted the urge to spit on the ground to rid himself of the taste of bile that rose in his throat.

'I'll ask her to come in tomorrow morning so I can speak to her in person, that way we can see her reaction. I might ask Lizzie to accompany me if you don't mind.' Dawn glanced over to where Lizzie and Faz were still chatting. It looked like they were getting on famously. 'I think she will be a good fit,' she added.

Alex nodded. 'Me too. Come on, I'm dying for a brew. Let's get back and find out what her tea-making skills are like.'

Chapter 18.

Then.
Tracy leaned her head against the window of the bus and closed her eyes. The rumble of the wheels on the road vibrated through her head, but it didn't bother her as much as the thought of seeing that pig again. It made her feel physically sick, and she fought to keep her dinner down. The bus arrived at Tracy's stop, and she took her time to get off.

'Come on, love, I haven't got all day!' the driver shouted as she dragged her feet getting off. He was pulling away from the kerb before she had time to get her balance, and she stumbled on the uneven pavement.

'Fuck!' She glanced around to see if anyone had seen her trip, but the people milling about were too engrossed in their own lives to notice her. She straightened her skirt and headed to the butcher's shop.

'Here she is, my little princess! I didn't think you were going to make it today.' Derek Donaldson wiped his hands on his apron and came round from behind the counter. He pulled Tracy into an awkward hug, risking a sneaky pinch of her bum at the same time. Tracy swallowed hard, trying not to gag at the fetid stench of stale sweat and bad breath that emanated from him.

'Are you okay, pet?' one of the women in the queue asked, seeing Tracy's pained look.

'She's a good girl, she works hard don't you, my love?' Derek gave Tracy a wink as she pulled away from him. He grinned, showing nicotine-stained teeth.

Tracy went through to the back room and hung her bag on one of the pegs that were screwed to the wall. She picked up a white overcoat and put it on over her school uniform. The stomach cramps were starting to ease off now, and she hoped the bleeding was slowing down. PE had been a nightmare, her pleas of stomach-ache fell on deaf ears and that cow, Miss Evans, had made her do an extra lap of the field.

As Tracy went back into the shop, the last customer was just saying goodbye. Derek was flirting with her, and she was lapping it up like a starving puppy. Tracy noticed the scrawny woman pass a piece of paper across the counter before she left. The butcher smiled as he followed the woman to the door, giving her bottom a pat as she left. He closed the door and slid the bolt across, then turned to Tracy, that familiar glint in his eye. He ran his fingers through his thin, black hair.

Derek followed her through to the back of the shop. He undid his trousers and pushed them down to his ankles, his underpants quickly following. He sat down on a stack of insulated boxes and pulled her onto his lap. She squirmed in his arms, trying not to let his small, stubby erection press against her leg.

'Please, I don't want to, not today,' Tracy pleaded.

'What's the matter? You're usually much more fun than this.' He looked annoyed but allowed her to stand up. Tracy tried not to look as he idly stroked himself.

'I've got my period, and it's a really bad one.' Tracy's cheeks flamed with embarrassment.

'Well, you can't leave me like this,' he said, gesturing to his erection.

Tracy shook her head, her cheeks flaming red. 'I don't feel well.'

'Are you pregnant?' Derek looked at her accusingly, trying to catch her eye.

'No. I mean I think I was, but something came away this morn-ing. My stomach hurts so much.' Tracy allowed a tear to roll down her face.

'Don't even think about trapping me with a trick like that! It must be someone else's.'

'There isn't anyone else, I swear.'

'Yeah, says you. You probably give it to every lad that comes sniff-ing round.' Derek looked at her in disgust as he stood up and hitched his pants and trousers back up. 'I never pegged you for a slag, Tracy.'

'I'm not a slag, I've never been with anyone else!' She sobbed.

'Well, you'd better not tell anyone about what we've been doing, or you'll regret it,' he sneered. He grabbed Tracy by the wrist and dragged her to the butcher's block in the middle of the room, picked up the large cleaver and placed it against her arm. 'These things are very sharp, and we wouldn't want any accidents in the workplace, would we?'

Tracy went white. 'No, of course not!'

'Good.' Derek let her go and she stumbled backwards, holding her wrist where he had gripped her. 'Now get out and don't come back.'

Tracy took off her white overcoat and picked up her bag. 'What about my wages?'

Derek pulled a wallet out of his back pocket, withdrew a handful of notes, and threw them on the ground at her feet. 'Here. Now fuck off. You were starting to bore me anyway.' He glared at her with dis-gust as she picked up the money.

Tracy wrestled with the front door, tears streaming down her face as she failed to flick the catch off. She shrieked as Derek's hand came over her shoulder, freeing the lock. She stumbled over the doorstep and ran down the street.

'Ta-ra, Princess,' he called after her. 'Say hello to your mum for me.'

BOBBIE LAY ON HER BED with her eyes tightly shut, hands clamped over her ears. The half-packed holdall had been stowed back under the bed, with a promise from her sister that it would all be okay.

The shouting had been going on for over an hour and didn't sound like it would stop anytime soon. Angie had been furious when Bobbie had told her some of the things her mother's boyfriend had been doing to her. It had started out as a game, bear hugs or tickling sessions, but soon escalated into something else. At 13, Bobbie wasn't completely naive, she knew what sex was but some of the things he'd made her do were beyond anything she could have imagined. The last time had been the worst, she had bled for ages, and was still sore down below.

The slam of the front door meant that either Angie had gone out or her mum's boyfriend was here. The silence told her it was the for-mer, and Bobbie allowed herself to breathe for a moment. A series of thuds cut her relief short, as Bobbie's mother made her way upstairs.

The door flew open. 'Here you are, you little slag, hiding in your bed! It makes a change from being in mine with my fella, though.'

Bobbie's mother looked round at the posters of cartoon charac-ters that plastered the walls. She gave a short laugh of derision. 'Bit old for cartoons now, aren't you?'

Bobbie scrambled further up the bed as her mum started mani-cally tearing the posters down, scattering them across the floor. Bob-bie held a pillow in front of her like a shield, watching as her belong-ings were systematically destroyed in front of her.

'Yes, you're not a baby anymore, are you? You're just a dirty little tramp who couldn't bear me having something for myself.'

She approached the bed, leaning in so close that Bobbie had to turn her face away from her mother's whisky-tainted breath.

'I'll teach you to go near my man, you filthy little whore.' Spittle flew from her mouth and landed on Bobbie's cheek as she drew her fist back, ready to strike.

'I wouldn't do that if I were you.'

Angie stood, stony-faced, by the door, watching her mother leaning over Bobbie. They surveyed each other for a moment before her mother straightened up again, the alcohol in her system making her feel brave.

'What do you want? I bet you've been teaching your sister the tricks of the trade, haven't you? It wasn't enough for you to tell tales and get your dad sent away, was it? No, you had to encourage her to do the same with my new man. You two hate me having any fun, I should never have had either of you. You're nothing but a pair of slags!'

'Are you done?' Angie pushed the bedroom door open wider and jerked her head towards it. 'If so, get out.'

Her mother opened her mouth ready to spout more insults but changed her mind when she saw the fury on her eldest daughter's face. She flinched as she walked past Angie, realising that the girl was now taller than her, and probably strong enough to take her on.

Angie slammed the bedroom door shut and rushed to her little sister, enveloping her in a hug. Bobbie sobbed in her arms, and Angie held her until she cried herself to sleep.

'Don't worry little one,' she whispered as she lay Bobbie down and covered her up with a blanket. 'I've got you.'

'HOW WAS YOUR DAY, LOVE?' Julie's mum asked as the front door opened. Her face fell when she saw her daughter's torn clothes and rushed over to hug her.

'Not more bullying? Really, the number of times I've been up there, you'd think they would have done something about it by now. Perhaps I should go up there again.'

'Leave it, Sandra, they have better things to do than listen to parents whining about their kids.' Julie's father turned the page of his newspaper, shaking it to straighten the sheets out.

'Come on, Reg, she can't keep going through this. Look at her blouse, it's ruined!'

'School is tough, you just have to ride it out until you leave. Look at me, I was bullied all through senior school and it hasn't done me any harm.'

'It's different for girls, though. They can't fight back in the same way that boys can.' Julie's mother gently pushed her daughter towards the stairs. 'Go and get changed, love. It's pie and mash for tea tonight, your favourite.'

Once Julie was out of sight, Sandra rounded on her husband. 'It would do her the world of good to know you were on her side, you know. Sitting there with your paper like you don't have a care in the world.'

Sandra gasped as Reg jumped up from his armchair, grabbed her roughly by the throat and pinned her against the wall. 'Don't ever speak to me like that again, you hear me?' He shook her once before letting her go. 'No wonder the girl's soft, with a pathetic excuse like you for her mother. Now get back in that kitchen and sort my dinner out. Jim's picking me up at six.' He sat back down and picked his paper up.

Sandra rubbed at her neck but said nothing and went back to preparing the dinner. She thought about her own mother's warnings about getting mixed up with Reg and his family when she was younger, but Sandra had been smitten by the handsome young man, so paid no heed. She regretted not listening now as she sliced the carrots, wishing each one was Reg's throat.

After dinner, Julie sat at the dining table, her head bent over her French homework. She really couldn't understand how irregular verbs worked. Why couldn't they just use regular ones instead?

She looked up when the doorbell rang, and Julie's father gestured for her to open it. 'Let Jim in, will you? I'm trying to sort out these blasted darts.'

Julie opened the front door and was immediately wrapped in a pair of strong arms. 'Hello, Juju, how's you?' Jim seemed amused by his own unintentional rhyme. He set her down again and sauntered into the small, open-plan lounge and dining area. Julie slid back into her seat and picked up her pen, trying to ignore the pain in her chest where Jim had hugged her.

'Oi, where are your manners, young lady? Make Jim a cuppa!'

'It's okay, Reg, I don't want one. Let the kid get on with her homework.' Jim smiled at Julie, and she smiled back. She noticed the scowl on her father's face and quickly looked away.

'Manners cost nothing, mate. It's time she learned some.' Reg fiddled with his darts, trying to get the plastic flight onto the stem. 'Damn it, why do they make these things so bloody fiddly?' He threw them on the dining table, making Julie jump.

'Give them here, you idiot.' Jim picked the darts up and soon had the flights fixed in place. 'Your hands are too big for such a delicate operation. Not like us, eh, Juju?' he smiled.

Her mother came in at the sound of Jim's deep voice. 'Hello, Jim, how are you?'

'All the better for seeing you, beautiful. Is that a new dress?' He indicated the faded green pinafore and orange cardigan.

Sandra blushed to the roots of her hair. 'Get away with you, Jim, you know I've had these for ages,' she giggled.

'But you still look a million dollars,' Jim said with a wink.

Reg glared at his wife for a second, then stood up and grabbed his jacket. 'Let's go, I want to get there early so we can see who we're playing tonight.'

'After you, mate. See you both later, ladies,' Jim said, bowing low to Julie and Sandra, making them both giggle.

'Don't forget to do my sandwiches for work before you go to bed tonight, and don't put cheese in them again, I'm not a mouse. I'll have ham and pickle.' Reg pulled the door closed with more force than necessary, stirring up dust motes which danced in the dappled light coming through the window.

Sandra smiled at her daughter. 'Peace at last, love. Now, shall we have some hot chocolate?'

Chapter 19.

N ow.
 Alison sat in the reception of the police station, arms folded, tapping her foot on the floor. She had asked to speak to Alex, but he was busy, so another officer was on their way down to talk to her instead. Her mind strayed to the meeting that evening and to the women who would be there. She was looking forward to getting to know them all better, and hopefully becoming friends with some of them.

'Hello again, Miss Munroe. I'm Detective Constable Maureen Ross, we met yesterday. I believe you wanted to speak to someone in Major Crimes?'

Alison jumped violently. She looked at Mo as if she'd never seen her before. 'Sorry, I was miles away.'

'Somewhere nice, I hope.' The detective crossed to the other side of the reception desk and opened a door. 'If you'd like to follow me, we can get started.'

Mo took Alison to the second of the nice interview suites, this one painted in a soft shade of lilac, with light brown carpet and cream curtains. It was a little chilly, so Mo turned the thermostat up on the wall before inviting Alison to take a seat on one of the two large plum-coloured sofas that faced each other.

'Right,' Mo said, opening a notepad and writing the date at the top. 'What can I help you with?'

Alison opened her handbag and took out the envelope that had been on her windscreen. She handed it to Mo. 'I was out with a friend earlier, and when I went back to my car, I found this underneath my wiper blade. I brought it to you because I think this might be linked to what happened to Jean Harrison.'

Mo opened the envelope and took out the card. On the front were four pictures – a lifejacket, a meat cleaver, an empty paint pot, and a car. Mo turned the card over, but it was blank.

Mo looked at the front of the card again, then at Alison. 'What do these pictures mean? Your friend's card only had one photo on the front, and there are no numbers or phrases on this one. Were you abused by four different people?'

'No, it was just one person. I only knew him as Uncle Geoff, and I don't know what he did for a living,' Alison said. 'But seeing as the group I'm running now is only in its second week, this must be to do with the previous one, the one that Jean was a part of. The only reason I can think of for this being left for me is because I'm the one who runs the group. Perhaps the person responsible is telling me about other abusers they've killed.'

'Or ones they plan to kill.' Mo put the card back in the envelope. 'I'm going to have to keep this if you don't mind. Can you tell me the names of the people these pictures might mean something to?'

Alison shook her head. 'I can't give you the names of the women because I'd be breaking their trust. All I can do is ask them personally if they will speak to you.'

'Okay, I see your point. I'll take this to my team and tell them what you've told me. Have we got your contact details?'

'You have, but I'll give them to you again.' Alison took a card out of her bag and passed it to her.

Mo took it with a smile. 'Thanks. Is there anything else at all that you can think of that we should know?'

Alison shook her head. 'No, but I'll call a meeting of the last group and tell them what's been going on.'

'Would you mind if we came and spoke to them as well?' Mo asked.

'I'll have to ask them first, and I can't make them stay if they feel uncomfortable with your presence.'

'Fair enough,' Mo agreed.

After she had shown Alison out, Mo headed back upstairs to the office. Les waggled a mug in her direction when she walked in and she gave him the thumbs up.

'Penny for them,' Les said as he came back with the drinks.

Mo showed him the card. He looked at it, then looked at the envelope. 'Maybe this is a warning of what's to come,' he said.

'It's possible. I'm certain she knew who these pictures relate to but didn't want to say.'

'Like she said, it would be a breach of confidentiality if she told you.'

'I know, but if I had the chance to save four lives, then I would.'

'Me too, but not everyone is like us.'

'Who's not like you?' Alex asked as he walked in, closely followed by Lizzie and Dawn.

Mo explained about Alison coming in, and the conversation they'd had.

'Bugger,' Dawn said. 'If I'd known she was here I would've asked you to hang on to her.'

'She's only just left; you might still catch her.'

'Good idea, back in a bit.' Dawn rushed out of the room.

'Does anyone want a brew?' Lizzie asked. Les and Mo declined as they still had full mugs.

'Now you're talking my language,' Alex smiled. 'There's a list on the cupboard in the break area of what everyone has and how they take it.'

Lizzie smiled back and went to put the kettle on.

Dawn came back in, puffing hard. 'No sign of her at all. I'll try ringing her.' She picked up the phone and made the call but replaced the receiver after a few seconds. 'It's going straight to voicemail.'

'I've said we'll go and talk to the group as soon as she sets up a meeting,' Mo said.

'I think I've found something,' Les said, looking up from his screen. He pressed a key and paper started coming out of a nearby printer. He went to retrieve it then brought it over to the big table and spread the sheets out so everyone could see them.

'I'm going through Alan Stanley's financial records, and it makes interesting reading. He has two savings accounts besides his current account, and he has three regular cash payments of two hundred pounds going into one of them every month.'

'Why is that so interesting?' Lizzie asked, as she came back with the drinks.

Les indicated a row on one of the statements. 'Look at the reference details for this one.'

Lizzie looked. 'It just says 'Green.''

'That's right. If it was someone's name it would have a prefix. Then here,' Les pointed to another line – 'This one just says 'Gold' and then further down there's 'Black' – again, no prefix.'

'Maybe they were code names,' Gary said, 'Like in that film, Reservoir Dogs.'

Dawn laughed. 'This is the Midlands, not MI5.'

'Think about it though,' Les said. 'What if each of these colours represent a person who's paying him for something that he wouldn't want to show up on his bank statement?'

'It's not that far of a stretch. People use film references for all kinds of things,' Craig pointed out.

Les nodded. 'I think he may have been part of a child pornography ring, and these payments are for services he provided to other paedophiles...'

'Services? Such as photos?' Lizzie asked.

'Exactly.' Les looked grim. 'They might not be code names for people, it could be he used a different colour for each type of service he was providing – green for photos, grey for videos and so on.'

'It's certainly worth looking into,' Mo said.

'Well done, Les. Let me know how you get on.' Alex put his empty mug down on the tray. 'That was a cracking cuppa,' he told Lizzie.

'Of course, it was. I'm a Yorkshire lass, everyone knows we make the best tea.'

'Careful, you'll end up making it all the time,' Gary laughed.

'It'll be a nice change from that swill you make,' Alex grinned. 'Now, I've got work to do and so have you lot, so let's get on with it.'

Chapter 20.

Tracy had already set out the chairs and was putting an assortment of biscuits on a plate when Alison arrived at the community centre that evening.

'I'm so sorry I'm late,' Alison panted as she dropped her bag and struggled out of her coat. She looked harassed.

'No problem at all. I was early because Brian's taken Callum to the cinema, so he dropped me off first,' Tracy said. 'Is everything okay?'

'Yes, everything's fine,' Alison said, finally managing to catch her breath. 'Mark was dragging out his leaving until the last minute, I think he was waiting for me to go out first, so he could help himself to anything he liked.'

'So, he's gone now? I hope you remembered to take his key.'

'Yes, and I did. I don't know if he's had copies made, so I bolted the front door and I came out through the patio door. He never had a key for that so he can't sneak back in once I'm out. First chance I get, I'm changing the locks.'

'Wise woman,' Tracy said. 'I bet it's a huge relief knowing he's gone.'

'It is,' Alison admitted. 'I just hope I've seen the back of him now.'

'I think the first thing you should do is book yourself a holiday. You look very pale, and your stress levels must be through the roof.'

'That's more to do with what happened after I left you this afternoon.' Alison explained about the card that she'd found on her windscreen.

'Do you know who it was?' Tracy asked. She filled the kettle and switched it on.

Alison shrugged. 'No idea. The police want to know who the pictures on the card might relate to, but I said it was confidential. I can't tell them without asking the group first.'

Tracy frowned. 'But what if it's one of them who's doing it? I mean, only the people in the room with Jean knew how scared she is of snakes, because of that tattoo. Those other photos don't seem so disturbing, but they could still be upsetting to someone. Have you any idea what they mean?'

'No,' Alison said, 'but the police have asked me to set up a meeting with everyone from that group so they can talk to them. I spent a couple of hours this afternoon ringing everyone from the last group to see if they can come along tomorrow evening. Are you free to help out?'

'Sure, count me in.'

The rattle of the door opening signalled the arrival of the group, so Alison and Tracy went to greet them. Once the usual pleasantries were out of the way, Alison clapped her hands and waited for everyone to be quiet before she spoke.

'Margaret would like to tell us her story tonight.' Everyone sat up a little straighter; a couple of them held hands, seeking strength from each other.

'Margaret, I'd like you to do something for me first, if you don't mind,' Tracy said. She handed the shaking woman a mirror and asked her to look at her reflection. Margaret put the mirror face-down on the arm of the chair.

'No,' Margaret replied. 'I can't look at myself.'

'Why not?'

'I just can't.'

'Please, just take a quick glance. It's important, trust me.'

Margaret looked wary but did as Tracy had asked. She looked terrified as she put the mirror down again.

'Well done, that was excellent. Now, whenever you're ready, tell us your story.'

Margaret spoke so quietly that the others had to strain to hear her. 'The first time I can remember was when I was four years old. My Uncle Phil used to look after me while my mum and dad went out. My dad worked long hours at the local car factory, but he and my mum used to go out once a week to the local social club to play bingo. One night, Uncle Phil said he had a special game to play with me, but we had to get into the bath to play it.' The small woman wrung her hands together and kept her eyes on her feet.

'Take your time, Margaret. You don't have to tell us the details if it's too painful.' Alison gently patted her hand. 'Just know that you are safe and amongst friends here.'

Margaret swallowed hard, trying to dislodge the lump that had formed in her throat before she continued.

'The first few times, he pretended his – thing – was the periscope of a submarine. He made me hold it; he said the sailors in the submarine needed me to move it around so they could see where they were going. After a few months, he got me to sit on his lap, so the periscope could hide from the enemy warships. I remember how warm it felt against my skin. He didn't, you know, put it inside me, he just rubbed it against me. I remember he kept cleaning the steam off the bathroom mirror, so he could look at my face. That's why I hate mirrors.'

Margaret took a few deep breaths. 'Anyway, my dad was in the bath one night and my mum asked me to tell him dinner was ready. I went up to the bathroom and walked straight in without knocking. My dad grabbed a towel to cover himself and shouted at me to get out. I ran back downstairs, crying my eyes out. When he came down, he told my mum what had happened, and they both told me off.

They said it was rude to see other people naked, so I told them that Uncle Phil had said it was okay.' Margaret took a breath so deep that it made her cough. 'I remember my mum sending me to bed with no supper that night.'

'Wow, that must have been horrible,' another woman said.

'It was, but my dad was a clever man and he knew something wasn't right. He put me to bed a couple of nights later and read me a story. Before he went downstairs, he asked me why Uncle Phil had said what he had, so I told him about the game in the bath, the submarine and so on.' Margaret wiped a tear that rolled down her cheek. One of the others, a thick-set girl called Tanya, handed her a tissue and she took it, squeezing Tanya's hand in thanks.

'Are you okay? Do you want to stop now?' Alison asked gently.

'No, it's fine. I need to get this out while I'm in the right mindset. Dad hugged me tightly for a long time, and I remember wondering why the top of my head was wet when I lay down to sleep. It was years later that I realised he'd been crying while he held me.'

'What happened next?' Another voice from the group piped up, willing her on.

'Well needless to say, I never saw Uncle Phil again. When I asked my mum about him, she said he had moved away because he had a new job. I didn't question it because that's what grown-ups do. I stopped thinking about him until we did sex education at school when I was around twelve. Then it all came rushing to the surface.' Margaret swallowed hard again. 'Could I please have a drink?'

Tracy jumped up and left the room, returning a few minutes later with a glass of water.

'Here you go, sweetheart.'

'Thank you.' Margaret took a couple of small sips before handing the glass back. 'I'd like to stop now if that's okay?'

'Of course. You've taken a huge step forward tonight,' Alison smiled.

'Yeah, well done Mags,' Tanya added. Her comment was backed up by murmurs of respect from the others present. A few of them were crying.

'You're all so kind, and I'm sorry to have taken up so much time.'

'No need to apologise, this is exactly what the group is for.' Tracy dismissed her comment with a shake of her head. 'How do you feel now, Margaret?'

'Lighter, as if the weight of the world has been lifted off my shoulders.'

'Then I'd like you to look in the mirror again.'

Margaret looked dubious but picked up the mirror and looked into it, at first a half-glance but then a proper look. She stared for almost a minute, then burst into tears and cried hard, as if she was emptying her very soul. Tracy came to sit on the arm of the chair and held her while she sobbed. After a few minutes, Margaret wiped her eyes, picked up the mirror again and stared into it.

'He's gone,' she said, her voice wavering, touching her face in wonder. 'I can see me again.'

Chapter 21.

I fear that I am beginning to enjoy myself a little too much. The last one is barely cold, but already I want to press on with the next task. I wonder if anyone has noticed they are missing, but these creatures are the lowest of the low, so I doubt it. I am satisfied with how they met their end, each one a fitting tribute to the person whose life they destroyed.

There are eight names on the list, and I keep detailed accounts of them all. I know their diseased lives inside out – where they live, where they work, and everything in between.

I think about my first extermination all those years ago. That one was an unemployed layabout, who had 'taken care' of his children while his wife worked two jobs to keep the wolf from the door. The eldest child suffered the most, putting herself forward every time to protect her little sister. Her mother couldn't understand her constant mood swings, putting it down to pressure at school. When she did find out, she sided with him, and the daughter bore the brunt of her rage.

I study my list to see who I should consider as my next subject. My plans for the butcher are complete, but I intend to save that one for last. Perhaps the fat gardener, who created beautiful landscapes but was rotten to the core. He used to take his daughter to work with him whenever he could, telling her mother that he needed her help. The things that little girl endured were horrific. I know that she still has the burn marks, which must be a constant reminder, but I will ensure that she never has to look over her shoulder again.

The name of the builder, a tall, skinny racist with a sharp tongue and cruel hands, catches my eye and I smile to myself. I know exactly how to prepare this one.

Chapter 22.

'What the hell happened to you?' Dawn asked Les when he arrived for work the next morning sporting a row of butterfly stitches on the top of his head and a ferocious bruise above his left eye.

'Don't bloody ask!' Les looked embarrassed as he shrugged his jacket off and hung it on the back of his chair.

'Fair enough, I won't. Do you want a brew?' Dawn asked as she headed towards the break area.

'Yes please.' Les took a packet of pills from his bag, popped two of the tablets into his mouth and swallowed them dry. He closed his eyes and sighed, dreading the reaction when everyone found out what had happened.

Craig breezed in, looking as sharp as ever in a navy suit, white shirt, and dark pink tie. A matching handkerchief was set at a perfect right-angle with the edge of his breast pocket.

'Good morning, you gorgeous lot,' he said, then noticed Les's injury. 'Blimey, have you had a run-in with your good lady? I bet she caught you looking at the adult channels again, didn't she?'

'Bugger off, Muir,' Les grumbled, 'You know my Ruth doesn't have a violent bone in her body.'

Craig laughed. 'That's true, she is a gentle soul.' He sat on the edge of the desk and peered at Les's head. 'So, what happened?'

'I don't want to talk about it,' Les said. He took the mug that Dawn held out to him and smiled at her. 'Thanks, Dawn.'

The door opened and Mo came in, deep in conversation with Lizzie. They spotted Les and were immediately concerned, both asking what had happened.

Les held his hands out in surrender. 'Fine, I'll tell you all. It was a bat.'

'You mean you were attacked with a baseball bat?' Mo asked.

'No.'

'A cricket bat?' Lizzie guessed.

'No.'

'Who was it? Have they been arrested? Is Ruth okay?' They all started talking at the same time, so Les stood up and waved his hands to silence them.

'If you must know, it was the animal variety. We've got a colony of bats roosting under the eaves of our house,' Les explained. 'One got into our bedroom through the open window last night while we were asleep. I was attempting to catch it so I could put it outside.' Les went red, waiting for the inevitable jibes to begin.

'Christ, I didn't know they could pack such a punch,' Craig sniggered.

'Don't be bloody daft,' Les said. 'It was flying round the bedroom in a panic...'

'A blind panic?' Dawn snorted.

'...So, I had to catch it in a bath towel,' Les continued, ignoring her. 'It was a nippy little bugger; it took me nearly half an hour to capture it.'

'So how did you get hurt?' Mo asked. 'Surely it didn't bite you?'

'No, of course not.' Les blushed again. 'I managed to catch it and was leaning out of the window, flapping the towel to shake it off, when the curtain pole fell down and walloped me on the head. It knocked me for six, but Ruth refused to call an ambulance until I got dressed.'

'You mean you were naked?' Craig looked horrified. 'No wonder the poor little thing was scared!'

'Get stuffed,' Les said. 'I had my underpants on. I wouldn't have attempted to catch it if there was a chance of it flying anywhere near my dangly bits, would I?'

'Ooh, that would have been painful, having to have a bat surgically removed from your bollocks!' Craig winced at the thought.

'Anyway, I've told you all now, so can we get back to work?'

'Anything you say, Batman,' Lizzie said, leaping out of Les's way as he stood up suddenly.

'Shut up, the kids have been calling me that since breakfast. Ruth thinks it's hilarious.'

'I can't wait to tell Deb,' Craig laughed.

'No doubt Ruth will tell her; they're going shopping together today to buy outfits for Gary's wedding.'

'Ooh, that's going to be expensive!' Dawn said, 'I hope you've got a bank balance like Bruce Wayne.'

'Don't be daft, she's only getting a dress.'

'Trust me, it won't just be a dress. There will also be new shoes, coat, handbag and so on. Then she will want her hair and nails done.'

'I feel sick,' Les mumbled, sitting down again with a thud.

'Morning,' Alex called out as he walked in. He was in stitches when he heard about Les's unfortunate encounter with the bat.

'Blimey, Les, you don't do things by halves, do you?' Alex remarked. 'Anyway, let's see where we are this morning.'

Craig went into Alex's office later to find his boss on the phone. Alex beckoned him forward and pointed to a chair, so Craig sat down. After a couple of minutes, Alex hung up, a look of concern on his face.

'Everything okay, boss? Not bad news, is it?'

Alex shook his head. 'No, not at all. That was the nurse who's looking after Jayne, she was just updating me. The scans show that the swelling has reduced even more. With any luck they should be able to operate soon.'

'That's great news. How long will it take?'

'She said it depends on how difficult the clot is to remove, but it could be a few hours.'

'Jayne's a tough cookie, I'm sure she'll be fine,' Craig said.

'Thank you, I hope so. I'd be lost without her,' Alex said. 'Now I just have to figure out what to do about my son.'

'That's a tough call, but if Debs or I can help at all...'

'I know, and thanks. Do you fancy a pint tonight? That band we saw before Christmas is on at the rugby club. God knows I could do with a distraction.'

'Yeah, why not? We can discuss Gary's stag do at the same time. I'll need to nip home and change first,' Craig said. 'I can't go out in my work clothes. Speaking of which, why don't you go home and get your head down for a bit? You look done in.'

Alex rubbed his hand over his face. 'That's not a bad idea, if you're sure you don't need me. I'll meet you at the club at 7pm. By the way, what did you come in for?'

'Oh, I almost forgot, I'm off out to speak to the manager of the rowing club. They've got CCTV so I'm going to have a look at the footage and see if they captured anything that we can use. I'll take Gary with me unless you need him for something else.'

'No, that's fine, and thanks again.'

Craig opened the door just as Les was about to knock on it. He stepped back so Craig could leave before he entered.

'I'm just nipping out for a sandwich; do you want one?'

'No thanks, I'm heading off in a minute. What's Mo doing?'

'She's about to go on lunch as well, but she's at her desk if you want me to get her,' Les offered, but Alex shook his head.

'No, don't disturb her, I'll pop out and have a word in a bit – oh, and Les, are you up for a pint at the rugby club later, around 7pm? Operation stag do.'

Les stuck his thumb up and disappeared.

The phone rang again, this time it was DCI Oliver. It was unusual for him to ring, he usually turned up when he wanted an update. Alex thought his voice sounded strained.

'Nothing significant to report yet, sir.' Alex filled him in on what they had so far, but Andy didn't sound impressed.

'I thought you might be further forward by now,' Andy complained. 'Especially now you have two bodies.'

'We're doing the best we can with what we've got, there are a lot of avenues to explore.'

'Then explore them faster, man.' The phone went dead, and Alex frowned. Andy Oliver was normally the epitome of calm; it was rare for him to lose his cool. Alex shrugged to himself and gathered his keys and phone before leaving his office. Mo was looking at pictures of cars on her computer. She spotted Alex approaching and started to close the page.

'No need to stop on my behalf,' Alex told her. 'You're on your lunch so it's fine. What are you looking at?' He carefully moved the double photo frame containing pictures of her fiancée, Isobel, and Mo's favourite actor, Lewis Collins, to one side and perched on the edge of her desk before peering at the screen.

Mo scrolled back up to the top of the page. 'I was just checking out scrap yards to see what they have in the way of parts for my poor car.'

'Is your brother fixing it for you?' Alex asked.

Mo sighed. 'He is, but he's not happy. He spent almost two years on that restoration for me, only for it to get smashed up a few weeks later. He says it's going to take at least six months.'

'It will be worth the wait, I promise.'

'I'm sure it will, it's just that I was planning to take Isobel away for Valentine's weekend, but it looks like that's not going to happen now.'

Alex patted her shoulder. 'If you're stuck you can borrow mine. Carol's using Jayne's car to ferry Joel backwards and forwards to his various clubs, so I can always use hers if I need to.'

'Thanks, boss, I really appreciate that.'

Mo closed her browser and stood up. 'I may as well show you where I'm up to while you're here.' She walked slowly over to the board and pointed to the things she'd added.

'I've run background checks on Alan Stanley and made a list of his known associates, right back from when he was at secondary school to the time he died. Then I cross-referenced that list against the sex offenders database. I got a couple of interesting connections, which I'm following up and I've also called in a favour from a colleague in the Sex Crimes Unit where I used to work, and they are checking the same names against their database.'

'Are you thinking that he could be part of an online pornography group?'

'Yes, and if he was, he may be connected to other child sex offenders. We often had paedophile rings that operated in more than one area.'

'Good work, keep it up. I'd like to think we can have this case all done and dusted before Gary's wedding, but I think that may be wishful thinking. Speaking of Gary, we're popping to the rugby club tonight to discuss his stag do, if you want to come. It won't be a late night,' Alex said, seeing her hesitation.

'Yeah, that would be nice. I'll get a taxi to save anyone having to pick me up. Isobel's on the night shift this week, so it'll do me good.'

Chapter 23.

Andy Oliver poured himself a coffee then sat down at his desk again and put his head in his hands. The spate of killings was all over the front pages of the newspapers, and he was being leaned on from upstairs to get his house in order, catch the perp and restore the public's faith in the police force. Sometimes Andy wondered whether promotion automatically turned you into a politician because it seemed to him that all anyone of a higher rank cared about were statistics. Sometimes Andy felt as if he were being squeezed from all directions, and now his ex-wife had resurfaced like a bad smell.

Andy had refused all contact with her since their divorce, except via his solicitor. She was the one who had chosen to have the affair which tore their family apart, and now she had the nerve to write and ask for his financial help. As far as Andy was concerned, she could crawl back under whichever rock she'd been hiding for the past twenty years.

He opened the letter out again and re-read it, feeling nothing but contempt for everything that woman had done, and not just to him.

Andy threw the letter onto his desk, stood up and walked over to the window, clenching and unclenching his fists until he felt calm again. A cornflake-like aroma from the nearby brewery wafted in, reminding Andy that he needed to pick up some more breakfast cereal on his way home.

His phone pinged with a text message from his daughter.

'Hi Dad, can I pop round to yours and use the computer again, please? Mine's still on the fritz x'

'Of course, why don't you all come for dinner? It's been ages since I saw any of you.'

'Sorry, I'm snowed under with work right now, but I promise we'll get together soon. Love you x'

'Love you, too x'

Andy smiled to himself. He went back to his desk and picked up the letter again. He read it through once more, then screwed it up and dropped it in the wastepaper basket.

Chapter 24.

Carol Peachey hummed to herself as she placed the plate of sandwiches on a large tray, along with a packet of chocolate wafers and a bowl of crisps. Tucking a couple of dog biscuits into her cardigan pocket, she picked up the tray and carried it carefully through to the large conservatory at the back of the house. The view from here was spectacular, looking out towards the nature reserve and stream that lay beyond, one of the reasons why Dave had chosen this spot to build their house. The trees and hedgerows that Dave had planted when they had first moved in were maturing nicely and were often teeming with birds. Carol had created a large wildflower meadow at the far end of the garden, which attracted bees and butterflies galore, and she loved nothing more than to sit outside and watch nature at work. Today it was cold and misty, but the conservatory was warm and inviting, thanks to the underfloor heating.

Joel sat at the big table in the centre of the room, head bent over a jigsaw puzzle, lost in concentration. He jumped violently as Carol put the tray down with a thud.

'I'm sorry, sunshine, I didn't mean to startle you.'

'You nearly gave me a heart attack.' Joel looked at the tray. 'Is it lunchtime already?'

'It is, and we'd better grab some food before greedy guts comes in, or there won't be anything left.' Carol took a dog biscuit out of her pocket and showed it to Buddy, who was hovering nearby, tail wagging in anticipation. She opened the conservatory door and threw the biscuit onto the lawn. The dog tore after it, yapping with delight.

Carol shut the door, leaving the dog outside. She put a ham sandwich, a chocolate wafer biscuit and a handful of crisps on a plate for Joel, then went back to the kitchen to get them both a drink. She set Joel's sports bottle of blackcurrant squash into the cup holder on his wheelchair.

'Is that okay there, or would you rather have it on the table?'

'No, that's fine, thank you.' Joel started eating his lunch, then stopped and stared into space.

'Hey, dreamer, what are you thinking about?' Carol nudged his elbow, making him jump again.

'Sorry. I was wondering how my mum is.'

Carol put her coffee mug down and placed her hand on his arm to reassure him.

'From what I can gather she's doing okay, so hopefully she will be home soon.' Carol noticed the sadness in her nephew's eyes and her heart ached. She knew what was coming next, and Joel didn't disappoint her.

'Auntie Carol, do you know when I can go home?'

Before Carol could answer, the door flew open and Dave burst in, face red with cold. He stamped his feet, leaving clods of earth all over the floor. Carol looked at the mud and sighed.

'Behold, I have returned!' he sang in a loud voice, causing Joel to laugh so hard he drooled half-chewed food down his front.

Carol punched Dave in the leg. 'Keep the noise down, you big oaf! Now look what you've made him do.' She picked up a handful of napkins and thrust them at Dave. 'Here, you can clean Joel up while I get you a drink. Do you want tea or coffee?'

'Tea please, my darling,' Dave said, planting a wet kiss on Carol's cheek as she pushed past him. Dave wiped Joel's face and clothes, then picked up the bits of food that had fallen on the floor. 'There you go, mate. Good as new.'

'Bloody hell, Dave! You've traipsed mud all the way through the house as well!' Carol shouted from the kitchen.

Dave pulled a face at Joel. 'Nag, nag, nag,' he mocked, opening and closing his hand like a mouth and causing Joel to splutter again.

Carol came back in with a mug of tea for Dave. She handed it to him then punched him in the arm. Dave looked shocked and held his arm with his free hand.

'What was that for?'

'That one's free, the next one will cost you a new handbag.' Carol winked at Joel.

'I didn't do anything! Joel, tell her to stop picking on me, will you?' He pleaded with his nephew, who couldn't say anything because he was laughing so hard, which made them both laugh too.

Dave sat at the table to eat his sandwiches and took a few moments to study the jigsaw puzzle on the table. It depicted a Devonshire village at Christmastime, the little thatched cottages covered in snow, and rosy-cheeked children building snowmen or having snowball fights. 'Hey, this is coming on a treat, mate, I'm impressed. At this rate you'll have finished it by the weekend.'

'I hope so, I've got another two to do yet and I haven't got a big enough table at home to do them on.'

'Well, we will have to fix that, won't we? Your new place is plenty big enough to fit another table in, and I know your Auntie Carol was on about getting rid of this one, so you can take it with you when you go home.'

'Joel was just asking when that would be.' Carol exchanged a look with Dave.

'I'm not sure, mate, but I'll have a chat with your dad later. He may want to wait until your mum is home because he will struggle to go to work if there's no one there to look after you.'

'I understand that, but I don't know why I can't have a live-in carer like some of my friends do. Is it because I haven't got a social worker?'

Dave scratched his head. 'I don't know, but I'll do some research and find out.' Seeing his wife giving him a warning look, Dave pulled himself to his feet, ruffled Joel's hair and picked up his mug. 'Let's talk about it at the weekend, so we've got time to do some digging – speaking of which, I have to get on with digging out a space for a new septic tank. I'll see you tonight, mate.'

Carol picked up the empty plates and followed Dave back through the house to the kitchen.

'What are we going to do, Dave? The lad needs answers, but I don't have any.'

Dave pulled Carol into his arms and hugged her against his broad chest. 'Neither do I, sweetheart. We don't know how long Jayne will be in hospital, or how long her recovery will take, but Joel needs to be in his own home. He manages to get around fairly well here, but it's not really designed for a disabled person.'

'You don't think Alex will press charges against Joel for assault? Is that even possible, given Joel's disabilities?' Carol sounded worried and it made Dave angry.

'I think if he was going to do that, he would've done it by now.' Dave kissed Carol and headed for the front door, a look of steely determination on his face. 'In fact, I'm going to go and see him right now. That boy in there has been through enough.'

Alex had crashed out on the sofa as soon as he got in and woke up an hour later, feeling rested and refreshed. A long, hot shower had eased much of the tension out of his shoulders, and he had just finished getting dressed in t-shirt and jeans when the doorbell rang. He grabbed a pair of socks from the chest of drawers and headed along the corridor to the front door. He was surprised to see his brother standing outside and held the door wide, beckoning him inside. He followed Dave to the kitchen and flicked the kettle on.

'Half day for you too, is it?' he asked as he pulled two mugs from the cupboard and made coffee for them both. He handed one to Dave and perched on the edge of the windowsill to drink his own. 'I'm off to see Jayne in a bit, then I'm heading to the club for a pint with the lads to discuss Gary's stag night. Why don't you come along?

'I wish I could, but I've got too much work on. I'm fully booked for the next two months.' Dave placed his mug on the counter without drinking any.

'What's up? Not enough milk in it?' Alex's smile faded at his brother's serious expression.

'I need to talk to you, and it can't wait.'

'If this is about Joel again...'

'I'm going to speak to social services and see if they can supply a live-in carer for Joel, so he can come back home as soon as possible.'

'Look, I really don't – '

Dave slammed his hand on the counter, causing some of the coffee to slop out of the mug.

'Damn it, Alex! The boy needs to be here, where he belongs! This is his home, and he has every right to be here – more than you, if truth be told, seeing as he's the one who paid for it!'

Alex looked stunned. Dave rarely raised his voice in temper, but he wasn't the only one who could shout.

'I know he paid for it, and he's made us pay for it too, every damned day! For years we've put up with his tantrums, walking on eggshells around him when he's got one on him. Jayne put up with his abuse for too long, and now look at her!' Alex threw his mug in temper, narrowly missing Dave. It smashed against the wall and shattered into pieces, spilling coffee everywhere.

Dave stood up and went to retrieve the broken pieces, then tore off a wad of kitchen roll to mop up the spilt liquid. He dropped everything in the bin and glared at Alex in disgust. 'And you wonder where he gets his temper from.'

Alex looked ashamed. 'I'm sorry, Dave. It's just that it's been hell, and I don't know what to do.' A tear rolled down his cheek and he brushed it away.

'You think I don't know that? Carol and I may not live with you, but we've been with you every step of the way since Joel was born.' Dave walked over and put his arm around his brother's shoulders. 'Look, I know Jayne didn't want social services involved, and I don't mean to be blunt, but if she hadn't been so stubborn then she wouldn't be lying in the hospital now.'

'The arguments we've had over that; you have no idea.' Alex shook his head in disbelief.

'I can imagine. Jayne and Carol are very alike, they're both incredibly strong women, which is why we love them. But what would you be telling me to do if you were in my shoes?'

Alex sighed. 'I don't know, Dave. If I involve them, Jayne will be so angry.'

'Well, Jayne isn't here right now, you are, and you have to do what's best for Joel. You don't have to be involved if you don't want to, Carol and I can take care of everything, but I hope you will be. Just promise me one thing – that you'll come and see Joel. You should at least hear his side of the story.'

Alex pulled away and busied himself refilling the kettle. 'Okay, but I want you to be there, too. I don't trust myself to be alone with him.'

'Fair enough, I'll ring social services now, before I carry on with that septic tank.' Dave held his mug out. 'Now, make yourself useful and get me a refill while I find their number.'

'No, I'll ring them,' Alex argued. 'It's about time I took some responsibility.'

'Okay but keep me in the loop so I can tell Carol,' Dave said. He looked at his watch. 'Forget the coffee, I'd better get back to work. I'll speak to you later.'

Alex went into the dining room and switched on his computer, which stood on a desk in the corner. After a quick internet search, he found what he was looking for. He keyed the number for social services into his phone, then closed his eyes and thought of his wife.

'Please forgive me, sweetheart,' he said, and pressed the call button.

Chapter 25.

The rugby club wasn't busy, but there were still enough people in to make it worthwhile for the band onstage. A group of women stood close to the stage, jumping up and down as 'Nowhere Fast' belted out a Sham 69 song. The lead singer, Dean Smith, spotted Alex and gave him a thumbs-up. Alex grinned and returned the gesture, remembering when he and Jayne had gone to see them together before Christmas. Jayne had been thrilled when the band had covered a Beatles song for her. Seeing them again without Jayne at his side made Alex miss her even more.

Lizzie hadn't been able to make it due to having a training session, but Alex didn't mind as he knew the others would fill her in the next day.

'Thanks for coming at such short notice,' Alex said as he put a fully-laden tray down on the table. He handed the drinks out then picked up his pint of Guinness, took a long pull and swallowed it with a smile of satisfaction. 'Ah, I needed that.'

Mo took a strip of pills out of her jacket pocket and popped two out into her hand, put them in her mouth and took a large swig of her fizzy pop. 'Ugh, I'll be glad when I can stop taking these, I'm dying for a beer,' she complained.

'I bet the cold weather's not helping,' Les sympathised. 'It affects my gout something chronic.'

'That's your age,' Craig quipped, ducking as Les went to slap him. 'I'm the same age as you, you know.'

'True, but I look good on it,' Craig said, sipping his lager. He tutted loudly when a drop of condensation dripped off the glass and onto his designer jeans. He pulled a white handkerchief out of his pocket and dabbed carefully at the wet patch.

Les rolled his eyes. 'God, you're such a neat freak, I don't know how your missus puts up with you.'

'There's no shame in taking care of your clothes,' Craig replied. He laid his hankie over his knee in case there were any more drips, which made Les roll his eyes again.

'Er, excuse me, but have you seen her? She's an even bigger fashionista than he is,' Alex said with a smile.

'Except she's much better looking,' Mo said, winking at Craig.

Alex looked around at his colleagues. 'Right, let's talk about Gary's stag do. I know he's disappointed that it's been cancelled, so I thought we should put our heads together and sort something out. We can't let him get married without some kind of send-off.'

'I still can't believe he thought his original stag do was a fishing weekend,' Dawn laughed. 'He was so excited about it, too. Can you imagine what he would have said if he'd known he was going to a pole-dancing club instead?'

'Gary would have preferred fishing, he's not much of a lad, is he?' Les said.

'I know, he's a sad git. If he's not careful, he'll end up like you.' Craig laughed as Les stuck two fingers up at him.

'Can we get back to the topic in hand? These tablets make me drowsy, so I don't want to be home too late,' Mo said.

Alex threw Mo a grateful look. 'As I was saying, we need to arrange another stag do. I know it's short notice, but even if we just take him out for a few drinks, it's better than nothing.'

'When are we thinking of doing it?' Craig asked.

'It will have to be next weekend, seeing as the wedding is the week after that,' Alex said. 'Jo will never forgive us if we do it the night before they tie the knot.'

'Good point.' A smile started to creep over Craig's face. 'I think I have an idea.' He pulled his phone out and went outside to make a call.

'What do you reckon he's up to now?' Les asked.

'I don't know, but it's your round,' Alex said as he put his empty glass down. 'I'll have a Coke this time, please.'

By the time Les got back with the drinks, Craig had returned and was grinning from ear to ear.

'All sorted, I've booked the Leamore club for next Friday night, and I've sorted out some entertainment as well.' He sat down and picked up his glass, leaning forward to avoid any more drips.

'It had better not be strippers,' Dawn warned. 'Not all of us want to look at naked women, writhing around all over the place.'

'Speak for yourself,' Mo laughed.

'No strippers, I promise, but it does involve a bit of glamour. I'm not saying anything else, but I guarantee you'll all have a great time.'

Chapter 26.

The next morning, Alex's team gathered around the large table in the centre of the open-plan office. The night out had done him good, and he felt much more like his old self.

'Right, I've got a couple of personal appointments in a bit, so let's go over what we have so far. Lizzie, why don't you start?'

Lizzie had taken each of the images on the card and copied them onto separate pieces of paper. She spread them out across the table. 'I've been going over these pictures from the card sent to Alison Munroe,' she began. 'And I think I've figured it out.'

'Go on,' Alex coaxed.

'Each picture seems to represent a career,' Lizzie said. 'I'd guess that the lifejacket is something to do with boats, the meat cleaver is for a butcher, and the paint pot means decorator. The car could be a taxi, I'm not sure. I think that some of the women in the group were abused by people with these professions.'

Alex nodded. 'That's a good assumption, and certainly makes sense.'

'But Alan Stanley was a retired shopkeeper, so I don't understand why the perp sent a card with a snake on, unless he wanted to upset Mrs Harrison,' Gary said.

'Maybe they didn't think about that until afterwards, so changed their style when they realised,' Dawn said. 'That could be why he sent the next card to Alison, because she's in charge of the group and he didn't want to scare the person it was intended for.'

'Or it could be so that we don't know which picture is for which woman,' Alex said. 'We've only just found victim number two, so once we've identified who they are, we can check to see if anyone in the group has received anything. Did we manage to get anything from the address label that was attached to the second victim?'

'Sadly not, the label was too smudged to read,' Dawn said.

'Never mind, it was worth a shot,' Alex said. 'Les, how are you getting on with Alan Stanley's bank accounts?'

'Not very well, I'm afraid. I still haven't figured out what the colours mean, nor have I solved the numbers puzzle from that first picture card.'

'Right, keep at it. Dawn, you go back and talk to his family again. See if you can find out where the cash was coming from, or if those colours mean anything to them.'

'Will do.'

'Craig, what did you and Gary get from the rowing club?'

'Not a fat lot, to be honest,' Craig said, looking at his notebook. 'There's a tramp who usually sleeps in that tunnel, but he seems to be AWOL at the moment. We did get CCTV footage from the rowing club, though. I'm going to watch it once we're done here.'

'Before you do that, I need you to go somewhere for me.' Alex tried not to smile.

Craig's face fell. 'Oh no, please don't do that to me, boss. I've had enough trauma for one week.'

Alex grinned. 'I'm afraid someone has to do it, so it may as well be you.'

Lizzie looked from one man to the other. 'What's up?' she asked, looking worried.

Craig looked grim. 'He wants me to go and pick up the PM report from Faz.'

'Faz? You mean Dr Farrow?' Lizzie asked. 'What's the matter, don't you like him? He seems friendly enough to me.'

Alex laughed. 'He is, but he has a habit of playing practical jokes on poor Craig.'

'I'll go instead if you like, call it penance for nearly running you over,' Lizzie grinned.

'Deal,' Craig said, looking relieved when Alex nodded his assent.

'Seeing as DC Brewster is doing your job, you can do hers,' Alex continued as Lizzie left the room.

'Name it, boss,'

'Put the kettle on and make us all a brew.'

Chapter 27.

Alex sat in his car outside Dave's house an hour later and gathered his thoughts. He was about to see his son for the first time since the night Jayne had been hurt, and it made his stomach churn.

A tap on the passenger window startled him. 'Hello, earth to Alex.' Dave opened the door and climbed in, his solid bulk making the car dip. 'Blimey, you need to give this car a good clean, it smells like sweaty socks in here.'

'It was fine until you got in,' Alex replied, earning himself a punch on the arm. 'Ow, assaulting a police officer is an offence, you know.'

'I'd better give you a doughnut then, and make it worth the sentence,' Dave said, grabbing his brother round the neck and rubbing his knuckles across his head.

'Pack it in, you big tit or I'll puncture your balls.'

'Big talk for a little man.' Dave took pride in being an inch taller than his brother. 'How are you feeling?'

Alex tried to flatten his hair down from where Dave had ruffled it. 'I don't know, to be honest. I'm not sure what's expected of me, and I'm shitting myself at the thought of seeing Joel again.'

'Ah, that explains the smell, then,' Dave joked. He got out of the car, went round to Alex's side, and opened the door for him. 'Come on, move your arse. There's chocolate cake in there and I'd like to get a piece before your boy scoffs it all.' He walked up the path to his front door, leaving Alex to trail along behind him.

'Here goes,' Alex said to himself as he followed Dave along the bright hallway and through the dining room into the conservatory where his son was. Alex's heart ached as he looked at him; so much like his mother but with the streak of Peachey genes that gave him his straw-coloured hair. Joel looked like he'd put some weight on; his clothes looked snugger than the last time Alex had seen him.

Joel sat in his wheelchair at the table, head bent over a jigsaw puzzle of Westminster Abbey, concentration written all over his face. Alex's heart pounded as he approached the table. Joel glanced up, then his eyes went straight back to his puzzle.

'Hello, Joel. How are you?'

'Hi dad. I'm fine, thank you.'

'Good. Are you ready for this meeting?'

'Yes.' Joel was a man of few words, which was typical of people with Asperger's syndrome. Alex stood and watched him, unsure of what else to say. Joel didn't seem bothered that he was there.

Carol came in with a mug of tea for Alex and a sports bottle full of squash for Joel. 'Are you two alright?' she asked.

'Yes, thank you Auntie Carol.' Joel looked at the clock on the wall. 'You said the social worker was coming at 1pm.'

'That's what she said, but it's only just turned quarter past.'

'That's not very professional. If you make an appointment, you should turn up on time.'

'Well, perhaps the traffic is bad, but she will be here.' Carol looked at Alex who confirmed what Carol had said.

'Your Auntie Carol's right, there are a lot of roadworks around the city at the moment, perhaps she's stuck in traffic.'

'Whatever,' Joel replied, picking up a piece of puzzle and slotting it into place. 'It means I get more time to work on my puzzle.'

'We'll leave you to it for a bit, I'll call you when she gets here, and we can sit at the big table in the dining room to talk.' Carol indicated for Alex to follow her back into the lounge, where Dave sat in his favourite armchair, reading his paper, and humming along to Planet Rock which was playing in the background. He looked up as they came in and sat down.

'You okay, little brother?'

'Yes, that wasn't as hard as I thought it would be.'

'Glad to hear it.' Dave folded his paper up and put it down the side of the chair. 'Have you decided on where we go from here?' Dave looked at his wife. 'We're more than happy to have him here, but it's not designed for a wheelchair user. He has a place of his own just down the road, and he should be living there where he has all his own things around him.'

'I know, and I've been thinking long and hard about it,' Alex said, putting his tea down on the side table. 'I think Joel should move back into the bungalow as soon as live-in carers can be arranged, and Jayne and I will move back into our old house. I think it's wise to have that degree of separation, it gives Joel much more independence, and I can go to work knowing my wife is safe.'

Carol nodded. 'That sounds like a very sensible plan,' she said. 'And it's exactly what we were going to suggest but didn't want you to feel that we were forcing you and Jayne out.'

'As Dave said before, it's Joel's house and he should be living in it. One day we'll be gone, so the sooner he gets used to independent living, the better.'

'Exactly,' Dave added. He glanced out of the window as a car pulled up. 'Look sharp, the social worker's here. Wahey, she's a bit fit! I'm looking forward to working with her.'

'Down, boy,' Carol warned, 'Or do I have to get the big stick out again?'

'Ooh, yes please,' Dave grinned, wagging his tongue like a dog.

Carol laughed and slapped him on the backside as he walked past to go and open the door. 'He can be a twat sometimes,' she said.

Alex laughed. 'But he's your twat and you love him,' he said. 'Come on, let's get this over with.'

Chapter 28.

Lizzie walked along the corridor of the large white cube that housed the city mortuary and the coroner's office. The money ploughed into the city had been well spent, and this building was just one of a few desperately needed additions. Usually, mortuaries were housed in hospitals, but when the plans for the new police station had been submitted, it was decided to move the coroner's offices and mortuary to within walking distance to the station. New Cross Hospital was a few miles away, and it saved a lot of time and was more efficient. The demolition of the old mortuary had freed up much-needed space in the hospital grounds for visitor parking, something that had become a problem since the new heart and lung department had opened.

Lizzie tapped on the door marked 'Dr Farrow' and heard a muffled voice call her in. She opened the door and raised an eyebrow in surprise at how old-fashioned the interior was compared to the rest of the place. Oak furniture and brass lamps were the order of the day in here, giving it an air of something from a fifties movie. Each wall displayed a different theme: one had framed certificates, another had anatomical drawings and the far wall was covered with photographs, mostly of a small girl and a huge dog. Lizzie suddenly realised the man seated behind the leather-topped desk was watching her.

'I'm so sorry, Dr Farrow,' she said, 'I didn't mean to stare. I just wasn't expecting something quite so traditional.'

'No need to apologise, and please call me Faz, everyone does. The truth is I don't like the clinical look, it's too much like my other workplace. Plus, I'm a huge fan of old tv shows, so wanted an air of nostalgia – apart from the record player of course,' he added, pointing at the smart Bang & Olufsen system that sat on the sideboard below the family photographs. He noticed Lizzie looking at them and smiled. 'My daughter, Maisie,' he said with pride in his voice. 'The mad dog is Luna, the loopiest boxer dog you'll ever meet. But she's fiercely protective of Maisie so I can't complain.'

'She's beautiful – your daughter I mean. The dog is cute too,' Lizzie added.

'Thank you, I'm a very lucky man. Now, I expect Alex has sent you because DS Muir was too scared to come.'

'Something like that,' Lizzie answered. 'But I am keen to familiarise myself with everyone in the team, so offered to come instead.'

'Very noble of you,' Faz said. 'Now, let's get down to business.' He opened a file on his desk and leafed through the contents. 'Mr Stanley's genitals and tongue were removed pre-mortem, with the hands and eyes removed post-mortem.'

Lizzie shuddered. 'What was the cause of death?'

'Exsanguination,' Faz said. 'He bled to death.'

'What a horrible way to go.'

'I suspect he would have been unconscious at that point, but I can't be certain. There were no defensive wounds, so he was probably given something to incapacitate him. Whatever it was, it was long gone by the time he graced my table.'

Lizzie thought for a minute. 'They wanted him to be awake and aware of what was happening.'

'It would seem so.' Faz closed the file and handed it to Lizzie. 'Between you and me, I hope he suffered. I'm sorry if that shocks you,' Faz added, seeing the look on Lizzie's face. 'But, speaking as a father, anyone who abuses children deserves everything that gets thrown at them. I do hope you catch the killer soon though, because while perverts like Mr Stanley are in the headlines, it's forcing their victims to relive the trauma of their childhood all over again.'

Faz walked Lizzie to the door and opened it for her. 'Now, if you'll excuse me, I've got a few things to do before I make a start on victim number two.'

As she walked back across the quadrangle that separated the police station, the mortuary, and the court buildings, Lizzie thought about what Faz had said. She could understand his anger; he had a young daughter, and there were predators out there who had the power to harm her. Lizzie suspected if she had children of her own, she would feel the same way. She was so lost in her thoughts that she walked straight into Mo, who was heading towards her. Mo stumbled and Lizzie managed to catch her before she fell over.

'I'm so sorry, I was miles away,' Lizzie spluttered. 'I'm not doing it on purpose, I swear.' She bent to retrieve the paperwork which had fallen out of her hand.

'It's fine, honest,' Mo said, 'I was just on my way to get warrants for Alan Stanley's phone records and so on. Why don't you come with me?'

As they walked towards the courthouse, Mo talked about the city and how it had changed over the years. She pointed out the Chubb building, former home of Chubb Locks and Safes, which was now home to the Lighthouse Media Centre. Its unusual shape reminded Lizzie of the flat iron building in New York.

Lizzie thought the combined court building was also impressive. Built of cream-coloured stone, the contrasting bright-blue steel framework added a touch of contemporary style.

Inside was bright and airy, with small groups of low tables and chairs for visitors to sit at whilst waiting for whatever service they required. Mo spoke to the man sitting in the reception booth, who signed them in then directed them towards an office on the first floor.

Mo headed for the stairs, paused, and then started up. Lizzie asked her how she was feeling.

'I'm getting there, still trying to do more than I should,' Mo said. 'I'm not the most patient person, so this is frustrating.'

'Are you seeing a physio? If not, I can recommend a brilliant one. She fixed my shoulder last year when I damaged it,' Lizzie offered.

'I am, but I'm not sure it's doing any good. The pain seems to be more general than just in my arm. I ache from head to toe,' Mo grumbled.

'You probably need an osteopath instead,' Lizzie said, 'You've had a nasty jolt to your whole frame so maybe it's knocked your body out of alignment.'

'I'll look into it, thanks. By the way, how did you get into wrestling?'

'I used to have a boyfriend who was handy with his fists, you know the sort, always sorry afterwards, swore never to do it again, etc. I was so in love with him that I believed him every time. Anyway, I saw a poster at my local gym and it sounded interesting, so I decided to give it a go. I really got into it and was invited onto the local women's team. When my boyfriend found out he wasn't happy, he kept belittling me, telling me I was no good, and even accused me of being a lesbian. One night after I came home from training he'd been drinking, so I knew what was coming. He grabbed my arm, so I picked him up and body slammed him to the floor. Then I packed my bags and walked out, head held high.'

'Good for you! It must have been scary though.'

'It was, especially when I had to go back and collect the rest of my stuff, but he sat in an armchair, a terrified look on his face while my brothers carted all the furniture out to the van. I wasn't mean, I left him the armchair and the bed, but everything else was mine, so I put it all into storage and moved back in with my parents.' Lizzie blushed, feeling embarrassed at sharing her personal life.

'I'm proud of you, girl. Wow, that's incredible,' Mo said as they reached the door to Judge Ramsay's chambers. 'Where are you living now?'

'I'm renting a flat in Newbridge on a six-month lease. It's not ideal and the furniture is cheap and nasty, but it has a garage so at least my bike is safe. I'd love to buy my own house, I've got some decent savings, so I just need to find the right place.'

'I'm happy to help you look for somewhere when you're ready.'

'That would be great, thank you.'

The door flew open before Mo had a chance to knock. Judge Ramsay let out a small gasp and stepped back at the sight of the two detectives.

'What on earth are you two doing lurking outside my door?' the woman demanded, a stern expression on her face.

'I'm so sorry, Your Honour, but we've come for the warrants that D.I. Peachey rang you about,' Mo said, after introducing her colleague.

'Ah yes. Well come in then, don't dither in the doorway.' The judge went back into the room and rifled through the stack of papers on her desk. She was a petite woman, and her gown looked at least two sizes too big for her, but Lizzie felt quite intimidated by her no-nonsense manner. As she handed Mo the warrants, a loud fart echoed round the room. The judge looked at Lizzie's expression, her blue eyes full of mirth.

'Don't look so shocked, detective,' she said, 'It's just Mathilda.' The judge pointed to the floor next to the desk where a large Staffordshire bull terrier was curled up asleep in a battered dog basket. The dog snuffled and farted again, then began snoring loudly.

Judge Ramsay followed them out of the room, locking the door behind her before striding off purposefully along the corridor, her long, blonde hair bouncing on her shoulders.

'Wow, she's intense!' Lizzie said.

Mo laughed. 'She's lovely once you get to know her. Most Glaswegians come across as brusque, but they have hearts of gold and a wicked sense of humour. Trust me, if she doesn't like you, you'll know about it.'

'Where have you two been? Les had to drink your tea!' Gary called out as Mo and Lizzie walked back into the office.

'Oi, leave me out of it,' Les protested. 'I've no desire to have my neck broken.'

'Don't worry Les,' Mo grinned. 'We know what Gary's like for causing trouble.'

'Me? Never!' Gary said with a wink.

Lizzie looked around the room. 'Where's the boss? I've got the post-mortem results for him.'

'He's got a meeting with social services, so he's gone home,' Craig answered, looking up from his computer.

'I know it's none of my business, but what happened to his wife?' Lizzie asked.

Craig filled her in on the situation.

'Wow, that's a lot to deal with.' Lizzie said. 'What will happen to him? His son, I mean?'

'That's where it gets more complicated. Alex is waiting until Jayne is awake so he can get her side of the story before he decides whether or not to press charges against Joel for assault.'

'The poor sod, having to deal with that all by himself.'

'He's not alone, his brother and sister-in-law are a huge help,' Les added. 'They practically live next door, so Alex has plenty of support.'

'Well, that's something at least,' Lizzie said. She looked at the folder in her hand. 'What should I do with this?'

Craig held out his hand. 'I'll have a look at it.' Lizzie handed it over and he leafed through the contents.

'Those are some brutal injuries,' Craig said. He asked Lizzie to write the new information up on the incident board, then suggested everyone grab some lunch while it was quiet.

'God knows what time we'll be here till, so let's crack on.'

Chapter 29.

Then.

Tracy giggled as she elbowed Gemma's arm. The student chemistry teacher really was cute, with his oversized tweed jacket, owlish glasses, and mousy hair slicked down with Brylcreem or whatever it was they used nowadays. She remembered her grandad used to slather that stuff all over his hair when he was going out, and her grandma constantly complaining about not being able to wash the greasy stains out of the pillowcases.

'You should chat him up, Gemma,' Tracy teased. 'He keeps looking at you.'

'Maybe that's because he can see my new lacy bra through my shirt.' Gemma crossed her arms and pushed her elbows together to make her cleavage look bigger. The poor teacher swallowed audibly and tried to avoid looking in their direction.

'I forgot to tell you, my mum said there was a part-time job going at Donaldson's butcher's shop. Have you quit?' Gemma asked as the bell rang for lunchtime.

Tracy blanched. 'Yeah, it wasn't working out for me. No time to get my homework done.'

'Since when did you give a shit about homework?' Gemma laughed.

'Well. Maybe I don't want to be stuck in this dump for the rest of my life,' Tracy snapped. 'First chance I get, I'm out of here.'

'Woah, steady on, no need to bite my head off,' Gemma complained. 'I was only teasing you.'

'Yeah, well don't. I'm sick of this place.' Tracy stuffed her books and pen in her schoolbag and stalked out, leaving Gemma sitting on her own and the student teacher calling after her that the lesson wasn't over yet.

Tracy slipped out of the school and trudged along the road, wondering what to do. A few times she'd thought about telling her dad but was worried he wouldn't believe her. Derek Donaldson was his oldest friend, and Tracy knew that it would break her dad's heart.

Tracy slid her key into the lock, frowning when it wouldn't turn. Walking round to the back of the house, Tracy stepped over the low wooden fence that ran around the edge of the back lawn. She peered through the front room window and drew her head back quickly, shocked at what she'd seen.

Derek and her mum were naked on the living room floor. Pam sat astride him, head tipped back, moaning loudly as she moved up and down on top of him. He had his eyes closed and his hands on her breasts. It made Tracy's stomach lurch.

Tracy stepped back from the window, tears running down her face in disgust. How could her mother do that to her poor dad, and with such a monster, too? She walked back along the road, not focusing on anything in particular until she approached the red phone box. Her disgust turning to delight, Tracy opened the door. The ripe scent of stale urine attacked her nostrils and she fought the gagging sensation in her throat. Picking up the phone, Tracy dialled 999 whilst trying to avoid the yellow puddle. When the call connected, she put the sleeve of her jumper over the mouthpiece to disguise her voice.

'I need the police. There's a woman being attacked by a man in her home. Please hurry.' Tracy gave the address then hung up before making another quick call. She headed home again and didn't have long to wait until a police car raced by and stopped outside her house. She ducked behind the hedge of next door's garden and watched from behind the overgrown privet as the police hammered on the door.

Tracy's mum threw the door open, clutching her dress in front of her to cover her nakedness, and yelped when she saw the two officers standing there. An argument was soon under way, which was when Tracy's second phone call bore fruit.

Her dad turned up.

EVERYONE LOOKED UP at the sound of a knock on the class-room door. Mrs Corcoran put down her pen and went to see who it was. A hushed conversation took place with someone outside before Mrs Corcoran looked at Bobbie.

'Bobbie, can you please go to the head's office? You may as well take your things, seeing as this lesson is almost over.' Her light, Scottish lilt carried across the room.

Whistles and catcalls from the other students echoed around the room before Mrs Corcoran banged on her desk. Her steely glare quickly brought order to the room, and silence fell.

'That's enough noise, you're not first years now. Back to your revision if you please.'

Bobbie shot a look of gratitude in Mrs Corcoran's direction before she slipped out of the room. She was surprised to see the head's secretary, Mrs Huntley, waiting for her.

'Am I in trouble, Miss?'

'No, not at all,' Mrs Huntley reassured her as she walked briskly towards the head teacher's office, leaving Bobbie to half-run along behind. 'He just wants a chat with you.'

They reached the headteacher's office. Mrs Huntley knocked firmly, then popped her head round the door and muttered a few words before opening it fully. She ushered Bobbie into the room then left, closing the door behind her. Bobbie could hear the click-clack of heels fading into the distance.

Mr McGeorge sat in a high-backed maroon leather chair behind a huge desk, both of which looked far too big for him. He stood up and came round to the small seating area as Bobbie shuffled in, and invited her to sit down.

'Please don't look worried, you've done nothing wrong,' he began. 'But I've had some information that concerns me. I need to talk to you about it before I decide what action to take. Would you like a female member of staff to be present while we talk?'

Bobbie shook her head and said nothing. She picked at the skin on her fingers to try and stop herself from shaking.

The head teacher looked as nervous as Bobbie felt. 'It's come to my attention that things are not so good at home.'

'I don't know what you mean, sir,' Bobbie said.

'I had a visit from your sister, Angela, earlier. She said that there are issues with your mother.'

Bobbie felt dread flood through her body. 'Oh, right.'

'Can you tell me what's been happening?'

'What did Angie tell you?'

'Look, we aren't going to get anywhere if we keep skirting around the issue. I'm not allowed to come out and say what I've been told because it's a breach of confidence. All I can do is ask you what's going on, so I can decide what's best for you, both as a student and as a person.'

'Can Angie sit with me while we talk?' Bobbie asked.

'I'm afraid that won't be possible in case she prompts you on what to say. She gave me a letter for you, she said to give it to you if you felt uncomfortable talking to me.' Mr McGeorge stood up and retrieved an envelope from his desk. He handed it to Bobbie and stood with his back to her at the large bay window, so Bobbie could read the letter in private.

After a few minutes, Bobbie looked up, tears running down her face. The head teacher turned when she spoke his name. He came over and sat down, concern etched all over his face. 'Are you okay, Bobbie?'

'I think I'd like you to see this, sir.' Bobbie wiped her face on her sleeve and handed the note to him. He read it in silence.

Handing the note back, he stood up again. 'If it's okay with you, I'm going to make a couple of phone calls first.'

JULIE LAY IN BED, WONDERING whether tonight would be when she'd be brave enough to use the scissors she'd secreted under her bed. Thanks to the recent lesson on sex education at school, she now knew what was being done to her. Julie didn't believe the constant reassurances from the monster that this was how it was for all girls – surely one of her friends would have mentioned it. Then again, the monster had said it needed to stay a secret between them, so maybe her friends had been sworn to secrecy, too.

Last time she'd been told it would soon be time to learn something new, something that would please her future husband. She had no idea what that could be, but if all girls had to be taught this sick ritual, then she didn't want to get married.

She sighed and turned to face the wall, feeling older than her years. She was tired, fed up, and so confused. The bedroom door opened, and Julie braced herself for another night of pain.

Chapter 30.

N ow.
　　The body lay on the table in the mortuary suite, limbs bent at unnatural angles, with bones poking through the mottled skin in places. His dark skin appeared more grey than black under the harsh lights

'Well, I really don't know where to start with this one, Ziggy.' Faz scratched his head in puzzlement as he walked round the table. 'He's a bit of a mess, that's for sure.'

The younger man tilted his head to one side then the other as he looked at the body. 'His positioning reminds me of an oven-ready chicken. Perhaps we should try to straighten him out first, then go from there, unless you'd rather wait until the detective arrives,' he suggested.

'I think we can afford to wait a few more minutes, although I thought someone would've been here by now. They knew what time we were starting.'

'I think DI Peachey has been a bit distracted lately, what with his wife being in hospital.'

'That's true, and I'd be the same if I were in his shoes, but time and tide wait for no man, as they say.' Faz flexed his fingers, stepped forward and grasped the victim's ankle.

The door swung open, and Dawn rushed in. 'I'm so sorry, I had a few things to finish off before I could leave.' Dawn wiped her sleeve across her face, removing the sheen of sweat.

Faz grinned. 'Don't worry, you've not missed anything important. Grab a stool behind the screen and park your backside while Ziggy and I try to untangle this man's limbs.'

'I don't envy you that job.' Dawn sat down and pulled a Mars bar out of her pocket. She tore open the wrapper with her teeth and bit into the chocolate. 'Mmm, I'd forgotten how good these were,' she sighed.

'Well, some of us have our waistlines to think of, especially those of us who may have overindulged during the festive season,' Faz joked, patting his stomach.

'Get lost, you look fabulous – for a man of your age. I mean, you're hardly as fit as your assistant, but I don't know many men who are.' Dawn winked at Ziggy, causing him to blush to the roots of his hair.

Faz laughed. 'You're a cheeky sod, that's for sure. Now look what you've done to the poor man, he's come over all peculiar. How is he supposed to concentrate with you sexually harassing him?'

Dawn looked horrified. 'I haven't done anything of the sort!'

'You did, you winked at him. That's grounds for complaint. If I were him, I'd be speaking to my union rep.'

'Bollocks! If it were you, you'd lap it up like a starving dog,' Dawn laughed. She looked at Ziggy, who suddenly became extremely interested in the instruments on the nearby trolley. 'Sorry if I embarrassed you, Ziggy. I meant no harm.'

Ziggy smiled shyly. 'You didn't, it's Dr Farrow who should apologise.'

'Hear, hear!' Dawn stuck her chocolate-coated tongue out at Faz.

Faz huffed in mock disgust. 'Fine, I apologise. Now, can we get back to the matter in hand? I'd like to try and straighten this poor bugger out so we can see the full extent of his injuries.'

After a lot of manipulation and swearing under their breath, Faz and Ziggy had the body back to its correct position. Dawn finished her snack and stuffed the wrapper back in her pocket before standing up to get a better look.

'Sheesh,' she said.

'You could say that, although I can think of stronger words to use,' Faz replied.

Now that the man was straightened out, they could see that large areas of skin had been removed, leaving patches of raw flesh.

'What could have caused that kind of injury?' Dawn asked.

Faz scraped gently with his scalpel. 'It's not been cut away. More than likely it's been rubbed off with a coarse material. I've never seen anything like this.'

'What about the first victim? Did he have wounds like this?'

'No, his skin was intact, apart from the areas where parts of him were removed.'

'Can you tell why it's been done? Is there something the perp didn't want us to see?'

Faz picked up a magnifying glass and looked closer. 'No, I don't think so. See here, where the damage is worse? I think a power tool has been used, and they were testing how much pressure to apply. These deeper wounds suggest to me that this is the starting point. Other areas are more uniform and not so deep, which tells us that the killer got more confident with practice.'

Dawn shook her head in disbelief. 'Wow, that's seriously disturbing.'

'I think I know what did this,' Ziggy piped up. 'When I was a teenager, I helped my dad restore some old furniture, and he caught his hand against the sanding belt. It left a similar mark to these ones.'

'You could be right.' Faz patted his young assistant on the shoulder. 'Now, let's look at the rest of him. Were any body parts found at the scene, detective?'

'Not yet, but they are still searching nearby, as well as in the canal. I'll let you know if we find anything.'

Faz continued with his examination. He hummed to himself as he went, dictating his findings into a Bluetooth microphone attached to his left ear. His calm, soothing lilt was almost hypnotic. A sudden outburst of expletives made Dawn jump so hard she almost fell off her stool.

'Is everything okay?'

'Don't bother looking for this man's fingers. I believe I may have found them.' Faz's face creased in concentration as he probed the victim's rectal cavity.

'Are you joking?' Dawn's face drained of colour, and she immediately regretted eating the Mars bar.

'I'm perfectly serious,' Faz replied. He asked Ziggy to bring him a shallow bowl. Reaching for a pair of long forceps, he pulled a series of fleshy lumps out of the victim's bottom and deposited them in the bowl. After a few minutes he put the forceps down and peered at the bowl's contents.

'Well?' Dawn asked, impatient to know what he'd found.

'We definitely have ten digits, but they don't belong to this chap.'

'How can you be so sure?'

Faz held up one of the dismembered fingers. 'Because black men don't tend to have white fingers.'

Chapter 31.

Alex kissed his wife gently on the forehead before the porters wheeled the bed away. The hospital had called to say that they were prepping Jayne for surgery just as he was leaving Dave's, so Alex had rushed to see her before she went to the operating theatre. He knew there was nothing more he could do but he couldn't bring himself to leave just yet, so he sat on the chair in Jayne's room in silence and tried to still his mind.

The meeting with the social worker had gone well but had left him mentally exhausted. It had been agreed that Alex and Jayne should move back into their old house, and for Joel to move back to his bungalow, with live-in carers. Alex knew that Jayne would be furious but the social worker – a vibrant, middle-aged woman named Ronnie, whose entire outfit was a violent shade of purple which perfectly matched her hair – had insisted that it was the right thing to do.

'Don't worry Mr Peachey, as soon as your wife sees how happy your son is, she will be glad of the help.'

'She was adamant that we wouldn't get social services involved. No offence,' he added, looking at Ronnie.

''None taken. I know it's not what she wanted, but – and I say this with the greatest respect – if she had involved us earlier, she might never have ended up in hospital.'

'It's no good dwelling on what might have been,' Dave butted in, seeing his brother's hackles starting to rise. 'Let's just concentrate on moving forward.'

'Agreed,' Carol added. 'Now, how do we find reputable carers?'

Ronnie rifled through her overstuffed briefcase and pulled out a stack of leaflets. She peeled off several and handed them to Alex. 'Have a look at some of these and see where you go from there. There are other agencies out there, so you don't have to go with any of these, you are free to employ anyone you consider suitable. I would strongly advise you check all credentials very thoroughly, and always go through a properly registered agency if possible. It's more expensive, but they will do all the necessary checks and make sure you get the right person for the job. In the meantime, I'll see if I can arrange for some respite care for Joel. I think a break away would do him good.' With that, she shook hands with everyone and swept out of the house, leaving only a faint whiff of lavender perfume in her wake.

The doctors had promised Alex that they would ring as soon as Jayne was out of surgery, so he left the hospital and walked across the car park. He paid the parking fee and drove through Heath Town, heading towards the ring road which led to the station. Work on the tower blocks in this area of the city had finally begun, and each tower sported a scaffold exoskeleton. It was a very run-down area and Alex was glad to see it was finally getting a facelift.

Alex's phone rang as he pulled up in the station car park and he fumbled in his pocket for it, finding it just as the call rang off. He checked the number but didn't recognise it, so put the phone away and got out of the car. Alex stood for a few minutes, breathing slowly to calm himself before heading inside.

He climbed the stairs, walked into the main office and glanced around the room, noticing only Les and Mo were at their desks. 'Where is everyone?'

'Hello, boss, we weren't expecting you back in today,' Les said, getting up from his desk. 'I'll put the kettle on.'

Mo looked up from her screen. 'Dawn's at the post-mortem, and the tramp who sometimes sleeps in the canal tunnels has been spotted, so Craig and Gary have gone to see if he'll talk to them. Gary filled that old thermos from the kitchen with tea and said he'd pick up some food on the way, in case the old guy's hungry.'

'Good idea, people often ignore the homeless, but they are still human beings and deserve to be treated as such. What are you up to?'

'I'm working my way through these lists of known paedophiles that live in a 50-mile radius, then checking to see if any of them have anything in common with Alan Stanley. Les is working on the number sequences and Alan Stanley's bank statements.'

'Where's our newest recruit?'

'She's gone to the shop to grab some more teabags as we were almost out. She shouldn't be long, though.'

'Right, I'll be in my office if anyone wants me.'

Chapter 32.

When Dawn got back to the office, she relayed what Faz had said.

'Just what we didn't need,' Alex complained. 'It's like some macabre Easter egg hunt but we don't have all the clues.'

'I really hope we catch them before they kill another four people.' Les grumbled. 'Although, we have five pictures and two bodies, so potentially we could be looking at three.'

'And they're not exactly helpful picture clues either,' Dawn added. 'The paint pot could mean anything from decorator to someone who works in a hardware shop.'

'Or they could be an artist, although then it would probably show a paint palette,' Mo said.

'I've not worked on anything this big before,' Lizzie said. 'It's both exciting and terrifying at the same time.'

'Don't worry, we all feel the same,' Les said. 'It's just a case of being organised.'

Lizzie smiled at him. 'Let's hope we can solve it before Gary leaves. He'll hate not being around to see the outcome.'

'Who's taking my name in vain?' Gary asked as he strolled in.

Lizzie repeated what she'd said. Gary nodded. 'Aye, I'd hate to leave you all in the lurch.' He turned to Craig. 'By the way, are we still going out on Friday for a pint?'

'Absolutely, mate. I'm just sorry that we couldn't have a proper stag do as we originally planned.'

'It's fine, we can always arrange a fishing trip later in the year, once the boss's wife is better. A few pints down the local working men's club will be just as good a way to celebrate.'

Craig struggled to keep the smirk from his face. 'We'll still do you proud, mate.'

When Gary went to the toilet, Lizzie poked Craig in the ribs. 'What are you up to? I saw the look on your face when Gary mentioned fishing.'

Craig laughed, unable to help himself. 'He thought we'd arranged a fishing trip, but it was actually a weekend away, involving a lot of drinking and a night at a pole-dancing club.'

Lizzie snorted. 'Oh, you wicked man! A night down the local pub will seem tame compared to that.'

Craig winked at her, a twinkle in his eye. 'Trust me, it may not be as extravagant, but I've still got a few surprises in store.'

'Really? Like what?'

'If you want to know you should come along. It may be a stag night, but Dawn and Mo are going to be there.'

'Sounds great, count me in.'

Craig grinned. 'I guarantee it will be a night to remember.'

'How did it go with the tramp at the canal?' Alex asked, changing the subject as Gary came back in.

'He wasn't able to recall much, thanks to some bright spark giving him a bottle of whisky to keep the cold out,' Craig complained. 'He took it to share with his pal, who lives in the next tunnel along, and they fell asleep there. He wasn't very happy when he came back to his usual spot to find someone had dumped a body in it, so he went back to his friend's and stayed with him for a few days.'

'He was grateful for the tea and sausage rolls we gave him, though,' Gary added.

'He also said that one of his blankets was missing. He asked if we had it, but I'm pretty sure we don't,' Craig said. 'I'll check with forensics to see if they've got it.'

'I've got an old duvet at home he can have. Jo said we need to declutter before we move,' Gary said. 'We've probably got some pillows, too.'

'Okay, let's move on,' Alex cut in. 'Les, how's it going with Alan Stanley's phone records?'

'He had two mobile phones, one for family and friends, then a second one with unregistered numbers on. I'm waiting for his service provider to get back to me with the details.'

'Good, keep on at them, remind them this is a murder enquiry if you have to. Mo, what about you?'

'Alan Stanley spent four hundred pounds every month on hotel bills, according to his credit card.'

'That seems extravagant,' Craig said. 'It must be a very fancy establishment if it costs that much.'

'It wasn't just the one guest house,' Mo said. 'He stayed in four different ones in Yorkshire on a rotational basis. He received three cash payments of two hundred pounds the same week the trips were made.'

'It sounds like he wasn't travelling alone,' Alex said.

'That's what I thought,' Mo agreed, 'So I looked them up and got in touch with the proprietors. Something else that's interesting is all the guest houses are very small, each one only has four rooms to let, so Alan's party had exclusivity. They all confirmed that Alan Stanley and his colleagues have stayed with them three times a year for the past couple of years.'

'Excellent. Did they give you the dates when he was staying?'

'Yes, they match up with the dates on his credit card. One of the owners was especially helpful. She said Alan Stanley told her he was a rep for an insurance company.'

'Really? I suppose it's as good a cover story as any,' Alex said. 'Did she give you their names?'

'She did – Mr Green, Mr Black, and Mr Gold. She said she was sure they were false names because she overheard one of them on the phone identify himself as Reg, yet he'd told her his name was Jim.'

'As Alan Stanley was the one paying the bill, he wouldn't be able to use a credit card with a different name,' Craig said.

'See, code names, just like I said,' Gary chipped in. 'I wonder why they chose insurance reps though?'

'Perhaps one of his mates is an insurance man. It always makes sense to keep a bit of truth in any story in case anyone slips up,' Lizzie said.

'It's possible, but we won't know for sure until we identify his travelling companions,' Dawn said.

'I can arrange for the landlords to go to their local station and work with a police sketch artist if it helps.'

'I can do that if you like,' Lizzie offered. 'They are all in North Yorkshire, so will come under my previous station. My old DI is a decent bloke and won't mind helping us out.'

'Thanks, Lizzie,' Alex said. 'Set it up and I'll clear it with Andy.'

Chapter 33.

How gullible are these people? It took no effort at all to persuade this one to come around on the pretext of giving me an estimate for some work. Boy, is it in for a shock – in more ways than one!

It took a long time to clean up after the last one, but it was so worth it. It always had the gift of the gab, but everything that came out of its mouth was shit, so it seemed fitting to feed it back to it. I like to make them see how it feels to be on the receiving end.

Everything is ready. The floor is covered with plastic and my instruments lie in neat rows in the order I plan to use them. The large car batteries are fully charged, so they should last for many hours. A van rolls slowly up the gravel driveway and the driver's door creaks open. It climbs out, big grin in place, and reaches for a toolbox. The stench of cheap body spray assaults my nostrils; it seems to be a common fragrance favoured by these animals.

I glance at the clock – it's half an hour early but I don't mind at all. It means I'll have more time to play with it.

Chapter 34.

Alison looked around at the faces of the women in the room. Some looked confused, others defiant. They had not been happy at all about the police wanting to know their private business, and all of them had flatly refused to attend if the police were there so Alison had not invited Dawn along. Instead, she hoped to persuade the group to give her the information that they needed so she could pass it along.

'No one is asking you to give away your anonymity,' Alison assured them. 'All the police are asking is that if any of these pictures connect in any way to your past abuse, can we let them know who the likely targets might be?'

'What if we don't want to?' one woman asked. 'I'd shake the hand of anyone who killed my abuser. It's one less monster on the streets.' There were murmurs of agreement around the room.

'I agree,' another said. 'I'd even pay for mine to die.'

'Ladies, please, let's be reasonable. Someone is committing brutal murders and they seem to be connected to our group. The police need our help to stop the killer, I think the least we can do is hear them out.'

'Why should we?' someone else argued. 'Those bastards ruined our lives, wrecked our childhoods and made us afraid of our own shadows. It's time those perverts found out what being scared feels like.' Loud cheers echoed around the room, and Alison knew she had lost them. Jean stood up and clapped loudly to quieten them down.

'Can I just say something please?' she pleaded. The room fell silent.

'Although I'm happy that my abuser got what he deserved, I'm worried about what the killer might do next. What if they turn their attention to us?'

'Why would they? We haven't abused anyone!' Everyone tried to speak at once and Jean clapped again.

'I'm not saying you have,' Jean continued. 'But whoever it is knows us very well. They know details that only we know, so what's to stop them from telling other people we care about what happened to us? I've worked so hard to hide my past, and I'd hate for that to become public knowledge. My mum doesn't know what happened to me and it would destroy her if she found out. My abuser's wife doesn't know either. It would ruin their lives and that's not fair.' Jean started to cry. 'I just think enough damage has been done by these vile creatures, so although they deserve it, we owe it to the innocent parties to help out.' She sat back down again and wiped her eyes.

'Maybe Alison could give us some time to discuss things amongst ourselves,' someone suggested.

Alison nodded. 'I think more tea and coffee is in order, so we'll give you all some privacy to discuss it while we put the kettle on again. Are you coming, Tracy?'

'If you don't mind, I think Tracy should stay,' Jean said, 'She was a part of this group so she should get a say in the discussion.'

'Fair enough,' Alison said. She left the room, closed the door, and went into the kitchen. She stood by the window and stared at the people walking by as she waited for the kettle to boil, mulling over what Jean had said. She was right, enough damage had been done. Maybe she should take that holiday as Tracy had suggested; she could definitely do with one, she was worn out emotionally and physically.

'Are you okay?' Tracy asked as she came into the room a few minutes later. 'I thought you might need a hand with the drinks.'

'Yeah, that would be great, thank you. I was just thinking about your suggestion of a holiday,' Alison replied. 'It depends on how much it's going to cost me to redecorate the spare room, but I think that getting away would do me good.'

'Does the spare room need doing straightaway?' Tracy asked as she filled the mugs with boiling water. 'You should put yourself first for once.'

'I'm tempted to leave it, but it smells terrible in there, so it must be done. Mark's still got some stuff to be collected, but one of his brothers is meant to be coming for that at the weekend. That's a meeting I'm not looking forward to.' Alison pulled a face at the thought of seeing Colin again. He had hated Alison from the beginning, but she had no idea why. She could only think it was because he and his wife had lost their free babysitter when Mark had moved in with her.

'Do you want me to be there when he calls round? I don't mind,' Tracy offered but Alison shook her head.

'No, it's fine. I'll wait until I know he's due then put everything out on the front porch, so I don't have to see him.'

'Have you heard from Mark since he left? I half expected him to be pestering you to let him come back by now'.

'It's only been a few days, but I know at some point he will. I wouldn't put it past him to come with Colin on Saturday,' Alison sighed. 'I don't half know how to pick them, don't I? Why can't I find a decent guy like you did?'

'Trust me, Brian's no angel, he has his moments,' Tracy laughed, 'But he is pretty awesome the rest of the time,'

Jean came to find them. 'Can you both come back in please?'

Tracy held the door open, and Alison carried the drinks tray through. She set it down on the table, aware that everyone was watching her.

'I hope you don't mind me acting as spokesperson,' Jean said after they had taken their seats, 'but we've come to an agreement of sorts. To respect everyone's privacy, the ladies have agreed that they will give the police the names of their abusers, but they themselves will only disclose their first names. The police can come in and speak to us as a group after that if they think it's necessary, but no one will give their names and none of them will identify which man abused them. Is that acceptable?'

Alison nodded, relief flooding through her veins. 'Yes, that's wonderful. Thank you all, I know this is difficult, but Jean is right about protecting your privacy. The police will get no details about any of you from me or Tracy, that much I can promise you.'

Tracy nodded her agreement. 'My lips are sealed.'

Jean passed an envelope to Alison. 'I asked everyone to write the name of their abuser on a piece of paper and put it in this envelope. I hope that's okay with you.'

'I think you should take charge of it,' Alison said, noticing the large 'X' on the seal. 'Can you take it to the police station, please?'

Jean agreed and slipped it into her bag. 'Of course, I'll pop along there tomorrow.'

Alison asked everyone to share something positive that had happened since they last saw each other. As they went around the room, the tension fell away and before they knew it, it was time to go home. One by one the women left until only Jean, Tracy and Alison remained.

Alison took the mugs through to the kitchen and started washing up, leaving the other two chatting quietly in the lounge. Just as she rinsed the last mug, Tracy came to join her.

'Has Jean gone? I thought she might have popped in to say goodnight before she went.'

'I think she was anxious about getting back to her mum, she doesn't like to leave her too long.' Tracy looked as if she would rather be somewhere else.

'Why don't you get going too, I can lock up here,' Alison suggested.

'Only if you're sure...' Tracy looked relieved, and Alison was quickly becoming irritated.

'Well, you seem preoccupied, so I won't keep you if you have something more pressing to do.' Alison spoke more sharply than she had intended to, and Tracy looked hurt.

'I'm so sorry, I didn't mean to snap at you,' Alison said, pushing a stray lock of hair behind her ear. 'It's just this whole business is getting to me. We offer a place of trust and safety here and it feels as though someone has trashed the whole thing. I understand why the group feel betrayed, but I get the feeling that they blame me in some way.' Alison looked at Tracy's face and saw that she'd hit the nail on the head. 'So, they do blame me. I hope you put them straight.'

When Tracy didn't answer straightaway, Alison lost her temper. 'Thanks a bunch, at least I know where I stand. Next, you'll be telling me that you think I've hired a hitman to bump off all the group's predators!' She turned back to the sink and started to dry the mugs, slamming them down on the worktop.

'Don't get so steamed up,' Tracy said, 'I was about to say that they wondered whether you may have shared information with someone without thinking, or maybe someone got access to the files without you knowing. I told them that your keys rarely leave your side, so the question came up about computer hacking. I said I didn't know if you'd uploaded anything onto your home computer or whether you just had hard copies of everything.' Tracy looked uncomfortable. 'I simply told them what I knew.'

Alison sighed and threw the tea towel on the counter. 'I guess I'd feel like that if I were in their position. Let's just leave the police to sort it all out. I'll suspend the current group for a couple of weeks, I think I need a break from it all.'

'I think that's a good idea, it will give you time to deal with all this business over Mark as well,' Tracy said. 'How about you and I go for a coffee next week, hopefully the police will have made some headway and we can decide where to go from here.'

'Sure, send me a text to remind me,' Alison replied. She felt drained and just wanted to go home and fall into bed. A pulse in her head had started to throb, threatening a migraine. 'I'm just going to put these mugs away then I'll be heading off. I'll see you next week, give my love to Brian and Callum.'

'Will do.' Tracy hugged her and left her to it.

A feeling of unease crept over Alison as she put the last of the crockery away. She wracked her brains to try and think how such sensitive information could have got out, especially when she knew that the only people who had seen it were herself, Tracy and Sonia. She had copies of everything on her computer at home, saved to the cloud, but it was of no value to anyone, so Alison had no idea how or why anyone would hack into it. Her passwords were strong, and she'd installed other security measures after catching Mark trying to use her computer.

Alison turned off the lights, grabbed her coat and left the building, making sure the outer door was firmly locked. She hurried to her car, wishing she had parked closer to the building, but there had been a weight loss club in one of the other rooms, so there had been no spaces left. She got into her car with a sigh of relief, feeling the adrenalin start to subside.

It took Alison twenty minutes to reach home, thanks to late-night roadworks on the A454, but her relief turned to despair when she spotted Mark sitting on the kerb at the front of the house. He stood up when he saw her, hope written all over his face and a bunch of flowers clutched in his hand.

'Just what I didn't need,' Alison said to herself as she swung the car onto the small patch of tarmac in front of the garage. She took a deep breath and got out.

'Hi babe,' he said in a small voice, the one he used when trying to sweet-talk her. 'I popped round to get some of my stuff, but you weren't here.'

'That's because I was at a meeting,' she replied. 'If you'd called me first, I could have saved you the trip.' Alison looked at Mark's bicycle, which leaned against the garage door. 'If you were coming for your stuff, how were you planning to carry it?'

Mark looked sheepish. 'Okay, I lied. I just needed to get out for a bit. My mum's doing my head in already. These are for you,' he said, holding out the flowers.

'Thank you, but you should have saved your money.'

'I tried to find another plant like the one that got broken, but they didn't have any, so I got these instead.'

Alison bit back the sarcastic comment that was forming in her head and waited in silence. She knew what he was leading up to and wished he would get on with it so she could go inside where it was warm.

'I've been thinking,' he began, 'Maybe we should go away for a bit and sort everything out. I'll look for a job and start paying my way, start being the man you want me to be.'

'It's too late, Mark,' she said. 'We've tried so many times to fix it, but we can't. You have to face the fact that it's over.'

Mark shook his head. 'No, it's not, we are really good together, but I know I've made mistakes and I'm willing to change if you are.' He stepped closer. 'Come on babe, you know you want to. Let's go to bed and make up like we used to.' He held his hand out and winked at her.

Alison threw the flowers at him, making him flinch as they bounced off his chest and scattered on the path. 'For fuck's sake, what part of 'It's over' do you not understand?' she shouted. 'I don't want you back and will never want you back, so get it through your thick skull and leave me alone!' She strode past him and opened the door, slamming it hard behind her. She stood with her back to it, bracing herself for the knocking to start. After ten minutes of silence, she opened the door a crack and peered outside. Mark and the flowers were gone, the street was deserted, and everything appeared normal.

Everything except the envelope tucked beneath her windscreen wiper.

Chapter 35.

When Alex pulled into the station car park, he felt more positive than he had in a while. Jayne's operation had gone smoothly, although it was too early to tell whether a second one would be necessary. She was still under sedation, but the plan was to wake her up over the next couple of days.

'If we bring her round too suddenly it could cause her a lot of distress. Trust me, we do this all the time,' the consultant had assured him.

Alex got out of his car and stood with his eyes closed, face turned upwards, enjoying a rare kiss of sun on his face. He smiled to himself. Things were finally starting to get better again. The sound of his name being called pulled him back to reality, and he looked around to see Les standing by the entrance door.

'Boss, we've got another one.'

Alex's heart sank. 'Please tell me you're joking.' He joined Les and they went upstairs together. When they entered the office, they were greeted with silence. A heavy atmosphere hung in the air, and they all looked defeated.

Alex took a deep breath and clapped his hands together. 'Come on, people. We're not going to let this get the better of us! Gather round and tell me what the situation is. Where is it?'

'It's in Wombourne Woods,' Dawn said.

Gary put the phone down that had rung while Alex was talking. 'Someone called to say they've received a card like the one Jean Harrison got. She wouldn't give her name, but she gave us the information from the card, and said she will ask a friend to drop it off later today.'

'We need to find out who she is, and quickly,' Alex said.

'Agreed, maybe we can ask Alison Munroe to help us out,' Lizzie suggested.

'Good idea, get on the phone and ask her to come in.' Alex said. 'Dawn and I will go to the crime scene.'

By the time they arrived at Wombourne woods, the obligatory white tent had been erected and a group of white-suited figures moved silently around the area, taking photos and collecting evidence. Alex unfolded himself from Dawn's Mini and stretched like a cat until he felt his spine pop. He signed them both in with the officer at the cordon and ducked under the tape as she held it up for them.

'PC Marshall, nice to see you again,' Alex said, receiving a smile and a nod in return.

'It amazes me how you remember everyone's name,' Dawn puffed as they pulled on their white coveralls. 'I have trouble remembering my own name some days, let alone anyone else's.'

'I try and make a point of it. I've done that job, and it can make you feel pretty unappreciated, Al,' he smiled.

'Who's Al and what does he have to do with anything?'

'Sorry, couldn't resist. It's a line from one of Jayne's favourite films. Maybe I should see if they can set up a TV and DVD player in her room. It might help with her recovery.'

'It's certainly worth a shot.' Dawn nodded towards the tent. 'Looks like Faz is ready for us.'

'Hello, you two, I hope you haven't had your dinner yet,' The coroner flashed them a brief smile as they approached. 'It's a juicy one.'

Alex sighed inwardly, regretting the scrambled eggs he'd had for breakfast. They stepped through the tent flaps, but the overpowering stench almost knocked them back out again.

'Holy shit!' Dawn exclaimed, clamping her hand over her nose.

'It is shit, detective, but I don't know if there's anything holy about it. I know it's not your usual scene of crime scent, but that's because the contents of his bowels have been plastered all over his face, hence the aroma. His mouth is also full of faeces.'

Alex peered as closely as he could whilst trying not to breathe. He pointed to the victim's neck.

'Correct me if I'm wrong, but is that a string of sausages?'

'Yes and no,' Faz said. 'They are his intestines, twisted to look like that.'

'That's a first. Is it the cause of death?'

'Now, you know I can't answer that until I get him on the table and have a good look at him, but first impressions would suggest the sausage necktie was done post-mortem. I can't check for petechiae yet until I get him cleaned up because of the killer's expressive use of excrement.'

'Bloody hell, what a way to go,' Alex murmured. 'Am I right in assuming he's also been castrated?'

'I'd say it's a safe bet but won't know for sure until he's cleaned up. Now, I think it's time we got this poor bugger moved before the smell in here renders us all unconscious. I'll let you know when the PM will be. I've already got a guest waiting for me when I get back, but I'll attend to this gentleman as soon as I can.'

'Cheers, Faz.' Alex stepped outside the tent and gulped down a lungful of fresh air. The smell was fainter out there, but not by much. He stripped off his coveralls and placed them in the bin provided before heading back to Dawn's car.

Dawn swung out of the parking area and drove slowly along the narrow track until she reached the road. She put her foot down and the Mini shot forward, causing Alex to grab at the door handle. He gave her a look and she slowed down a fraction.

'Sorry, I forgot you drive like a granny.'

'I don't, I just stick to the speed limit.'

'Yeah, the speed limit as it was in Queen Victoria's time.'

Dawn's smile faded as they approached the entrance to Mason Manor. Once the country home of some long-dead aristocrat, it had fallen into disrepair until being snapped up at auction by the local casino mogul, Glyn Mason. He'd promptly handed the keys over to his beloved goddaughter, Hope, and moved to Spain, leaving her to restore the house to its former glory.

Hope's father, male stripper Ray Diamond, had taken full advantage of his daughter's good nature and moved in, enjoying free board and lodgings until being convicted of the manslaughter of promoter Steve Gifford, who he'd recently confessed to killing in a hit and run years before.

'I wonder how Ray's coping with life on remand,' Dawn said.

'Probably got them eating out of his hand by now.' Alex gazed out of the window. 'It looks like someone's been busy; the gardens are much tidier than when we were last here.'

'I heard that Glyn was moving back from Spain because of Brexit looming, so Hope's probably been getting it ready for his return.' Dawn turned into Beggar's Bush Lane, then left onto the Stourbridge Road. It was quiet at this time of day, so they were back at the station only ten minutes later.

Alex got out of the car and stood with his hands on his hips, staring at the ground.

'You okay, boss?'

Alex looked up. 'Sorry, Dawn. I was just thinking about that body back there. Talk about overkill.'

'It was a bit over the top, wasn't it? Do you think they are escalating?'

'I bloody hope not. How much further can they go?'

Dawn shrugged. 'No use asking me, I've never been abused so I can't say what I'd do to someone to exact revenge. That level of torture takes time, which makes me think they have access to somewhere remote.'

They crossed the car park and Dawn opened the station door, allowing Alex to go first. The officer on reception called out to Dawn, and Alex waited while she approached the counter. When she came back, she was carrying a large brown envelope.

'Jean Harrison dropped this off just now. I'm hoping it contains the answers we're looking for.'

Chapter 36.

Les sat at his desk, coffee cooling rapidly in front of him as he read through the copious sheets of paper that the printer had spewed out. After a couple of hours, he was starting to feel peckish, so he picked up his mug and wandered to the kitchen area, put the kettle on again and took one of the ham and cheese rolls out of his lunch-box, figuring it would keep him going until lunchtime.

Mo came over to join him, choosing the chair opposite Les, and eased herself into it. She made several attempts to open her sandwich wrapper before handing it to Les. He grinned at her as he tore the cardboard strip off and opened the packet out, creating a makeshift plate, and placed it on her lap.

'How are you feeling?' Les asked through a mouthful of bread.

'Not too bad, just a bit stiff here and there.' Mo bit into her sandwich and chewed slowly. 'It's frustrating more than anything, not being able to move as quickly as I used to.'

'You scared the life out of us all, I thought we'd lost you.' Les screwed up the cling film from his roll and got up to put it in the bin. 'Do you want a brew?'

Mo nodded. 'I scared myself, too, but my guardian angel was looking after me,' she added.

'Well, I'm glad they were. This team won't function without you.' Les brought two mugs of coffee over and sat down again. 'What's the latest on your car?'

'It's in a sorry state, but the chassis seems okay. My brother was furious when he saw it, it took him almost two years to restore it the first time.'

'Sourcing the parts will be the biggest problem,' Les said. 'Ford Capri parts are rarer than hen's teeth.'

'Tell me about it. I spent most of my lunch break yesterday trawling scrapyards and online dealers.'

'Have you got one you can use in the meantime?'

'No, but Alex has said I can borrow his if I'm stuck. I won't be able to drive for a while yet, so I'll cross that bridge when I come to it.'

'If you need taking to the shops, or anything like that, just shout,' Les said as he got up and headed back towards his desk.

'Thanks, Les, I really appreciate it.' Mo struggled out of the chair and brushed crumbs off her shirt. She followed Les back to his desk and picked up the sheets of paper he'd been looking at. 'Have you had any luck with these numbers?'

'Not yet. I know I've seen that sequence somewhere before though.'

'The mix of numbers and letters remind me of a crossword. Could they be across and down clues?'

'Mo, you're a bloody genius.' Les grabbed her and planted a sloppy kiss on her cheek. 'Stay right there, I'll be back in a flash.' He rushed out of the room, narrowly avoiding colliding with Craig who was coming in.

'Whoa, where's the fire?' Craig looked at the door then at Mo. 'What did I miss?'

'Just a flash of brilliance from me, of course,' Mo said, wiping her cheek with a grin. 'Although I have no idea what I've done.'

Craig laughed. 'I've never seen him move so quickly, so whatever it was must have been spectacular.'

The door swung open as Les rushed back in a few minutes later, brandishing a UK road atlas. He bent over to catch his breath. 'Bugger me, those stairs are a killer.'

Once he'd recovered, he held up the book. 'When my kids were little, I used to give them the map to look at when we were going on a long journey.'

'Wow, you really knew how to keep them entertained,' Craig said drily, heading for the kitchen area.

'Shut up and listen, smart arse,' Les said. 'Whenever we had a long journey to do, I used to give the boys the atlas and the journey details, and they would sit with this on the seat between them and follow the road lines. I'd ask them which junctions were coming up, how far the next service station was and so on. It passed the time and stopped them from punching each other. It also taught them how to read maps.'

'Are you thinking that the numbers on the cards are road numbers? They don't look like any I've seen,' Craig called from the kitchen.

'Not exactly. Mo, give me the first set of numbers and let me check if I'm right.' Les put the atlas on the big table and opened it, flicking quickly to the page covering the West Midlands. Craig came back in with his coffee and perched on the edge of the table, intrigued.

'Nineteen, then a capital P, then thirty-nine,' Mo said.

Les ran his finger along the page until it settled on a spot near the crease. He grinned from ear to ear.

'I knew it! See that first number? It's not nineteen, it's one point nine. Now, look here.' Les pointed to the edge of the page.

Mo looked. There were a series of numbers from one to sixteen down the side of each page. She put her finger close to the number two.

'So, one point nine would be just about here, yes?'

'Correct. Now, look along the bottom of the page. There are letters instead of numbers here. I'll put my finger on the letter P. Now, move yours across in a straight line from left to right.' Les moved his finger up the page at the same time until they touched.

'Look at where they meet,' Les said.

Mo looked. The point where their fingers met was where the first body had been discovered. 'Bugger me, Les, you've cracked it,' Mo gave him a playful shove. 'And thirty-nine is the page number. You clever old sausage.'

Les blushed. 'Less of the old if you don't mind. It was you who cracked it, you mentioned crossword clues going across and down, and that's what made me think of this.'

Does this mean we're looking for an older person?' Craig chipped in. 'Someone who doesn't have a satnav, perhaps?'

'Not necessarily. I think the atlas has been used because they either don't drive, or thought they were being clever. Most people rely on satnavs these days and wouldn't have a clue what these numbers mean – let's face it, it took us a while to figure it out. What interests me is why they bothered to send these numbers in the first place. Unless they wanted to send us clues, like a scavenger hunt.'

Mo shuddered. 'Ugh, that's gruesome. It's lucky you had one of these in your car.'

'To be honest, I rarely use it since I got the satnav, I just like to have it for back up. No one has come forward yet about the second victim, so we don't know what the coordinates are on their card, assuming he sent one,' Les said. 'But we do know where that one was found, so we can mark it on the map and cross-reference it if anyone comes in about them.'

'We should check where the victims lived or worked in relation to the dump sites. It could be they walked home that way, or maybe that area had special meaning to either them or the person they abused,' Mo said.

'That's going to be difficult to find out. I can't see the women in that group being very forthcoming with that sort of information,' Les said. 'Don't get me wrong, I can understand why they don't want to revisit such a dark place in their past.'

'I'll talk to Alison Munroe again and push her to sort out a meeting so we can speak to them as a group.' Mo picked up the phone and started to dial.

'It's certainly worth a try, the more information we have, the better.' Les pulled up a map on the computer and pressed print. 'It certainly won't do any harm.'

He attached the map to a separate board, then stuck a pin in the place where the first body had been found. Next to the map he wrote the co-ordinates that had been on the first card.

'Mo, can you read out those co-ordinates that were phoned in, please?'

'Seventy-two, capital B, forty.'

Les entered the details onto his map. 'That puts us in Oxley, where the second victim was found. If I've worked this out correctly, the next lot of co-ordinates should be forty-three, capital Q, thirty-nine, which is Wombourne Woods.'

'I hope that's the last one now,' Mo said.

'I doubt it,' Les said, 'I don't think this killer is anywhere near to being finished yet.'

Chapter 37.

Alison hit the snooze button on her alarm clock and lay back against her pillows. She felt drained, both physically and mentally. Taking over the running of the group had been a welcome challenge to start with, and Alison didn't mind giving up two evenings a week to help these women rebuild their lives, but lately it felt like it was starting to encroach into her day job. Yesterday morning she'd been called into Mrs Addison's office to explain why it had been necessary to bellow at a classroom full of six-year-olds, reducing some of them to tears.

'I appreciate that you're having some personal problems, Miss Munroe,' the head teacher had said, 'but I would much rather you leave them at home and not bring them into the school. Take tomorrow off as well, and we will see you bright and early on Monday morning. Have a good weekend.' With that, she had been dismissed with hints about using up some of her accrued holiday.

Alison had worked hard to get Mark's old room sorted out. The carpet had been heavily stained, and the wallpaper was torn from where Mark had taken down his posters of monster trucks. Alison decided to completely gut the room and start from scratch. It would also erase any memory of Mark ever being there. She enlisted the help of the couple next door to help her bring everything downstairs and outside onto the drive, ready for collection by the local council later that week.

Now it had been redecorated and had new carpet fitted it looked very smart. All that was left was to hang some new blinds. Alison intended to use it as an office as it was bigger than the one at the community centre, and she could be sure that everything was kept confidential.

Alison had driven to a Swedish furniture store on the retail park near Wednesbury. She wandered around the huge shop, picking up tickets for a new desk, chair, bookshelves and filing cabinets. She added a pinboard, a whiteboard and pens, two reams of paper and a new printer to her trolley. One of the bargain shelves caught her eye, so she selected some notebooks and pencils that were half price. She had no idea what she would use these for yet, but they would come in handy for something.

At the checkout, Alison arranged for the larger items to be delivered, then left the shop. As she loaded her car, she spotted the same woman and child she'd seen in the street after having coffee with Tracy. The woman avoided her gaze as they hurried by and got into their car, an older-model Volvo. Alison wondered if they were following her, then shook the idea from her mind as she climbed into her own car and drove away.

The next morning, Alison was up bright and early, and looking forward to the new furniture delivery. When the van turned up at midday, she was disappointed to find only one person in the cab, a short, pot-bellied man of around fifty years old. He explained that he wasn't allowed to help her carry the items upstairs.

'It's not me, love, it's all health and safety these days.'

'Well, I can't possibly manage it all on my own, can I?'

'What about your husband? Can't it wait until he gets home?'

'I'm single, so that's not an option.' She looked at her feet in despair.

The man took off his woolly hat and scratched his stubble-covered head, then smiled, showing crooked teeth.

'Look love, I'm not supposed to do this, but you seem to be in a bit of a fix.' He winked at her. 'Maybe if you make it worth my while, I'll give you a hand.'

'How much?' Alison asked. 'I don't carry much cash.' Her eyes widened as she realised he might mean something else.

'Don't look so scared, I was thinking a cup of tea would be nice,' he smiled. 'We don't get much chance to have a brew in this job, it's all go until clocking off time.'

Alison's face broke into a grin. 'I'm sure I can manage that.'

The delivery driver put his hat back on. 'Champion,' he said. 'Now, how about I start unloading this stuff while you put the kettle on?'

Chapter 38.

Andy Oliver stood by his office window, watching the rain as it ran down the glass. He looked at the letter in his hand again and felt his stomach churn. The memo from the Chief Constable explaining about the need to cut back on manpower in all departments had wound him up tighter than a watch spring. It seemed to Andy that it was always the ones who did the hard work who were squeezed the hardest, but the ones at the top always managed to emerge unscathed. Having come up through the ranks himself, the endless politics you were expected to take part in further up the ladder was one of the reasons he had refused further promotion.

Screwing the letter up, he threw it across the room in temper, narrowly missing his secretary who had chosen that moment to enter the room. She gave him a frosty look, placed the white box she was carrying on his desk, and left in silence.

Andy walked over and picked up the ball of paper, dropping it into the wastepaper basket before turning his attention to the box. He took a penknife from his top drawer and slit the box open, then peered inside. The colour drained from Andy's face when he saw the contents.

Nestled on a bed of blue tissue paper was a cow's horn, still stained with blood from where it had been sawn off. Andy put on his jacket, picked up the box and went downstairs to his car. Opening the boot, Andy carefully stored the box, making sure it was secure before closing the boot and returning to his office.

After he'd slipped his jacket off and made himself a coffee, Andy picked up the card that had accompanied the box. On one side was a picture of a pair of lips, with a finger pressed to them. His blood ran cold as he read the words printed on the other side:

'GOODNIGHT, GOD BLESS.'

Chapter 39.

I am amazed the police have not figured out who I am yet. After all, I've given them ample opportunity to catch me. Maybe they aren't trying hard enough, or maybe they are simply incompetent. You'd think someone would have reported their loved ones missing, but perhaps they have no one left to love them.

Of course, it could be that I've not been caught because the police are secretly pleased that I'm removing this scum from the face of the earth. Some of them have children too. I heard the red-haired coroner say he would kill anyone who touched his little girl. This pleases me greatly, knowing he is a kindred spirit.

Chapter 40.

Alex was delighted to hear that Mo and Les had cracked the numbers puzzle. 'Well done, that's a massive leap forward,' he said. 'Jean Harrison had left this at reception for us, so let's see if it contains any more. Dawn, would you do the honours?'

Dawn opened the envelope and tipped it up on the table. Several pieces of paper fell out and she picked them up. She shuffled the pieces of paper around. 'No numbers. Sorry, boss.'

'Never mind, at least if we do get any more we know what to do, and hopefully we can get one step ahead. Are they just names, Dawn?'

'Yes, and to be honest I don't know how helpful they are.' Dawn looked through the pieces of paper. 'Most of these are just one name, or what could be a nickname.'

'That's fine, just read them out anyway. Something might pop out.'

'Okay. We've got 'Chippy Jim', 'Uncle Phil', 'Monster', 'Black Joe', 'Kelly', 'Daddy', and 'DD'. Dawn turned the pieces of paper over. 'No clue as to who they were abusing.'

'Black Joe could be the guy who had the fingers up his bum,' Gary suggested.

'True, but it might not have anything to do with the colour of his skin,' Lizzie said. 'Maybe he was a miner or a coal man.'

'Blimey, Lizzie, don't make it more complicated than it already is,' Craig pleaded.

'She's right, though,' Alex said. 'Let's not jump to any obvious conclusions.' He looked at Dawn. 'Is that all we've got?'

'Looks like it,' she said, peering into the envelope.

'Well, it's more than we had yesterday. Craig, whereabouts are you with things?'

'Not much further forward, I'm afraid. We've canvassed the area around the rowing club again, and we've spoken to the tramp's pal but no luck. The diving team didn't find anything of use in the canal, either.'

'I'm surprised they could see anything in there, it's so full of rubbish,' Les said.

'Mo, where were those guest houses where Alan Stanley and his mates stayed?' Alex asked.

'Dalton, Oulston, Bagby, and Crakehill, all in the Thirsk area. Lizzie's old boss, DI Tony Millington, is arranging for the owners of the guest houses to sit down with a sketch artist, which we can give to the press. He's also sending us the names of any persons of interest or known paedophiles in or around those areas that are on their radar.'

'Excellent, let's hope we can find a connection quickly. In the meantime, see if you can figure out these names from the group. I need to go out, but if you get any breakthroughs before then, ring me.'

Chapter 41.

Andy Oliver walked along the corridor, deep in thought. The contents of the box currently sitting in the boot of his car had unnerved him, and something distant stirred in his memory, but he couldn't shake it loose. Dismissing it for now, he pushed open the door to the Major Crime Unit.

'Seeing as no one has bothered to update me, I thought I'd better come and see for myself.' He looked around the room. 'Where is DI Peachey?'

'He had some personal business to attend to, sir,' Dawn said. 'He said he'd be away for a couple of hours.'

'Well then, you'd better fill me in, DS Redwood.'

Andy was unhappy to hear there was a third body, and even more so when Dawn told him they still hadn't identified the second one.

'If you ask me, I reckon the perp's doing us a favour,' Les said. 'These scumbags are lower than a snake's belly, and nobody wants their kind loose on the streets.'

Andy gave Les a glacial stare. 'That is not the attitude I expect from this team, detective. No matter what these men did in the past, they are victims and deserve justice.'

'The kids they abused were the real victims, but they didn't get any justice,' Les said, his temper starting to rise. 'It boils my piss, it really does. Don't worry, I'll do my job and catch the perp, but don't expect me to have any sympathy for those perverts. I'm going out, I need some fresh air.' Les snatched his jacket from the back of his chair and strode out.

'You can't blame him, sir,' Gary said, shrugging his shoulders. 'He's only saying what we're all thinking.'

'It doesn't matter what we think, we must put our own feelings aside and find this vigilante. Having their demise splashed across the tabloids isn't just distressing for these men's families, but it's dragging up painful memories for the people they abused, too. The sooner we put a stop to the killings, the sooner these women can start to move forward again,' Andy said. 'Does anyone else have anything useful to add?'

Craig spoke up. 'Alan Stanley stayed in four different guest houses close to Thirsk, in Yorkshire.'

'I know where Thirsk is, sergeant. Get on with it.'

'We've arranged for the owners of the guest houses to go to Thirsk station and sit down with a sketch artist. With any luck, it will help us identify who Alan Stanley's companions were. DI Tony Millington is overseeing that for us, he's DC Brewster's old boss. He's going to email them to us as soon as they are done so we can release them to the press.'

'I'm combing through Alan Stanley's finances and phone records,' Mo said, unwilling to say anything further.

The vein on Andy's temple began to pulse as his temper rose. He turned his attention to Lizzie. 'I hope you've got something more useful to add.'

Lizzie swallowed hard. 'I'm working on the names we got from the group members, and we're setting up a meeting with the group so we can talk to them.'

'I see.' He looked around the room. 'Well, it's very disappointing, that's all I can say.'

'We're doing our best sir,' Dawn protested.

'Well, if this is you at your best then I'd hate to see you at your worst!' Andy snapped.

Leaving orders that Alex was to come and see him the minute he got back, Andy left the room, slamming the door behind him. A stony silence ensued.

'Coffee, anyone?' Gary asked, clapping his hands together to break the tension in the room.

'Can I have tea instead?' Lizzie asked.

'I suppose so, but only because I'm worried that you'll hurt me again if I refuse.'

'As if I would!' Lizzie's face held a mock look of horror. 'I wouldn't want to upset Jo. She won't be happy if she has to spend her wedding night giving you a bed bath.'

'Don't go giving him daft ideas,' Dawn said, seeing the grin spread across Gary's face.

Craig put his fingers in his mouth and pretended to vomit. 'Imagine having to wash that big numpty. It would be like sponging down a grizzly bear.'

'Here, I'll have you know that Jo loves my manly physique.' Gary pulled his shirt up to show off his hairy chest. 'Look at that, pure beefcake,' he grinned.

Mo pointed at him and turned to Lizzie. 'And that, my friend, is why I prefer women. I couldn't deal with all that hair and stuff.'

'But you love Lewis Collins, don't you? I bet he had a smattering of fuzz,' Lizzie said.

'Possibly, but unlike our Gary, he was gorgeous, so I would've made an exception,' Mo added, earning a shout of indignation from Gary.

'Men are supposed to look like men, not Ken dolls, all smooth and plastic-looking. You wouldn't catch me doing all that poncy grooming,' Gary said.

'It's called manscaping, and there's nothing wrong with looking after yourself.' Craig brushed an imaginary speck of dirt off his tie and ran his hand over his flat abdomen. 'My body is a temple.'

'Aye, Shirley Temple,' Gary quipped.

'Shut up and get on with your kitchen duties. My throat's as rough as a badger's bum,' Craig said.

'Matches your face,' Gary laughed, ducking as Craig launched a highlighter pen at him.

Les came back in, looking calmer than before.

'Just in time, Gary's making a brew.'

'Crikey, did he win the pools or something?'

'Do you want one or not?' Gary shouted from the kitchen.

'Of course, and I've brought a peace offering. Sorry for storming off like that.' Les pulled two packets of bourbon biscuits from his jacket pocket.

'Nothing to apologise for, we all feel the same,' Dawn said. She opened one of the packets and took a deep sniff. She sighed with pleasure. 'There's no finer smell than chocolate biscuits,' she murmured.

Alex walked in and surveyed the scene in front of him.

'Gary, tuck your shirt in, you look like you've been on the lash. Dawn, what are you doing?'

'I'm sniffing Les's bourbons.'

'That doesn't sound dodgy at all, does it?' Alex said. 'Gary, make me a cuppa as well while you're at it, please,' he called.

Mo's phone started ringing, and she propped it on her shoulder while she wrote down what the other person was saying. When she hung up, she looked grim. 'That was DI Tony Millington from the Major Crimes Unit in North Yorkshire. He's emailed a list of local paedophiles over, along with a list of their proclivities.'

'That'll make delightful bedtime reading,' Dawn said.

'That's not all. He said that the injuries sustained by our victims rang a bell with him, so he spoke to their coroner, Dr Fiona Quinn, and she confirmed there was an unidentified male victim a few years back with similar injuries. I asked if a copy of the PM could be sent to Faz so he can compare them.'

'Dr Quinn – is she a medicine woman?' Gary sniggered, referring to the popular TV show from the nineties.

'Very original,' Dawn said, rolling her eyes. 'I bet she's never heard that one before.'

'Well, I thought it was funny,' Gary mumbled, his ears going red.

'Christ, that's all we need, a cold case linked to this one.' Alex scratched his head. 'Anything else?'

'The DCI wants you to go and see him, and he's in a foul mood,' Craig said, revealing what had happened earlier.

'I see,' Alex said, his face like thunder. 'Well, I'd best not keep him waiting, then.'

Chapter 42.

Alex didn't go straight to Andy's office because he was afraid he would say something he'd regret. Instead, he went outside, sat in his car and put a Gary Moore CD into the player. When he walked in half an hour later, the DCI's face was purple with rage.

'Where the hell have you been?' he spluttered. 'I left word that I wanted to see you as soon as you came in, yet I saw you go outside and sit in your car!'

'I figured you needed to calm down a bit. I know I did. I'd appreciate it if you didn't shout at my team in future, sir, they're doing the best they can.'

'Watch your tone, detective,' Andy warned.

Alex bit back a retort. Instead, he told Andy about the call from DI Millington. 'He's going to ask Dr Quinn to send a copy of the PM to Dr Farrow so he can compare the injuries.'

'It's a development we could have done without. I'm already being pressured to keep the budget down; the press are snapping at my heels and now you tell me there's a possible cold case as well!' Andy paced up and down, clenching and unclenching his fists.

'I'm afraid so, but if we find a link between North Yorkshire and us, we'll need to turn over a lot of rocks between here and there to see what crawls out.'

'Damn it, man, stop making it any bigger than it already is!' Andy slammed his fist down on the desk, causing the pen pot to topple over and scatter its contents. 'I don't care about their case; I care about this one! I want the person responsible found!'

'As do I!' Alex said, scratching his head in frustration. 'Look, it's clear we're not going to get anywhere if we just keep bellowing at each other.' He dropped into a chair and closed his eyes, wishing he'd stayed at the hospital with Jayne.

'As if we hadn't got enough on our plates already. It's a bloody joke, that's what it is and it's not good enough!'

'Hey, don't get your knickers in a twist, we're doing the best we can!' It was Alex's turn to shout now. 'Me and my team are out there, working their arses off to try and solve this case, so how about you get off our backs and let us do our jobs?'

'That's the problem, Alex, they may be working hard, but I don't think you are. You're only here half the time, and when you are, your mind's not on work. Maybe I should bring someone else in to take over while you sort your life out.' As soon as the words left his mouth, Andy realised he'd gone too far.

Alex stood up abruptly, his temper boiling over. He leaned over the desk, his pointed finger inches from Andy's face. 'Fuck you, sir,' he snarled.

With that, he turned and walked out, slamming the door behind him.

Chapter 43.

Whilst Alex was dealing with the DCI, Gary and Craig left for a fitting for their wedding suits, Dawn went to get some lunch and Lizzie had gone for a run, leaving Les and Mo alone.

After half an hour, Mo stood up and stretched, tilting her head from side to side to work the kinks out of her neck. She took a couple of steps and gasped as a bolt of pain shot through her ankle.

'Sit down, I'll make the coffee,' Les said. 'Is your leg still giving you gyp?'

'No, I'm fine. It just gets stiff if I don't remember to stretch it regularly.'

'Hey, what's with the pervy talk?' Dawn asked as she came in, armed with a carrier bag. It had the name of a local butcher on the side.

'It's not pervy talk, so get your mind out of the gutter, Redwood, and tell us what's in the bag,' Les said, catching a whiff of something tasty.

'Nothing for you, Morris, just some bones for Barney and a big fat steak for me.' Dawn stuck her tongue out and gave a thumbs-up to Mo, who waggled a mug in the air at her.

'Well, they smell like they're already cooked to me.'

'Fine, I've bought everyone a pasty, satisfied now?' She took some paper bags out of the carrier and tossed one to Les.

He caught it and peered inside, examining the contents. 'I hope it tastes as good as it smells.'

'It should do, it cost a bomb. It's from that posh new bakery in Queen Street.'

'Isobel usually goes there whenever she's in town. They do lovely carrot cake,' Mo said.

'Now you're talking. Did you get any of that as well?' Les looked hopefully at Dawn.

'Busted. Here you go.' She reached into the bag again, pulled out a large, white box and handed it to Les. 'There's a piece for everyone, so don't go scoffing them all.'

'I think you're confusing me with DC Temple, he's the champion cake eater.' Les took a bite of his pasty and chewed. 'Damn, that's good. What's in it?'

'It's lamb, mint and vegetables. Wholemeal pastry too.'

'Very fancy.' Les took another mouthful, dropping crumbs down his front.

Mo came over with the coffee just as Alex threw the door open and marched across the room. He disappeared into his office, a thunderous look on his face.

'It looks like that didn't go too well,' she said, picking up her pasty and going back to her desk.

Several crashes, accompanied by loud swearing, emanated from the office, followed by a silence that was almost deafening. Dawn popped the last piece of her pasty in her mouth and stood up with a sigh.

'Do you want me to go?' Les asked.

'No, I'll be fine. It sounds like he's finished letting off steam now.'

'Okay, I'll make him a brew. Do you want one?'

Dawn shook her head and went over to the office. She knocked the door but there was no answer. Feeling brave, she opened the door and went in, closing it firmly behind her. Les heard raised voices as he waited for the kettle to boil, but they subsided again quickly. He smiled to himself. Dawn could talk anyone out of a bad mood, and if she couldn't, she'd been known to resort to physical persuasion.

Les carried a mug of tea across to Alex's office and opened the door. Dawn sat on Alex's desk, her arms round him as he sobbed quietly into her shoulder. Les put the mug down and withdrew, knowing that Dawn could handle whatever was going on.

'Hey up, where's our coffee?' Gary called out as he and Craig came in.

'Nowt wrong with your legs, lad. In fact, you should be on kitchen duty for the rest of the time you're with us.' Les laughed as Gary gave him a rude gesture in return.

Sitting down at his computer again, Les continued trawling through a list of online paedophile rings that DI Millington had sent over. It made him feel physically sick to think how many children might be suffering at that very moment.

'Can I help with anything, Les?' Lizzie asked when she came back. Her face was flushed from her run and her hair was damp from the shower.

Les handed her a stack of paper. 'You can help me go through these if you like, I'll be here all day otherwise.'

'Sure.' She glanced at the information and shuddered. 'Are all these websites still active?'

'That's what we need to figure out,' Les said. 'I'm cross-referencing the name of the first victim to see if he shows up in any of these, as that may give us a link to the other bodies.'

'Which may link back to the survivor's group,' Lizzie added.

They both turned as Alex's door opened and Dawn came out. She gave a small shake of her head as Alex followed a few minutes later, jacket on and keys in his hand. He left the office without a word to anyone, and Dawn visibly relaxed.

'Christ, that was tense. I've had to send him home before he commits murder.' She told the others what had happened.

'The DCI is a twat,' Gary said, his face going red. 'I should go along there and punch him in the face.'

'That won't do any good, and you'll end up suspended,' Les said. 'Trust me, you're not alone in wanting to batter him.'

'Poor Alex,' Mo said. 'He's barely holding it together as it is.'

Craig agreed. 'I know he didn't have to come back to work yet but he did, and that shows how committed he is, not only to the job but to us as well.'

'I don't know Alex that well, but he seems like a great boss so far,' Lizzie said. 'If anyone's going to knock the DCI's lights out it should be me.'

'I'd pay good money to see that,' Dawn smiled, 'but the best thing we can do is to plough on.'

Chapter 44.

Alex locked his car and headed into the hospital, rehearsing the words in his head as he waited for the lift to take him to ICU. He was still fuming after his exchange with Andy, but all he wanted to do was to hold his wife in his arms and bury his face in her hair.

The meeting with Ronnie had been productive; she had arranged for Joel to attend a taster session at a respite care facility in Stourport the weekend of Gary and Jo's wedding, with a view to him going on a regular basis once Jayne was home. Alex was worried about how Jayne would take the news about the arrangements regarding Joel. He knew all she would focus on would be the words 'social services'. Sometimes he hated himself for not putting his foot down and insisting they get help when Joel was younger, but work had been so demanding since Alex's promotion to DI that it had been easier to leave all the decisions to her. Joel had been happy and settled at school and Alex hadn't given a second thought to what might be going on beneath the surface.

He stepped out of the lift and walked along the corridor to the high dependency unit, which was as busy as ever. Machines beeped, alarms sounded and in some of the rooms, radios played music to help aid the patient's recovery. The door to Jayne's room was closed, so Alex waited outside until a nurse came out.

'Hello, Mr Peachey, how are you today?' she asked. She looked closely at him and he wondered if she could tell he'd been crying.

'I'm fine thanks, Lisa,' Alex said, recognising her from previous visits. 'Is everything okay in there?' Alex asked, his stomach turning over.

Lisa smiled at him and opened the door. 'Come in and see for yourself.'

Jayne lay on her back, tubes and wires protruding from both arms and a couple from somewhere beneath the covers. A large bandage was wrapped around her head and over one eye. The bruises on her face had started to turn yellow and her nose didn't look so swollen.

Alex smiled as he leaned in to kiss her. 'Hey, beautiful.'

Jayne's eye fluttered open. She let out a cry and shrank away from him, a look of terror on her face as she tried to hit out at him.

'Sorry, sweetheart, I didn't mean to scare you,' Alex said, taking a few steps back.

'Nooo!' The sound came out disjointed, and Alex's heart broke. He retreated to the back of the room, tears rolling down his face as Lisa tried to calm Jayne down.

'It's okay, Jayne, he's not going to hurt you, I promise,' Lisa said, but Jayne started to thrash around in panic. Lisa pushed the buzzer and another nurse came in and held Jayne steady while Lisa administered a sedative. Jayne's movements slowed and she sank into a deep sleep. The two nurses straightened Jayne's bedding and wires out and the second nurse left the room.

'Hey, it's okay,' Lisa said as she approached Alex. 'That's quite a normal reaction. I promise you she will get there.' She rubbed his arm as he tried to regain his composure.

'I'm sorry, it's just that – I didn't expect that,' he said, his voice shaking.

'Just give her time,' Lisa said. 'That's all she needs now.'

'Is it okay if I sit with her for a bit? I won't disturb her, I promise.'

'Of course, but I've given her quite a powerful sedative, so she'll be asleep for a while.'

'I'll only stay for ten minutes.'

Alex waited until the nurse had left the room before he sat down next to Jayne. He lay his head on her lap and stroked her hand as he told her about his day, the case and everything in between. He was sure her fingers moved when he mentioned Joel but dismissed it afterwards as a reflex reaction.

Alex was too upset to go home, so he drove to the old house to check for any stray post and to make sure there were no problems. He wandered through the empty rooms, thinking of how happy they'd been living here, back when Joel was a baby. His temper rose as he thought about how many times Jayne had explained away the numerous bruises over the years, brushing off his and other people's concerns and saying everything was fine. Although he loved Joel, Alex was looking forward to moving back here when it would be just him and Jayne again. He stood in their old bedroom and looked out over the cul-de-sac. The house opposite had been sold since his last visit, and the driveway was currently occupied by a builder's van. The bungalow at the end sported smart new UPVC windows. Life was going on wherever he looked, but for him it seemed to have stopped.

He shook himself out of his reverie and made his way downstairs. He collected the small bundle of letters and flyers together and stepped outside, locking up carefully behind him. He waved to Roy across the way, who was out in his garden deadheading something or other – Alex was no gardener and couldn't tell one plant from another. He got in his car and headed back to the bungalow, stopping only for fish and chips at Codsall Fish Bar on Station Road.

When he got in, Jack rubbed around his legs, purring loudly and eyes shining brightly.

'Okay, okay, I'll give you some. Now move out of the way before I step on you.' He broke off a small piece of fish, put it in the cat's bowl and placed it on the floor. Jack attacked it as if he was starving. When he'd finished, he looked at Alex in anticipation.

'That's your lot, mate, this is mine.'

Alex grabbed a beer out of the fridge and sat at the kitchen counter to eat his dinner. The doorbell rang and he wiped his hands on a nearby tea towel before he answered.

'Hi boss, I've just dropped Mo off, so thought I'd come and see how you were doing.'

'I'm fine, thanks.' He went back inside, indicating for Dawn to follow him.

'Hey, get down from there!' Alex shouted, shooing Jack from off the counter where he was attempting to steal Alex's fish. The cat jumped down, gave him a dirty look and stalked off in a huff, tail held high.

'Ooh, you've been to Codsall chippy.' Dawn stole a couple of chips as she sat at the counter opposite Alex.

'Help yourself, why don't you? he said in a sarcastic voice, huffing when she took a couple more.

'I shouldn't have any really, I've got a steak in the car for my tea, but I can't resist their chips.'

'Next time, bring me a steak as well and I'll cook it while you fetch the chips.'

'Deal,' Dawn smiled. She chewed quickly, then took a swig of Alex's beer to wash it down. 'It's common knowledge that other people's food always tastes better,' she said, laughing at his expression. 'How's Jayne doing?'

Alex pushed his food away, his appetite suddenly gone. He told Dawn what had happened. 'It was awful, she was so terrified. I just froze, I didn't know what to do. The nurse had to sedate her before she had a chance to pull any tubes out.'

'Poor Jayne, it must be so confusing.'

'I hope next time she will be more lucid,' Alex said. 'Were there any developments after I left?'

'Apart from me having to stop the whole team from stringing Andy up by his balls, you mean?' Dawn smiled briefly. 'I spoke to

Jean Harrison; she's arranged a meeting for Monday. I told her Mo and I would be there. I figure Mo could put her Rainman skills to work.'

'Good idea. It does come in handy sometimes, having someone with an eidetic memory on the team,' he laughed.

Dawn stood up and headed for the front door. 'I'd better go home and walk Barney before he craps all over the place.'

'I don't envy you having to pick up after him.'

Dawn laughed. 'You do need a JCB sometimes. Are you in tomorrow?'

'Yes, I'll be in first thing. I'll go and see Jayne on my lunch hour, seeing as we've got Gary's stag do tomorrow night.'

'I'm really looking forward to that, I think it will do us all good.'

Dawn climbed into her car, closed the door and wound her window down. 'Don't take any notice of what Andy Oliver said. He's being a complete dick.'

'The problem is, he's right. My mind should be on the job. Jayne's in good hands, so I should make solving this case my priority.'

'I still think he's a dick.'

Alex smiled as she started the engine. 'That makes two of us, Dawn.'

Chapter 45.

Andy Oliver arrived home later than planned, due to the temporary traffic lights on the A464 near the Summer House pub. He got out of his car and hurried to his front door, trying not to think about the box in his boot. There was a small stack of mail waiting in the porch, so he picked it up and put it in his study before going to get changed out of his work clothes. It still seemed strange that Elaine wasn't there when he got home at night, but he was slowly getting used to it. Her decision to leave hadn't been totally unexpected, Andy had seen it coming for a while, but it had still hurt when she had moved out just after New Year. The only positive thing about her leaving was that he didn't have to put up with her unwavering obsession with soap operas anymore.

After a simple meal of homemade vegetable soup and crusty bread, Andy made himself a coffee and went into his study. The walls were lined with shelves and filled with an assortment of books, trophies for various sports from his younger days, and knick-knacks from his children. The window looked out over the back garden, which was starting to show results after all the hard work Andy had put in since he'd bought the cottage a couple of years before. It had been completely overgrown, but he had cleared the entire area and laid a new lawn, put in some raised beds to grow produce in, and had bought himself a greenhouse. The flowerbeds were currently empty, but Andy was planning a trip to the garden centre as soon as the weather was warmer.

Andy drank his coffee as he sorted through his mail. Most were circulars from advertising companies and holiday firms, so Andy put

them aside for recycling. He turned his attention to a padded envelope and tore it open eagerly, anticipating the new packets of seeds
he'd ordered. He tipped the envelope up but let out a cry of alarm
and shoved his chair back hurriedly as a shrivelled human tongue fell
out onto his desk.

With a shaking hand, he picked up the card that had fallen out
with it. The picture on the front was the same as the one from the
box, with the same one-line message:

'GOODNIGHT, GOD BLESS.'

Chapter 46.

Then.

After all the drama at the house, Tracy had wandered down to an area of the local park where the other kids who bunked off school went. It was deserted today, which was a surprise as the weather was warm and dry. Butterflies danced in and out of the wild bluebells, and Tracy felt happier than she had in a long time. Pulling off her jumper, she lay down in the long grass, using her school bag as a pillow, and closed her eyes.

'Oi, skiver.'

A deep voice startled her, and Tracy raised her hand to her eyes to see who was standing over her.

'Brian?'

The skinny young man grinned and sat down beside her. 'How did you guess?'

'Easy, dummy. You weren't at registration today.'

'Fair point. What are you doing here? School's not over yet.' Brian flicked his collar-length black hair out of his face and grinned, his brown eyes glittering in the sunshine.

Tracy looked at the boy and wondered whether to tell him. She grinned back.

'Well, it's like this...'

Brian threw his head back and roared with laughter until tears ran down his face. He wasn't what most would call good-looking, but Tracy liked his slightly crooked teeth and the way the skin around his eyes crinkled when he smiled. His school uniform bore the signs of repair, but it was clean and well-pressed.

'I wish I'd been there. The look on your mum's face must have been priceless.' Brian wiped his face with the sleeve of his blazer.

Tracy smiled. 'Oh, it was, especially when my dad turned up. It's just a shame that Derek had somehow managed to escape undetected. I spotted him hiding behind the bins at the side of the houses. He was trying to get dressed without being seen.'

'I wonder what your mum told him.'

'I don't know, and I don't care. She deserves all she gets.' Tracy stood up and paced back and forth, a dark expression clouding her features.

'Hey, I know it stinks, finding out your mum's cheating on your dad, but it's their problem, not yours. I'm sure they'll sort it out.'

'It's not that, it's just...' Tracy burst into tears.

'Don't cry, it'll all be okay. What's up with your stomach? You keep holding it. Is it that time of the month?'

'No, it's not that. Oh God, it's such a mess. I don't know what to do about it.' Tracy sat down again and hid her face in her hands. 'I'm so scared.'

'Look, I know I'm no expert, but you can talk to me if you want.' Brian sat behind her, his back against Tracy's. 'Just spill it, it will make you feel better.'

Eventually, Tracy told Brian everything, including the part about the miscarriage.

'What kind of sick fuck does that?' Brian stood up and kicked a nearby tree stump.

'I'm so sorry, I wish I'd never said anything.'

'Hey, you have nothing to say sorry for, you hear me?' Brian dropped back onto the grass and grabbed her by the shoulders. 'He's the one who should be sorry.'

'Fat chance of that happening. I only wish that my dad would give him a pasting, but I doubt he will.'

'Why not? If my dad caught my mum shagging another bloke, he'd kick his head in. He'd probably give her a slap as well. Is your old man a wuss or something?'

'No, he's not. He's a copper.'

THE POLICE OFFICER and the social worker spoke to Mr Mc-George in his office, while Bobbie waited in reception with Mrs Huntley.

'Do you want a cup of tea, love? I'm making one for myself, so it's no bother.'

Bobbie smiled and shook her head, and the secretary went out through the door behind her desk into the staff room. Bobbie could hear the clink of cups and the low tones of gossip filtering through the half-open door. She took a small bottle of rose-scented perfume out of her bag and squirted it on her wrists. It wasn't as nice as the perfume Mrs Huntley wore, but Bobbie found the smell comforting. She and Angie should have had a mother who smelled like flowers, not the sweat-stained, whisky-swigging embarrassment that they had to put up with.

'I told you, I don't know what it's about,' Mrs Huntley said to another member of staff. 'He just told me to look after her while he phones social services and the police.'

'He must have given you some inkling, Glynis. Have you asked the girl what's going on?' another female voice said. The history teacher, Bobbie thought.

'I can't do that, he'll go mad!' Mrs Huntley sounded shocked at the suggestion.

'Maybe her mum's done a runner with that fancy man of hers and left her on her own,' Miss Read said.

'Don't be ridiculous, Kim, what sort of parent does something like that?'

'I wouldn't be surprised; she was a complete slut when she was younger. Since her husband went to prison she's been spreading her legs for all and sundry.'

'Keep your voice down!' Mrs Huntley was louder than Miss Read, which Bobbie thought was hilarious. She coughed loudly, halting the conversation abruptly.

'Everything okay, dear?' Mrs Huntley asked as she came back through and sat down behind her desk, humming to herself as she flicked through some paperwork.

'Did you change your mind?' Bobbie asked, forcing a look of innocence.

'Pardon me?'

'You said you were getting a cup of tea.'

'Bugger – I mean, so I was. I got talking to another staff member and forgot all about that.'

'You can go and make one if you like, I'm fine here.' Bobbie struggled to keep the smile off her face.

Mrs Huntley shook her head, making her carefully constructed hairdo wobble dangerously. 'Maybe later, I need to get these notes done first.'

JULIE DRAGGED HER FEET as she walked along the corridor, eyes fixed firmly on the floor. Last night had been the worst yet, and there wasn't a part of her that didn't hurt. Her pleas to stop had fallen on deaf ears, and the monster was even rougher than before.

Julie turned the corner and headed for her locker, which was opposite the reception area. She removed the padlock and began putting her books in, trying not to look at her reflection in the small mirror on the back of the locker door, ashamed that the damage the monster had done last night would be visible on her face. Julie couldn't help herself and risked a quick glance, surprised when she saw another girl behind her across the hallway, sitting on one of the chairs outside the head's office. A harassed-looking woman and a young policeman arrived at the reception desk, spoke softly to Mrs Huntley, then were swiftly ushered into Mr McGeorge's office. Julie wondered what trouble the girl could be in that would warrant the police being called.

At that moment, Bobbie looked up and their eyes met briefly. Julie recognised the dead look in her eyes. A glance at the bruises on the girl's arm confirmed what she was thinking. She turned away again but watched her reflection.

Bobbie saw Julie looking at her in the locker mirror, trying not to be noticed. She half-raised a hand in greeting and the girl smiled nervously at her. Bobbie stood up and walked over.

'Hi. You live near me, don't you? I've seen you walking to school.' Bobbie introduced herself and Julie did the same.

'Hi, yes I think I've seen you too. Are you in trouble?' Julie asked, gesturing towards the closed door.

'Not exactly,' Bobbie sighed. 'It's complicated, you wouldn't understand.'

'Really?' Julie closed her locker door and turned to face Bobbie.

Bobbie spotted the wince as Julie leaned back against the locker. She gently took Julie's arm and steered her towards the row of chairs so she could sit down. 'What happened to you? You look like you're in pain.'

'It's nothing, I fell down the stairs.' Julie looked at her feet, cheeks reddening with shame.

'How long have you been falling down the stairs?' Bobbie drew quotation marks in the air.

Julie didn't answer, so Bobbie didn't pursue it. She wondered whether she should mention it to the people in the office but didn't want to upset Julie.

'I wish they would hurry up and make a decision, I'm getting nervous here.' Bobbie stood up and paced up and down, arms wrapped round herself.

'Why, what's happening?'

Bobbie nodded towards the office door. 'They're trying to find me a foster family. I'm not allowed home because of...well, stuff that's been going on with my mum's boyfriend.'

'Is your mum okay?'

Bobbie closed her eyes briefly before looking at Julie again. 'She's the biggest part of the problem. Her boyfriend has been doing things to me, and she blames me for it.'

'What kind of things?'

'Sexual stuff, you know, touching me, getting me to touch him, then the other night he forced me to do other things. My sister caught me packing a bag to run away, that's when she guessed what was going on.' Bobbie shrugged her shoulders. 'My dad had done similar things to her when she was little. He's in prison now.'

Julie said nothing, but a tear rolled down her face. She wished she had a big sister to look out for her.

The door opened, making them both jump. Julie scrambled to her feet and hurried away.

The door to the head teacher's office opened and Mr McGeorge leaned out.

'Come in, Bobbie, we're ready for you now.'

Chapter 47.

Now. The cold snap overnight had left a sheen of frost on everything, and Alex had to scrape his windscreen before he could head to work. Alex had only just taken his jacket off and sat down at his desk when Les stuck his head round the door.

'Alison Munroe is downstairs, boss. She's asking for you.'

Alex sighed and stood up again. 'Mo, can you come with me, please?' he called as he put his jacket back on.

'I want you to watch her every reaction,' Alex told her as they headed slowly downstairs. 'I'm sure she's more involved than she's letting on – and feel free to jump in if you think of anything.'

'Poor choice of words, boss,' Mo said, 'I don't think I'm going to be jumping for a while.'

'Oh God, I'm sorry,' Alex said, his face going red. 'I didn't think.'

'I'm only kidding,' Mo smiled. She spotted Alison sitting on one of the chairs in reception. Her knee was bouncing up and down, and she kept pushing her hair behind her ear, only for it to fall back down again.

'I must say, she looks terrified,' Mo said.

'Some people get like that around the police. I remember seeing coppers when I was a kid and automatically assuming I was in trouble,' Alex said.

'So did I,' Mo laughed. 'I never dreamed I'd become one.'

Alison stood up when she saw the two officers approaching. They exchanged greetings and Alex led them through to the same interview suite as before.

'How can we help you?' Alex asked, once they were all seated.

'I thought I'd better bring this in,' Alison said, handing over an envelope. 'I meant to do it earlier, but I've been busy.'

'When did you receive it?' Alex asked as he opened the envelope and took out a card. The pictures were of a similar nature to the last one Alison had received. This time there was a tyre iron, a lawnmower, a set of darts and a police car.

'Last week sometime, Thursday I think.'

'You don't sound too sure,' Mo said.

'It's been crazy these past few days. My ex has moved out and I've been getting grief from his family.' She explained about the fight with Mark. 'To be honest, I thought he'd left it on my car as a joke.'

'You really should have brought this is as soon as you got it,' Alex scolded. 'It could be vital to our case.'

Alison looked at her feet, sniffing back tears. 'I know, and I'm sorry. I feel like my whole life is going through a washing machine, everything's getting churned up.' She rummaged in her handbag for a tissue.

Alex decided to change tack. 'Tell me about the survivors' group. How long have you been running it?'

Alison told them about her own abuse and how she had gone off the rails as a teenager. 'You've probably got a copy of my record; I was arrested once for shoplifting.'

'When was that?'

Alison thought for a moment. 'Around fifteen or sixteen years ago? I can't really remember much about it, apart from the dressing-down I got from my dad. Social services got involved because I was under eighteen, and I remember my mum being worried in case the neighbours found out.'

'Do you remember who your social worker was?' Alex asked.

'Yes, it was Sonia Jameson, the same woman who used to run the group. She helped me turn my life around. Later, when she set the group up she contacted me and asked if I wanted to come along, but I wasn't interested. It was a few years before I felt ready to face my past.'

'Where is she now?'

'I'm not sure, her plan was to travel around the world when she retired. Last time I heard from her she was sunning herself in the Bahamas or somewhere like that. I can give you her phone number and email address if you like.'

'That would be very useful,' Mo said. 'How do people join? Can people find your details on a website or on a community notice board?'

Alison shook her head. 'No, it's referral only, usually by a social worker, doctor, or psychiatrist. When I'm putting the groups together, I try to ensure the attendees don't know each other prior to starting. A lot of people won't speak in front of someone they know, even if they've had the same abuser. Obviously, I keep a close eye on numbers and never have more than eight as a rule.'

'How many groups do you run a week?' Alex asked.

'Just the one. It's a shame, but I have a job as well so don't have the time to do any more. I wish I did, the waiting list is huge.'

''Do you know if any of the women from Jean's group kept in touch with each other after it finished?'

Alison looked uncomfortable. 'I don't know if I should give you their names, not without their permission, anyway.'

'You don't have to, but we will treat everything you tell us in the strictest confidence,' Alex assured her.

'I think Bobbie and Julie meet up to go walking, but I don't know about the others,' Alison said. 'Tracy and Jean would be able to tell you more, they were in that group together. I may have been the one running it, but I always keep myself one degree apart from everyone, if you know what I mean. It helps me to stay objective.'

'We could do with speaking to Tracy. Can you give us her details?' Mo asked.

Alison recited Tracy's phone number. 'I haven't spoken to her for a few days, I think she might be avoiding me.' She looked at Alex. 'Please hurry up and catch whoever's doing this, because it's not just those men who are suffering.'

'We're doing our best,' Alex said as they got up to leave, 'But if you get any more cards, or think of anything else, please let us know immediately.'

Once they were back in the office, Alex gave Lizzie the new card to add to the rest. She printed out the pictures separately then added them to the others.

'I've been thinking about that cold case up in Yorkshire,' Les said, 'I'm wondering whether any of the women from the group have connections to the area.'

'In what way?'

'Well, maybe one of them used to live there.'

Alex's phone rang so he hurried off to answer it.

'The DCI has summoned me, so can you finish the briefing? I shouldn't be too long, but I don't want everyone held up waiting for me.'

Dawn nodded. 'Do you think he wants to apologise?'

'Doubtful, but we'll soon see.'

Chapter 48.

When Alex knocked on the door there was no reply. He looked at Andy's secretary in puzzlement.

'He's in there, so just go in.' She lowered her voice as if to impart a secret. 'I'm a bit worried, he's been acting strangely since he got here.'

'In what way?'

'He seems on edge. When I took his mail in just now, he looked at me as if I was there to steal his soul.'

'I'm sure it's just the pressure of this case,' Alex assured her.

'Hopefully that's all it is,' she answered.

Alex knocked again then opened the door and went into Andy's office. His boss was standing by the window, deep in thought. He jumped violently when Alex walked over and put a hand on his shoulder.

'Sorry, I didn't mean to startle you, sir.'

Andy looked at Alex for a minute before he seemed to recognise him. 'I'm sorry, I was miles away.'

Alex had never seen his boss so rattled. 'Are you okay? Has something happened at home?' He steered Andy to his seat and poured him a coffee from the machine on the sideboard. Alex set the cup down on the desk in front of him and watched as Andy picked it up with a shaking hand. After a few minutes, Andy seemed to have regained his composure.

'What's going on, sir?'

Andy put his cup down and pointed to a white box standing on the desk. 'This was delivered yesterday; I'm just waiting for someone to come and collect it. However, I thought I should make you aware of it.'

Alex removed the lid and nearly gagged when he saw the contents. 'Why would someone send you something like that?'

'I have no idea. Don't ask me why, but I took it home with me. Then, when I got home last night, I had another nasty surprise.' He seemed to drift off into his own thoughts.

Alex was becoming impatient. 'Well, spit it out, man! What was it?'

Andy gave a small laugh. 'Excellent choice of words.' He took a padded envelope out of his desk drawer and placed it in front of Alex. 'Someone sent me a human tongue through the post.'

'Good God!' The colour drained from Alex's face. He looked at the envelope but didn't touch it.

'Indeed. I'm assuming the tongue belonged to one of your victims, but I'm sure Dr Farrow will be able to confirm that.'

'Well, he has three bodies all missing their tongues, so there's a good chance that it came from one of them.'

'There was a card with each gift.' Andy passed the cards over and Alex studied them in turn.

'Just like the ones the women received,' he said.

Andy looked up as the door opened and Ziggy came in. He greeted them both, then picked up the envelope with gloved hands and placed it into a small, insulated carrier. Andy signed the chain of custody sheet and the young man left, passing a woman who came to collect the cow's horn. Once she had gone, Alex got up and poured himself a coffee, refilling his boss's cup at the same time. He returned to his seat and looked at Andy. The man appeared to have aged ten years overnight.

'Why would someone send you such a thing? Does the cow horn have any significance that you can think of?'

'No, nothing springs to mind.'

'What about the tongue?'

'I'm guessing that is connected to this case, but what concerns me more is how they got my home address.' Andy sighed and rubbed his hand over his face.

'I'm wondering if this is more personal. Can you think of anyone who you or Elaine may have upset? Shit, I should have asked about her first. She didn't open it, did she?'

'We separated just after New Year,' Andy said, 'Things had been difficult between us for a while, but I kept it to myself because I don't like to air my dirty laundry in public. We're both happier now, she's moved back to Birmingham to be closer to work.'

'I'm sorry to hear that, sir.'

Andy waved his hand dismissively. 'Water under the bridge, Alex. Now, let's get back to the matter in hand. Until tests are complete, we can't be certain that the tongue belongs to one of our victims.'

'Well, I hardly think it's going to have come from anyone else, unless there's something you're not telling me.'

Andy didn't answer, so Alex gave up and left.

'Christ on a bike,' Les exclaimed when Alex told them all what had happened. 'Does that mean we're all going to be getting body parts in the post?'

'I doubt it very much but be vigilant. Whoever sent it knows the DCI's address, and that's not common knowledge.'

'You don't think he's a paedophile, do you?' Gary said, 'Andy Oliver, I mean.'

'Don't be ridiculous, Gary,' Alex said.

'I'm just thinking that maybe the killer wants to share his trophies.'

'Stranger things have been known to happen,' Craig added. 'What if Gary's right?'

'Don't encourage him!' Dawn scolded.

'The question remains though,' Les said, 'What other reason could the perp have for sending something like that?'

Lizzie hurried into the room, looking pale and sweaty. 'Sorry, I had to nip to the loo a bit sharpish, I think last night's Chinese disagreed with me. What have I missed?'

'Gary thinks the DCI is a nonce,' Craig said.

'No I don't, I just wondered if he could be.' Gary wished he'd kept his mouth shut.

'Can we stop making assumptions and try to figure this out?' Alex told Lizzie about the packages sent to Andy.

'Why send him a cow's horn?' Craig asked. 'That's a bit random.'

'You should have seen it; it was horrible. I didn't even know horns had blood in them.'

'Horns are full of blood vessels. Farmers used to saw the horns off their cows, supposedly to stop them goring each other. It's really cruel, it bleeds for ages and takes weeks to heal,' Lizzie explained. 'Nowadays it's done only if it's absolutely necessary, when the cows are still young, and only then by a trained professional.' Lizzie looked at the stunned expressions of her colleagues and smiled. 'I used to go out with a farmer's son; his dad was prosecuted for it. I dumped him when I found out.'

'That's horrible!' Mo looked like she was going to be sick. 'How can people get away with it?'

'They can't anymore, it's closely regulated.'

'Wow, you are a real fount of knowledge,' Les said. 'I'm impressed.'

'Thank you,' Lizzie smiled. 'I'm full of useless trivia.' She looked at the cards on the board. 'None of these pictures have anything to do with farming, unless you think the butcher could be a link.'

'It's a bit of a stretch, but we can't discount anything,' Alex said. 'Mo, when is the meeting with the survivor's group?'

'It's on Monday evening. That was the earliest we could get every-one together.'

'Excellent.' Alex looked at the board. 'It's unlikely that we're go-ing to put this case to bed before next Saturday as I'd hoped. At least Charlie Baldwin's team are covering us over the weekend, so we can go to Gary's wedding.'

'I think the break will do us good,' Les said. He rubbed his hand over the stubble on his head. 'I know I'm knackered.'

'I think we all are,' Alex agreed. 'I'm just so frustrated with it all. It seems we're being led a merry dance and none of us know the tune. Anyway,' he said, noticing the time, 'I'm nipping home to get changed, I'll see you all at the Leamore club later.'

Chapter 49.

The working men's club was heaving, much to the delight of manager Sally Cameron. Business had been slow since the ladies night before Christmas. People had been reluctant to drink in a place that had been associated with the murder of a young woman, whose body had been found at the back of the club. Since then, Sally had spent more money than she'd liked on extra advertising, drinks promotions and offering free use of the function room. Sally had been worried that the evening would be a wash-out, but thanks to that handsome detective wanting a bar extension, she had a decent crowd in, requiring her to bring in extra staff.

The entertainment that DS Muir had hired had also helped to draw the crowds in. Kitty McLane, real name Neil Stone, was a drag queen, a local legend with a huge fan base of all ages and genders. She also performed at old people's homes and was a regular at the bingo hall, calling the numbers. When Craig had explained it was his colleague's stag evening, Kitty had made sure to include some of DC Temple's favourite songs and had met up with Craig in order to learn more about Gary.

Neil glanced round the small, windowless dressing room and tried not to think about the last time he'd performed here. That poor girl had lost her life just outside the door at the back of the room. Neil said a silent prayer for her as he started to unpack his make-up case. His usual dresser, Ruby, was ill with the 'flu, so Craig had volunteered to help with costume changes tonight. Neil arranged everything in the right order on the table. Dresses and feather boas were hung up and jewellery laid out so that Craig would be able to find the right items quickly and easily. Finally, Neil placed a neatly-folded set of clothes on a nearby stool, stripped down to his underpants and threw on a thin satin robe. He sat down in front of the mirror and smoothed his hands over his freshly-shaved head.

'Hello Neil, how's it going?' Craig asked as he walked in. He looked around the tiny room, impressed at how organised everything was. He set a glass of iced water down nearby, complete with straw as requested.

'Hello yourself,' Neil replied with a wink as he placed a thin nylon hairnet on his head. 'It gives the wig something to grip on to,' Neil explained when Craig asked why it was necessary.

Neil started applying a thick layer of foundation to his face, neck, and upper chest, expertly working it into every crease. Craig pulled up a stool and watched as Kitty was created. It was a fascinating process to watch.

'How did you come up with your drag name?'

'It was quite simple, really,' Neil said as he drew on a pair of eyebrows. 'My mum's name is Katherine, but everyone calls her Kitty for short. The McLane part comes from 'Die Hard', which is my favourite film. Bruce Willis in that white vest still makes me swoon.' Neil carefully edged his mouth with a dark pink lip liner. 'I loved Alan Rickman too, but Kitty Gruber sounds like a cheap German floozy.'

Neil looked at Craig's reflection in the mirror. 'Fancy yourself as a queen, do you? You'd make a good one to be fair, you've got lovely bone structure. I bet your legs are fabulous, too.'

Craig grinned. 'I'd love to have a go; I've always liked fancy dress.'

'There is a lot more to it than putting on a bit of slap and a frock,' Neil remarked, raising one expertly-plucked eyebrow. 'You have to learn to become a woman, to walk, talk and think like one.'

'I never thought about it like that,' Craig admitted.

'You'd be amazed at how many bad queens there are out there; they're the ones who give the rest of us a bad name.' Neil finished his make-up and gave his face a final dusting of powder, then stood up and removed the robe. 'Right, that's the tricky part done. Pass me those two pairs of tights, would you?'

Craig passed Neil the items and watched as he put them on, one pair over the top of the other. As he did, he carefully tucked his genitals back between his legs so that nothing was showing at the front, then put on a tight-fitting leotard which kept everything in place. He laughed when he saw Craig's pained expression.

'Don't pull that face, it doesn't hurt if you do it right. Mind you, get it wrong and...' Neil gave a high-pitched whistle.

'I can imagine,' Craig said.

Neil picked up two soft, balloon-shaped cotton bags and popped them into the cups of the leotard to create a pair of breasts. He jiggled them around until he was satisfied, then stepped into the dress that Craig held ready. Craig pulled the long zipper up and straightened out the spaghetti-thin straps.

'Almost ready,' Neil said. He carefully lifted a long, brunette wig from the Styrofoam stand and put it on. He arranged the hair carefully around his face and stepped into a pair of white patent leather platform shoes. A pair of long white gloves and a white feather boa completed the look. Finally, Neil applied a squirt of floral perfume.

'Voila,' he said with a curtsey. 'Kitty McLane at your service.'

'Wow, I am seriously impressed,' Craig said, a broad grin on his face.

Kitty picked up the glass of water and sipped it. 'Using a straw saves you having to re-apply your lipstick and doesn't leave nasty smudges on the glass.'

'I did wonder about that. Right, what's next?'

'Next, you go and sit down with your friends, but be ready to follow me when I head backstage. I'm planning two changes tonight.

One is that red dress hanging there, the other is what we call a de-drag.'

'What's that?'

Kitty pointed to the wooden stool with the set of clothes on top. 'During the last number of the night, I'll remove my drag and put my own clothes on. I'll use a screen so the audience can only see my silhouette. Trust me, the last thing your friend wants to see is my wrinkly old plums, especially if he's had a skinful.'

Craig laughed at the thought of Gary's face. 'Got it. What about music and stuff?'

'Don't worry, DJ Dan has my playlist. I've worked with him before, so he knows what to do.' Kitty blew Craig a kiss. 'Now, go and greet your guests.'

Craig had reserved a table near the stage at Kitty's request and was halfway through his first pint when the rest of the team arrived. Mo made her way towards Craig while Lizzie followed Les to the bar to get the drinks in.

'Blimey, you're eager,' Mo said, squeezing into a seat behind the table so she wouldn't get bumped by anyone. She glanced around the room. 'Why's it so busy? They can't all be here for Gary's stag do.'

Craig grinned at her. 'Special guest act tonight, arranged by yours truly and paid for out of the stag weekend pot. I can't let my mate get married without marking the occasion properly.'

'What have you done?'

'Just a little treat for my pal, which I'm sure we will all enjoy.'

Les and Lizzie fought their way to the table, each carrying a tray filled with beer glasses.

'Gordon Bennett, it's mad in here tonight,' Les complained.

'Blame laughing boy here,' Mo said. 'He's got something special arranged for Gary.'

'Oh, bloody hell, it's not strippers, is it? Ruth will kill me.'

'No, nothing like that, although there is a special lady making an appearance.'

'Sounds ominous,' Lizzie said, slurping her pint. 'Where's the guest of honour?'

'Dawn's picking him up, they should be here in a minute. Alex sent a text to say he will do his best to pop in for an hour if he can.'

'Hey up,' Gary said as he approached them, cheeks rosy from the cold but his eyes full of smiles. He wore black jeans, and a t-shirt with the words 'GROOM TO BE' printed on the front. Dawn followed behind him, a big grin on her face.

'Hey, big man, sit down and get that inside you,' Craig shouted over the increasing chatter. He handed Gary a pint of dark beer and Gary took a huge swig.

'Ahh, that's hit the spot,' he said, smacking his lips. He looked around. 'Bugger me, it's busy in here.'

Mo and Craig exchanged glances but said nothing.

The group steadily grew in numbers as more of Gary's colleagues arrived. He was an amiable man, and had many friends, having been a beat copper before joining Major Crimes.

'All here to celebrate the loss of your freedom and to wish you well in your new post,' Craig said. 'You're a popular lad, especially with the ladies.'

'Give over, you're making me blush,' Gary laughed, going beet-root red. 'There's only one woman for me, you know that.'

'That may be true but wait until you see what we've got lined up for you tonight, you might change your mind.'

'Have I missed anything?' Alex pulled the remaining free chair out and dropped into it.

A massive cheer went up round the table, and Gary grabbed him in a bear hug. 'Glad you could make it, boss. How's Jayne?'

Alex wriggled out of Gary's vice-like grip and pulled at his collar to loosen it. 'Christ, you nearly broke my neck. She's okay. It's early days, but they're confident they won't need to operate again.'

Another cheer went round the table and Alex struggled to swallow the lump in his throat. 'Enough talk about my missus, give me a beer.'

The drinks were replenished just as the lights went down. Everyone at the table cheered except Gary, who had no clue what was about to happen.

The curtains parted and a shapely leg came into view. Gary went white as the others whooped. He looked at Alex helplessly. 'Boss, please tell me that's not a stripper.'

'Don't look at me, ask your best man,' Alex grinned.

Craig laughed so hard he nearly fell off his chair. He put an arm around Gary. 'Don't worry mate, you're in safe hands.'

As Kitty McLane stepped fully into view and blew a kiss at the group, Gary let out a sigh of relief. He looked at Craig, who was doubled over as he tried to take photos. 'You git, you had me worried for a minute there.'

'Hello everyone, and thank you for the warm welcome,' Kitty said. 'It's lovely to be back again. Let's all say hello to a special man, Detective Constable Gary Temple, who has a double celebration going on tonight – really, some people aren't satisfied with just the one. He's not only moving away, but he's getting married as well.'

Once the applause had died down, Kitty entertained them all with songs and jokes, most of them at poor Gary's expense, then nodded to Craig and disappeared backstage.

'Oh man, that was brilliant,' Gary said, still clapping. 'Where are you off to? Don't tell me you're finally getting a round in?' he said as Craig stood up.

'Shut your face, you cheeky sod,' Craig said, punching him on the arm. 'I am assistant to Miss McLane tonight, so be nice to me or

I'll tell her some really raucous stuff about you.' With a wink he shot through the side door that led backstage.

'My round,' Mo announced, slapping twenty pounds on the table. 'But someone else will have to get them for me.'

'I'll go,' Dawn said, 'If someone will give me a hand.' Alex went with her, and the rest of the group chatted amongst themselves.

'Are the wedding plans all in place?' Mo asked.

'Yeah, you know Jo, she's got everything sorted out, including me.'

'That's not difficult,' Les quipped, dodging to avoid Gary's attempt to slap him. 'My missus was the same when we got married. Ruth said, 'Get there early and wear what I tell you to.' Easiest day of my life.'

'Same instructions as me,' Gary nodded. 'Nowt to it, this getting married lark.'

'Jo might disagree with you,' Mo said.

'What about you, Mo? Have you set a date yet?' Lizzie asked.

'No, but we've only just got engaged, so we haven't had a chance to discuss it yet. Don't worry, you'll all be invited.'

'I should hope so, it's a chance for me to come back and see you all,' Gary said.

Alex squeezed between them and put a tray of beer down. 'Dig in, the second half should be starting in a minute, and I hear that Kitty has something special in store for you.'

Chapter 50.

I wipe the sweat from my brow and stand back to admire my hand-iwork. This one was difficult to control due to its size, and it took a lot of drugs before it became compliant. I know I'm running out of time, so I won't embellish it as much as I'd like to. There is only one more name on my list after this, and it's one I've been looking forward to for a long time.

Chapter 51.

Backstage at the Leamore Club, things were not going to plan. Craig had found Kitty on the phone, tears streaming down her face. He busied himself checking through the photos he'd taken while he waited for Kitty to finish her call.

Kitty hung up and sat down heavily on a stool. Craig knelt in front of her, his eyes searching hers.

'What's the matter?'

'It's my mum, she's dying. The manager at the care home says she won't last the night.'

'Oh no, I'm so sorry.'

Kitty stroked Craig's face. 'Dear boy, that's so kind of you to say. I never thought it would be so soon.'

'You were expecting it, then?'

'Yes, she's had dementia for a few years, so I knew it would happen eventually.'

'I remember you had to rush off over Christmas because she wasn't well.' Craig held Kitty's hand, patting it softly.

Kitty gave him a sad smile. 'She was convinced she'd had a miscarriage, poor thing. She lost a baby when I was young, and I don't think she ever got over it.'

'That's awful,' Craig said. 'What about your dad?'

'He left years ago, after I came out. He said he wouldn't have a shirt-lifter under his roof, but mum stood by me, so he left. He already had a bit on the side to warm his bed, and I think mum was glad when he went.'

'She sounds amazing,' Craig said.

'She is. She didn't deserve to go out like this.' Kitty wiped her eyes on the back of her glove. 'Oops, now I've got mascara on my new gloves. It's a bugger to wash out, you know. Can you tell everyone there will be a delay? I need to redo my make-up.'

'No, you can take it off and get yourself away. That lot won't mind.'

'But I've got a duet to sing with the groom, I can't leave now.' Kitty protested.

Craig pulled her to her feet. 'Yes, you can, I insist.' He looked at Kitty's dresses hanging up and grinned. 'I have an idea, but I might need a bit of help.'

Chapter 52.

The beer was flowing freely, and everyone was having such a good time that no one noticed that Craig was missing until Dawn looked around for him.

'He's helping Kitty with her costumes,' Les said as he slurped the froth off his beer. 'It was a good call, booking her for tonight.'

Alex agreed. 'We all needed a laugh, and what better time than at our esteemed colleague's stag do.'

A cheer went round the table and Gary blushed to the roots of his hair. He stood up, almost knocking the drinks over, and announced he wanted to make a speech.

'Aw, don't spoil it now!' Dawn shouted.

'Shut your face, Redwood,' Gary waved his finger in her direction.

'That's Detective Sergeant Redwood to you, matey. And don't point that thing at me, I don't know where it's been.'

'I bet that's what Jo says to him on their wedding night,' quipped Mo, causing Les to choke on his beer. Lizzie slapped him hard on the back, almost knocking him off his chair.

'Anyway, as I was about to say...' Gary shouted over the top of the noise, but his voice was drowned out by the cheers as the lights dimmed. Les pulled him to his seat as the curtains opened again. A tall, glamourous woman stood there in a red sequinned dress and matching elbow-length gloves, her long blonde hair cascading down her back in a waterfall effect. As she stepped forward, she winked at Gary and blew him a kiss.

'Who's that? It's not Kitty,' Dawn said.

'I don't know, but I think I fancy her,' Gary replied.

'Sorry for the delay, but there has been an unexpected change to tonight's entertainment,' the drag queen said in a sultry voice. 'Kitty has had some bad news, so has had to rush off, but I hope you'll be happy with me instead. My name is Muffy Sparkles. Be gentle with me though, it's my first time, and I wasn't prepared. Kitty has given me permission to use her music, so let's get this party started.' She looked at the DJ and signalled for him to play the next track in Kitty's set. A round of applause went round the packed room in as she belted out the hit song by Pink.

'Wow, what a set of pipes! I wish I could sing like that,' Lizzie said, standing up to dance at the table.

'Me too,' Mo said, joining her. She looked around. 'It's a shame Craig's disappeared; he'd love this.'

Alex looked closely at the woman on stage. When she looked back at him, a huge grin spread across his face. 'Don't worry about Craig, I'm sure he's enjoying it as much as we are,' Alex said.

When the song finished, Muffy took a bow and dabbed her forehead with a tissue she'd pulled from her cleavage. Tucking it away again, she clapped back at the audience.

'Thank you all so much, you are all too kind. Now, I understand we have some of Wolverhampton's finest in tonight.' She turned to the party. 'What's the occasion, darlings? Oh, stag night – sounds like fun, loads of rutting and so on, I imagine. Now, where's the groom? Let's have him up here on stage so we can get a better look at him.'

A big cheer sounded as Gary stepped up onto the stage, his face beetroot red.

The drag queen looked him up and down. 'You're a big lad, aren't you?' She squeezed Gary's bicep. 'Ooh, solid through and through. Are you hard like that everywhere?' she asked, running her hand over Gary's abdomen before feeling his bum. 'Hmm, plenty of junk in your trunk. Speaking of which...' Muffy cupped Gary's crotch. 'Ooh, hello big boy! I'm impressed.' She gave him an exaggerated wink and stuck her tongue in his ear.

Gary jumped and moved away, laughing. 'Easy, tiger.'

Muffy made a growling noise and rubbed up against him. 'So macho,' she said, which was the DJ's cue to play the next song, making Gary pose with his muscles flexed as she sang to him. Gary's workmates were killing themselves laughing, some so hard they had tears rolling down their faces.

Dawn leaned over and spoke in Alex's ear. 'Maybe I've had too much to drink, but does that drag queen look familiar to you?'

Alex wiped his eyes. 'Oh, this is priceless, my chest hurts from laughing so much.'

'What's the matter with you, boss?' Lizzie asked.

'Really? Have none of you clocked who that is up there?'

Les looked hard at the couple on the stage, then did a double take.

'No!' he said with disbelief.

'Yes!' Alex wiped his eyes again.

'Oh, my word, this just got so much better!' Les said, clapping his hands with glee.

'Come on, boss, spill the beans,' Dawn said. 'What are we missing?'

'Oh, this is just too good,' Alex wheezed. He had a coughing fit and took a few minutes to catch his breath before he could continue. 'Muffy Sparkles,' he said, pointing towards the stage, 'It's Craig.'

Muffy Sparkles was going down a storm, yet Gary had still not realised that the gorgeous drag queen was his work colleague. He couldn't understand why everyone seemed to be constantly laughing.

'Stop taking the piss out of her, she's doing brilliantly,' he scolded.

'We know, she's fabulous,' Mo said, wiping away tears of laughter at Muffy's jokes.

Muffy called for quiet, then addressed the crowd. 'I know tonight was not as planned, but I am so grateful to you all for popping my cherry in style. I have one final number to do, and this one is especially for the groom in the room, Mr Gary Temple. Please give him a round of applause.'

The lighting changed to a single white spotlight on Muffy. The DJ pressed play and Muffy clipped the microphone onto its stand as she started to sing the slow version of 'I Am What I Am'. A member of staff carried a room divider and a silk robe to the centre of the stage, and Muffy stepped behind it, her silhouette clearly visible through the thin fabric. As she began to disrobe, the wolf whistles and cat calls grew louder, the loudest ones coming from Gary.

Muffy appeared from behind the screen, now wearing a thin robe. She grinned at the audience, lifted her wig off then took a bow as the audience gave her a standing ovation. She turned to Gary and blew him a kiss before disappearing through the stage door at the back.

Gary stopped clapping and stared. 'What the...was that...' he spluttered. The rest of the team fell about at the look on his face. 'Did you lot know about this?'

'No, none of us did,' Alex said. 'I only realised when she started singing.'

'She squeezed my arse and groped my balls,' Gary said, 'I mean he, oh I don't know what I mean.' He sat down, looking confused, causing more laughter.

Mo stood up. 'Being the only sober one among you, I'm going backstage to take Miss Sparkles a well-deserved drink,' she said. She picked up Craig's untouched pint from the beer-spattered table and headed towards the stage door.

'I have to say, that was fantastic,' Lizzie said. 'I wonder if Craig's found a new vocation.'

'Wait until Deb hears about this; she will love it,' Les said. 'Did anyone get photos?'

'Mo took loads, we'll get them up on the computer tomorrow and have a proper look.'

'I got some video, too,' Dawn beamed. 'I hope it comes out alright.'

'Excellent. If this is a typical night out with you lot, sign me up for more,' Lizzie said, draining her beer. 'Have we got time for another?'

'They've just called time, so no. Still, there's the wedding to look forward to, so plenty of opportunity for more beer then,' Alex said.

'I'm not going to the wedding,' Lizzie said, 'But maybe we can sort out another night out soon.'

'You are coming to the wedding, you're part of the team now,' Gary said. 'It wouldn't be right, not having you there.' He hugged Lizzie and kissed her cheek.

'Thanks mate, I'd love to come.' Lizzie ran her hand through her unruly mane of curls. 'I'd better book a hair appointment; this lot takes some taming I can tell you.'

'That's sorted then. Now, who fancies a curry?' Gary rubbed his stomach. 'I could eat a scabby horse.'

Craig was removing the last traces of make up when Mo walked in. She handed him his beer and he took a grateful gulp.

'Thanks, I needed that. I never knew that it could get so hot up there,' he said as he started to get dressed.

'You were absolutely brilliant,' Mo said, giving Craig a hug. 'How did that all come about?'

Craig explained about the phone call that Kitty had received. 'It seemed like the right thing to do. She didn't want to let everyone down, but I couldn't let her go on for the second half. She was in a terrible state.'

'I bet, poor thing. Well, you definitely did her proud.'

'I did my best. Did Gary enjoy it?'

'He didn't have a clue it was you, not until you turned around at the end. He's totally gobsmacked now.'

Craig giggled as he pulled his jumper on. 'It doesn't take much to confuse our Gary,' he laughed, stepping into his shoes. 'Can you give me a hand to pack everything away? Kitty said to leave it here and she will pick it up when she gets back, but I'd feel more comfortable taking it with me, so I know it's all safe.'

'Sure, just tell me what goes where. Gary's keen to go for a curry now, so the sooner we get it done, the sooner we can head off.'

Chapter 53.

Alex walked across the green towards the coroner's office. He didn't know if Faz would have the post-mortem results yet, but it was worth a shot. The sun was out, but there was still a nip of winter around and Alex wished he'd put a big coat on over his suit jacket.

Gary's stag night had been a welcome distraction and, apart from a dull headache all day on Saturday, Alex had enjoyed it far more than he expected. Sunday had been spent having lunch with Charlie Baldwin and his family, which gave Alex a chance to talk to Charlie's daughter about Joel. Lucy Baldwin was the manager of a private care company and had been able to answer a lot of his questions.

As Alex approached Faz's office, he could hear loud music and smiled to himself. He knocked once then opened the door.

'Alex, you must have read my mind, I was about to call you. Come in and park your backside. Coffee?' Faz stood at his fancy coffee machine, conical flask poised.

'Yes please.' Alex sat down in one of the chairs in front of Faz's desk. The coroner's office was coveted by all who set foot in it, with its heavy dark furniture and plush carpets. The turntable that stood on the sideboard against the far wall was playing the new AC/DC vinyl, which Alex had given him for Christmas.

'This is a cracking album; I'm surprised I haven't worn it out by now.' Faz's face split into a grin as he put a steaming mug in front of Alex before turning the record player off and sitting down behind his desk. Alex recounted the events of Friday night, and Faz howled with laughter at the thought of Craig in drag.

'That must have been a sight to see,' he said, wiping tears from his eyes. 'I wish I'd been free to come along, but I had a personal issue to deal with.'

'Anything I can help with?' Alex asked as he sipped his coffee.

Faz waved his hand in dismissal. 'No, it was nothing, just a minor domestic quarrel. Steph was upset because I got home late, and we were meant to be going to her mother's for a meal. Then, I had to sit through dinner listening to her mum droning on and on about how I was failing to look after her daughter properly. It didn't go down too well when I suggested that maybe her daughter should get up off her lazy backside and find a job. That way, she could start contributing toward the household expenses, so I wouldn't have to work all hours.'

'I never realised Steph didn't work.'

'She gave up work when Maisie was born and is still using it as an excuse.'

'How old is Maisie now?'

'Old enough to have her own mobile phone.'

'Ah, I see.'

Faz smirked. 'Like I said, it's nothing I haven't heard a dozen times before; you learn to tune it out eventually.'

'If you ever need an ear to bend, you know where I am.'

'I do and I appreciate it, my friend.' Faz handed a folder across the desk before settling back in his leather-backed wing chair. 'This is for you. I'll read through the PM that Dr Quinn sent over later today.'

Alex thought the only thing Faz was missing was a white cat on his knee to complete the Bond villain look. 'Is there anything unusual in here?'

'You mean apart from the copious amounts of poop? Not really, although both the poop and the intestines came from different people.'

'This gets weirder by the minute,' Alex said. He read the first couple of pages. 'The injuries appear to be similar in all the cases so far, which suggests to me that the same tools are being used.'

'I would agree. I found minute traces of DNA from victims one and two in the wound tracts of this chap.' Faz opened one of his desk drawers and took out a tin. He pulled the lid off and offered it to Alex.

Alex looked inside. 'Mars Bars?' He shook his head. 'No thanks, I'm not really a chocolate bar person.'

'You can blame DS Redwood for that. She brought one into the PM and I've been craving them ever since.' Faz selected one and unwrapped it. He bit into the chocolate and closed his eyes. 'Bloody delicious.'

'Just be careful you don't put all that weight back on that you lost last year.'

'Why do you think I bought mini ones? I'd be as big as a house if I had the standard-sized bars.'

Alex read through the report while Faz turned the record player off and busied himself watering his plants, then sat back down and waited.

Alex looked up. 'That's quite a catalogue of damage. The consensus in the office is not sympathetic, but part of me can't help feeling a bit sorry for the guy.'

'I don't,' Faz said, draining his mug. 'While I'm against taking a life, I can tell you now that anyone, regardless of gender, who dared to breathe on her the wrong way would be autopsied whilst still alive,' he said, pointing to the photo of his daughter on the wall.

'I agree he gets no sympathy, but we must abide by the law. What can you tell me about him, apart from what's in your report?'

Faz had his finger in his mouth, picking chocolate out of his teeth so it was a minute before he answered. 'It took him a long time to die, but whatever he had in his system was long gone by the time I got to see him.'

'Do you think he was kept alive to prolong the torture?'

'I would say so, yes. A lot of the injuries sustained were superficial enough not to kill him but would have inflicted a considerable amount of pain. In the end, it was the blood loss that finished him off, just like the others.'

Alex closed the file and stood up, his knees cracking as he did so. 'Thanks for this, I'll catch up with you soon.'

'Not too soon, I hope. The mess that last one created was phenomenal. Poor Ziggy was run ragged,' Faz grinned, walking over and opening the door for Alex.

'He's young, he's got more energy than we'll ever have again.' Alex said, shaking the coroner's hand.

'Speak for yourself! I'm in great shape, I'll have you know,' Faz argued.

'You won't be if you keep eating that chocolate, but I suppose round is a shape.' Alex ducked to avoid the pen that Faz lobbed at him and left the room, Faz's laughter echoing behind him.

'Faz's report makes interesting reading,' Alex said when he got back to the office. 'It suggests that this man was held captive for a considerable length of time, as were the others. Faz thinks the victim was systematically tortured over a period of several hours, possibly more than a day. Eventually, the blood loss was too great, and he died. He also said that it's possible he was drugged, but there was nothing left in his system to prove it. Any thoughts?'

'He would have made a lot of noise, so he must have been kept somewhere remote, or somewhere that had been soundproofed.'

'Good, Lizzie. Anything else?'

'They would have needed transport big enough to carry a grown man, who was probably unconscious at the time. I can't see anyone going of their own accord.'

'Unless they had an accomplice,' Craig said, 'Although I think they'd go willingly if they had the right incentive.'

'Such as?'

'These victims are all paedophiles, so if you offer them something they might like they might go along.'

'You mean like a child?' Alex looked horrified.

'Not necessarily, but if you've hinted that you belong to a club that shares their interests, they might be persuaded.'

'I see. Yes, that makes more sense. Mo, have you got anything from your pals in Vice?'

'Yes, I have, they've been really helpful. There are loads of specialist groups online, usually disguised as something else to avoid suspicion. The more hardcore ones tend to favour the dark web. There are a few that are bold enough to meet up in person, to trade experiences, photos, videos and in some instances sharing a child,' Mo said.

'Sick bastards,' Les muttered.

'Is that what we think was going on at the guest houses, sharing of illicit material?'

'Either that or they could have been there to participate in something that was happening in that particular area at the time,' Mo said.

'Christ, it gets worse by the minute. Anything else?' Alex asked.

'Copies of the artist's impressions from the guest house owner were forwarded to the press officer yesterday, so all the local papers are running it today. Hopefully someone will come forward and identify them so we can cross-reference them with the victims,' Dawn said.

'We're going to take the sketches with us later, to see if someone from the survivor's group recognises them,' Mo said.

'Let's hope they do, I've had about as much as I can take from this case,' Alex said. 'Make it known that we are considering bringing everyone in for formal interviews. I hate to put the pressure on, but needs must when the devil drives.'

Chapter 54.

Dawn and Alex sat in the break area the following day, throwing ideas back and forth whilst Alex devoured a chicken sandwich as if his life depended on it.

He banged his chest to dislodge a piece of food that had been too big to go down. 'Sorry, I didn't have time for breakfast this morning.'

Dawn laughed and patted Alex hard on the back as he started to choke. 'Just slow down and take your time. You don't want to end up in the morgue, with Faz poking around your insides, do you?'

'Christ, no. He'd take photos and put them on Instagram.' Alex took a gulp of tea to help the last of his sandwich down. 'How's Lizzie fitting in?' Alex raised his mug to his lips, but it was empty. He got up to make another drink. 'Do you want one?'

'Yes please. She's doing great, still a bit green but the team all like her, and she's not afraid to speak up when she has an idea or if something's bothering her.'

'That's brilliant. I will miss Gary, him transferring out will leave a huge gap, but it's nice to know that his replacement is capable of filling it.'

'Yeah, he's one of a kind, that's for sure. But we've got the wedding to look forward to before he goes.'

'I'm not sure if I'll go, to be honest. It won't feel right while Jayne is in hospital.'

'Gary and Jo will both be gutted if you're not there.'

'I know, but it seems wrong to be spending the whole day away from her.'

'No disrespect boss, but didn't you say she was struggling to recognise you? Maybe a break will do you both good.'

Alex sipped his tea. 'I don't know, Dawn. Maybe you're right. Lord knows I could use the distraction.'

'Talk to Jayne's doctors and see what they say. That way, you can make an informed decision.'

'That's a good idea. I'd hate to let the happy couple down on their big day.'

'That's settled, then. Right, I'll go and find out how Mo's getting on.'

Alex headed back to his office just as his phone started to ring.

It was Andy. 'Could you come along to my office please, Alex? It's rather important.' The phone went dead and Alex hung up, irked at his rudeness.

'You off home, boss?' Dawn asked when he came out of his office and started heading for the door.

'No, I've been summoned by the DCI. Apparently, it's urgent.'

'I appreciate you responding so quickly,' Andy said when Alex walked in.

'You said it was important so I thought I'd better not dither.' Alex's voice was cool, and Andy looked sheepish.

'I realise I never apologised for my behaviour the other day. I am sorry about that, it's just the pressure getting to me.'

'It's getting to us all but losing our rag won't get us anywhere.'

'You're right, and I apologise again.' Andy kept glancing at the white box that stood on his desk.

'Is that another gift from our perp, sir?'

'It is.' Andy pointed at the box. 'Take a look.'

'It's not a severed head, is it?' Alex joked as he pulled a pair of gloves out of his pocket and put them on. He removed the lid of the box, looked inside and stepped backwards in shock.

'Jesus!' Alex went a shade of green and quickly put the lid back on. He took some deep breaths and sat down.

'Precisely,' Andy said.

'Are they...?'

'Yes, from the quick glance I took, there appears to be at least three sets of male genitalia. I didn't look too closely.'

'Was there a note?'

'There was a card, same message as last time.' Andy passed it over. 'This package was sitting on the bonnet of my car just now when I popped outside to get my lunchbox. I soon lost my appetite when I opened it.'

'I bet you did.' Alex looked at his boss. 'Do you know why any-one would want to send you these trophies?'

'If I knew that, Alex, I would tell you.'

Alex gave him a sympathetic look. 'I'll check the CCTV from the car park to see if it caught whoever left it.'

'Thank you, I appreciate that.'

There was a knock at the door, and a tall, serious-looking man walked in. He placed the box and the card in an evidence bag. Andy signed it over and the man took it away.

'This might not have anything to do with our case,' Alex said. 'Maybe they're sending you a personal message to do with your past.'

Andy stood up suddenly, making Alex jump.

'What is it?'

Andy went to say something, then stopped himself. 'It's nothing. Let's just concentrate on what we have and worry about this later.' He took up his customary position in front of the window and stared out. After a moment, Alex got up and went back to his office.

After he'd told his team about the DCI's latest unwanted gift, Alex went into his office and closed the door. He mulled over their conversation and the more he did, the more he was certain that Andy had lied to him. Although they had known each other for years, Alex having been a part of Andy's team when he first made detective, Alex thought about how much he really knew about the man and realised it was very little. Andy never attended social events, such as weddings or birthday parties, and Alex couldn't recall him ever going for a celebratory drink with his team when they closed a case. He'd always accepted that his boss was a very private man and had chalked it up to him just preferring his own company. Now, he wondered whether or not there was a more sinister reason.

Alex jumped at the loud knock. 'Come in,' he called.

The door opened, and Dawn stuck her head into the room. 'Sorry, boss, is this a bad time?'

'No, not at all,' he replied with a smile, 'I was miles away. What's up?'

'We've got another victim.'

Alex groaned and buried his head in his hands. 'For fuck's sake,' he said. 'Where?'

'Pelshall Common.'

Alex sighed and stood up. 'Come on then, let's go and take a look.'

Chapter 55.

Faz was standing to one side of the white tent when Alex and Dawn arrived, and he walked over to them as they struggled into the white paper suits and bootees.

'Please tell me this one's not covered in shit,' Alex said.

Faz shook his head. 'No, this one is surprisingly dull compared to previous victims, but it's almost certainly the same person responsible, judging by the injuries I can see so far. I'll be able to tell you more once I've done the PM.'

They ducked into the tent and looked at the body. It was hanging upside-down from a tree, the thick chain attached to bolts screwed into the legs just behind the kneecaps. The arms had been removed at the shoulders, leaving small stumps of protruding bone.

'That's new,' Alex said, pointing to the victim's legs. 'They've not removed the feet before.'

'They've also never removed the ears before either, which suggests to me that he had an aural fixation – he liked to listen,' Faz explained. 'And then there's this.' He crouched down and pointed to the body's abdomen. It had been cut open and there was a clear plastic bag filled with something bloody inside sitting neatly in the opening.

'At this rate there'll be less and less to find each time,' Alex complained. 'By the way, the DCI had another package, one of your guys picked it up.'

'What was it this time, a spleen, a liver, or something more exciting?'

'Bollocks.'

'Charming,' Faz said, looking affronted. 'I only asked.'

'No, I meant actual bollocks - more than one set from what I could see.'

'Ooh, intriguing. Anyway, this one seems straightforward enough, so once I've got him back to the mortuary, I'll have a look at him and get back to you.'

The team sat round the table, drinking coffee and eating biscuits as they tossed ideas back and forth between each other.

'So, what body parts is the latest victim missing?' Craig asked, reaching for a bourbon biscuit.

'Hands, feet, eyes, tongue, and ears so far, but Faz said he will let us know about the genitals once he's examined him back at the morgue. They might be in that box that Andy received earlier,' Alex said, sipping his tea.

'It sounds like they're escalating if that's even possible,' Mo said. 'But why remove the ears?'

'Faz said he may have liked to listen.'

'Perhaps he refused to listen, didn't lift a finger to help and didn't take steps to stop it happening, which are what the amputations signify,' Les said.

'Those poor kids,' Lizzie said. 'It's too awful to think about.'

'Unfortunately, we do have to think about it, painful though it is,' Alex said.

'I know, but...' Lizzie burst into tears and ran from the room. Dawn went after her.

Alex looked at the rest of his team. 'I know this case is taking its toll on all of you, so if anyone needs to step away for a while then please do. No one will judge you. Your mental health is more important than anything else.'

A murmur of appreciation went round the table, and Alex was about to say something when Dawn came back in.

'She's fine, it's just a lot for her to take in,' Dawn said. 'It's her first case.'

'Poor kid,' Les said, making a mental note to keep a closer eye on Lizzie in future.

Alex stretched his arms up towards the ceiling, feeling all the vertebrae click in his back as he did so.

'That didn't sound good,' Dawn said.

'It didn't feel good either.' Alex rotated his head from side to side and his neck crunched like a bowl of dry cereal. 'Sleeping on that sofa is killing me.'

'How many more murders do you think there will be?' Les asked.

'I hope there aren't any more but given there are eight women in the group, and if we count the one up in Yorkshire, I'm anticipating at least three.'

They were discussing the similarities between the different victims when Lizzie came back in. She gave an embarrassed smile. 'I'm sorry about that,' she said.

'No need for apologies,' Alex assured her. 'We've all reacted like that at some time. It just means you're human. Anyway, I'm having dinner with Dave and Carol tonight, we've got some things to discuss, so I'll see you all tomorrow.'

After Alex had left, Dawn read through the notes she'd made to take to the group meeting later.

'Mo, are there any co-ordinates on the cards that the DCI received?'

'Nope, just the same picture and message on all of them. I think the first few were sent to help us find the bodies so the women they were linked to can get some closure.'

'Maybe you're right. Can you print off some copies of the photofits, please? We'll take them with us tonight and see if anyone recognises them.'

Chapter 56.

After dinner, when Joel had gone into the conservatory to carry on with his jigsaw puzzle and Wayne had gone to the cinema, Alex and Dave sat in the lounge enjoying a glass of single malt whisky whilst Carol was at the hospital visiting Jayne. Alex had wanted to go, but Carol had thought it best if he waited until Jayne wasn't so confused.

'Maybe she thought you were Joel and was frightened you were going to hit her. I'm sorry if that upsets you, Alex, it's just my opinion,' Carol had said, seeing Alex's face fall. In the end he'd agreed, and Carol had gone alone.

Alex drained his glass and set it on the table. 'So, that's the gist of it so far. I can't go into specifics, but the artist's impressions will be in the papers again tomorrow. We've had no luck with them so far, not even a crank call.'

'Sounds like you're making some progress, which is more than I am with that damned septic tank,' Dave said. 'The bloody digger broke down, so we're having to dig it out by hand while we wait for replacement parts to arrive. At least you get to work indoors.'

'Not all the time. You should have been at the scene I had to attend the other day; it was like something out of a horror film. The guy had someone else's intestines tied round his neck and he was covered in shit, some of which he'd been forced to eat.'

'Christ, that's sick. I wonder if they planned it all out in advance, or it was a spur of the moment thing.' Dave refilled both their glasses. 'Damn, that's the last of my Laphroaig. I guess I'll have to start on the Balvenie next,' he said.

'That's an interesting point,' Alex said, 'About the planning, I mean. You wouldn't keep intestines from a victim unless you knew you were going to use them for something else.'

'Plus,' Dave added,' you'd need somewhere to keep the spare parts, like a big fridge or freezer, otherwise they'd go off.'

'That's true.'

'Have you decided when you're going to move back to your old place yet?' Dave asked as he sipped his whisky.

'I'd like to do it soon, so Joel can go home. If you're free, would you be able to give me a hand to move my stuff next week?'

'Sure, I can probably do next Friday. We should be finished at the farm by then if the digger parts arrive on schedule.'

'Great stuff, I'll get started on the packing and take the first lot over on Sunday after Gary's wedding.' Alex looked up as the front door opened and Carol came in.

'It's raining again, and bloody freezing, too.' She shrugged her coat off and hung it up in the hallway. Dave got up and took a new bottle of whisky and a glass from the sideboard. He poured her a generous measure and Carol took it gratefully, sinking into the armchair closest to the hearth so she could take advantage of the dancing flames of the open fire.

'How is she?' Alex asked, unable to wait any longer.

Carol swallowed the whisky slowly, enjoying the warmth as it went down. 'She's still traumatised whenever she comes round, but they said they can't keep sedating her as it's not good for her long-term. They're arranging a consultation with the mental health team, so they can decide what to do next.' Carol smiled sadly. 'It's going to be a very long road, I'm afraid.'

'We'll get through it, we always do,' Alex said. He looked at the clock on the mantelpiece. 'I'd better get going, I've got a lot to discuss with my team tomorrow. Thanks for the dinner and the conversation, it was much appreciated.'

'Anytime,' Dave said. 'See you tomorrow.'

Despite only living a few hundred yards from Dave and Carol, Alex was drenched by the time he got back. Jack was huddled under the nearest bush, clearly unimpressed at being left out in the rain. As soon as Alex opened the front door, the cat pushed past him, leaving a stripe of wet fur and mud on Alex's trousers.

'Cheers, mate, these were clean on this morning,' he muttered.

Alex fed the cat then had a quick shower. When he came out, Jack was lying in the centre of their king-size bed, washing his leg. Alex put on some jogging bottoms and a t-shirt, then went into the lounge and switched on the CD player, choosing Queen's Flash Gordon soundtrack. He lay down on the sofa, letting the music wash over him while he made mental lists of what needed to be done while Jayne was in hospital. Tomorrow he would start packing up the books and ornaments, ready for the move back to their old house. Then, he would chase up the social worker and find out where they were regarding Joel's case.

At some point he drifted off to sleep, dreaming that all his belongings were walking down the street by themselves, serenaded by Dave who was dressed like a ninja turtle and playing a trombone. He turned over in his sleep and was mumbling about pizza when loud sirens woke him with a start. He leapt off the sofa, startling Jack and gaining claw marks in his shins that would make Wolverine proud. He slipped his feet into his trainers and went outside.

The sky was full of orange smoke, and it was a few seconds before Alex realised that Dave's house was on fire.

Chapter 57.

'I know none of you wanted to speak to the police about your experiences, but if we don't talk to them now, they may think we've got something to do with the murders,' Jean said, 'So we need to co-operate as much as we can.'

'What kind of things will they be asking us?' one woman asked. 'I don't want to relive my experiences.'

'I don't know, to be honest,' Jean replied. 'They know my story, but I asked Alison to tell them. I was too busy being sick in the toilets, because of the shock of it all.'

There was a soft knock at the door, and Jean got up to open it. She ushered Dawn and Mo into the room and closed the door again.

'Is Alison not joining us?' Dawn asked as they took their seats.

'No, we all felt it best not to invite her, because she runs the groups,' Tracy explained.

'I thought you ran them with her?' Mo asked.

'Yes, I do, but I was a participant in this group. I only began working alongside Alison when the latest one started up.'

Oh, I see.' Dawn smiled round at the faces staring back at her. 'Can we start with introductions? I'm DS Dawn Redwood, I'm with the Major Crimes Unit in Wolverhampton. My colleague is DC Mo Ross. If we can go round the group, and you can tell us who you are. You don't have to use your real names, but it would help us a great deal if you would.'

'Can we trust you to keep our names out of the press?' Tracy asked.

'Yes, you can.' Dawn assured her.

'Fair enough.' Tracy looked around the room. 'Is everyone comfortable with first names? Good.' She looked at Dawn then pointed to each woman in turn. 'Starting on your left is Anne, Julie, Bobbie, Jean, Patricia, Mandy, and Samantha.'

Once Mo had written the names down, Dawn began. 'We are here tonight to see if anyone can help us identify the four victims...'

'Er, they're not victims, they're paedos,' Anne interrupted. 'We are the victims.'

'We're not victims, we're survivors, and we don't allow them any control over us anymore,' Tracy said.

'I'm so sorry, that was insensitive of me,' Dawn said, her cheeks reddening. 'Let me start again. So far, we've had four bodies turn up, each one tortured before death and mutilated afterwards.'

'Good, I hope they suffered,' Mandy said. The others nodded in agreement.

'Oh, they suffered alright,' Mo said. 'They all got what they deserved.' She glanced sideways at Dawn, who looked surprised but said nothing.

'Jean, how much have you told everyone about your recent experience? Is it okay for me to go over it with everyone?' Dawn asked.

'I have no secrets from anyone here, so feel free to tell them anything.'

Dawn explained the circumstances surrounding the card Jean had received, and how it linked her to the first body. A collective shudder and noises of disgust went round the room.

'Jean was able to tell us who it could be from the description we gave her, and his identity was later confirmed by a member of his family. Now, we haven't told them about the connection he had to Jean, as we don't want anything leading back to her.'

'Did they know he was a paedophile?' Tracy asked.

'No, they knew nothing about it, which is often the case.'

'Are you going to tell his family what he did?' Julie asked.

'That's not really any of our business,' Tracy said softly.

Julie looked at her feet, her cheeks burning. 'You're right.' She looked at the two officers. 'I'm sorry. I was just wondering if he'd messed with his own kids.'

'No need to apologise, it's only natural to express concern,' Mo said, 'And you raise a valid point. We will be investigating to see if he did abuse his own children. They are boys, though, so it's doubtful.'

'That doesn't mean a thing,' Anne said. 'Just because he abused Jean doesn't mean he didn't like abusing boys, too.'

'True, but tonight we just want to try and find out who these other three are.' Dawn looked at Jean. 'Is it okay to show everyone the card you received?'

Jean nodded, so Dawn handed the card to the woman sitting nearest to her. She studied it and passed it on, until everyone had seen it. Tracy gave it back to Mo, who put it on the coffee table in case anyone wanted to look at it again.

'I've also brought along some sketches of four men who stayed in various guest houses in Yorkshire with Jean's abuser. We think they may have been part of a paedophile ring that met up regularly.' Dawn handed the printouts to Anne, who looked at them before passing them on. 'We don't know if these guys are ones that abused any of you, so apologies if their pictures cause any distress.'

'Why can't you just check the bodies against the sketches?' Bobbie asked, 'It would be less upsetting for us.'

'We haven't been able to identify three of the bodies as they were badly mutilated,' Mo said. 'Someone did a really good job of making them unrecognisable, but if we get a name for them, we can let people know that they are no longer a threat to children.'

'Fair enough,' Bobbie said. Mo noticed that she barely glanced at the pictures before handing them to someone else.

'Can we take a quick break, please?' Jean asked. 'I need to use the loo, and I'm sure some of us could use some refreshments.'

Dawn and Mo exchanged glances, then stood up. 'No problem, let's take fifteen minutes so that everyone can grab a drink, have a quick smoke or go to the toilet.'

Tracy went towards the kitchen to make some drinks, with Anne in tow. Dawn excused herself, saying she needed to get some stuff from her car. She signalled for Mo to follow her outside.

'Sorry if I spoke out of turn in there,' Mo said. 'I just thought if we showed a bit of solidarity, they might open up to us a bit more.'

'No need to apologise, though it did surprise me. What's your impression so far? Did you pick up on anything in particular?' Dawn asked as she rummaged around in her boot for contact cards.

'Hard to tell yet, but they've all spent years keeping the worst secrets, so I doubt anyone will have trouble keeping a neutral expression,' Mo replied. The temperature had dropped since they'd arrived, and she shoved her hands deep in her jacket pockets, trying to stave off the cold.

'True.' Dawn finally located the cards and handed them to a shivering Mo. She closed the boot and locked her car. 'Sorry that took so long, I really should be more organised,' she added.

Mo shuffled her feet. 'Can we go back in, now?'

'Sure.' Dawn looked at her. 'Are you okay? You look a bit peaky.'

'I'm fine, I just want to get this over with so I can go home.'

'We should be able to wrap up in about an hour, but if you want to go now, I can finish this on my own.'

'No, I'll stay,' Mo said. Seeing Dawn's concerned expression, she smiled. 'My ankle's playing up, that's all.'

'Have you got any painkillers with you? I might have some in the car if you haven't.'

'I have, but they knock me out, so I'd rather take them when I get home,' Mo said. 'Thanks, anyway,' she added.

They hurried inside again, and Mo went to stand by the radiator to warm herself up. The atmosphere seemed more relaxed than before, and Dawn hoped they might make some progress. She handed her contact cards round so they could each take one.

'I hope you've all had a chance to look at the sketches and the card which Jean received. You can see what I meant when I said it appeared to be unique to Jean and to the person who abused her. Has anyone here had a card like that, either recently or in the last few weeks?'

There was a low murmur, then two hands went up.

Chapter 58.

Alex ran as fast as he could along the lane towards Dave's house, praying under his breath that everyone was safe. The fire crew surrounded the house, spraying powerful jets of water at the inferno. Two ambulances stood nearby, ready to tend to potential injuries. Alex dodged round a few people, desperately trying to see what was going on, but a burly fire officer grabbed his arms and firmly steered him away from the blaze.

'Stay there, we have enough to do without having you getting in our way,' he said, giving Alex a warning look. Alex looked around in frustration, trying to spot his family but there was no sign of anyone he recognised through the thick smoke.

'Uncle Alex!'

The shout came from Alex's left, and he turned to see Wayne, carrying someone over his shoulder. The lad lowered the inert figure gently to the ground then leaned over, hands on his knees, coughing harshly.

Alex pulled the young man into a rough hug before turning his attention to his sister-in-law. He just had time to brush smoke-blackened hair out of her face before being moved aside by a team of paramedics. Wayne stood nearby, tears streaming down his face.

'Well done, mate. Where's everyone else? Did they get out?' Alex asked as he pulled the lad to one side and checked him over. 'Are you hurt?'

Wayne coughed hard and vomited on the grass before taking a big gulp of air.

'I'm fine, Uncle Alex. We were in bed when it started. Dad got me and mum to the door before going back in for Joel.'

'What about your brothers?'

'They're in London at a party.' Wayne started coughing again. 'Is she alright?' he asked one of the paramedics.

'She will be, thanks to you,' The paramedic stood up and took Wayne's arm. 'Come on, you can go in the ambulance with her. That way we can get you checked out at the same time.'

Wayne started to protest, but Alex stopped him. 'Go on, your mum needs you. I'll stay here and find your dad.'

As the ambulance pulled away, Alex heard a shout from behind him. He spotted a figure stumbling out of the building, carrying someone in his arms. Alex ran over to take an unconscious Joel from Dave just before his brother's legs gave way and he crumpled to the ground.

Another team of paramedics rushed over to intervene, and Alex stood by helplessly while they worked on his brother and son. A soft bump against the back of his legs made him jump, and Alex glanced down to see Buddy looking up at him, tail wagging fiercely and tongue lolling out. Alex sank to the floor, wrapped his arms around the dog and sobbed into his soot-stained fur. After a couple of minutes, a paramedic tapped him on the shoulder. Alex wiped his eyes and stood up, embarrassed at his outburst of emotion.

'Look, mate, why don't you go and sort the dog out, then meet us at the hospital?'

Alex nodded, too numb to speak. With a backwards glance at his family, Alex ushered Buddy down the lane and into the bunga-low, only noticing that he had left the front door wide open when he'd run out. He put the dog in Joel's bedroom and went to get him a bowl of water. When he came back, Buddy was curled up on Joel's bed, fast asleep. Alex made sure the door was closed firmly then grabbed his coat and keys and went outside. He drove along the lane, trying not to look in the rear-view mirror at the flames devouring his brother's house.

Chapter 59.

A lex sat in the waiting room of the accident and emergency department at New Cross Hospital, with a distinct sense of déjà vu. He was becoming sick of the sight of the pale grey walls and the scuffed vinyl floor marked with lines showing directions to different departments. There was a strong smell of disinfectant from where one of the cleaners had recently mopped up after someone who had regurgitated their last meal. Alex knew from bitter experience the pitfalls of eating greasy kebabs after consuming vast quantities of booze. He smiled to himself, thinking of some of the benders he and Dave had been on years before when his brother had been home on leave from the army. He made a mental note to remind Dave of some of their antics at some point, including the time they raced around the Co-op car park in shopping trollies, both of them drunk. It was great fun until they had crashed down the embankment at the end of the car park into a ditch, and Alex had broken his arm.

A harassed-looking doctor came into the waiting room and glanced around before spotting Alex. She beckoned to him, and he followed her to a quiet room. Alex's heart sank. He'd been in rooms like this when they had needed to deliver bad news, and he clenched his fists tightly to stop the tremors in his hands.

'Don't worry, Mr Peachey, everyone is fine,' she said, 'I just need details of everyone who came in from the fire, it makes more sense to talk in here so you can give us what we need all in one go.'

'Of course.' Alex breathed a sigh of relief. 'Who do you want to start with?'

Chapter 60.

Alex was in the office before anyone else the next morning after spending the night in the hospital, sitting by his son's bedside. Apart from smoke inhalation, Joel, Carol, and Wayne were otherwise uninjured but had been kept in overnight for observation. Dave had suffered burns on his legs, arms, and face, and had a dislocated shoulder from breaking Joel's bedroom door down. Luckily, the burns hadn't been full-thickness and the doctor said he would have minimal scarring. Wayne had agreed to sit with Joel while Alex went home to check on Buddy. He also needed to pop into work but had promised his nephew he'd be back as soon as he'd briefed his team. Wayne had pulled out his phone to show Joel some funny videos and Alex had smiled as Joel's laughter echoed down the corridor behind him.

Alex used the quiet time to re-read Faz's latest PM report, adding notes to those he'd written the day before. He called a briefing as soon as the rest of the team arrived and explained what had happened the night before.

'Wow, Dave's a brave man,' Lizzie said. She held a mug of tea out and Alex took it gratefully.

'He's the best brother in the world, and I'm lucky to have him.' Alex cleared a lump from his throat. 'Now, let's focus on work. Dawn, how did you and Mo get on with the group last night?'

'It was tense at first, but fine once they knew we weren't going to drag up anything personal. Two women admitted they'd had cards like the one Jean received, they're going to drop them off for us later today.'

'That's excellent, well done both of you,' Alex beamed. 'Did you give a general description of the bodies we're trying to identify?'

'We did, and we showed them the sketches, but no one admitted to recognising them.'

'Have we had any luck via the media?'

'Just the usual cranks, hoping for their fifteen minutes of fame,' Les said. He scratched at his ear. 'You'd think someone would be missing them.'

'Unless they live alone, in which case the only people missing them would be work colleagues,' Lizzie said.

'They might be unemployed, or run their own businesses,' Mo said.

'There's certainly a lot of avenues yet to explore,' Alex said.

'We've found another connection between the group and the victims,' Dawn said. 'Some of the injuries sustained were similar to the kind of abuse they inflicted.'

'Go on.'

'Victim number two was found near the river, and it looked like he had been in water at some point.'

'Was drowning the cause of death for that one?' Les asked.

'No, but he had been submerged prior to death, and Faz says it wasn't river water. One of the women said her abuse took place at bath times, so there could be a link there.'

'It's possible. Did you find any other such connections?'

'Stop interrupting me and you'll find out.' Dawn stuck her tongue out at Alex, and he grinned at her over the rim of his mug.

'A couple of the women said their abuse took place at night, in the dark, another said she was blindfolded. That could point to the subsequent removal of the victim's eyes,' Dawn said, 'And I'm thinking that the one who had the fingers in his rectum may have been into sodomy.'

'I dread to think what number three was into, if that's the case,' Craig said, pulling a disgusted face.

'Did anyone mention if they were abused in that way?' Alex said, ignoring Craig.

'No, we didn't really discuss their abuse in detail, we just wrote down everything they said so we could go over it later,' Mo said.

'Victim number four had his internal organs removed and placed in a plastic bag, which was then stuffed inside his body cavity. I reckon he was a butcher, and the abuse could have taken place in the shop,' Dawn said.

'How did you work that one out?' Lizzie asked.

'Years ago, butchers used to have carcasses hanging up in their shops, displayed in the same manner as this guy, with the offal in a bag inside the body,' Les told her.

Lizzie gave a shudder of disgust.

'What else have you got, Dawn?' Alex asked as he drank the last dregs of his tea. He could still taste soot in his mouth.

'Apart from that, not much, I'm afraid. I'll go through everything we got last night to see if I can add any more to the board. We may have to interview Alison Munroe and Tracy Downey again, to see if they can give us any more information.'

'Good idea. I know we have to be sensitive, but people are dying.' Alex looked at his watch. 'I need to pick Carol and Wayne up in a bit but keep me in the loop. I spoke to Charlie Baldwin first thing this morning; he's not back officially until next week, but he's offered to come in and lend a hand while I try to sort out all this business with the fire.'

'How bad is the damage to the house? Is there anything we can do to help?' Dawn asked.

'I haven't been to look, but I don't think there's much left, going by how fierce it was burning last night.'

'I think I speak for all of us when I say that we'll come and help out with sorting through to see if anything can be salvaged,' Craig said. The others nodded in agreement.

'Just name it, boss, we'll be there,' Gary said. 'I'm sure we could get a few others to pitch in as well.'

'Thanks, guys, I do appreciate it, but for now everything is fine. I'm going to the hospital now, so I'll leave Dawn in charge again as I might be gone all day. I meant to say earlier, Dave and I were talking about the case last night before all the drama happened, and he raised an interesting point. As we know, the intestines tied around victim number three's neck were not his own. Dave said they must have been kept somewhere like a fridge or freezer, otherwise they would have started to decompose. Any thoughts?'

'You'd hardly be inclined to keep a bucket of guts in your domestic fridge, so I reckon they've got access to a larger facility,' Craig said.

'What about industrial places, like meat-packing plants? They would have gigantic fridges and freezers,' Lizzie said.

'They'd also have to have transport big enough to carry a possibly unconscious man. No one would question a van going in and out of somewhere like that,' Les added.

'Supermarkets and restaurants also have walk-in fridges and freezers,' Mo said, 'Maybe they work in the food industry.'

'I've been thinking about something,' Gary said.

'Ooh, careful lad, you'll set the smoke alarms off,' Les quipped, then winced when he realised what he'd said. He threw an apologetic look at Alex.

'No, seriously,' Gary said, waving his hand at Les to shut him up. 'How long has the survivor's group been running for?'

Dawn checked her notes. 'I don't know, to be honest. I think Alison Munroe said it was six or seven years, with each course being ten weeks long. Why, what are you thinking?'

'I'm just wondering why this particular group is being targeted and not any of the others.'

Alex sat forward, sensing that Gary was on to something. 'Go on.'

'So, that's what – three or four courses a year?' Gary said, getting into his stride now. 'If each course is attended by eight women, that's how many people?' He looked at Mo.

'If you calculate it at four courses a year, that's thirty-two women. Over six years that's one hundred and ninety-two,' she said.

'Thank you. What I'm wondering is, out of nearly two hundred women, what makes these eight so special? Maybe the women in this group aren't there by accident, I think they were put in the same one deliberately. Either that, or it's someone in that group taking revenge for their new friends.'

Alex was impressed. 'Wow, that's some deep thinking there. Well done, Gary.'

'Cheers, boss,' Gary said, blushing to the roots of his hair.

'I have to go now, but when I get back we'll go through everything again, piece by piece.'

Chapter 61.

Alex's first stop when he arrived at the hospital was to the high dependency unit to see his wife, but she was sleeping, so he left a message to say he'd been in, then headed down to see his son. As he was buzzed into the ward, he could hear Joel shouting angrily.

'Hey, what's the matter?' Alex asked as he threw the door open, startling Joel into silence. A young male nurse stood at the end of the bed, looking unsure of himself.

'I'm sorry, Dad. He was trying to pull my shirt up and he's a stranger.' Joel's eyes blazed with anger.

'Joel, he is a nurse, and he's trying to take your temperature to see if you're well enough to go home. He can't put the thermometer in your mouth as you might bite down on it, so he has to put it under your arm instead.' Alex looked at the nurse's name badge. 'I'm so sorry, Martin. Did no one tell you about Joel's special needs?'

Martin looked annoyed. 'No, they didn't, but that's beside the point. He's been very unpleasant to the staff. He should have a carer with him.'

'Joel has cerebral palsy and Asperger's syndrome. I agree that he should have had someone with him to interpret his concerns and fears, but there simply wasn't time to put anything in place.' Alex turned to Joel. 'I think you owe Martin an apology, son.'

'I'm sorry,' Joel said. 'I thought only women could be nurses, that's why I didn't trust you.'

'Nurses can be any gender nowadays,' Alex said, 'Now, can you please behave and let Martin finish his observations?'

'Yes.'

'Thank you,' Martin said. He still looked annoyed but he completed his checks.

Joel sat in silence until Martin had left. 'I'm sorry.'

'Forget it; but remember that the hospital staff have a job to do, and that is trying to help you get better, so no more shouting. Now, can you sit quietly and watch TV while I go and see how Uncle Dave is doing? I'll be half an hour.'

Joel looked at the clock that hung on the wall opposite his bed. 'See you at 11.37am.'

Alex smiled and made his way to the burns unit, where he found Carol sitting outside Dave's room, talking quietly with Wayne. They both stood up when Alex walked towards them. He hugged them both, noticing a faint smell of smoke clinging to them.

'Are you two alright?'

'We're fine, thank you for being there last night.' Carol gave Wayne her purse. 'Go and get us some coffee, will you please?'

Wayne frowned and opened the purse. He took a handful of coins out and handed the purse back. 'I'm not carrying that around the hospital. What if I see a fit woman?'

Alex laughed. 'Good to see you've got your priorities right, mate.'

'Always. Back in a bit.' Wayne strode off in the direction that Alex had just come from.

'He's the spit of his father,' Alex said, watching him go.

'He is, and if it wasn't for his quick thinking, none of us would be here today.'

'What happened? How did it start?'

'I don't know yet. Wayne said he heard Joel shouting and got up to see what was wrong. He noticed smoke coming from under the lounge door as he came down the stairs, so ran back up to wake us. By the time we got downstairs the whole ground floor was ablaze. I tried to find the dog, but the smoke was too thick. Dave told us to get out while he went to get Joel. I passed out before I could go out-side, but Wayne carried me.'

'Was Joel shouting to alert you of the fire?'

Carol gave a small laugh. 'No, he said that Buddy was in his room, and was trying to nick his crisps. You know how Joel is with his snacks; he won't share them with anyone.' She stopped for a moment. 'Oh God, tell me the dog's okay.'

'He's fine, I took him home and put him in Joel's room. I walked him this morning before I went to work, but he had to have cat food for his breakfast because I didn't have anything else.'

'I'm sure he won't care; that dog will eat anything.'

'Just like his owner,' Alex laughed, nodding towards the door. 'Shall we go and see how he's doing?'

Dave lay back against the starchy white pillows, a smile on his face as a nurse sponged his feet. Both arms were bandaged up to the elbows, and one side of his face was covered in padded white dress-ings. The sheets were draped over a frame to keep them off Dave's legs.

'Jesus, it's the Phantom of the bloody Opera!' Alex exclaimed.

'Oops, the wife's here, we'd better be careful or she'll get jealous, Daphne.'

The nurse laughed at him. 'Behave yourself, Mr Peachey, you old flatterer.'

'Hey, less of the old! I'm in the prime of my life.'

'Yeah, keep telling yourself that, buster.' Carol smiled at the nurse. 'You have my permission to slap him if he misbehaves.'

'Ooh, bondage, count me in!' Dave started to grin but groaned when it pulled at his dressings.

'Serves you right, you randy old goat.'

'Eww, Mum, that's gross,' Wayne said as he came in carrying two polystyrene cups. Alex took them from him and passed one to Car-ol. He took the lid off his and blew on the steaming liquid before attempting a sip and giving up. He stood the cup on the windowsill to cool down further and sat down in the high-backed chair in the corner of the room.

'So, what have they said?'

'Well, I won't be entering any more beauty contests, that's for sure. But I was lucky that it's only first-degree burns on my face, arms, and lower legs.'

'Thank fuck for that, I didn't fancy being related to Freddy Krueger,' Alex laughed.

'Piss off, you cheeky git! I'll still be better looking than you, even with a melted face.'

'Pack it in, will you?' Carol shouted, bursting into tears.

Wayne put an arm around her shoulders. 'You two can be such knobheads sometimes,' he scolded. 'Mum's been worried sick.'

The brothers both looked sheepish. 'Sorry, Carol. I was just trying to lighten the situation,' Alex said.

'I'm sorry too, love. Stop worrying, we're all safe.'

'That's as maybe, but what about the house?' she sobbed. 'What are we going to do about that?'

'We're insured, and I can rebuild it so stop fretting.' Dave tried to placate her, but she put her hand up to stop him.

'Really? How are you going to do that? Look at the state of you, it'll be months before you can go back to work. You've got commitments to fulfil before you even think about starting on a rebuild.'

'My lads are competent enough to finish the stuff that's ongoing, we just won't be able to take on anything else for a while. If money gets tight, we've got savings we can use if necessary.'

'There's no need to panic, the bungalow is available for you all, for as long as you need it,' Alex said. 'We can start looking for carers for Joel at the same time.'

Carol wiped her eyes. 'That's wonderful, thank you Alex.'

'I'll move back into the old house tomorrow. I was going to wait until Jayne was out of hospital, but I may as well go now.'

'What about your furniture?'

'You guys need it more than I do. I'll sort out some more for me. I'll take my computer and such, but the rest is yours.'

Dave and Carol exchanged looks of gratitude. 'Thanks, Alex. Once our house is finished, we'll move out and Joel can be fully independent.'

'Just take your time, there's no rush,' Alex said. He glanced at the clock and stood up. 'I'd better get back to Joel before he kicks off again.' He recounted what had happened earlier.

'I'm sorry, Uncle Alex, I should have stayed with him until you got back, but I wanted to see how Mum and Dad were doing. He said he was okay on his own for a bit.'

'You don't need to apologise; I appreciate you watching him for me.'

'Is he being discharged?' Carol asked.

'I think so, they can't wait to be rid of him due to his behaviour.'

'Do yourself a favour and give the social worker a ring,' Dave said. 'See if she can get that respite place sorted out sooner.'

'Good idea, I'll do it when I get back. Take care, big brother and I'll come and see you later and draw on your facial dressings while you sleep.'

Carol smiled at them both. 'You two are a pair of idiots.'

'But you love us,' Dave said. The pain from his injuries was starting to show on his face from where the drugs were starting to wear off.

Carol stood up and kissed Dave on the top of his head. 'Somebody has to. Come on, Wayne, let's go and see if your cousin is ready to go home.'

Chapter 62.

The lengthy conversation with the coroner from Yorkshire had been interesting to say the least, and Faz made himself a coffee while he waited for her email to come through. The sleek black and chrome machine that stood on the cupboard behind his desk was another one of his indulgences. Faz was a firm believer in quality over quantity, unless it was about biscuits. Chocolate hobnobs were his kryptonite, and he had to ration himself recently on account of his waistband becoming too tight.

The computer pinged to announce the arrival of the files, and Faz printed off the numerous pages so he could read them more thoroughly. There were definite similarities in the type of injuries inflicted on the remains discovered up there, but if what Dr Quinn was saying was true, then Alex had a problem.

Picking up the phone, Faz dialled the Major Crime unit. Craig answered and Faz grinned. He loved nothing more than winding Craig up.

'Well, if it isn't Muffy Sparkles herself!'

'Sorry, Faz, Muffy's busy at the moment. Will I do?'

Faz sighed dramatically. 'I suppose you'll have to. Is your intrepid boss around?'

'Not at the moment, he's at the hospital. Is it important?'

'It's important enough for you to come and see me instead. I've got the file from Dr Quinn, the coroner from Yorkshire.'

'Has that only just come through?'

'It has. I've just been speaking to her and she apologised for the delay, but she had several victims from a pile-up on the A19 to deal with and forgot to send it. To be fair, I've been so busy with all these guests that keep gracing my table that I wouldn't have had much chance to read it if she'd sent it earlier.'

'Better late than never, I suppose. Let's hope it's useful.'

'I'm not sure about that. I think it may muddy the waters even further.'

'Oh bugger,' Craig said. 'Is it bad?'

'I'd say so. Dr Quinn doesn't have just one set of remains, she has two.'

'Faz, this had better not be a joke.'

'Trust me, I would never joke about something like this.'

'Make me a cappuccino, I'm on my way over.'

Chapter 63.

'I'm so sorry to hear about the fire at your brother's house, Mr Peachey,' the social worker said. 'I'm certain we can sort something out for Joel short-term. Can I call you back in a couple of hours? I need to make some enquiries so we find the right solution.' The phone clicked in Alex's ear as the social worker hung up.

'What did she say?' Carol asked as they sat in the kitchen of the bungalow. Joel was in the lounge, playing cards with Wayne. By the sound of it, Joel was winning.

'She's going to call back in a bit, but that it shouldn't be a problem,' Alex said, getting up to refill his mug from the teapot on the counter.

'I'm so sorry we couldn't save his wheelchair,' Carol said. 'I think Dave would have if he could.'

'I know, but wheelchairs can be replaced, you guys can't. It was insured, so Joel won't lose out. Ronnie's going to speak to the occupational therapist and arrange for a manual wheelchair to be delivered today, which will do until a new electric one can be supplied. He won't be happy, but it beats being carried around like a sack of potatoes.'

'True,' Carol said. She tapped her forehead. 'I've had it up to here with one thing and another, so if he does moan about it, he'll have me to deal with.'

'Let's hope Ronnie can sort out some respite for him, then we can all get a break,' Alex said. 'You and Dave have been fantastic with him while Jayne's been in hospital. I couldn't have coped at all without you.'

'Don't be daft, that's what family is for. Are you going to see her today?'

'I looked in on her this morning, there's no change, so I'm going furniture shopping.' Alex put his empty mug in the sink. 'When are you going to see Dave?'

'I'll pop up tonight once you're home. No disrespect, Alex, but I don't want to leave Joel here alone with Wayne.'

'That's fine. Craig and Gary are coming round tonight for role-playing, and we normally order pizza, so I'll get some for the boys, too.'

'Thanks, Alex, it's much appreciated.' Carol picked up her phone. 'Now I suppose I'd better speak to our insurers and get the ball rolling.'

It was good to be back in the old house, although he was the only one who felt that way if the low growls coming from the cat basket were anything to go by. Alex had visited the local British Heart Foundation shop after leaving Carol, and had bought a nearly new three-piece suite, dining table and chairs and a coffee table. The manager was so thrilled that Alex had spent so much money that she agreed to his request to have it delivered later that day. She had also thrown in a large, padded ottoman for free. After that, Alex had gone to the nearby Co-op for a few basics that would tide him over until he could do an online shop.

Alex bent down and unlatched the front of the cage and Jack stalked out, looking very cross at being cooped up in such an undignified manner. He sniffed the air suspiciously, confused by the familiar smells. He wandered off into the lounge, where Alex found him sitting in front of the large patio doors, looking out at the garden which he knew so well.

'Sorry, but you'll have to stay in for a couple of weeks,' Alex said, crouching down to stroke the cat's thick fur. Jack started to purr, then remembered he was upset with Alex and turned his back on him.

Alex chuckled to himself, then went to set up Jack's litter tray and food bowls before putting the kettle on. Leaving it to boil, he carried his suitcase upstairs and unpacked his things, grateful for the built-in wardrobes. Once everything was put away, he went back downstairs and made himself a coffee. Jack was curled up in the roomy armchair.

'Oi, I got the ottoman for you, mister,' Alex said. He scooped Jack up and put him gently on the padded seat, then picked up his mug. Jack glared at him, ran back over to the chair and lay down on his back, legs akimbo, his white furry belly with the big black patch on display. He looked at Alex, silently daring him to try again.

'Fine, I'll sit here,' Alex laughed, choosing one of the two sofas. He sipped his coffee and made notes on his phone of the things he needed to do tomorrow.

At some point he must have nodded off, waking only when the doorbell rang. He tried to sit up but was pinned by Jack, who had decided to lie across Alex's chest. Shooing the sleepy animal down, Alex hurried to the door and opened it.

'Hey boss. Sorry, were you asleep?' Dawn grinned up at him.

'I was, but it's fine. Come in.'

Dawn went through to the lounge and sat in the armchair. 'I like this, it's really comfy.'

'I wouldn't know, I've not had a chance to try it yet. Do you want a drink?'

'No, I'm okay. You don't mind me coming round, do you?'

'Of course not,' Alex said, sitting back down. 'Is everything okay?'

'Yeah, I think so. I've just dropped Mo off and thought I'd pop in on my way back. Hey, big guy, how are you?' She rubbed Jack's tummy as he ran over and flopped onto his back in front of her. 'Is it nice to be back, huh? Who's a good boy?' she cooed at him, earning loud purrs in return.

'This is nowhere near your place, and Mo's is even further out.' Alex said. He narrowed his eyes. 'What's going on, Dawn?'

'I was worried about you, alright? We haven't talked about your meltdown at work the other day, so I wanted to check in with you. You're being pulled in so many directions that I'm afraid you'll snap.'

'I'm alright, I guess. It's a case of having to be, as my gran used to say,' Alex said. 'I am looking forward to taking some time off once we've solved this, though.'

'Jayne will get better, and although she might be upset about the whole social services thing to start with, hopefully she will be fine once she sees how much happier Joel is.' Dawn stroked Jack once more then stood up to leave. 'I'd better let you go if you've got Craig and Gary coming round,' she said. 'Are you still playing Doomhammer?'

'It's called Deathwatch,' Alex laughed, 'Yes, we are. A typical game can go on for weeks, even months sometimes.'

'Jeez, how thrilling.' Dawn rolled her eyes then grinned at him. 'Still, each to their own.'

'You should give it a go, you might even enjoy yourself,' Alex said. He picked up his coat and followed her outside, making sure that Jack didn't follow him. 'I'd better get back to the bungalow so Carol can go and see Dave. I'll see you tomorrow, Dawn.'

Chapter 64.

Alex was furious when he heard about the post-mortem report from Dr Quinn the following morning, which had shown that the dismembered hands found with her victim belonged to someone else.

'For fuck's sake, can we not get a break instead of a kick in the teeth?' he snapped.

'To be fair, it's not Dr Quinn's fault. The PM was done by her predecessor,' Les said.

'I know, but it's another layer of crap we could have done without.' Alex looked around the room at the team. They all looked as fed up as he felt.

'Faz said he wouldn't have connected it to our case if the injuries on the victims hadn't been almost identical to our first find.'

'I know, Craig, I'm just bloody frustrated with it.'

'We all are, but we'll crack it just like we always do.'

'I just wish I hadn't got all this other bollocks going on at the same time.' Alex pushed his hair back off his face. 'And now I've realised that I need a haircut, too.'

'Not a problem I have these days,' Les muttered, making them all laugh and breaking the tension.

The office door flew open. 'Stand by your beds!' DI Baldwin strode in, a big smile on his face. He shook hands with everyone. 'Ah, it's good to be back,' he said.

'Perfect timing, Charlie, we're chasing our own tails here,' Alex said. 'I would say we need a fresh pair of eyes, but that's probably not very appropriate, given that our killer likes to remove them.'

'Sounds like I've walked into a Stephen King novel,' Charlie joked. He rubbed his hands together. 'Right, I know nothing about the case, so let's start at the very beginning, and see where we end up. I know it seems like a waste of time, but sometimes it's the tiny details that slip through the cracks when you're not fully paying attention that can make or break a case.'

'Agreed,' Alex said.

Craig pinned several blank sheets of paper up on the boards and the whole team spent the rest of the day sifting through everything, dissecting and cross-referencing everything they had accumulated since day one.

'The injuries to the victim found in Yorkshire correspond with the ones sustained by ours. All have had their tongues removed and their genitals mutilated pre-mortem. The removal of hands, feet and eyes appear to have been done after death,' Alex said.

'Did Dr Quinn's victim have fingers up their bum?' Gary asked.

Alex glanced at the notes. 'No, but the fingers were missing. Lizzie, why is that interesting?'

'Because the first two victims were missing their whole hands, not just the fingers. We also know that the hands found with that body couldn't have come from any of our victims because they were much older, suggesting that there's another victim somewhere that was killed around the same time, and is missing their hands.'

'Very good, but we won't worry about who those hands belonged to, we'll just focus on the fact it was probably the same perp. Les, talk to me about the area where the bodies were found.'

'An aircraft hangar, the canal towpath and the woods – all fairly remote.'

'Whereabouts in Yorkshire was that body found?' Lizzie asked.

'It was in Husthwaite, close to Newburgh Priory,' Dawn said.

'I know that area, I used to live in Sowerby. Could stately homes be important?'

'There are no stately homes near to where the other victims were found,' Les said.

'True, but we can't rule it out as being important to our perp,' Alex said. 'Craig, add it to the list of theories.'

'I know the answer is here in front of us, but we just can't see it.' Alex's eyes roamed over the boards, but it was all starting to blur at the edges like a watercolour painting left out in the rain. He rubbed his eyes, feeling exhausted.

Charlie stood in front of the board next to Alex, hands on hips and eyes narrowing in concentration as he looked at the evidence. After a few minutes, he pointed to one of the names.

'I think you should bring Alison Munroe in again,' he said. 'She puts these groups together so she will have background on them that we may not be aware of. We need to push her harder. And what about this Tracy Downey? You say she works alongside Alison, but it doesn't look like anyone's interviewed her yet.'

'Alison Munroe gave us all the information we asked for. We didn't think anything of it as she's the one in charge of the group,' Dawn said.

'But didn't Tracy attend the group before she helped with the running of it? That makes her doubly interesting to me,' Charlie said.

'You're right. Mo, get in touch with her and ask her to come in as soon as possible. In fact, let's get the woman in who identified the first body – what was her name?'

'Jean Harrison,' Dawn said. 'She was in a right state when she came in with that first card, all nerves and tears.'

'That proves nothing,' Charlie said. 'She could still be a killer.'

'She's over fifty as well, so she's old enough to have committed the earlier murder,' Les said.

'Good point, Les,' Alex said.

'I was joking, boss. A woman of her age couldn't have committed such brutal murders, could she?'

'I'm not joking, and she could.' Alex looked at everyone. 'As far as I'm concerned, every single woman in that group is a suspect.'

'I'll ring them now,' Mo said, picking up her phone, 'They know me, so it should be easy enough to get them to come in.'

'Craig, did Faz mention when he would have the PM report on the fourth victim?'

'He said he'll have it ready by Monday.'

'That's fine, I don't think I could take any more at the moment, and I think the DCI will resign if I throw anything else at him.'

Mo put the phone down. 'Jean Harrison must have read my mind, she's already on her way here.'

'I'll head down and talk to her,' Dawn said.

'You go too, Lizzie, it'll be good practice for you,' Alex said.

Lizzie grabbed her notebook and followed Dawn out of the room.

'Boss, we've got a possible ID on victim number two,' Gary called, holding his phone against his shoulder. 'I've got a Mr Andrew Wroe on the phone, he says he recognises one of the sketches we ran in the papers.'

'Did he give you a name?'

'No, but he's certain it's the taxi driver who picked him up a couple of weeks ago from the train station.'

'Get the taxi company's details, then ring them and see if they're missing a driver. Get Mr Wroe's details as well in case we need to speak to him again.'

'Will do.' Gary returned to his call.

'Does Faz say whether the tools used on our victims are the same ones used on the one up north?' Charlie asked.

'He says they could be, but he can't be certain without seeing the injuries first-hand, and I imagine that after seven years, the level of decomposition may be too advanced for toolmark comparison.'

'Fine, let's just leave that for now and concentrate on what we have here. Les, can you get in touch with Alan Stanley's family and find out about any organisations that he belonged to? I want to know if he played any sports, belonged to any clubs, or volunteered anywhere where he could have crossed paths with anyone else in that group.'

'Okie dokie.'

'Boss, it says here that Faz suspects the victims could've been drugged, which is how the killer was able to subdue them, is that right?' Mo said.

'Yes, that's right. What are you thinking?'

'That the perp might have a medical background. I think we should run a check on everyone from the group to find out what their jobs are,' Mo suggested. 'It'll be difficult, seeing as we don't know their full names.'

'We could always ask someone who knows them,' Alex said. He sent Dawn a text to ask her to ring him straightaway and a few minutes later his mobile phone rang.

'Dawn, can you find out what Jean does for a living, and see if she knows what the others in the group do? I'll explain when you come back upstairs. No, just work it into the conversation somehow. Okay, thanks.' Alex hung up.

'I can't believe how we missed that,' Alex said, scratching his ear. 'It's such a rookie mistake.'

'Don't beat yourself up about it, you've had more than enough on your plate with your family, and now there's the fire as well.' Charlie put his hand on Alex's arm. 'I don't even know how you're still standing.'

'Neither do I, mate,' Alex said, 'I guess it's just pure adrenalin.' He stretched his arms up towards the ceiling and several of his joints cracked loudly. 'Yikes, that didn't feel good.'

'I bet it didn't.' Charlie roared with laughter, 'You sound like you're ready for the knacker's yard. Have you seen anyone about that?'

'No, it's just stress. My joints seize up when I'm tense.'

'Even so, you should go and get a sports massage or something, to get rid of those knots. I can recommend someone if you like,' Charlie said.

'No, it's fine. Once this case is over, I'll be taking that leave I'm owed.'

'Make sure you do because you're no good to man nor beast otherwise.'

Mo punched the air with a whoop, causing them all to look at her.

'I've got the names and last known addresses for two of the men who stayed at the guest houses with Alan Stanley. One is Reg Clements from Tipton and the other is Kelly Norman from Bradley.'

'Excellent, Mo, well done. Now we just need to pick them up,' Alex said.

'We've already got them, they're in the morgue.'

'Are you sure?' Alex went to look at Mo's screen and saw she was right.

'How on earth did you get their names?'

'I've been working on this at home, trawling social media sites and going through missing persons while Isobel's been on nights,' Mo said. 'I did go on the dark web a couple of times, pretending to have something interesting, and a couple of people pointed me towards men who were into that kind of thing.'

'Right, we'll need to follow this up. Craig, you and Gary take one address and Dawn and I will go to the other. I want both families spoken to at the same time, they may all be linked in other ways, and I don't want to give them the chance to warn each other.'

'What about the third man?' Lizzie asked. 'Do you think he could be the one up in Yorkshire?'

'No, he was killed long before Alan Stanley started going away with his pals, but hopefully we'll be able to find him now we know who his friends are.'

Chapter 65.

A lex and Dawn pulled up outside a tired-looking row of houses in Tipton. Some of the residents had made a reasonable effort to make their homes look nice, painting the front of their houses and making sure their gardens had well-tended borders and weed-free lawns. Others had replaced the grass with stone chippings or block paving, but every so often there would be a car up on bricks in the front garden, with a lawn so overgrown it was impossible to see the footpath that led to the front door. A couple of houses still had exterior Christmas decorations up, as if trying to cling on to a happier time in their lives.

The two detectives got out of the car, aware that more than one curtain was twitching.

'I'm glad we brought your car, boss. No one's going to nick that.'

'That's a very biased remark,' Alex scolded. 'You shouldn't assume that just because an area has a reputation for being rough, everyone who lives there is a criminal.'

A young boy of around seven years old, dressed in ripped tracksuit bottoms and a t-shirt three sizes too big for him, rode past on an ancient-looking bicycle. 'Pig scumbags!' he yelled, sticking his middle finger up at them.

Dawn raised an eyebrow. 'You were saying…?' she said sarcastically.

Alex shook his head and opened the gate to the house they'd come to visit. The yellow paint on the front door was faded, but the windowsills were clean and there was no trace of rubbish outside. He knocked loudly and waited for a response.

The door opened a crack, the chain still in place, and a small woman with brown hair peered out at them. 'Yes?'

Alex introduced himself and Dawn, then asked if she was the owner.

'I don't own it, I'm a tenant. Have I done something wrong?'

'Not at all, we'd just like a quick word with you if you don't mind, Mrs...'

'Clements, Sandra Clements. What about?'

'It's probably better if we come in, Mrs Clements,' Dawn said. 'It's a delicate matter.'

Sandra Clements pushed the door to with a sigh, then slipped the chain off. 'Hurry up then, you're letting the heat out.'

Alex and Dawn followed her through to a small but very tidy room, with two armchairs facing the fireplace in one half of the room and a table and two dining chairs standing against the back wall in the other half. A sideboard with a portable radio on the top stood in the place usually occupied by a TV. The furniture was old but well-kept, and the roaring fire made the room feel very cosy. Sandra indicated for them to sit down at the table while she made some tea.

Once she had returned from the kitchen with a laden tray, Sandra poured each of them a drink then sat down in the armchair nearest the fire.

'We need to ask you about your husband, Mrs Clements,' Dawn began, but Sandra put her hand up to stop her.

'Ex-husband, and if he's in trouble then it's his own fault. My mother warned me about him when I was a girl, and she was right.'

'How long have you been divorced?' Alex asked.

'Oh, it's got to be getting on for ten years, now. I got shut of him as soon as I found out what he was up to.'

'And what was he up to?' Dawn asked.

'It doesn't matter now, it's in the past. Why do you want to know about him?' Sandra put her arm under her bosom and hoisted it up, a haughty look on her face. It reminded Alex of an old Les Dawson sketch.

'There's no easy way to say this, Mrs Clements...' Alex began, but Sandra cut him off.

'He's dead, isn't he? Well, I'm glad. It's no less than he deserves.'

Alex and Dawn looked at each other, not sure what to say.

'Well? Are you going to tell me what's happened, or do I have to guess? Has he been stabbed by some jealous husband? I wouldn't be surprised, the dirty dog.'

'We can't tell you for definite that it's him yet, but we do have a body that matches a photo we found of him online. Do you have any photos of your husband we could look at?'

'No, I don't, I burned them all when we got divorced. Do you want me to come and identify him?'

The way Sandra Clements asked threw Alex for a moment, because she seemed so unnerved about it.

'That would be helpful, but I should warn you it may not be him.'

Sandra stood up and left the room, returning with her coat in her hand. 'There's only one way to find out, so let's get on with it, shall we?'

Chapter 66.

Sandra Clements viewed the body laid out on the table with disdain. 'That's him, that's Reg. I recognise the tattoos on his arms.' She turned to Dawn. 'Do you need me for anything else or can I go now?' Her face was devoid of any emotion. Alex's phone rang and he apologised before going outside to answer it, leaving Dawn to speak to Mrs Clements.

'Do you have any family we can contact for you, Mrs Clements?' Dawn asked.

'I've got a daughter, but she won't care either. She was as relieved as me when he buggered off. He made the poor girl's life a misery, always snapping at her, or blaming her when things didn't go his way.'

'We'll still need her details, for elimination purposes.'

Sandra Clements looked at Dawn, shock written all over her face. 'You're not seriously suggesting that my Julie would do something like that, are you?'

'Not at all, but we have to look at every angle.'

'I'm telling you now that she didn't kill him! She was a squeamish child, frightened of her own shadow most of the time.' Sandra fussed with her coat collar. 'He treated her like shit most of the time, apart from when his mate was there, when he was slightly more human. Jimmy was so nice to our Julie; she got more kindness from him than she ever did from that monster. Don't expect me to pay for his funeral either, because he's been dead to me for years.' Refusing a lift home, Sandra walked out of the mortuary suite and headed for the tram stop.

'Where's Mrs Clements?' Alex asked when he came back in.

'She's gone, and she had some choice words to say about her ex-husband, too.'

'Damn it, I hadn't finished speaking to her. Did you get anything useful?'

Dawn smiled. 'You'd better believe I did. Let's go back to the office so I can fill everyone in at the same time.'

Lizzie updated the incident board while Les made drinks and Charlie went to the canteen. Craig was on the phone with someone from forensics.

'Where do all the women come from?' Les asked as he put Lizzie's tea down on the table. He slurped his coffee, realising too late that it was boiling hot. 'Ooh, you bugger!' he exclaimed, fanning his mouth.

'Steady on, Les,' Lizzie laughed. 'It's a bit early for strong language.'

'I'll give you strong language, you cheeky mare,' Les grinned, pretending to clip her round the ear.

'Violence too – whatever next?'

'I'd never hit you, Lizzie.'

'Aww, such a gentleman.'

'Not at all, I saw what you did to Gary. I like my arms attached to my body, thanks.'

They were all laughing when Alex and Dawn walked in. 'Hey, I don't pay you lot to laugh.'

'You don't pay us at all,' Lizzie said with a grin.

'Ba dum tish,' Les said, pretending to play the drums.

'Ha ha, very funny,' Alex said, rubbing his neck. The new sofa was shorter than the one in the bungalow and, although comfortable, it wasn't designed to be slept on by a six-foot-plus man.

'What are you all doing?' Dawn asked.

'I was just updating the information we have so far,' Lizzie said.

'Then Les burnt his mouth,' Mo added, making Lizzie giggle.

'Never mind Les, this is more important,' Alex said, ignoring the pained look on Les's face. 'Have those other women brought their calling cards in yet?'

'Yes, I've got them here,' Les said, 'The first one was received by Bobbie Mathieson. It has a picture of a car on the front, and the co-ordinates are sixty-two, capital D, forty. That matches up with the victim found at Pelshall Common.'

'Did she say what her abuser's profession was, or what the picture could be a reference to?' Alex asked.

'No, I don't think she knew what he did. She told us he was her mum's boyfriend, a guy from the local pub. Her dad was a pae-dophile, too.'

'Poor kid,' Lizzie said. 'Was her dad abusive towards her?'

'No, he only picked on her older sister. She told one of her teach-ers, which resulted in the dad going to prison. It was the sister who reported Bobbie's situation to the school, and they got social services involved,' Dawn said. 'She was sent to live with a foster family until she was sixteen, when she moved in with her sister.'

'What a lucky escape,' Les said.

'I suppose, but it's a lot of upheaval at such an important age.'

'True, but better than staying in that situation.'

'We've got a positive ID on body number three, it's Reginald Clements. His ex-wife didn't have anything good to say about him, but what she did say was very interesting.' Dawn relayed the conver-sation between her and Sandra Clements.

'There was a Julie at the group,' Mo said, 'And there's also a Jim on the list of names. I wonder if he's her abuser.'

'Make a note of it to be followed up,' Alex said. The door opened and Charlie came in with bacon and sausage sandwiches for every-one. 'I hope none of you are vegetarian, I forgot to ask before I went.' He handed the food out, and they all sat round the big table to eat.

'Mrs Clements said her ex was always horrible to Julie. Her exact words were 'He treated her like shit'. I wonder if that's relevant to how he was found,' Dawn said, her mouth full of food.

'It could be, anything's possible at this stage,' Alex said. He pulled a piece of bacon rind out of his sandwich and put it back in the paper bag.

'Sandra Clements also referred to her ex as a monster, that was another name on the list,' Dawn added. 'So, he could be either one of them.'

'What about the second card?'

'That was sent to Samantha, we don't know her surname. Her card matches the Oxley location. She didn't name him or say what his occupation was.'

'Craig, how did you and Gary get on with the second address?' Alex asked.

Craig got his notebook out. 'There was no one in, but the neighbour said the chap who lived there had done so for over twenty years. He never saw a wife or children, but there were sometimes children at his house.'

'Interesting. Did they say what his name was?'

'They just knew him as Norman, but they confirmed that he was the guy in one of the sketches, which puts him with Alan Stanley at the guest houses.'

'Excellent. So now we have names for three of the four,' Alex said. 'What did Norman do for a living?'

'He was a swimming coach,' Craig said, 'So he may have abused children who went to him for swimming lessons.'

'It would explain the water in his lungs, someone wanted him to feel like he was drowning,' Gary added.

'Did we find out what all the women from the group do for a living?' Charlie asked.

'Oh, sorry I forgot to tell you,' Lizzie said. 'Jean was a secretary; she took early retirement to look after her mother. Jean said that Alison's a primary school teacher, and Samantha works in a shop. She wasn't sure about the others, so I'm going to speak to Alison and ask her.'

'Good work.' Alex's phone pinged with a text message. 'That's Carol, she says Dave's being discharged from hospital, so I need to look after Joel. Can I leave you all to it? I'll be as quick as I can.'

'No problem, we can manage just fine without you,' Charlie said. 'Give my regards to Dave.'

Chapter 67.

Carol read the text from Alex then slipped her phone back in her bag.

'Is everything okay?' Dave asked as he struggled into a loose-fitting t-shirt, wincing as his dressings pulled.

'That was Alex, apologising for not being back before I left, but he's on his way home now. He was telling me that Andy Oliver has been getting gruesome presents from the killer; body parts and so on.'

Dave pulled a face. 'I wouldn't be surprised if he wasn't involved in some way, there's always been something shifty about that bloke.'

'Don't be daft, Andy's lovely. He's been so good to Alex, always happy to accommodate hospital appointments and such. And look at how he's given Alex so much leeway since Jayne's been in here.'

'I still don't like him,' Dave grumbled. 'Can you help me get these damn socks on? I can't grip them properly. God knows how I'm going to get my pants on.'

'You can just go commando for now.' Carol soon had Dave dressed and ready to leave. 'Now, have you got to collect any medication before you're discharged?'

'One of the nurses picked it up for me earlier, to save us sitting in the pharmacy department for ages.' Dave sat down on the bed and closed his eyes, his face the colour of putty.

'Are you okay, love?' Carol rubbed his arm gently.

'Yeah, I'm just tired. Getting dressed really took it out of me.'

'You can have a proper rest when we get home. I'll make you some cheese on toast.'

'Have you heard from the insurance company yet?'

'They said they were sending someone out to do an assessment.'

'One of us should be there when they do that in case they miss anything.' Dave stood up and walked slowly towards the door just as a nurse opened it.

'Where do you think you're going?' the nurse asked.

'Home. I'm sick of looking at these four walls now.'

'Wait there.' He disappeared and came back with a wheelchair a minute later. 'Sit down, I'll take you to the car park.'

Carol smiled gratefully at the nurse and picked up Dave's bag. She ducked past the wheelchair so she could open the door.

'Come on, let's get out of here.' Alex sat at the dining table, watching his son doing a maths puzzle in one of his books and marvelling at his level of concentration. The experts had told them Joel would be intelligent, but Alex hadn't believed it. Watching him now, doing a sudoku that would make most men weep, Alex felt proud at how far Joel had come.

The phone call from the social worker earlier confirmed that a two-week placement had been found, and Joel had wasted no time in packing his things.

'Dad, will Uncle Dave be back before I go?'

'He should be, it depends on the traffic.' Alex looked at his watch. 'I'm expecting them anytime now.'

'Was the fire my fault?'

Alex smiled at him. 'No, you are the hero, you shouted loud enough to wake Wayne up.'

'I was shouting because Buddy was in my room, nicking my crisps. He's a bad dog.'

Alex smiled. 'Okay, think about it like this. If Buddy hadn't made you shout, Wayne wouldn't have woken up and discovered the fire.'

'Buddy is really the hero then, because he made me shout. Maybe he nicked my crisps on purpose.'

'Maybe he did.' Alex heard a car pull up. 'I think that's your Auntie Carol now. I'll go and help her get Uncle Dave out of the car.'

Joel undid his seat belt and lowered himself to the floor. 'Take my wheelchair.'

Alex wasn't in the mood to argue, so he grabbed the handles and headed outside. Carol had the car door open and was helping Dave to his feet.

'Hey, knobhead!' Dave called, forcing a smile.

'Shut your fat face,' Alex grinned. 'Joel insisted you borrow his wheels.' He held the chair steady so Dave could squeeze himself into it, then turned the chair round and wheeled him along the path.

'Whoa, slow down, you'll break the land speed record in a minute!'

Alex started to tip the chair back, making Dave panic for real.

'Okay, I'm sorry!'

'I should think so, too. Your poor disabled nephew is sitting on the floor so you can use his wheelchair. Shame on you.'

Carol caught up with them. 'Alex, you take the bags and I'll push him.'

'Jesus, no, anything but that!' Dave shrieked. 'She drives like Lewis Hamilton on HRT!'

'Fine, Alex can push you, but any more cheek and you'll be needing another ambulance,' Carol threatened.

'I guess this means I'm not getting any cheese on toast now,' Dave sulked.

'It's your own fault, you will insist on winding people up,' Alex laughed, stopping at the front door. 'Can you manage from here or shall I wheel you all the way inside?'

'I could manage from back there but didn't want to seem ungrateful.' Dave slowly stood up. 'Thanks, little brother.' Dave moved slowly along the hallway, grateful for the handrails that lined the walls.

Joel crawled out to meet them. 'Hi Uncle Dave, are you okay?'

'I'm fine thanks, mate. I just need to get plenty of rest.'

'You can use my room if you want to, but only until I get back from my holiday.'

'That's great, but I think I'll be okay. Your bed is a bit small for me.'

'True,' Joel started laughing. 'Your bum is much bigger than mine.' He crawled off along the hallway, giggling loudly.

'You wait till I'm better; I'll sit on your head and fart in your ear,' Dave called after him, a big grin on his face.

Once Dave was settled, Carol went to make some drinks, leaving the Peachey brothers alone.

'How are you really?' Alex asked, as he watched Dave trying to get comfortable.

'I'm okay. It'll take more than a little fire to keep me down.'

'There was nothing little about it, mate. I've seen the wreckage and it's not a pretty sight. You could have all been killed.'

'We weren't though, were we? Stop worrying about what might have been and let's talk about what lies ahead.' Dave shuffled in his chair. 'I take it you heard back from Ronnie?'

'Yes, she's been brilliant, to be honest,' Alex admitted. 'I'm glad you forced my hand and got her involved. I know Jayne won't be happy, but...'

'Stop worrying about Jayne for once and concentrate on what's right for you two – well, all of us, really. It's going to be a bit chaotic with all of us under one roof, but I hope it won't be for too long.'

'Shut up, you stay as long as you need to. There are enough rooms here to house a small army, as you well know. I've already moved back to the old house, so I won't be under your feet, and Joel is away for a couple of weeks from today, so you'll have time to rest and start to heal. Do you need any help with the insurance stuff?'

'No, it should be straightforward. Carol's already spoken to them, but I'll give Brian Downey a ring and check if he needs anything else. If not, my lads can make a start on clearing the site next week.'

'Did you say Downey? That's the same surname as one of the women in our case.'

'Yes, Brian Downey is our insurance man, I've known him for years. Well, ever since he moved to these parts.'

'Where's he originally from?'

'I don't know, somewhere up north. He's a decent bloke, very dependable.'

Alex stood up as Carol staggered in under the weight of a large tray, laden with mugs of tea, a tin of shortbread and a large plate of fruit cake. He took it from her and put it on the large coffee table, and she sat down next to Dave.

'Wayne was asking if he could go and look through the rubble, to see if he can salvage anything. I told him to wait until the fire officers had finished and Brian had been to look at it.' Carol poured drinks for everyone and held Dave's up to his mouth for him.

'It's okay love, I can manage.'

'Are you sure? I don't mind,' Carol said.

Dave held the mug carefully in his bandaged hands and brought the mug slowly to his lips. 'Ah, that's great. That stuff they gave me in the hospital was horrible.' He handed the mug back and gently rolled his shoulder. 'It's already feeling better than yesterday.'

'Just don't get overdoing it, you don't want to end up going back in.' Carol picked up a piece of shortbread and bit into it.

'What have they said about the fire? Do they know how it started?' Alex asked, helping himself to a handful of custard creams.

'Not yet, but they said they'd get back to us as soon as they could,' Carol said. 'I've been thinking about it since it happened. I'm wondering if I left a candle burning in the lounge. I was watching TV in there and I dozed off on the sofa for a while. When I woke up the film had finished, so I just dragged myself up to bed. Dave had gone up before me as he'd had an early start that day.' Carol looked ready to burst into tears. 'I could have killed everyone.'

'Hey, pack that in,' Dave scolded. 'It might not have been that at all, so let's wait and see what the experts say.'

'Dave's right,' Alex said. 'Now is not the time for blame.' The doorbell rang and Alex got up to answer it but was almost knocked over as Joel raced past in his wheelchair, propelled by his cousin.

'Wayne, slow down!' Carol shouted, but her warning fell on deaf ears. Wayne ran down the driveway, Joel bouncing around in his chair and laughing wildly.

'Kids, who'd have them?' she complained. She helped Alex take Joel's belongings out to the minivan, where Ronnie stood waiting, today dressed entirely in yellow, with hair to match. The three of them chatted as the taxi driver secured the wheelchair and stowed the luggage.

'I bought a present for Mum, can you take it to her, please?' Joel asked Alex. 'It's in my room.'

'Sure. Have a good time, mate,' Alex said as the driver closed the minivan door.

'Don't worry about him, he'll be well cared for,' Ronnie assured Alex.

'I'm sure he will be. Thank you again, we really appreciate this.'

Ronnie flapped her hand at him. 'Don't be daft, that's what I'm here for.'

Once Joel had been waved off, Alex and Carol walked back up the path. A roar from inside made them both break into a run.

Dave stood unsteadily on his feet, looking embarrassed. His loose jogging bottoms were soaked, and a broken mug lay on the floor.

'Bloody hell, Dave!' Carol started picking up the broken pieces.

Alex looked at his brother and burst out laughing.

'Alex, pack it in and help me get these trousers off,' Dave yelped, trying to hold the hot fabric away from his crotch.

Alex had tears rolling down his face as he helped his brother to strip off. 'I'm sorry, I know I shouldn't laugh, but you've got to admit that was hilarious.'

Dave grimaced. 'Easy for you to say, you didn't get your plums poached with scalding hot tea.'

'True. I'll go and get you some dry clothes.' Alex left the room, passing Wayne who was just coming in.

'Dad – what the hell?' Wayne stood in the doorway, a look of horror on his face at the sight of his father standing with his trousers round his ankles, and his mother on her knees beside him. 'Can't you two at least wait till Uncle Alex has gone home?'

'Chance would be a fine thing,' grumbled Dave, earning a dirty look from Carol.

'Actually, Uncle Alex was the one who took his clothes off,' Carol said. Wayne looked even more disgusted until she explained the situation.

'Thank God for that, I was starting to wonder if you were all perverts,' Wayne said.

'Not all of us, just your father,' Alex said as he came back into the lounge. He handed Dave's clean clothes to Wayne and picked up his keys. 'I'm off now but call me if you need me. Dave, behave yourself and do as Carol tells you.'

Chapter 68.

Dawn's ear was aching from spending so long on the phone, but she knew it was vital to get the information they needed. They didn't have time to call another meeting of the group, so she had decided to ring Alison Munroe rather than wait for her to come in.

After what seemed like ages, Alison picked up the phone. 'Hello?'

'Hello, Miss Munroe, it's DS Dawn Redwood. We've made some headway but I'm hoping you can help me with some information.'

'I'm not discussing the group's members with you, that would be...'

'A breach of confidentiality, yes I know,' Dawn interrupted, 'But that's not why I called, well, not exactly. Don't worry, we're not going to harass anyone, we just need to narrow down where their paths may have crossed with the killer.'

'Okay.' There was a loud noise in the background and Alison waited until it had gone quiet again. 'Sorry, just a tractor going by.'

'Are you away from home?'

'Yes, a friend of mine has a little cottage near Bewdley that she rents out on Air BnB, and she offered me the use of it. I've been very stressed as you can imagine, so I thought it would do me good.'

'Very nice. I just need to know what everyone does for a living, or used to do if they are retired now?'

'Jean was a secretary in a firm of solicitors, Tracy is a full-time carer, Sam works in a supermarket and Julie is a veterinary nurse.'

'Brilliant, thank you,' Dawn said, scribbling everything down in her special form of shorthand. 'What about Mandy, Patricia, Bobbie, and Anne?'

'Mandy is a cleaner, she works at the school where I teach. Patricia is a pharmacist, Bobbie works for an animal charity and Anne is a nurse.'

'Which hospital does Anne work at?' Dawn asked, a prickling sensation creeping up her spine.

'New Cross Hospital.'

'Thank you, that's very helpful. I'm sorry to have disturbed you when you're trying to rest.'

'It's not been very restful up to now, the bloody cows keep waking me up at the crack of dawn. Serves me right for renting a cottage on a working farm.'

Dawn thanked Alison again and hung up. She looked at the list and wondered if things had just got even more complicated. Dawn took the list to Charlie, who was working in Alex's office.

'Sorry to bother you sir, but I thought you'd want to know about this straightaway.' Dawn told him about her conversation with Alison.

'That's a big help, we've now got three possible suspects who all have access to drugs. Let's dig deeper into them and see what we find.'

There was a knock on the door and Mo came in. 'Sorry, Dawn, I didn't know you were in here. Boss, can I have a word? I think I've got something.'

'Come on in, Mo, have a seat,' Charlie said, signalling for Dawn to clear off a chair for her. Mo sat down, wincing slightly when she bumped her ankle on the chair leg.

'What have you got?' Charlie asked.

'A few years ago, Alison Munroe was interviewed by the police as a witness to a murder in the shopping centre.'

'Really? Who was the victim?' Charlie asked.

'His name was Philip Albany. He was out with his girlfriend and her daughter when he was attacked by Alison's friend, who stabbed him in the neck with a pen then ran off. The shopping centre was sealed off while they looked for her, but they couldn't find her. Alison was taken to the station so she could give a statement. A few hours later, Alison's friend committed suicide by jumping off the top of the multi-storey car park.'

'What was her name?'

'Angela Mathieson,' Mo said. 'She was Bobbie Mathieson's sister.'

'Christ on a bike!' Charlie rubbed his hand over his face.

'I'm afraid it gets worse,' Mo said. 'The officer in charge was Andy Oliver.'

Charlie, Dawn, and Mo went into the main room. Craig was printing something off, Gary was concentrating hard at something on his computer screen and Les was on the phone.

Charlie called everyone together, waiting until Les had finished his call before telling them the latest developments.

Alex walked in to find the entire team sitting in the break area, drinking tea, and looking glum.

'What's up? Has someone eaten all the bourbons again?' he quipped.

'No, boss, it's worse. Mo's found something and we're all pretty shaken up by it.' Dawn filled him in on the revelations.

Alex was furious. 'For crying out loud, that's something he should have disclosed! He must have known we'd find out, so why didn't he tell me?'

'I might be able to answer that, boss,' Les said. 'I was just double-checking I had my facts straight before I said anything.'

'Said anything about what?' Alex asked.

'Tracy Downey is Andy Oliver's daughter.'

Chapter 69.

Andy Oliver sat on the bench in his back garden, trying to stem the churning in the pit of his stomach. He'd left work early claiming he had an appointment, but the truth was he didn't feel safe at work, nor anywhere else for that matter. Even when he'd stopped to fill the car with petrol on the way home he'd had the distinct feeling he was being watched.

'Get a grip, man,' he told himself as he sipped his coffee and watched the various birds dancing on his lawn, pecking for worms and insects. Marvelling at their sheer determination to break through the hard ground to find food, he only wished he had their tenacity.

He raised his mug to his lips, and as he did so, he felt the air move behind him, followed by a sharp scratch on his neck. The mug slipped from his fingers and his vision started to swim. Just as he slipped into unconsciousness, he heard a familiar voice in his ear.

'Guess who?'

Chapter 70.

Alex looked at Les in disbelief. 'How certain are you?'

'As certain as I can be, but I'm happy for someone else to double check. I don't know what made me suspicious, there was just something about the way he's been acting with this case that got me thinking. I did some digging and I discovered he was stationed in Sowerby when he was in uniform. Then I looked at his personnel file and noticed he'd been married at the time and had two children.'

'I never even knew he had a family,' Craig said. 'He never talks about them and there are no photos in his office.'

'It was a long time ago,' Alex said. 'He transferred to another county after his divorce.'

'How old were his kids when he got divorced?' Les asked.

'His daughter was fourteen and his son was nine,' Alex said

'You don't think he abused his daughter, do you?' Les asked, his face darkening. He stood up and gripped the back of his chair so tightly that his knuckles went white.

'I sincerely hope not,' Dawn said.

'If I find out he did...' Les replied.

'Let's not cast aspersions just yet.' Alex rested a hand on Les's shoulder to calm him down. 'We need solid proof before we start slinging accusations around.'

'Of course, now it makes sense!' Mo exclaimed. Everyone turned to look at her.

'What makes sense? At the moment, nothing's making sense to me,' Charlie said.

'Ever since we went to the group I had a feeling I'd missed something important but couldn't figure out what. Now I know what it was.'

'Well, don't just sit there, put us out of our misery!' Dawn said.

'I couldn't sleep that night because my ankle was aching, so I got up to make a drink and I was thinking about the women in the group. One of them kept clenching and unclenching her fists.'

'Did you figure out who she was just from that?' Craig asked.

'Yes, I did. I remembered at the briefing last week that the DCI did the same thing when he was getting agitated. I don't even think he's aware of it.'

'Thousands of people pick up habits from their parents, like biting their nails,' Dawn said. 'It doesn't necessarily prove she's his daughter.'

'It stuck in my mind because it was so unusual,' Mo explained. 'I've never seen anyone else do it before.'

'Tracy Downey can't be our perp. For a start, she's a full-time carer, she won't have access to drugs,' Lizzie said.

'That's where you're wrong,' Alex said. 'Joel has drugs for all sorts of things, including sleeping tablets. She could have got them from one of the people she looks after.'

'If her dad did molest her this could be her way of taking him down, along with those who abused her friends,' Gary said.

'She would be privy to all the women's contact information, so would know where to send the cards,' Les added.

'The DCI's been on edge ever since this case started, and he bit your head off the other day,' Gary said. 'Do you think the victims are friends of his?'

'They could be, he doesn't seem very sympathetic towards the women in the group,' Lizzie offered.

'Okay, enough!' Alex clapped his hands as everyone started talking over each other. 'There's only one way to settle this, I'll go and fetch him, then he can answer all of our questions.'

'I rang him earlier to bring him up to speed, but his secretary said he went home early yesterday, and hadn't come in today. No warning or anything,' Charlie said.

'Now that's strange. I'll go over to his house and check if everything is okay.'

'Do you want one of us to come with you? Just in case things get complicated,' Gary asked.

'No, I'll be fine, thanks though,' Alex said as he strode towards the door. 'Get round to Tracy Downey's house and pick her up.'

Alex jogged down the stairs and out of the building, his mind racing. He knew there were incidents of police officers being involved in child pornography but the mere thought of Andy Oliver being involved just beggared belief.

It was a short drive to Andy's house out near the golf course but the temporary traffic lights that had annoyed Andy were still in force, so it took him twice as long as usual to get there. He drove up the short driveway and parked behind Andy's Volvo. There was no answer when Alex rang the doorbell, so he walked round to the back of the house.

The patio doors were open and the pale grey curtains flapped in the breeze. A coffee mug bearing the words 'World's Best Grandpa', lay in a pool of brown liquid. Alex called it in, then pulled a pair of disposable gloves out of his pocket. He moved the flapping curtain back and peered into the lounge, checking it was clear before stepping through the doors. There was no sign of a struggle, so Alex walked carefully through each room in turn, but there was no sign of Andy. He retraced his steps, looking for clues that might suggest his team's suspicions that Andy was a paedophile, but there was nothing untoward at all.

Alex smiled as he looked at the mementos in Andy's study. There were pictures of him with his children at their graduations, then their subsequent weddings and finally several pictures of his beloved grandson. Alex had never met his boss's family but could see the resemblance between them all. One photo caught Alex's eye and he picked it up to take a closer look.

Two girls stood with their arms around each other, both wearing huge grins. In the background, Alex could see a field full of cows, with what looked like farm buildings to one side. He carefully took the picture out of the frame and turned it over. There was a sticker on the back with a message that made Alex's blood run cold.

'Goodnight, God Bless xx'

Chapter 71.

Then.
    'Wow, this looks great,' Angie said as they all got out of Sonia Jameson's ancient car.

Bobbie looked around, captivated by how quiet it was, just the rumble of a combine harvester in the distance breaking the silence. A strange sound came from the other side of the hedge that bordered the huge garden, and Bobbie ran over to investigate, closely followed by her big sister.

'This is a lovely place,' Andy Oliver said, taking in the white-painted farmhouse and generous garden, which was dotted with flowerbeds full of rose bushes. A dog ran out of the house and headed for the girls, who squealed in delight as the dog bounded around their legs in excitement.

'Yes, it's one of my favourite foster families,' Sonia said as she opened the boot. 'They are very experienced at looking after abused children, so Bobbie will be in good hands.'

Andy and Sonia carried Bobbie's belongings up to the open front door, where a middle-aged couple stood watching the girls playing with the dog,

'Mr and Mrs Williamson, nice to see you again. This is PC Andrew Oliver; he's been working with me on this case.'

'Nice to meet you, PC Oliver,' the woman said as they all shook hands, 'and please call us Janet and Keith, we don't stand on ceremony here.'

'Nice to meet you, too. Thank you for taking Bobbie in at such short notice, it's much appreciated.'

'Well she could hardly stay where she was, it sounded terrible,' Keith said, gesturing for them to come in. The house was as lovely on the inside, with dozens of framed photos lining the walls. The lounge was bright and sunny, and Janet wasted no time in giving them a tour of their home. Keith led them through to the dining room, where they had put out sandwiches and cakes. The girls were still outside, so the adults were able to talk freely.

'What made you become foster parents?' Andy asked.

'Sadly we weren't able to have children of our own, so we opened our home to those who needed it,' Janet said. 'I worked as a nurse on a children's ward years ago, and I remember this little girl coming in one night. She was around six years old, very underweight and covered in bruises. She also had some old rib fractures that had been left untreated. I slowly gained her trust and she told me what had happened to her. When she was discharged she was sent back home. The next time I saw her she was lying on the mortuary slab, her poor little body completely broken. She was so badly damaged internally from where she'd been brutalised, that she'd slowly bled to death.' A tear rolled down Janet's cheek and Keith reached across to squeeze her hand.

'That's horrific!' Andy swallowed hard, feeling angry and sad at the same time.

'It broke my heart, and I came home that night and said to Keith we should try to do something to help children like her. Bobbie will be our seventh rescue, and she'll be as well cared for as if she was the first.'

'I'm glad to hear it,' Andy said as he finished his coffee. 'I'll call Bobbie in so she can come and meet you properly.'

Andy went outside and found the girls sitting on the grass, stroking the dog, and talking animatedly.

'So, what do you think, Bobbie?' he asked.

'I love it, but I was just telling Angie how much I'll miss her.' Bobbie brushed her hair out of her face and looked up at Andy. 'Why can't Angie come and live here with me?'

'Hey, we won't be apart forever. I've got a better chance of finding a job where I am now, and I'll be saving hard to get my own place so you can come and live with me.'

Keith and Janet came to join them. 'Hello, Bobbie. I hope you like our home because it's yours too now, for as long as you want.'

'It's lovely, but I'll miss Angie loads.' Bobbie buried her face in her sister's shoulder and Angie hugged her.

'I've said that I'll visit when I can, I hope that was okay,' Angie said.

'Of course, just give us a couple of weeks so we can get Bobbie settled into a new school,' Janet said. 'Then we'll sort something out.'

'See, I'll see you again very soon,' Angie put her hand under Bobbie's chin and tilted her head up so she could see her face. 'I promise.'

Keith held up a Polaroid camera. 'Shall we get a couple of photos for you both?'

The girls posed with their arms round each other, grinning madly as he took the photos. He handed a copy to each of them. 'There you go, now you can still see each other every day. Okay, shall we go inside and have something to eat? Then you can show Angie your new bedroom.'

Chapter 72.

Now. Alex sat on the bench outside Andy's house while the forensics team got to work. He tapped the photo against the palm of his hand, then put it in his pocket and headed back to the station.

Dawn looked up as he walked into the office. 'We've got Tracy Downey in an interview room downstairs, boss. Do you want to speak to her?'

'Not yet, I've got another lead which I think might put her in the clear.' Alex showed them the photo. 'This was in Andy Oliver's study. Neither one of these girls is Tracy, but the message on the back is what interests me the most,' he said, reading it out loud.

'That's the same as the message that was on the calling cards,' Les said. 'Do you think that Bobbie Mathieson is who we're looking for?'

'It certainly looks that way. Can you get me her sister's case file please? And I know it's a very long shot, but we need to know where this foster home is.'

'Social services should have a file on Bobbie, it will be in there,' Mo said, 'But it might take us a while to get through the red tape.'

'Leave that with me, I'll see if Joel's new social worker can point us in the right direction.' Alex went into his office to call Ronnie. A few minutes later he came back. 'She said we'll need a warrant, so I've called Judge Ramsay and ask her to sort one out if someone can go and pick it up.'

Lizzie offered to go and started walking towards the door, but Alex called her back and gave her some money.

'What's that for?'

Alex smiled. 'The judge said it would cost me, so can you pop to the shop on your way and pick up a jar of Marmite for her, please? She's very partial to it.'

Lizzie laughed. 'No problem, back in a bit.'

'Right, come on Dawn, let's go and speak to Tracy Downey.'

Tracy Downey wept when she heard her father was missing. 'This is all my fault!' she sobbed.

'What's your fault, Tracy?' Dawn asked gently, passing her a box of tissues. They sat in one of the comfortable interview suites instead of one of the stark, functional rooms they usually used. Dawn had felt they would get further if they took a softer approach, and Alex had agreed.

'If I'd told him about Bobbie being part of the group, none of this would have happened.'

'I understand, you couldn't tell him without breaking that bond of trust, but Bobbie would have probably still committed these crimes.'

'That's if it is Bobbie,' Alex said, 'We still haven't ruled out someone else being responsible.'

Tracy looked at him, her fists clenching and unclenching, reminding him of Andy. 'What? Do you think I did it?' She gave a snort of derision. 'I thought my father said you were a brilliant detective.'

Alex's temper started to rise and he sat forward in his seat. 'I suggest you cut the attitude and have some respect unless you plan to keep beating around the bush until your dad's reduced to a mutilated corpse!'

'Boss, why don't you step out and get some fresh air?' Dawn said. Her eyes flicked from Tracy to Alex and back again nervously.

Tracy looked at her feet. 'I'm sorry, that was out of order. I'm just worried about him, that's all.'

'We all are, so let's work together so we can find him and bring him home safely,' Alex said, sitting back again. He gave Dawn a small nod to let her know he was okay.

'Tell us about Bobbie and how she's linked to your dad,' Dawn said.

'It was years ago when my parents were still together. Dad was working with a social worker on Bobbie's case, and he stayed in touch with her after she went to live with foster parents. Shortly afterwards, him and my mum split up. Now, that was my fault,' Tracy admitted. 'I left school halfway through the day and went home. I thought she would be at work, but when I tried my key in the door it was double-locked, so I went round the back and saw her having sex with dad's best friend on the living room floor.'

'How is that your fault?' Dawn asked.

'I rang the police anonymously and said there was a woman being attacked in her house, and then I rang him and pretended to be a concerned neighbour. After that, I went to the common and stayed out of the way until it was my usual time to get home.' Tracy wiped a stray tear away. 'If I had kept my mouth shut they wouldn't have split up, but I couldn't stand the thought of that pervert shagging my mum behind my dad's back.'

'You can't blame yourself for that, you were just doing what you thought was right at the time,' Dawn said, reaching out and taking Tracy's hand.

'Anyway,' Tracy went on, 'my dad lost touch with Bobbie shortly afterwards because he transferred to a different area, so was taken off the case.'

'Did you meet Bobbie through the group?' Alex asked.

'Yes, she told us all about her big sister when we did an exercise about what you would say to your abuser if you came face to face with them as an adult. She said she didn't need to think about him anymore, as her sister had killed him years before.'

'That must have been awful.'

Tracy nodded. 'She said if the police had locked him up like they'd promised, her sister wouldn't have had to stab him. Whoever took over the case from my dad had decided there wasn't enough to press charges, so he walked free. I know my dad was so upset when he found out that Angie had killed herself. He said it was his fault for moving away.'

Alex took the photograph out of his pocket and gave it to Tracy. 'We found this photo in your dad's house. Do you recognise it?'

Tracy looked at the photograph and nodded. 'Yes, that's Bobbie and Angie, taken the day Bobbie moved to her foster home. Dad said it was one of his happiest moments, knowing he'd saved someone from any more abuse.' Tracy handed the photo back to Alex. 'I should have told him I was in touch with Bobbie, but I couldn't.'

'He wouldn't blame you, you had to respect her privacy,' Dawn said.

'No, that's not why. It's because I'd have to tell him that I'd been abused, too.'

'Who were you abused by? Was it one of the men who have been murdered?' Alex asked.

'No, his name was Derek Donaldson, he was my dad's best friend. The same friend who was sleeping with my mum.'

Chapter 73.

By the time Alex and Dawn got back to the office, Lizzie was back with the warrant.

'Judge Ramsay said to say thank you for the Marmite but asked where the bread was to go with it.'

'That woman is never satisfied,' he smiled. 'Right, I'll call Ronnie again and ask her to email the file across. While we're waiting, can somebody make a brew?'

'I'll do it, seeing as I'm off in a couple of days,' Gary said, heading towards the kitchen.

'Good lad,' Charlie said, 'I feel like my throat's been cut.'

'Nothing stopping you making one, you know,' Alex quipped.

'I would, but I've recently had life-saving surgery.'

'You'll need life-saving surgery in a minute,' Alex laughed, throwing a pen at him.

'Is he always this violent?' Charlie asked Mo.

'No, he's usually much worse. He must be going easy on you because of your age.'

'Cheeky bugger, I didn't come here to be insulted, you know!'

'Where do you usually go?' three people said at once, making everyone laugh.

Alex clapped his hands. 'Excuse me, we've still got a missing person to find so let's get back to it.'

'Boss, we've got an email with a file attached from social services,' Les said.

Gary brought a tray of drinks through just as Les had finished printing off the file. Alex took it from him and read it out loud while Lizzie wrote relevant points on the board.

'Bobbie Mathieson, daughter of Rachel Burgess and John Mathieson. Originally from Yorkshire, Bobbie was moved to Bewdley after being removed from her mother's care. Father sentenced to five years in prison for sexually abusing his eldest daughter, Angela. Bobbie is not allowed to have contact with any other family members apart from Angela. It looks like Bobbie left foster care aged sixteen and moved to Wednesbury in the West Midlands, to live with her sister.'

'How old was she when her sister committed suicide?' Craig asked.

Alex looked at the dates down the side. 'Angie was twenty-four when she died, so Bobbie would have been twenty-one.'

'So why wait until now to exact revenge?' Charlie asked.

'Maybe the timing wasn't right before, or...' Alex stopped speaking for a moment, and Charlie had to prompt him to start again.

'Sorry, I've just noticed that Angie would have been thirty this year, so perhaps that was it.'

'I doubt it,' Mo said. 'It's too random. There must have been something more specific than that for her to start murdering people.'

'Agreed,' Charlie said. 'There must have been a bigger catalyst than that.'

Alex read through the file then shook his head. 'I can't see anything in there, but feel free to take a look, maybe you'll spot something I missed.'

Mo picked up the file and read through it while everyone had their drinks. Alex looked up and saw her frowning.

'I know that look, what have you found?'

'It may be nothing, but have you seen where this foster home is?'

'Yes, it was just outside Bewdley. Why?'

'Alison Munroe is staying in a cottage on a working farm in Bewdley at the moment. She said it belongs to a friend of hers.'

'Well done, Mo. Find out who owns it, will you?'

Mo tapped at her keyboard then looked at Alex. 'It's owned by Keith and Janet Williamson. They live in a big house nearby, on the other side of the farm.'

'Bloody hell, we need to get out there as soon as possible,' Alex said, leaping to his feet. Everyone stopped speaking and looked at him.

'Get out where?'

'I know where Andy is, he's at Bobbie Mathieson's old foster home.'

'You lot get moving,' Charlie said. 'I'll call it in.'

Alex, Dawn, and Craig rushed downstairs and into the car park. Alex climbed into Dawn's car and they drove off. Lizzie was a few minutes behind them, due to her having to put her leathers on first. When she got outside, she found Craig swearing loudly.

'What's the matter?' Lizzie asked as she pulled her gloves on

'Someone's boxed me in,' he complained. 'I can't get my car out of there.'

'No problem,' Lizzie said, 'You can ride with me.'

'Not bloody likely!'

'We don't have time for you to be soft,' Lizzie scolded. She opened one of the panniers, took out a spare helmet and gloves and thrust them at Craig's abdomen, knocking the wind out of him. She swung her leg over the powerful machine. 'Now, get on.'

Chapter 74.

Andy Oliver opened his eyes and gasped as the artificial light blinded him. He tried to raise his hand to block it out, but his arms were tied. He turned his head as far away from the brightness as he could, then opened his eyes again.

'Good afternoon. I'm glad to see you're awake at last.'

'Who's there?' Andy tried to see who the voice belonged to, but the spotlights prevented him from seeing more than a few yards.

'All will be revealed in good time, but only if you don't try to interfere with my plan.'

'You do know that I'm a police officer, don't you, and that by imprisoning me you're breaking the law?'

'I know very well who you are. Please forgive the theatrics, but it was vital that I completed my work before I revealed my identity. Now, if you'll excuse me, I need to make sure everything is ready.'

A shadow moved beyond the spotlights and Andy felt a draught as a door was opened then closed again. Flexing his neck and shoulders, he looked around and tried to avoid the glare of the lamps. He was sitting on the floor of a large barn, arms tied firmly behind him to a stout support beam that held the cross beams up. Wriggling his wrists made them sore, so Andy tried to stand up by inching his way up the post so he could get his feet underneath him. His shoulders burned from the effort, and he bit his lip to prevent himself from shouting with pain.

Andy had just managed to get fully upright when the door opened again. The spotlights meant he didn't know where his captor was until they were right behind him. As a cloth hood was pulled over his head, he caught a whiff of a familiar fragrance, and he broke down.

'No, please, no,' he sobbed as his bonds were cut, all the fight gone from him. His captor led him out of the barn and re-tied him to what felt like a stout tree. Blinking rapidly as the hood was re-moved, Andy looked around at the overgrown garden, recognising it immediately. The once well-tended rose bushes were straggly and out of control, the grass looked like a cheap toupee and the old metal railings that separated the garden from the neighbouring field were twisted and bent from where the cows who used to inhabit the field had bumped against them.

Andy stood silently, head bent in shame. Any fight he had once harboured was all gone.

Bobbie Mathieson looked at Andy as she picked up the portable sander.

'Showtime,' she said.

The screams rang out across the sweet afternoon air, each one of a higher pitch than the last.

'All this concentration makes you sweat,' Bobbie said as she wiped her brow on her sleeve.

'Please stop, you don't have to do this!' Andy begged, a hitch in his voice from crying so much. 'I promise I won't say a word.'

Bobbie smiled at him as she picked up an old towel and wiped away the snot and tears that were running down his face.

'Don't worry, it will all be over soon. Your team aren't stupid, they'll soon connect the dots and come to your rescue.'

'You still have time to get away, so go while you can. I'll tell them I didn't see your face.'

'No, I want to finish this. I owe it to those women and to myself.'

'None of this is your fault, please don't throw your life away.' Andy started to cry again.

'I know it's not my fault!' Bobbie shouted. 'It's yours!' She dropped the sander on the ground and wiped her face with the back of her hand. 'You were supposed to protect them all, not just me!'

'I know, and I'm sorry.'

'After you left, the case against my abuser was thrown out on a technicality and he was let go, allowing him to continue abusing other girls.'

'Angie wouldn't want you to get into trouble.'

'Even if I stop, it won't bring Angie back, will it? You told me that that man would never be allowed to hurt anyone else, but you lot fucked up and he got off. Did you know he moved to Wolverhampton after meeting another woman online? If Angie hadn't seen him in the shopping centre and killed him, how many others would he have abused?'

'You're right, and I'm sorry!' Andy's knees buckled but his bonds prevented him from sliding down the tree trunk. His words became incoherent as he sobbed.

Bobbie looked at him. Her eyes filled with tears as she picked up the sander. 'I'm sorry, too.'

Chapter 75.

'How much further?' Craig shouted as Lizzie zipped past the traffic on the narrow roads. The cold bit into him and he wished he was wearing something more appropriate. His suit may have been made of pure new wool, but it did nothing to keep him warm. Then again, Craig doubted it had been made to withstand an 80mph bike ride.

'Nearly there, and you don't need to shout, I can hear you perfectly well through the internal headphones,' she replied. 'Hold on tighter, the last thing I want is you flying off into a ditch. That suit will cost me a month's wages to replace.'

Craig hugged Lizzie as hard as he could and swallowed a scream as she overtook a lorry so fast that he didn't have time to register what colour it was. He was grateful that she could handle the powerful bike but prayed that Dawn would give him a lift back in her car.

Lizzie pointed to a cottage up ahead. 'There it is. Let's hope we're not too late.' She changed gear and turned a hard left, thankful that the flimsy wooden gate was already open. She swerved to a stop, almost jettisoning Craig off, and kicked the stand into place.

The cottage stood in the middle of a large garden, with overgrown lawns running around both sides, bordered by a wild-looking hedgerow. Lizzie removed her helmet and gloves, dropped them on the grass and ran across the overgrown lawn, indicating for Craig to go the other way. He ditched his helmet and gloves and headed round the back of the cottage.

As he reached the bottom of the garden, Craig saw an oak tree so wide that he didn't notice the man bound to the trunk until he came round the other side of it.

'Jesus Christ!' Craig said when he saw the state of the man. He was completely naked, and his torso glistened where large patches of skin had been sanded away. The barbed wire holding him in place bit into his body, making it impossible for him to move. He made a keening sound when he saw the two detectives. Blood trickled down his chin from where his tongue had been cut out, the offending object nailed to the trunk next to his face. Craig gave a sharp intake of breath when he noticed the man's genitals were bloodied and unrecognisable.

Bobbie stood in front of the man, holding a bucket of liquid. Craig's arrival had startled her, and she jumped, causing some of the contents to slop over the sides of the bucket. She hadn't seen Lizzie, who was creeping along the hedgerow. Craig stepped forwards and she raised the bucket, a defiant look on her face.

'That's close enough! One more step and he gets this all over him.'

Craig held his hands up. 'Back up is on its way, so put the bucket down and let's talk about this.'

Bobbie shook her head. 'This is the only language wankers like him understand. They thrive on hurting people, especially children. I bet if I showed him a picture of a naked child right now, he'd still get a hard-on. Well, he would if he still had a dick.'

Lizzie moved slowly along the edge of the field, being careful not to make a sound.

'This is not the man who abused you, is it? I thought he was already dead,' Craig said, keeping Bobbie focused on him.

'That's right, thanks to my sister, he's rotting in the ground, but this one is particularly special. He not only abused children, but he also slept with his best friend's wife and broke up his marriage. Isn't that right, Andy?' she said, turning round and looking behind her.

Craig's eyes followed Bobbie's and saw Andy Oliver tied to a second tree, staring blankly into the distance. His face was blotchy and red, and his clothes were torn in places, but he appeared otherwise unharmed.

'Why all those other men?'

'Why not them? They deserved what they got. Julie's dad treated her like shit, so he got a taste of it. He did nothing to keep Julie safe, because as far as he was concerned, she wasn't worth it. He used her as a punching bag, and he turned a blind eye to his mate Jim violating her, all because she wasn't born a boy.' Bobbie wiped her face again; Craig could see she was beginning to tire.

'Then there's Alan Stanley, who had started his own little club, travelling up north to where this piece of crap is from, so they could have movie nights in the back of his shop. Andy would have been standing here instead of me if he'd known that some of those films starred his little girl.'

A loud bellow from behind her made Bobbie smile. 'Don't worry, I destroyed the films, for her sake, not yours. Did you know he got her pregnant when she was fourteen, Andy?' Bobbie said loudly. 'Lucky for her she lost it, but it's the reason it took her and Brian so long to conceive your grandson, and probably the reason she can't have any more children.'

Faint sobbing from Andy made Craig's heart break. Hearing such terrible things about his daughter had clearly broken him.

'What about Norman?' Craig asked, drawing Bobbie's eyes back to him. 'The one by the canal.'

'You mean Kelly Norman, Sam's abuser? He liked to hold her face under the bathwater while he sodomized her.' Bobbie rolled her shoulders. 'I'm tired of talking to you now, I need to finish this.'

'I'm so sorry for everything you've been through, but it's over now. Please put the bucket down and let's sort it all out.'

Craig's eyes flicked to one side and Bobbie stiffened as she realised that someone else was there. She just had time to hurl the contents of the bucket all over her captive before Lizzie barrelled into her and pinned her to the ground. She grinned up at Lizzie as screams echoed all around them.

'Justice is served,' she said.

Craig sat on the edge of the garden path, watching as the paramedics did their best to save Derek Donaldson's life. He'd gone into cardiac arrest when they had removed the wire holding him prisoner, and now they had him flat on the cold ground, frantically trying to find an area on the man's chest where there was enough skin to place the paddles to resuscitate him.

A second crew were helping Andy Oliver onto a stretcher. As he was wheeled past them, Craig noticed Andy's blank stare. It was as if someone had turned the lights off inside his head.

'This is seriously messed up,' he said to Lizzie as she approached with two bottles of water from her bike panniers.

She handed Craig one of the bottles and sat down next to him. 'You could say that. Personally, I think he got off lightly.' She opened the bottle and drank half of it in one go.

'What was in that bucket, was it acid?' Craig asked, 'I've never heard anyone scream like that before, it was chilling.'

'It was vinegar, believe it or not. I know how much that stings if you get it in a cut, so I can't even imagine how painful it was to get a bucket full of it all over you when most of your skin's been removed.' Lizzie drained the rest of her water and screwed the cap back on the bottle. 'Bobbie said it was the best way to deal with slugs.'

'It was certainly brutal. Do you think he will pull through?'

I think it might be better for him if he doesn't. She scorched his wedding tackle with a blowtorch, and I'm quite sure that's a big deal for a bloke.'

'Yikes, thanks for that.' Craig crossed his legs hastily. 'By the way, thanks for not killing me on that beast of yours.'

'You're very welcome, and I think you meant to say thanks for being such a competent and experienced biker.'

'That too. I'm not fond of bikes, I find four wheels more reassuring than two. Plus, your clothes don't get ruined in a car.'

Lizzie nudged him, almost knocking him over. 'That all depends on what you're doing in the car,' she laughed, winking at him.

They looked over to where the paramedics were silently packing away their equipment. The body of Derek Donaldson lay on the grass beneath the canopy of the old oak tree.

He wasn't screaming any more.

Chapter 76.

'I'm glad you got here when you did,' Alex told Lizzie when he and Dawn finally arrived. 'That bloody accident on the ring road in Kidderminster caused no end of problems.'

'We weren't far behind you, so I spotted the traffic slowing down and knew there was a problem. I took a slight detour through a housing estate and was able to get back on the dual carriageway further down.'

'Well, I'm very grateful, although Craig may need some time to recover.'

Lizzie looked over to where Craig was talking to the local uniforms, who were cordoning off the area. 'He's fine, at least he didn't fall off. Mind you, I'll have finger-marks on my ribs where he clung on so tightly,' she laughed.

The forensics team arrived and got straight to work. Once they were ready, Alex and Dawn were summoned to have a preliminary look at the scenes. Although it had originally been for storing cattle feed, the barn had been converted into a woodworking shop. It was very well equipped; a turning lathe, circular saw, and bandsaw stood against one wall, and a vast array of tools hung on the others. There were cabinets containing nails, screws and fixings, and a large wooden bench which took centre stage in the middle of the barn. From the patches of blood that had pooled on the floor beneath it, it was evident that this was where Bobbie Mathieson had performed her gruesome acts. After a quick look around, Alex and Dawn went to look at the house.

The inside of the farmhouse looked like many other homes. The furniture was dated but still in good condition, and there were photos and ornaments everywhere you looked. Dawn called Alex through to the back of the house and pointed to a shed.

'What do you suppose is in there?' she asked.

'I hope it's not the owners,' Alex said as he walked across and pulled open the door.

There were two chest freezers inside. One had various cuts of meat and plastic tubs, all carefully wrapped and labelled. Dawn lifted the lid of the second freezer and raised her eyebrows.

'I'd guess that this is where Bobbie kept the bits she planned to use.'

Alex looked inside. There were three sets of hands, one set of feet, and various bags of something brown and lumpy.

'I'm glad I won't be the one who has to analyse whatever that is,' he said, closing the lid again.

They headed upstairs and looked in the bedrooms. It was clear that Bobbie had been staying here, judging by the clothes strewn on the bed and chair. Another room was set up as an office, and photos of the victims were pinned to the corkboard on the wall. The master bedroom was neat and tidy but there was no sign of Mr and Mrs Williamson.

'You don't think she killed her foster parents, do you?'

'There's no sign she has, and from what I can gather, she thought the world of them.'

'Maybe they've moved out.'

'I think it's more likely that they're on holiday,' Alex said. 'But we can ask Bobbie when we interview her.'

'What a day, but what a result, too,' Craig said when Alex and Dawn came back outside to join him and Lizzie. 'Let's hope we can put this one to bed, now.'

'Don't mention bed, I'm shattered as it is.' Dawn yawned widely, setting everyone else off. She opened her car door. 'Come on, let's go before it gets any darker.'

'Can I get a lift back with you, please?' Craig asked.

'Aren't you going back with Lizzie?'

'Not even a personal appointment with Michael Kors could get me back on that thing.'

'Give over,' Lizzie laughed. 'You're still in one piece.'

'Only just. My poor balls are still throbbing, I bet they're a lovely shade of purple.'

'Eww, too much information,' Dawn said, wrinkling her nose. 'You can get a lift back with me.'

'Do you fancy riding pillion this time, boss?' Lizzie asked, offering Alex the spare helmet.

Alex grinned. 'I thought you'd never ask.'

The accident had been cleared by the time they passed back through Kidderminster, so it didn't take long until they were all back at the station. Alex climbed off the back of Lizzie's bike and removed his helmet with a big grin. 'That was exhilarating, thank you, DC Brewster.'

'You're very welcome, DI Peachey,' she replied with a smile. She stowed the spare helmet and gloves away and headed towards the back door as Dawn drove into the car park.

'Did you enjoy that, boss?' Craig asked as he climbed out of Dawn's Mini.

'I did, so much in fact that I'd consider getting one myself if I knew Jayne wouldn't kill me.'

'I have to give Lizzie credit; she handles that bike really well.'

Alex grinned. 'Are you saying you secretly liked it?'

Craig smiled back. 'Maybe just a tiny bit, but if you ever tell her I'll deny all knowledge.'

Once everyone was back in the office, Gary made drinks while Alex filled the rest of the team in on the developments in Bewdley.

'Bloody hell, what a mess!'

'You could say that, Les,' Craig replied, 'I've never seen anything like that and hope I never do again.'

'How's the DCI?' Mo asked.

'He was mostly uninjured, he had rope burns on his wrists and a few scratches here and there, but otherwise he was physically fine. His mental state is another matter, I think he's going to be off work for some time,' Alex said

'Does his daughter know?'

'Yes, I called her before we left the scene, she was heading to the hospital so she could be there when he arrives. What's left of Derek Donaldson is winging its way to Faz.'

'Was Alison Munroe at the cottage as well?' Les asked.

Alex shook his head. 'No, she was staying at another place just down the road. As far as we know she's in the clear, but we'll interview her again, just to be sure.' He yawned then looked at his watch. 'Let's all go home and get some sleep before we all drop where we stand. We can tie up the loose ends in the morning.'

Chapter 77.

Alex had been too tired to eat when he got home, so he fed the cat and had a quick shower before stretching out as much as he could on the sofa. He wrote a reminder on his phone about buying a new bed, then closed his eyes and slept soundly until Jack woke him at 6am the next morning, by sitting on Alex's chest and patting his face with his paws. When Alex refused to wake up, Jack bit the end of his nose, causing Alex to jump so hard he cricked his neck.

'Jesus Christ, Jack!' Alex complained, not sure whether to rub his face or his neck first. The cat eyed him dolefully from the doorway and Alex felt guilty for shouting. He patted the sofa next to him. 'I'm sorry, old man. Come and have some fuss.'

Jack turned his back and stalked out of the room, tail in the air and Alex swore under his breath when he saw the time. 'You'd better have a good reason for waking me half an hour before the alarm, matey.' He got off the sofa and stretched, feeling everything click. Maybe Charlie was right about getting a massage.

A loud meowing came from the kitchen so Alex went to see what was so urgent. Jack sat next to an overflowing litter tray and looked at Alex expectantly.

'Just what I didn't need first thing in the morning,' Alex grumbled to himself. He dealt with the tray, then put fresh food and water down before going to shower and get dressed.

When Alex came back down, Jack was sprawled in the middle of the duvet on the sofa, fast asleep. Alex stroked him, then went to make himself a coffee. He sat at the breakfast counter, sipping his drink and flicking through bed shops online. He found one close to the hospital, so saved the page. He drained his mug, said goodbye to Jack and headed out the front door.

Alex arrived at work twenty minutes later, having been stopped by a couple of the neighbours who wanted to enquire after Jayne. He wondered how they knew about it, but he put it down to small village life, where everyone knew everyone else's business.

When he walked into the office, everyone else was already there, apart from one member of the team. 'Where's Gary?'

'He's off today,' Craig said. 'He's got a final fitting for his suit then he's going for a haircut and hot towel shave, followed by a facial, hot stone massage, manicure and pedicure.'

'Bloody hell, he's gone over to the dark side,' Dawn laughed.

'No, it's just a little present from me. As his best man, I figured he could use a bit of pampering. Trust me, I've seen the state of his toenails.' Craig shuddered visibly.

'That's a lovely thing to do, Craig,' Mo said. 'Maybe I'll get you to be my best man when it's my turn.'

'You don't need any pampering, Mo, you're beautiful enough already,' he said.

'Flatterer,' Mo said, blowing him a kiss.

'I can't believe Gary's getting married on Saturday,' Dawn said, suddenly looking emotional.

'I know, they grow up so fast,' Les said, giving her a hug. 'I must admit I'll miss the big lump.'

'Has he had his exam results back?' Mo asked.

'I've not heard anything yet, but I'll chase them up,' Alex said. 'Now, let's get on. There are still a lot of loose ends to tie up.'

After dividing up various tasks, Alex left them all to it and went into his office to catch up on some paperwork, so he didn't have to think about how guilty he felt for not seeing Jayne the day before. After an hour he gave up.

Craig knocked the door and stuck his head in. 'Coffee?'

'Yes please.' Alex smiled gratefully and threw down his pen. 'I'm getting nowhere with this lot. I'm just making silly mistakes.'

'Ask Mo to do it for you, she's pretty much deskbound while she's recovering, and she'll have that lot done in a jiffy.'

'That will make me a hypocrite, I'm always telling you lot not to take advantage of her phenomenal typing skills,' Alex laughed. 'It's tempting though.'

'Boss, given the circumstances no one will think bad of you, and Mo won't mind at all. Plus, if anyone does say anything, you can fire them.'

'That's true, but I'll manage for now.'

Craig disappeared to make the coffee, but it was Dawn who brought it in.

'How's things at home? I expect you haven't had much time to think lately, have you?'

'It's been chaotic, what with one thing and another,' Alex said, 'But Joel being away for a couple of weeks is one less thing to worry about. I'm popping in to see Dave and Carol later, then I'm going to visit Jayne. I feel like I've not seen her for weeks.'

'How's she doing? Is she still getting stressed?'

'Yes, but the nurse suggested I take some photos in later to put by her bed, so she can familiarise herself with everyone again. Apparently, the amnesia is normal but I'm still scared.'

'You wouldn't be human if you weren't,' Dawn said. 'While I hate to pile anything else on your plate, don't forget we still have a body from Yorkshire to identify.'

'I hadn't forgotten, but thanks for reminding me. Has Bobbie Mathieson's solicitor arrived yet?'

'No, she refused one, she said she just wants to get it all off her chest so she can put it behind her. She did request that Alison Munroe sit in on the interview.'

'Fair enough, let's get in touch with her. Is Charlie here yet?'

'Yes, he got here a few minutes ago. Are you ready to brief everyone?'

Alex stood up. 'No time like the present. Once that's done we'll go and talk to Bobbie.'

'Well done everyone on yesterday's result, I know it wasn't easy on some of you, but you did a brilliant job. Now, let's see what's left to do. Who wants to start?'

Les stuck his hand up. 'I've got confirmation that the four men who stayed at the guest houses are Alan Stanley, Kelly Norman, Reg Clements, and Jim Hall. They used to meet up with Derek Donaldson to exchange pornographic material and to watch movies. A search of Jim Hall's and Kelly Norman's homes turned up evidence that incriminates all of them. It seems that each member of their little club was responsible for different things. Alan booked the accommodation, Jim oversaw travel, Kelly looked after the website and Reg sourced new material. DI Millington's team in Thirsk are searching Donaldson's home and work premises as we speak.'

'Excellent, thank you. Mo, what have you got?'

'Alan Stanley was involved with several paedophile groups, both online and in person. I've linked him to Yorkshire, Shropshire and Oxfordshire. I've notified the relevant police forces in those areas.'

'Faz came back to me with reports on the body parts sent to the DCI,' Charlie said. 'He confirmed that everything came from our victims. The three sets of genitalia belonged to Reg, Jim, and Kelly. The intestines belonged to Jim, the fingers in victim two were Alan's and the tongue was Jim's. Faz said next time can you just get him a regular jigsaw puzzle and not a 3D one?'

Alex smiled. 'I'll see what I can do.' He looked round the room. 'I get the feeling we're missing something.' He clicked his fingers. 'The body from Yorkshire. I don't want to assume it was Bobbie who did that, but do we have an ID for it yet?'

'No, Faz is still waiting on a few tests to come back, but he said he'll let us know the minute he's got something,' Charlie said.

'Fair enough, I'll leave you to it while Dawn and I go and interview Bobbie.'

Chapter 78.

Bobbie Mathieson sat on a straight-backed chair on one side of a grey metal table in interview room one. The artificial lighting gave everything a dirty yellow tinge and made the walls look like wet clay.

Alex sat down opposite Bobbie whilst Dawn set up the recording equipment. Once they had all identified themselves, Alex read through the list of charges.

'I don't want to say anything until Alison gets here,' Bobbie said. 'I owe her an explanation, and I'd rather she heard it first-hand.'

'I have spoken to her, she's on her way here now,' Dawn said.

'Then we have nothing else to discuss, do we?' Bobbie sat back and folded her arms. In her paper suit she looked like a teenager, and Alex wondered aloud how she had managed to overpower and transport four men who were twice her size.

Bobbie smirked. 'Typical man, thinking women are such delicate creatures.' She leaned forwards in her seat. 'The difference between men and women is that we know how to use our brains instead of relying on brute strength. In my job I have to hump animal cages in and out of my van, so I'm a lot stronger than I look. I also carry tranquilisers, which made things easier. Men can be so compliant if they think there's a sweet reward to be had.'

Alex's phone pinged to say Alison Munroe had arrived, so he went to meet her in reception, leaving Dawn with Bobbie. It was evident Alison had been crying and Alex felt sorry for her.

'This will put an end to the group,' she said, a wobble in her voice. 'It took a lot of hard work to get it running, and now it's all been destroyed.'

'I hope you can continue, because you do an amazing job. Don't let one person tear down everything you've worked so hard for.' Alex motioned for Alison to follow him through the double doors towards the interview rooms. 'Those women need you. If you give up, who will help them put their lives back together?'

Alison nodded. 'You're right. We are not victims, we are survivors.'

'Exactly,' Alex smiled.

Bobbie sat chewing her nails when the door opened and Alex came in, followed by Alison. She rushed over and hugged Bobbie, then took a seat next to her. Dawn started the tape and updated the details.

'Firstly, I'd like to apologise to Alison for all the trouble I've caused her. I know this will have a massive impact on the group moving forward, but please don't stop because of me. You helped me so much, and I feel terrible for hurting you.'

'You didn't just hurt me, you hurt everyone else, too,' Alison said. 'By taking matters into your own hands, you've stirred up painful memories for people who thought you were their friend.'

'I didn't want them to ever feel afraid again. Plus, those monsters were still abusing kids, so I've saved countless others from becoming victims.'

'Can you tell us about the people you killed and the methods you used?' Alex asked.

Bobbie cleared her throat and sat up straighter. 'The first one was up in Yorkshire around seven years ago...'

Chapter 79.

'So Bobbie Mathieson confessed to all the murders?' Charlie asked as they sat in the break area later.

'Yes, she told us everything in great detail. She started seven years ago, when she went back to visit a friend in Yorkshire – it was Julie Clements, as it happens. The taxi driver who picked Bobbie up from the train station was her own father, who had been released from prison early on good behaviour. Bobbie said he didn't recognise her, but something just snapped inside her head when she saw him. She took one of his business cards, then arranged for him to take her to Newburgh Priory a couple of days later, saying she had to go and collect her niece. She knew the thought of a little girl riding in his cab would appeal to him.'

'But how did she overpower him?'

'There was a coffee shop at the Priory, so she offered to buy them both while they waited for her niece. She said if her niece came out before she was back with the drinks to tell her she said to ask her to wait, then she gave him a photo of a little girl in a short dress. Bobbie said he practically drooled over it. When she came back with the coffee, she said her niece had asked to be picked up on the other side of the lake, so would he mind driving round there? Once they had parked up, he drank his coffee and passed out because it was laced with Rohypnol. Then it was a matter of shoving him into the boot and taking him back to the cottage she was renting, where she killed him.'

'What about the hands that were found with him?'

'She added those a few days later, after she'd been to visit her mother.'

Charlie nearly choked on his egg sandwich. 'You mean she killed her mum as well?'

Alex pulled a face. 'No, she said she left her alive, next to the train tracks. There was a report in the local news that a woman was hit by a train that same week, a local alcoholic named Rachel Burgess.'

'Bugger me, that's cold, to chop your mum's hands off then shove her under a train.'

'I don't know; if I'd gone through what she has I may have acted the same.' Alex screwed up his paper napkin and launched it towards the bin. 'Anyway, Bobbie was happy to confess to protect the anonymity of the other group members.'

'What about her foster parents, did she kill them, too?'

Alex laughed. 'No, Bobbie paid for them to go on a cruise for six weeks. She said Janet and Keith were the best thing that ever happened to her. She's only sorry that she didn't clean the tools properly, she said Keith was meticulous about it. He taught her some woodworking skills when she was living there.'

'That's a relief, they sound like good people. One other thing puzzles me, though. What on earth did she send Andy Oliver a cow's horn for?'

'That was a clue to her identity. When she first arrived at the Williamson's, there were cows in the field next to their house. Some of them had had their horns removed, and Bobbie got quite upset about it. Keith explained to her that the farmer did it every year, so Bobbie reported the farmer to the RSPCA. She says it's one of the reasons she wanted to work with animals, to put an end to such practices.'

'Good for her.' Charlie swallowed the last bit of his sandwich. 'It's a shame that this will affect the group. Do you think they will be able to come back from this and keep running?'

Alex picked up his mug and downed the last of his tea. 'I think so, yes. Let's face it, they've all survived worse.'

Chapter 80.

The heavy rain had eased off, leaving a light drizzle by the time the cream and grey Rolls Royce pulled up outside Saint Peter's church in Telford. The couple had chosen it because it had a decent-sized car park, but also because it had the ancient ruins of an abbey in the grounds, which were a photographer's delight. The old spire glittered where the light bounced off the wet stone, turning it the colour of parchment. Jo's friends had decorated the archway with fresh greenery, giving it a woodland look. The ends of the pews sported peacock-blue ribbons and cream roses, which matched the bouquets of the bridesmaids.

Craig stood outside, umbrella at the ready to protect the bride from getting wet. As soon as the car door opened, he dashed out and held the umbrella over her head with one hand and the back of her dress off the ground with the other as they hurried into the porch. Craig closed the umbrella and stood it in the corner of the porch, took a plain white handkerchief out of his jacket pocket and patted his face dry.

'That's a bit understated for you, isn't it?' Jo remarked, standing still so her brother could straighten out her train.

'I'm not risking ruining my silk one, even if it is your wedding day,' he joked, kissing Jo on the cheek. 'You look beautiful,' he added.

'Thank you, you scrub up nicely, too,' she replied, taking in Craig's charcoal-coloured suit and peacock-blue cravat, which nestled against his white shirt. 'I hope the groom is as well turned out.'

'He wishes,' Craig laughed. 'But he does look smart. It took some effort, though. You know how he is.'

'I wouldn't want him any other way. Right, bugger off so I can make my grand entrance without being overshadowed by you.'

Craig kissed her again before striding back to the front, where a terrified-looking Gary waited. His face was damp with sweat and his previously neatly styled hair stuck up at the front. Craig tutted as he flattened Gary's hair down again, then mopped the sweat from his brow with his trusty white hanky.

'Is everything okay?' Gary whispered, flapping his arms to stop Craig fussing.

'Nah, she took one look at me and changed her mind.' Craig yelped when Gary punched him on the arm in response. 'Relax and enjoy it, man, it will all be over before you know it.'

Before Gary could respond, the organ started up and everyone turned to watch Jo walk up the aisle, proudly escorted by her brother. As she passed Alex, she winked at him and he winked back.

Dawn bumped her shoulder against Alex's arm. 'Alright, boss?'

'Yes, I'm fine. It still feels wrong being here without Jayne, but Carol is spending the day there and has promised to ring me if there are any problems, so I can relax and enjoy myself for a change.'

A hush fell over the church as the vicar began to speak, and it seemed only seconds before the newlyweds were taken off to sign the register.

'Didn't Gary do well?' Dawn said. 'Only one little stumble over the words.'

'He excelled himself, and everyone fluffs their lines, it's to be expected when there are so many people watching you,' Alex smiled. 'I remember forgetting Jayne's middle name, the vicar had to prompt me.'

'And she still married you? I'm amazed.'

'She wasn't going to get rid of me that easily. Her mum wasn't best pleased, but she forgave me after a few sherries.'

The bride and groom returned and made their way back down the aisle. Alex had never seen Gary smile so much, and as they passed him he saw that the younger man's eyes were brimming with tears of joy. It brought a lump to Alex's throat and he heard Dawn sniff loudly beside him.

'If my mascara runs I'll thump him,' she croaked, her voice husky with emotion. She felt around in her handbag. 'Bugger, I've got no tissues, either.'

'Here you go, I always carry spares.' Ruth Morris reached past Les to offer Dawn a packet of tissues.

'Cheers, Ruth, you're a lifesaver,' Dawn said, pulling one from the packet and dabbing at her eyes carefully, trying not to disturb her eyeliner.

'I always carry tissues, sticking plasters and safety pins in my bag. And that's just for Les,' she giggled.

'Oi, I heard that,' Les grumbled. 'She's right, though.'

'Do you remember our wedding day?' Ruth laughed and turned back to Dawn. 'There was a big dog running around the cemetery, covered in mud as we came out of the church. Les rushed in front of me to protect my dress and went arse over tit.' They all started laughing as Les went beetroot-red.

'Yeah, yeah, it wasn't so funny when I sat on your dress in the car though, was it?' he replied. 'It was a different story then.'

'Oh, stop being so grumpy, you know I'm only teasing you.' Ruth planted a big kiss on his bald head, leaving a lipstick print behind, and he grinned from ear to ear.

'Fine, you're forgiven. Now, let's get out of here. There's a pint at the reception with my name on it.'

The congregation made its way to the car park, then followed the wedding car to where the reception was being held. Ushers were on standby to help everyone find their seat, and once everyone was settled, Craig got to his feet. He straightened his cravat and took a sheaf of paper out of his inside pocket.

'Unaccustomed as I am to making speeches,' Craig began, amid the cheers and whoops, 'it's my job to stand here, as Gary's best – and I think you'll agree, better-dressed – man, and tell you all a few tales about him, but we'll get to those in a minute. He's also transferring to a different police force, so I want to take a moment to say that Gary is not only a brilliant police officer; he's also a top bloke, the best mate anyone could wish for and he will be sorely missed.' Craig stopped speaking and took a sip of champagne to disguise the crack in his voice. 'So, before I continue, I have some official business to conduct. Gary, would you please stand up?'

Silence fell as Gary put down his champagne flute and stood up, looking worried. Craig handed him an envelope. 'On behalf of the Wolverhampton Major Crimes Unit, it is my absolute pleasure to give you this. Congratulations on your promotion, Detective Sergeant Temple.' Everyone cheered as Gary took the envelope with a stunned expression on his face.

'Seriously?' He looked at Alex for confirmation. When Alex nodded, he raised his arms above his head and gave a shout of joy. 'Get in!' He pulled Jo to her feet and hugged her so tightly she struggled to breathe.

'Gary, get off me,' she protested.

Craig laughed. 'She won't be saying that later.' He winked at Gary, who blushed all the way down to his collar.

'Watch it, you!' Gary pulled his friend in for a hug, patting him hard on the back.

Craig tapped a spoon on the edge of his glass and silence fell. 'Now that's out of the way, let me tell you what happened when Gary met Muffy...'

'What a wonderful day it's been,' Mo said, her arm wrapped around Isobel's waist.

'It has been great, and I couldn't be happier for the lad either,' Alex said, pointing towards Gary, who was on the dance floor, attempting to waltz with his new wife to a Bon Jovi song. He still had his cravat fastened around his head from earlier in the evening when he and some of the other guys from the station had been dancing to 'Kung Fu Fighting'.

'Bless him, he's not stopped smiling all day,' Isobel said, 'Apart from in the church. Then he looked terrified.'

'It's really nerve-wracking, as I'm sure you two will soon find out,' Alex said. 'Have you set a date yet?'

Mo and Isobel smiled at each other. 'Not yet, but as soon as we do you'll be one of the first to know.'

'Blimey, boss, give us a chance to get over this one first,' Dawn exclaimed. 'If I have to wear a dress too often I might start to like it!'

'Don't worry, Dawn, when we get married, we'll make it compulsory for the women to wear trousers and the men can wear the dresses,' Mo laughed.

'Oh no, don't do that, Craig's already planning his next drag show!'

'Are you serious?' Isobel asked.

'Deadly serious. Kitty McLane was so impressed with him that she's offered to give him a couple of guest spots at her shows. Mind you, he will never look as good as his wife,' Dawn added.

They all looked over to where Craig and Deb were dancing. Deb's peacock-blue satin dress hugged her in all the right places, and her matching stilettos meant she towered over Craig. He didn't seem to mind, he was content to rest his head against his wife's ample bosom, eyes closed and a look of pure happiness on his face. They made a beautiful couple.

'She really is stunning,' breathed Isobel, a look of envy in her eyes.

'And she's not into women as far as I know, so eyes front, please,' Mo said. 'Anyway, I saw her first.'

'Now, now, let's not have a fight, even though it's customary at weddings. Who wants another drink?' Alex asked.

'Not for us, we're going to head off,' Mo said, struggling into her jacket. 'I want to get in early tomorrow and get some of that paperwork done. With Gary off it will take longer than usual.'

'Nonsense. With Gary off there won't be so many mistakes to correct.'

'Hey, I heard that!' Gary wandered over, bringing Jo with him. 'My paperwork is exempt, no, it's exams...'

'Do you mean exemplary, darling?' Jo giggled, her smile lighting up the room.

'Yes, that word.'

'Excuse my husband, he's had a couple too many.'

'He'd better not have any more or he won't be any use to you later,' Dawn snorted.

'I'll have you know I am a man who can pre-form under pleasure.'

'I think you mean perform under pressure, dear.'

'Yes, that too.' Gary grinned at everyone, his eyes not quite focusing properly.

'I think we'd better take our leave, before he says something he'll regret,' Jo laughed. She hugged everyone, then prodded her husband, who had Isobel in a bear hug.

'Put her down, Gary, it's time to go.' Jo looked round them all, tears forming in her eyes. 'I'm so glad to have all of you in our lives, you really are family to us and we love you.'

'We love you too, thank you for a wonderful day,' Alex said, his voice giving away the emotion he was feeling.

'Bugger, there goes my mascara again,' Dawn muttered, wiping her eyes with her knuckles, making her look like a panda.

Lizzie had finished headbanging with Ziggy and came over to join them. 'Thanks for the invite, I've had a lovely day,' she said as she hugged Jo.

'Lizzie, it was a pleasure to have you here, even if you nearly crippled my husband when you first met him,' Jo laughed, a twinkle in her eye.

'Yeah, sorry about that,' Lizzie said awkwardly. 'To be fair, he did ask me to show him some moves.'

'Then it serves him right,' Jo laughed. After another round of hugs, the newlyweds went to say goodbye to another group of friends.

'I'm going to head off now too, does anyone want to share my taxi?' Dawn asked.

'Yes please,' Lizzie said. 'I'll just go and say goodnight to Ziggy and Dr Faz.'

Alex pulled his phone out of his pocket. 'I'm going to head over to New Cross and kiss my wife goodnight.'

'You sure about that?' Dawn said, 'You've had a few drinks and you don't exactly smell like a rose.'

Alex sniffed his armpit. 'Jeez, you're right. Maybe I'll pop by first thing instead before I come to work.'

'Good plan. You don't want to knock her out again with your boozy fumes.'

'Bugger off,' Alex joked. He waved them off as he rang Dave's number.

Dave answered on the first ring. 'Hey, knobhead! Are you having a good time?'

'Yes, I am, but I was wondering if Carol would come and pick me up.'

'Sure, give her half an hour, I'm just thrashing her at Scrabble.'

'Is that what you call it nowadays?' Alex laughed.

'Shut your face, Carol's put me on rations until my burns are healed.'

'I'm not surprised, it must be like shagging a Mummy.' Alex hung up with a smile, cutting off Dave's colourful reply mid-flow. He went back inside to say goodnight to everyone, then sat on the wall outside to wait for his lift home.

Chapter 81.

Alison Munroe sat at her kitchen counter and sipped her coffee while she waited for the washing machine to finish. The sun was out and she could see crocuses poking their heads through the soil, indicating spring was on its way. She thought about the past few weeks, shaking her head in disbelief at all that had happened. Bobbie had played her cards very close to her chest, even hiding the fact that she was related to Angie. She had often mentioned being from Yorkshire, but Alison hadn't made the connection, not even when Bobbie had given her a hamper from Betty's of York. It was somewhere Angie had promised her they would visit together one day.

The doorbell rang and Alison's heart sank. She went to answer it, hoping it wasn't Mark. She hadn't seen him since the night he'd turned up after the group meeting, but Alison knew he wouldn't give up that easily.

A woman stood on the doorstep, accompanied by a young girl aged around eleven years old. Alison recognised her as the one who'd been outside the café and the furniture store.

'Can I help you?'

The woman fidgeted with her bag strap, which kept sliding off her shoulder. She was clearly very nervous, so Alison smiled and invited them both in. They went into the lounge and sat down. The girl wandered around the room, looking at the bookshelves. She pulled out a book, sat on the floor and started to read it.

'My name is Nicky, and this is Debbie, my daughter,' the woman said. 'I'm so sorry for coming here, I wanted to say something to you when I saw you before but didn't know whether you'd be receptive.'

'It's okay, you can talk to me,' Alison said.

'You probably don't recognise me, but we've met before. I was with Debbie and my partner in the shopping centre a few years back...'

Alison's face must have registered the shock she felt when she realised who it was.

'You were with the man who died.'

'Yes, that's right. His name was John Mathieson. He had proposed that morning, so we were shopping for an engagement ring.'

'I'm so sorry, that must have been awful for you,' Alison said, reaching out for Nicky's hand.

Nicky gave a half-smile. 'It was at the time, especially for Debbie, but I actually came to thank you.'

'Whatever for?'

'It was only after your friend killed him that I found out what he was,' she said, lowering her voice so Debbie couldn't hear.

'Mum!' Nicky looked up at the sound of her daughter's shout. Debbie pointed to a photo that had slipped out of the book she'd been reading. Her face was pale and she looked terrified.

'What's the matter, darling?' Nicky asked, going over to her daughter. She put her arms around the girl and looked at the picture that lay on the floor. Nicky drew her breath in sharply. 'It's okay, you don't need to be scared.'

Nicky indicated for Alison to follow her into the kitchen. 'How do you know this man?' she demanded, thrusting the photo at Alison.

Alison looked at the photo. It showed her and Mark at a funfair just after they had got together. They were both smiling into the camera as he took a selfie. Mark had won a prize on the shooting gallery, and a green monkey with long arms was draped around his neck.

'That's my ex-boyfriend,' Alison said, 'Why do you ask?'

'Because his sister is a friend of mine. He used to babysit for me when Molly and I went out,' Nicky said, 'I haven't seen him for a couple of years, so I'm assuming that's when he met you.'

'We met two and a half years ago, at a music tribute night,' Alison admitted.

'I thought he must have met someone,' Nicky said. 'Well, judging by Debbie's reaction just now, I'd say this was the man who was abusing her.'

After Nicky and Debbie had gone, Alison rushed to the toilet and vomited until there was nothing left to bring up. She knelt on the floor and wiped her face on the hand towel, her mind racing. Mark had never given any indication that he was interested in children, so Alison struggled to comprehend what Nicky had said.

She thought back to when she'd broken into Mark's bedroom, and the files she had copied from his computer. Alison got to her feet and walked slowly upstairs to her new office. Booting up her computer, she opened her emails and was relieved to see they were all there, waiting to be opened.

Not trusting her legs to make it back downstairs, Alison pulled her phone out of her pocket and scrolled through until she found the number she was looking for.

'Hello, this is Alison Munroe. I'd like to speak to PC Penny Marshall, please.'

82.

Alex woke up the next morning, still clad in his shirt, socks, and boxer shorts. His mouth was bone-dry and his tongue was stuck to the roof of his mouth.

He groaned as he rolled off the sofa, promising himself that today would be the day he bought a new bed. Jack was asleep in the armchair, half on his back and half sitting up, his mouth open and his tongue lolling out. Alex smiled as he realised how alike they were, then stripped the duvet cover off, bundled his discarded clothes up and carried them all through to the utility room. He dumped everything on the floor and went upstairs to stand under the shower until he felt human again.

An hour later, Alex pulled up in the hospital car park, feeling much better after grabbing coffee and a bacon roll from the local drive-through. He headed up to the high-dependency unit, armed with a carrier bag full of photographs, a bottle of Jayne's favourite perfume, Joel's gift, and the new Jeffery Deaver novel.

Morning rounds had just ended, so Alex took the opportunity to speak to the doctor before going to see his wife.

'Everything looks satisfactory,' the doctor said as he flicked through Jayne's notes. 'There are no signs of any secondary clots, and her breaks are healing nicely. We have slowly reduced her sedation, so she's only on a light dose. She just needs time, now.' He smiled at Alex and handed the chart back to Jayne's nurse, before heading off to his next patient.

'Is there anything that's worrying you, Alex?' Lisa asked.

'What if she gets distressed like last time? I don't want to make things worse.'

'Relax.' Lisa's soothing tone did little to settle the butterflies in Alex's stomach. 'The more times we try, the sooner she will start to remember. It might seem cruel, but it's the best way, believe me.'

Jayne stirred and tried to lift her head when Lisa opened the door. She saw Alex and made a moaning sound, her eyes flitting around the room, as if looking for an escape route.

Lisa went to the bed and spoke softly to Jayne. 'Jayne, this is Alex, your husband. Don't get upset, he's not going to hurt you,' she said, wiping away the tears that were forming in Jayne's uncovered eye. 'Is it okay if Alex sits next to you for a little while? Maybe he can help you to remember some things.'

Jayne nodded slowly, so Lisa signalled for Alex to bring the high-backed armchair from the corner of the room and sit at Jayne's bedside. Jayne still looked wary, but Lisa sat on the edge of the bed, stroking her hand and smiling to reassure her.

Alex opened the bag he was holding and took out a photograph in a frame. It showed a much younger Jayne and Joel in a swimming pool on holiday. Joel was grinning from ear to ear as he bounced in his swim ring while Jayne watched him, a steadying hand firmly on his back and a proud smile plastered on her face.

'This is one of your favourite photos,' he said, 'It was taken when we went on holiday, around fifteen years ago. This was the first time Joel had been in a swimming pool and we were both worried he'd be scared, but he loved it as you can see from his face.' Alex held the photo up so Jayne could see it. She looked confused and tried to point at it.

'That's you, sweetheart.'

Jayne looked at the photo again, then back at Alex. 'Who?' she whispered.

'That's our son, Joel. He's all grown up now.'

A tear rolled down her face and Alex grabbed a tissue from the box on the bedside cabinet. Jayne flinched but allowed Alex to wipe it away. She opened her mouth, but no words came out. She closed her eye, sighed heavily and lifted a shaking hand, pointing towards the water jug that stood on the table over the bed.

'Do you want a drink? If it's okay, I'll let Alex help you with that, I've got to go and check on my other patients. I promise I won't be long.' Lisa walked towards the open door and waited until Jayne gave a small thumbs up.

When the nurse had gone, Alex reached for the jug and poured a small amount of water into a plastic cup. He picked up one of the straws next to the cup and angled it so his wife could take a sip. His hand trembled and she looked up at him as if worried he would spill

it on her. She swallowed a few more sips before lying back on the pillows and closing her eye. She looked exhausted from the effort.

'I also brought a teddy bear from Joel. I've sprayed a bit of your
favourite perfume on it, I thought you might be sick of the smell of
disinfectant by now.' Alex placed the bear next to Jayne's arm and she
reached over and stroked the soft fur.

Alex smiled and pulled another picture out of the bag and set it
on the bedside cabinet, next to the first one. 'This is us on our wedding day,' he smiled. 'I hadn't realised how young we looked, but we
were only in our twenties. We've been married almost twenty-five
years this year, but it only seems like five minutes. Oh, I also picked
up the new Lincoln Rhyme book. It's by your favourite author.'

Jayne's mouth moved and Alex leaned closer to hear her. 'Jeff?'

Alex smiled. 'That's right, Jeffery Deaver. I could read to you if
you like, I know how much you love him.'

Jayne nodded, so Alex opened the book and started to read. By
the time he got to the end of the first chapter, Jayne's eye was starting
to close.

'Do you want me to go so you can get some rest?' Alex asked,
smoothing the sheets where they had rucked up. Jayne slowly moved
her hand and placed it on top of his.

'Stay.'

Acknowledgements.

Tarrow his book was incredibly difficult to write, but I'm glad I did as it's proved a great catharsis for me. I was sexually abused for over ten years by a family member, and I was only able to come to terms with it and begin to heal after going to a survivor's group like the one that Alison runs in this book. The women I met and the stories we shared were the most harrowing things I've ever heard and done, and I am so very grateful to each and every one of them. I have not used any of their experiences in the book as they are not my stories to tell, and I would never disrespect any of them in such a way. I have deliberately kept any descriptions to a minimum, as I had a lot of flashbacks and nightmares during the writing of this book, and I have no desire to subject anyone else to such horrors. I have used some of my own accounts, but not in any great detail. I do, however, get to finally kill my own abuser, something I'm unable to do in real life.

I have a load of people to thank, so forgive me if I miss anyone out – it's not intentional.

Conrad Jones, owner of Red Dragon Publishing Ltd, and author extraordinaire; for taking a leap of faith and signing me. I will be forever grateful to you.

My editor, Dr Karen Ankers; for making this book so much better and for your kind words.

My cover designer, Emmy Ellis; you are a genius, and always know exactly what works.

The Twisted Sisters; Irene Paterson, Linda Wright, Fiona Quinn, Hayley Kershaw, Jackie Baldwin, Sonia Sandbach, Beth Corcoran,

Christine Huntley, Jo Abbott and Kriss Nichol. I am blessed to have you all in my life.

My Crime & Publishment family, especially Graham Smith; I will never be able to thank you enough for your continued support and advice.

Authors Rob Parker, Mik Brown and Robert Scragg; three men who are the brothers I would have chosen. I love you all so much.

Les Morris, a dear friend and fantastic author, who never minds the predicaments I put his alter ego in. In fact, he usually encourages them.

David and Carol Peachey, you are true superstars and I'm grateful that you allowed me to recreate you both in my books.

My beloved Auntie Mo, who I love more than she will ever know.

My dear friend, David Skinner, who was so desperate to read this book. It breaks my heart that you're not here to do that. I miss you every day.

My wonderful husband, Paul, for the many nights when you held me tight during my nightmares, and who gave me space when I needed it. I love you from the ground up.

My amazing children, all of whom make me so proud. Thank you for encouraging me to follow my dreams, and for being the finest gift a mother could wish for. You are the happy
thoughts that enable me to fly.

Milton Keynes UK
Ingram Content Group UK Ltd.
UKHW012021201023
431041UK00001B/94